Author of *Witch Bound*, a 2014 Romance Writers of America RITA® Award nominee for Best Paranormal Romance

"I very much enjoyed this read and would recommend it to anyone looking to branch out of their historical and contemporary rut and try something different."
—*FictionVixen.com* on *Reaper's Touch*

"Overall, *Reaper's Touch* is a solid, enjoyable fantasy western, with a romance that is fresh, interesting and brought to the boil at just the right pace. Consider me bitten/smitten."
—*Fantasy-Faction.com*

"*Reaper's Touch* is well worth your time if you like postapocalyptic romance. The worldbuilding in this story is wonderful and *Reaper's Touch* is the beginning of what will hopefully be a standout paranormal romance series."
—*TyngasReviews.com*

"A great read that is hard to put down. The world Stone is creating is complex and wonderful. The next book in this series will definitely be on my preorder list."
—*BookChickCity.com*, 4.5 stars

Also available from Eleri Stone and Carina Press

LOST CITY SHIFTERS: MERCY
LOST CITY SHIFTERS: REDEMPTION
LOST CITY SHIFTERS: REBELLION

Twilight of the Gods series:
DEMON CROSSINGS
WITCH BOUND

THREADS OF DESIRE
GUN SHY

Coming Soon from Eleri Stone
and Carina Press
THE SHAPE OF LONGING

ELERI STONE

REAPER'S TOUCH

carina press®

carina press®

Recycling programs for this product may not exist in your area.

ISBN-13: 978-0-373-00256-6

Reaper's Touch

This edition published by arrangement with Harlequin Books S.A.

www.CarinaPress.com

www.EleriStone.com

Printed in U.S.A.

Dear Reader,

I've always been a fan of unlikely couples, the kind who have seemingly insurmountable obstacles standing between them and a happy-ever-after. Jake and Abby, the hero and heroine of *Reaper's Touch*, are about as unlikely as they come. Jake's a Reaper, infected with a parasite that fights him for control of his own body, and Abby's a woman whose only job is to hunt Reapers down.

They're not exactly a match made in heaven, but they have more in common than you might think. Inside, they're both honorable and courageous people who are determined to make their world a better place. They both put their lives on the line again and again in order to protect those who can't protect themselves. And somewhere along the way, they both figure out that maybe there's more to life than just a fight for survival.

I had such a wonderful time writing about Jake and Abby's adventure through a very wild west. I hope you enjoy their story.

Happy reading!

Eleri Stone

Dedication

To G.F., S.K. and C.A.

REAPER'S TOUCH

Chapter One

CAM WAS PUKING outside the tent. Not only could she hear that awful noise which made her own stomach cramp in sympathy, but she could see him too, a hunched silhouette of misery outlined by the glory of another sunrise. She should be glad of it—the sun, that is. Mason was still alive, the Reapers were lurching back to their dens and ditches, and Cam never started puking until it was time to bury the dead.

"Abby." Doc's sharp voice snapped her attention back to the task at hand. "Don't let up the pressure. Do I need to dose you?"

"No." Even if they did help her stay awake, she hated the way Doc's injections made her feel—jittery, violent and damn near invincible. A dangerous delusion in their line of work.

"I need you here, so mind your hands."

He tossed the limb into the barrel and she fought a dizzy feeling as her brain tried to reject what her eyes were seeing. She *hated* medical duty. The captain thought it might toughen her up, but this—assisting with amputations and restorations—had nothing to do with toughness and everything to do with being able to ignore the fact you were cutting off pieces of your friends and replacing them with pieces of monsters. She'd never learned the trick of it and she didn't want to.

Mason moaned and she pressed harder, turning her head as Doc picked up an arm harvested from a fresh kill to fit it to Mason's bleeding stump. Stepping aside, she dropped the rag into the barrel and reluctantly—because she could never help it—looked back, fascinated and repulsed as the veins and tissue from the severed limb stretched like a thousand seeking worms to plant themselves in Mason's wound. He moaned again and Doc laid a rag soaked in chloroform over his face. No one should remember feeling this. Her skin crawled. She clenched her hand into a fist and forced her gaze away.

Silence stretched inside the tent as they waited to see if the graft would take. Twenty seconds. Twenty seconds and they'd know—either Mason would go into convulsions as the parasite entered his body or his wounds would begin to heal.

Mason was a Ranger, star-marked and one of the few people with a natural immunity to Reaper bite. The limb had been harvested from a fresh kill. There was no reason the graft shouldn't take. *It should work.*

Except…sometimes it didn't. Every once in a while the parasitic infection that turned men into Reapers caused convulsions and death, even in the people who were supposed to be immune.

Dust motes danced above the table. Doc gripped the edge of the scarred wood, his arms braced, lips moving slightly as he ticked off the seconds. When he was done, he drew a deep breath and bent to examine the wound.

Abby lifted the lamp higher and when Doc grunted in satisfaction, a wave of relief coursed through her so strong her legs nearly buckled.

"Looks good," he said. "I'll clean him up. You can go. Cam sounded like he might need help."

Cam was long gone. He was in charge of the cleanup crew, and she could already hear the thump of the axes falling as they decapitated the dead.

She frowned, looking at Mason's still body. "I should stay."

Doc shook his head. "You get too attached to these young ones. It's going to get you killed one of these days."

"I don't get too attached."

The look he gave her could have spoiled milk.

Last night, when the battle had swung close, she'd gone outside to make certain no Reapers came their way. She'd been showing off with that last shot, hitting the top of the Reaper's skull peeking above a fallen tree. A headshot. But she must have only sheared through the bone, not damaged the brain tissue enough to kill the thing. Tricky shooting at night with only the fires and moonlight to guide you. Mason had waved to her, turning his back on the not-quite-dead Reaper who lunged up and clamped its teeth around his wrist, tearing an artery.

If Mason hadn't been a Ranger he would have died or turned, but because he was a Ranger, the parasite in the Reaper's saliva had begun to heal him even as Mason's body fought the infection. She'd shot the thing dead and then dragged Mason up the hill herself. Doc was only angry with her because she'd had to abandon her gun to do it.

"I promised his mother I'd look after him."

Doc scowled. "That was a promise you shouldn't have made and you know it."

"Would you rather I'd left him out there?"

The noise he made was downright eloquent. She ground her teeth, trying to hold back an argument. He always raged like a bear with a sore tooth whenever anyone got hurt.

When he turned to scoop fresh water from the barrel, she touched Mason's wrist. Already, warmth had returned to the limb, and she could feel his pulse beating strong and steady beneath her fingertips. The wound, just above his elbow, was beginning to heal from the inside out. Blood vessels and nerves, then bone and muscle. Within the next half hour, the skin would pucker and seal. Within an hour, there wouldn't even be a scar.

Setting the bowl on the table, Doc shouldered her aside and set to work cleaning the wound.

"You're sure you don't need me?"

He placed the rag in the bowl and swirled it around before wringing it out. "If Cap gives you trouble, tell him I sent you. Just be careful."

She was always careful. "I'm still alive, aren't I?"

Looping the leather belt holding her ammunition over her head, she moved to leave.

"Abby."

One hand on the flap, she glanced over her shoulder. Doc fixed her with a hard look. Some of the men called him "the Butcher." He looked it right then—a bloody rag in his hand and his apron stained black. His shirtsleeves were rolled back and there were dried bits of gore stuck to his tanned skin. "Hold on to your gun this time."

Refusing to honor that with a response, she ducked outside, squinting against the bright light. They'd set the medical tent atop a hill beside an old bur oak. As she waited for her eyes to adjust, a finch flittered through the dry leaves, dropping to land beside a clump of meadow sage at her feet.

The battlefield spread out below. Gun smoke hugged the low ground, forming a shroud for the dead. About twenty of them, all Reapers. As the cleanup crew passed between bodies, the smoke drifted up, curling around their ankles like ghostly fingers. Flies buzzed above in little black clouds. There were no crows though. Animals tended to avoid Reaper flesh. No vultures unless you counted the human kind circling above the field on airships. Three of them today, each at a slightly different elevation. The first had arrived less than an hour after the first shot was fired. Even with the skirmish nearly over, there was still a crowd hanging at the rails to watch the show.

She wasn't helping Cam with cleanup. Instead, she took the trail leading north toward the sound of gunfire. Keeping to the high ground, she loped over the broken terrain, leaping across a narrow ravine and skirting a pile of rock that might once have been part of some farmer's wall. It was less than a two-mile jog and by the time she'd reached the other Rangers, she was already beginning to feel better.

She spotted the lieutenant right off, lying in the dirt with the rest of his men. They were positioned along the bluff. Reapers were gathered below, between the river and a line of mounted Rangers slowly closing in on them. When she called out to announce herself, Lyle waved her over before returning his attention to his rifle.

"Cap's going to have your ass."

Wiping the dust from her eyes, she sprawled out on her stomach, set her rifle in front and adjusted the angle of her hat. Her hair was fine. The long braid tucked into her shirt collar held most of it back, but a few stray wisps clung to her cheeks. "I got kicked out. If he has a problem with that, he'll have to take it up with Doc."

"What did you do?"

"We had to do a restoration on Mason. Apparently Doc thought I could use the fresh air." More likely he thought it would do her good to shoot something, but she never relished that.

Lyle studied her face for a minute, his frown easing. "Damn. Abby, I'm sorry. I thought he'd be okay back there."

"He should have been."

Looking away, she lifted her rifle and sighted down the barrel. There were a dozen Reapers left, most of them naked and covered in layers of filth. Old. When Reapers first turned, before all their clothes rotted from their bodies, they could sometimes be mistaken for human. There was no mistaking that these were monsters. The one she took aim at was stocky, with a thick knot of greasy black hair trailing down his spine. The muscles in his shoulders bunched as he crouched down in the mud, eyes fixed on the wall of mounted Rangers preventing escape across the open plain.

Its lips were pulled back in a snarl that exposed its teeth. Black, but not with rot. Nothing rotted on a Reaper. She'd seen sketches in the papers of Reapers with blood dripping from their cracked and pointed teeth. Skin hanging from their bones, missing noses, ears, all sorts of parts, but that wasn't the truth. Well, the blood was truth, but it was hardly ever their own.

She pulled the trigger, keeping her body relaxed to absorb the recoil. It rolled through her as she watched the Reaper she'd hit crumple to the ground. Headshot. Still...after Mason, she put another bullet in him just to be on the safe side.

There weren't any easy shots left after that. The Reapers had figured out where the bullets were coming from and hugged the base of the bluff. There was plenty of cover there, tangles of briars and deadfall washed up by the river.

She worked with Lyle just as they'd done a hundred times before. He would shoot at one of the hiding Reapers to force it out. She'd try to anticipate its movement and fire immediately after, hoping to hit it before it could recover.

Reapers were fast and smart in their own way. These had dug in, waiting for the Rangers to pry them out. *That* would be an incredibly stupid thing to do and all the Rangers on this patrol knew it. They held their ground. They had time and plenty of ammunition. As a last resort, they'd dump oil on the brush and burn them out, but before they did that they had to wait for the cleanup crew to clear out.

As she stopped to reload, a shadow moved across the canyon, sliding narrow and wide as it flowed over the rock. The sweat on her face chilled and she glanced up in annoyance. One of the airships, the largest of the group, passed in front of the sun, blocking it out as completely as a thunderhead. Much closer than it ought to be. She couldn't quite make out the lettering on the gleaming hull, but the flag—navy-and-white—marked it as one of the Eyrion fleet. Likely full of diplomats and debutantes. The observation deck on this one was one of the largest she'd seen.

The ship was far too low. Too close. They were supposed to stay at least five miles out, though they rarely did. Eyrion ships especially seemed to think the rules didn't apply to them.

She glanced over at Lyle, who was also staring up. "What the hell do they think they're doing?"

"Trying to get a better angle on the fighting, I imagine."

"They'll frenzy the Reapers." The sound of the engine always seemed to get them riled. Even as she said it, she looked down and saw the pack surge forward. As soon as they broke cover, they met with a wall of bullets that pushed them back. Eight left, three of them hit but still moving.

"Something's wrong with it," Lyle said, still watching the ship as he climbed to his feet, his duster settling around his legs. His sandy brown hair touched his collar as he tipped back his head. "It's listing. See there."

To starboard. The rudder seemed to be caught at an odd angle. More troubling, the ship was beginning to sink. A steady, smooth loss of altitude she hadn't noticed right off. The balloon holding the ship aloft appeared slightly misshapen. As she watched, a shudder ran down the length of the inflated skin. Her stomach turned. There wasn't enough space for a ship of that size to land on the bank without tipping and that would be disastrous. A bunch of unmarked Scrapers spilling into a pack of Reapers. Like throwing slop to pigs. The people aboard ship weren't immune. One little nibble and they'd die or turn.

"Hold your fire," Lyle shouted down the line. He was immediately obeyed. The other Rangers climbed to their feet just as she did, eyeing the faltering ship warily and then looking to Lyle for direction.

Fire was always a concern with the ships. They usually went to ground if there was so much as a dark cloud on the horizon. Crashes were rare.

Lyle grimaced. "And with a deck full of lords and ladies. Someone's going to lose his head over this."

"What do we do?"

"Be ready to catch? I'm staying the hell out of its way." He grabbed on to her arm and pulled her back as the ship suddenly swung in their direction. Rangers scrambled back, cursing and tripping to get out of its path. The ship was close enough that she could see the frantic movement of the crew, though she couldn't see that any of it was making one bit of difference. The steady whirr and thump coming from the ship said the engines were still working, but it continued to descend in a long, lazy spiral. Right before it struck the cliff, the wind kicked up again and sent it drifting south over the battlefield.

At that point, the observation deck was nearly at eye level and as it slipped past, Abby could see the pale, terrified faces of the passengers. A crowd of people, wide-eyed and clutching each other in fear. They might have been screaming, but the whoosh of air from the passing ship drowned out the sound.

All the Scrapers were dressed for the opera in black top hats and jewel-colored silk gowns. Peacock feathers bobbed from hats of various shapes and sizes. One woman still held a gleaming flute of champagne in her hands.

The ship itself was a beauty. Polished walnut trim. Private viewing compartments shielded from one another by velvet curtains. Large field scopes that were mounted to carved posts. That equipment was far finer than anything the Rangers had available to them.

A mighty wrenching noise came from deep within the bowels of the ship as a mechanical device squealed into position. At the same time, drag sails released from portholes set every few feet along the decking. That actually seemed to help somewhat, maybe not to control the descent, but at least to slow them down a bit.

It was awful, seeing those people pass by. When they were so far above the earth, it was easy to forget that there were people on board the ships watching them. To see their faces so close turned Abby's stomach. As if he could read her thoughts, Lyle placed a hand on her shoulder. Whether he meant to comfort her or keep her from shooting, she wasn't sure.

Together, they watched the ship descend. It was headed for the flat stretch of field where the cleanup crew had been working. If they were able to set down before they reached the hill, she thought they might stand a chance at landing it safely. If they hit the hill, they'd roll for sure. She sucked in a breath of air that tasted like gun smoke and stifled the flare of pity in her heart.

The ship seemed to sink faster as it neared the ground, though she suspected that was an illusion. An eerie silence filled the valley as the engine cut off. The guns were all silent and even the Reapers seemed to hold their breath at the prospect of fresh meat.

Twenty feet. Ten. And the ship touched down with a terrific crash of splintering wood. The bow tipped ever so slightly upward as if it were riding a wave. It swayed for a moment and Abby held her breath, thinking it might go over. But after a teetering pause it settled back almost with a sigh. That might have been the collective exhalation of the hundred souls clinging to the deck.

It almost looked like they'd landed it on purpose right there in the middle of a field of dead Reapers. If not for the odd dent in the side of the inflated skin above the ship, you wouldn't think anything was wrong. They were damn lucky, is what they were. Which was why she was so surprised when the wind shifted direction, carrying the sound of screaming along with a faint whiff of battlefield stench. She frowned and looked to Lyle.

"Are they hurt? They can't be hurt. Not *that* bad."

He opened his mouth to answer but before he could speak, a shout went up from below, and all hell broke loose.

The surviving Reapers, very much riled by the commotion, were taking turns darting forward, lunging at the horses' legs trying to get past. Before she could raise her rifle, one of them charged straight at Ignatius and his horse reared. Ignatius, young and city-bred, never had liked horses much. As well-trained as the Ranger horses were, they needed a steady hand when going up against Reapers. Ignatius tried to regain control, but it was no use. He went down hard, and Jack dismounted like the softhearted fool he was to make sure his friend was all right.

The other two Reapers made for the break in the line. And they were fast, so stinking fast. No matter how often she saw Reapers run, she could never quite get used to the sight. Men didn't move like they had lightning in their blood. But then, these weren't men. They were Reapers. And they were headed straight toward the ship.

Lyle pushed past her, heading for the steep ravine that cut down to the riverbank. She followed. Abby didn't know how he managed to keep to his feet. She slid down the sandy soil mostly on her ass so she could keep hold of her weapon. Lyle hit the ground running and quickly outpaced her. Gunshots exploded ahead as the mounted Rangers took off after the fleeing Reapers. Even though the Scrapers would be safe so long as they stayed aboard ship, they still made an unholy clamor when they saw Reapers coming at them.

The other Rangers remained on the ridge, not wanting to get in the way. There were only three Reapers left after all. Lyle felt responsible though. He was the lieutenant, and she'd seen Cap break away earlier to deal with the airship. She should get her ass back to medical before the captain saw her, but Lyle needed someone to watch his back and Doc *had* told her to find someone who needed help. She chased after Lyle, heart pounding in her chest and eyes stinging from the dust kicked up by the crash and the chase.

The thunder of a buffalo gun made her stumble. When she regained her feet, she paused, thinking maybe she'd misheard the sound, but the echo of it still hung in the air. None of the Rangers had buffalo guns. They were too unwieldy, too heavy to carry on patrol. Which meant that someone was firing from the ship. Some idiot untrained Scraper who wanted to brag to his friends about how he shot a Reaper. With all the smoke and dust stirred up by the landing, he was just as likely to hit a Ranger. He had to know that. He simply didn't give a damn.

While she stood there with her blood boiling, looking for a sign of Lyle and thinking about turning back, a dark shape separated itself from the smoke and came toward her at a dead run. Scrawny and wild-eyed, the Reaper seemed as surprised to see her as she was to see it. It slid to a stop, bare feet cutting furrows in the sand. Her gun came up, but the Reaper dodged to the right before she could fire.

It didn't attack her directly. They did have some sense of self-preservation and this one was looking to escape. When it turned to run, she dropped to a knee, took aim at the retreating back and squeezed the trigger. A hit to the shoulder. When they were close enough to hear you pull the trigger, sometimes they were able to move quick enough to avoid a direct hit. That bullet didn't even slow it down, but the next did. Its leg this time. Even then it still ran, though not as quickly. The next shot to the back took it down, but it wasn't dead. She'd hit its spine and it was still moving. At least its upper half was still moving, clawed hands trying to drag forward legs that had become deadweight. Standing up slowly, she glanced behind her to make sure she was clear.

No other Reapers. The mounted Rangers bearing down on her position saw her in time to rein in. Lyle swung off the back of one of the horses and stormed toward her. He was angry she followed him down. If he meant to holler at her, he'd have to wait.

She walked over to the Reaper. It hissed as she approached. Blood bubbled from the wound on its back. Sometimes those types of wounds were fatal for Reapers but usually not. It wasn't bubbling like that from the blood loss. The tissue was trying to reknit itself from the inside out. Half an hour would likely seal up all the holes she'd put in it. It would take only slightly longer to repair the severed spinal cord. That wasn't going to happen. She put a bullet in its brain, and then turned to face Lyle.

"That's the last one," he growled. He'd lost his hat

and raked his hair out of his eyes. "Ignatius broke his neck in that fall and Ben is hurt. The asshole on the ship shot the horse right out from under him and he twisted his knee going down. He's by the creek. Can you take him back to medical with you? I'm sure there'll be others."

"Is it bad on the ship? How many of the Scrapers were injured?"

Lyle's lip curled in a snarl. "None. They weren't screaming because they were hurt. They were screaming because they dropped into a field of Reapers."

She stared at him, disbelief mixing with outrage. "*Dead* Reapers. We killed every last one of them."

Lyle jerked his head in a nod and she cursed vehemently. They'd had everything under control until a useless bunch of Scrapers dropped their party into the middle of the battlefield. She glared at the sorry-looking pile of wood, metal and sail. They'd thrown ladders over the side of the broken deck, but only one brave man had moved to disembark. Crashed down so close to the border, all the Scrapers were probably still shaking in their spit-polished boots. Nodding to Lyle, she swung her rifle over her shoulder and turned her back on the airship. "We should have just let the Reapers have at them."

DOC RETURNED TO the medical tent as soon as "all those thin-blooded whoreson Scrapers overran the damn camp." Abby was starving and hoping for food, but he came back empty-handed. Well, not completely. He did bring back an order for her to report to the captain before turning in for the night.

Shoving aside her uneasiness over that summons, Abby waited to leave until Mason had fallen into a deep and natural sleep. The wound had mended perfectly well and his slight fever was gone. Already he could move most of his fingers and by dawn, they'd send him back to resume his duties. Rangers tended to heal faster than normal. The scientists speculated that an unusually strong constitution was the reason they were immune to Reaper infection in the first place. Or "freakishness," as the Scrapers called it.

While she and Doc had been busy patching up those who needed minor wounds tended, the other men cleared the field. Smoke from the pyres fogged the sky, bringing an early nightfall. All of the stranded passengers had been lifted to other ships and were well on their way back to their fortress cities in the mountains. The ship's pilot, according to Doc, had stayed behind with his crew to repair the damage, unwilling to take the loss. Airships were expensive and the pilot didn't want to take the chance that the Rangers would abandon his property.

The Rangers were under no real obligation to protect it. They received a yearly tithe from the City-States to guard the food sources and supply lines, but beyond that they were autonomous. Diplomat that he was, Cap wasn't going to stir up trouble if he could help it. Not when this ship flew under one of the most powerful flags in the federation. So, bottom line: the patrol was staying until the ship was repaired. No leave time in

New Providence, which meant she wouldn't be able to sneak off for the day to see Amy and the kids.

"You should go talk to him before he gets ticked off," Doc said, yanking off his boots. "When he said 'at your earliest convenience' he was just being polite. It doesn't make it any less of an order."

"I know. It doesn't mean I have to run onto the firing range either."

Doc's brows rose. "Did he see you chase Lyle into a pack of Reapers or is there something else I should know about?"

Abby laughed. "I'm his least troublesome recruit. You and I both know what his problem is and, besides, he's likely still busy kissing Scraper—"

She choked on the word when Doc stood and started working at his belt. He never slept in his skivvies. This was just his not-so-subtle way of chasing her out of the tent. He grinned. "Kissing Scraper ass means his mood will be more foul tonight, not less. The sooner you give him an excuse to hide in his tent, the better."

She turned around when he hooked his thumbs into the waistband of his pants. "I'm going. I'm going. Just give me a minute to get out."

"Eat something while you're there, will you? Nothing worse than a scrawny woman."

She smiled as she lifted the tent flap. "I am not courting your favor, Doc. Besides, there's something about sawing off body parts all day that always spoils my appetite. It disturbs me greatly that it always seems to make you horny."

"Eat anyway, love, and I promise not to importune

you. I can wait until we reach New Providence for that sort of companionship."

Laughing at his disgruntled tone, she let the flap fall behind her. He'd said it would be at least a week before the Scrapers retrieved the parts they needed. Another full day in the saddle to reach New Providence, but once they reached the tiny border town they'd get a warm welcome. Most border towns treated Rangers like gods. They wanted to make sure the Rangers remembered them fondly enough to come running the next time their town was under attack. Even if the patrol only bedded down for one night instead of the four they'd planned, there would be free food and whiskey. Eager women hoping to conceive a star-marked child because of the generous allowance the forts paid out to rear the new crop of Rangers. She'd seen men push their own wives and daughters on Rangers for a shot at that kind of money.

Doc liked to tease her about her lack of curves, but truth was she never lacked for male interest in the border towns. The other Rangers left her alone but the men in town seemed to view bedding her as a challenge, a mark of their virility even if they wouldn't earn a child price if she were to become pregnant.

She rarely availed herself of that interest. Rangers begat Rangers, and female offspring were rare. Female Rangers were confined to the fort once they became pregnant and encouraged to produce as many star-marked children as possible. She didn't want that life—not for herself and certainly not for any children she might bear.

Pulling her jacket tighter, she picked her way over the rocks toward the main camp, being careful not to step on any likely snake hidey-holes. She liked the cold; it meant winter was coming. The Reapers would retreat south soon. The night temperatures even in this dusty, rock-strewn, barren stretch of the border would drop too low for them to stay much longer. She'd survived ten summers so far. This one—God willing—would make eleven.

She didn't have far to walk. She could hear them up ahead—the deep roll of men's voices, the stomp and neigh of penned horses, the metallic clatter of bowls and spoons that told her she wasn't too late to eat. Once she turned the corner on the rocky outcrop, she could see light from the fires. Tonight, camp was no more than packed dirt ringed by a scattering of large sandstone boulders. They'd been fighting since before dawn and maybe their discipline wasn't quite what it should be. Exhausted Rangers had rolled into their blankets and slept where they dropped. Less than a half dozen men had been ambitious enough to erect their tents. One of those belonged to the captain.

As she approached, she spotted the airship crew gathered in a knot on the far side of the camp, huddled like children afraid of the dark. It was clear who the owner was by the elegantly tailored black suit he wore. It was clear who the pilot was too, by the way his shoulders slumped. She'd seen that same glazed look in the eyes of young men after their first Reaper attack and did not envy him. Even if he somehow managed to prove that he wasn't responsible for the crash, his career was likely over.

She wasn't going to waste much pity on him though, not a Scraper. He'd survive just fine. Unlike Ignatius.

Nodding to old Jasper, who sat cleaning his gun beside the fire, she pushed open the tent flap and stepped inside.

The captain's tent was large, not only to befit his station but because it was used for camp business as well as his personal use. The first chamber was empty save for a cold lantern set on a long folding table beside a few rolled maps. A sliver of light from the partition was all she had to see by as she crossed the space and rapped on the center pole to announce her presence. Cap called out a welcome and she entered.

He rose from behind his desk and she shifted uneasily beneath his intense regard. A great bear of a man, he had a neatly trimmed beard, the dark skin of an African and eyes that missed nothing. She'd been terrified of him when she was first assigned to his care. Sometimes, like now, she still was.

Fingers to heart, she saluted and he gestured to the chair across from him. "Please be seated, Abigail."

Abigail. Sometimes he addressed her as private, but never Abby. His manners always made her feel like a heathen. She'd once accused him of being raised mountaintop and his denial had been so scornful she believed it. He was very polite for a man who could rip the head off a Reaper with his bare hands. Very educated for a man still running patrols. Very outwardly calm for a man with a temper like a wildfire.

He'd never wanted her to join his patrol and while he'd always been fair enough to her, he made no secret of the fact that he thought she should be tucked away inside the fort. Truth was, she wasn't the best fighter, only a fair shot and an indifferent rider. But the same could be said of any number of the other Rangers and none of them was forced to endure these little chats.

He sat only when she did, shuffled some papers to the side and folded his meaty hands atop the scarred slab of wood he used as a portable desk. "In the morning, you'll leave for Fort Hill. I need you to deliver the message that we'll be delayed until the ship is repaired."

The blood drained from her face. It was the sort of errand they used the unmarked for. They wouldn't even send a first-year Ranger out on courier duty into secure territory unless it was as punishment.

"Have I done something wrong?"

"Not at all. I need a messenger and you've made it abundantly clear how you feel about assisting Doc."

"I don't mind helping Doc." *Not if this is the alternative.*

His bushy brows rose. "Fort Hill's a decent place. The captain's a good man and they're located farther from the border so they have more civilian contact than we do at Dougan. I'd like for you to have the opportunity to see it. They can afford any number of luxuries that we can't provide."

"I'm not interested in a transfer."

"Then you'll deliver the message and wait for us to join you. It shouldn't take us more than a fortnight."

A fortnight in a place that was basically one big research facility. They experimented on Reapers there, trying to come up with a cure for the contagion that turned ordinary men into ravening beasts. She wouldn't be able to sleep at night knowing what was locked in a cage on the other side of the wall, listening to her heartbeat and scenting her blood just waiting for a chance to get at her.

The people who worked there were nearly as bad. As one of the few star-marked women, she'd met her share of scientists. They always regarded her with a disturbing mix of fascination and plain lust. She was going to kill Doc for not warning her about this, for not talking the captain out of this fool-brained idea. As it was, her mind was too numb to even attempt to come up with an argument. Not that she'd ever successfully argued Cap out of anything once his mind was made up. Doc could manage it sometimes.

She stood stiffly. "Is there anything else?"

Cap was quiet for a long moment and then said, "This is not a punishment, Abigail."

"What is it then? You didn't want me here in the first place. This is just an excuse for you to send me back where you think I belong. It's bullshit and you know it."

If he was going to punish her for not having a dick between her legs, she might as well give him a better reason to do it. His jaw set. "I need someone to deliver the message and it's a good time for you to be away from the camp."

"Because of the Scrapers?"

That was why Doc hadn't been able to change his mind. He likely hadn't even tried because he agreed with the captain on this one. Cap inclined his head. “There’s renewed interest in placing us under Council control. When we sent noticc of an increase in the yearly tithe, several cities threatened refusal without an accounting of funds. They’re asking for a census of the star-marked children and now isn’t the time—”

“They have no right to that.”

He held up a hand to silence her. “Agreed. But it’s best if the Scrapers here have as little contact with you as possible.”

She shook her head. “Why bother? When you think the same as them, that I should be locked up making baby Rangers, whoring myself out in the name of duty.”

“Nobody’s asking that.”

“Aren’t they?”

She said it just to rile him. The captain fancied himself civilized and this was an old argument. He’d tell her she should be safe at the fort making baby Rangers and she’d accuse him of trying to turn her into a whore. His hands clasped together on the table were pale at the knuckles, and she felt a petty flare of triumph that she’d managed to get to him.

“You could marry just like any other woman,” he said. “You’d have your pick of men, I’d see to it. No one would force you to do anything.”

She made a rude noise and the captain sighed, leaned back in his chair and fixed her with a look of such abject disappointment it made her cringe inside. The worst part about these conversations was his sincerity. His determined paternal kindness meant she couldn’t completely hate him even though he held some truly asinine opinions.

"It's not what I want," she said simply, willing him to accept her choice and knowing that wish was futile.

"I only want what's best for you."

"I know it."

"You can wait until tomorrow to set out if you wish. They're not expecting us for a few days. Cam will be able to get you whatever supplies you need."

She waited for him to nod a dismissal and she was out of there like a shot, storming out of the tent and then stopping short when she got outside, undecided about where she wanted to be. Lyle looked up from where he was talking to Cam and flinched at whatever he saw on her face. He said something to Cam, who shook his head. She walked in the opposite direction. She didn't want to talk to either of them now. She didn't want to talk to anyone.

She kept to a brisk pace, not caring where she was going as long as it was away from everyone. She was marked and had no choice about being a Ranger, but she wasn't about to give up the freedom she had left. Some days it felt as if she was walking down a tunnel that collapsed behind her as she went. And no matter how much she dragged her feet or how hard she looked for a way out, there was only the one way forward. Angrily, she swiped the tears from her face.

Eventually she found herself standing on the one patch of ground that everyone would avoid. A slight breeze sent ashes dancing over the tops of her boots and she stepped back. It was stupid to want to stay here. Riding patrol meant that you were surrounded by death. Always.

Why cling to it?

It was a question she'd asked a million times, and she always came back to the same answer. Because the only alternative was for her to close herself behind the tall wooden walls of the fort and bear star-marked children, raise them, *love them* and then send them out here to this.

She wasn't going to let the captain push her to that. Doc either. Fuck them. *Fuck them all.*

She turned around and was surprised to find Lyle standing there, not more than a dozen feet away.

"I tried to talk him out of it."

"Not hard enough."

He swallowed a sound that was caught somewhere between a laugh and a groan. "It's a holiday not a firing squad."

"That's what you said when I went up with the delegation to the capital."

He scratched at his whiskers. "Yeah, well. That was not one of my finer ideas, I'll admit it. But this? What could possibly go wrong? It's a straight shot up to Fort Hill. No one will be the wiser if you make a little detour over to your sister's place. Visit with your nephews, get caught up with your family. Lord knows, you might not have the chance again for another year with the way they've been running patrols."

She sighed and closed her eyes, not wanting him to see how much that idea appealed to her. She hadn't seen Amy or the kids for months. She tried to hold on to her anger but felt it slipping away. "I had no choice but to say yes."

"I know, but that doesn't mean you can't make the best of it."

He wrapped an arm around her shoulders and turned her around. Away from smoldering ash and land that would be considered cursed for the next several generations. "It'll seem better in the morning, you'll see."

She held her silence as they started back to camp. She had enormous respect for Lyle and while she generally accepted his word as law, this time around she couldn't make herself believe him. Lyle was full of shit. Well-intentioned shit, but shit all the same. It wasn't going to be better in the morning. She wanted out of this life, and they both knew damned well that there was only one sure way to escape it.

Chapter Two

Abby tipped her hat down to block out the late afternoon sun. The saddle creaked as she shifted her weight, reaching for a clean handkerchief from her pack to wipe the worst of the sweat and road dust from her face. No point in alarming the locals. She'd never be pretty, but she could make herself presentable.

She'd hoped to make New Providence by midday, buy a few things for the kids and still reach her sister's ranch by nightfall. She would have made it too, if not for the damned airship crew monopolizing the captain's time all morning. They hadn't cleared out of his tent until nearly noon and then, she suspected, only because it was time for a meal. She'd have to stay overnight in New Providence now. As a Ranger she was safe, even alone, in any of the border towns. No one in their right mind would dare lay a hand on a Ranger. She'd buy her things when the shops opened in the morning and be on her way.

New Providence was one of the larger towns along their patrol route, located within a four-day ride of Fort Hill. She'd been here more times than she could count, but she'd never ridden in alone. As she passed down the main thoroughfare, she gathered more than a few curious stares along with an entourage of children who recognized her as a Ranger and didn't know enough to care that she was a woman too. They danced along almost under Marley's feet. Marley, trained not to panic even in the face of Reaper attack, paid the children no mind. Abby patted her mare's shoulder and Marley snorted by way of comment.

"Where's the rest of you?" The nearest boy asked. A smudge of dirt slashed across his cheekbone and he was barefoot.

"This is all of me."

He scowled. "I mean the other *Rangers*."

"They'll be along in another week or two. I'm a messenger passing through to Hill in the morning."

His mouth formed an O but his forehead wrinkled in confusion because even little kids knew it wasn't right to send a Ranger out as a courier. He shoved his hands in his pockets and did a little half jog, half skip to keep up. "Is there trouble?"

Her smiled faded at the concern that furrowed his brow. "No. No trouble. Not for you anyway." Since he didn't look convinced by that, she added, "There was an airship crash near Webster. I'm bringing news of it to Hill."

"You're pulling my leg."

She traced a cross over her heart. "God's honest truth."

"Did it catch fire? Did they all die?"

"No fire." *Thank God.* "And no injuries either, except to the pilot's pride. The patrol is stuck until it's repaired. You want to do me a favor?" When he nodded, she continued, "You go tell your sheriff the news for me. Tell him he'll want to put out an extra watch until the patrol comes through and gives the all clear. You got that?" It would be one less thing she'd have to do before she went to sleep. Caleb could just as efficiently spread the word, but the boy would surely enjoy the errand better. "If he wants to talk, I'll be at the Barrel."

The boy scurried off on his errand but the rest of his gang stuck, following her into the center of town where the general store, inn and saloon were clustered. When she dismounted and they realized she wasn't going to do anything exciting or dangerous, they drifted off to find other entertainment.

The Red Barrel was the pride of New Providence—a three-story inn the townspeople boasted as the finest establishment on the plains. The old structure had burned to the ground during a Reaper scare three years ago. This one smelled of new wood...and gin. The old one had smelled strongly of gin too, which was probably why it had taken them so long to put out the fire. The saloon took up most of the ground floor and judging by the number of horses tied outside, business was good. Leaving Marley in the care of a stable boy, Abby took her rifle and saddlebag and headed inside.

She'd visited New Providence often enough that the barkeep recognized her when she came through the doors. He lifted a hand in greeting as she approached the bar but his welcoming grin faltered a bit when he realized that she was alone. She didn't take it personally. The forts paid generously for housing a patrol, and he'd be disappointed in a solitary rider.

"Alone?" He kept glancing over her shoulder as if waiting for the rest of the patrol to appear.

"It's only me today, Caleb. Do you have a room?"

"I have a dozen. These riffraff only come for the gin. Ranchers pay out on Fridays, you know. It's bound to get lively later. You sure you don't want May's?"

She slung her bag over an empty stool and sat down beside it. "You turning away paying business?"

"No," he rushed to assure her. "Oh, no. We'll be glad to put you up, as always. Hey, Lou. Take Abby's things up to the honeymoon suite."

She raised her eyebrows and he shrugged. "It's where the captain always stays and it's empty. The fort will pay, eh?"

"Sure they will." Like Lyle had said, she might as well make the best of this.

He poured a dram of whiskey and pushed it across the bar. Leaning forward to rest his arms on the scarred wood, he lowered his voice. "Behind you, at the table by the window, that's Gallagher's eldest. Rich family, you know them?" When she shook her head, his frown deepened. "They'll be moving up soon. He and his crew have been in here all day, bored and looking for trouble. You watch out for him. His name's Nelson and he's been staring at you since you walked in. I don't care for the look in his eyes, but I don't want any trouble. You understand?"

"Are you worried about me or about him?"

Caleb snorted. "I'm only making the kindly request that if you do *have* to hurt him, you do it outside."

"Is he truly that stupid?"

"He's truly that drunk."

Abby lifted her glass in salute and Caleb nodded before moving down the bar to fill another order. She let the liquid burn down her throat before searching the mirror for her unwanted admirer. As irritating and overzealous as the other Rangers could be, it was strange and somewhat disturbing not to have them there. No one messed with a woman who had two dozen violently inclined and heavily armed brothers at her back. Of course, it would be beyond foolish for anyone to interfere with a Ranger at all.

Plenty of fools in the world. She could almost hear the sound of Doc's voice in her ear. God help her.

It took her a minute to spot Gallagher. He sat in the corner, back to the wall, cradling a full glass of gin. His long legs were stretched out beneath the table, the boots worn and still coated with dust from the road. Lean and wiry like the wolves that came down from the north during a hard winter. The bones in his shoulders poked against the thin fabric of his shirt and, where his sleeves were cuffed back, the muscles in his forearms were sharply defined. One gun at his hip but no other weapon that she could see, unless she counted his hands. And she'd have to do that. They were big, with thick fingers and rocks for knuckles.

His head was downcast and his worn hat hid most of his features. His clothes were dirty, but his black hair looked clean. Cut badly. The uneven ends touched his collar and a day's worth of stubble covered his angular jaw. Gallagher didn't look like a rich man's son, a drunk or a fool. He looked rough, dirty and not at all sociable.

As if he sensed her scrutiny, he lifted his head and looked right at her. Cool amusement flickered in his dark eyes and he nodded—a slight, mocking inclination of his head.

Embarrassed to have been caught staring, she downed the last of her drink and set her glass on the sticky bar top. She signaled to Caleb for another. One more drink. A good night's sleep and she'd be on her way in the morning. She wasn't looking for trouble and Gallagher had trouble written all over him. She didn't need to check the mirror to know he was still watching her. She could feel his gaze like an itch between her shoulder blades. Somehow, she knew if she looked up again, he'd be smiling.

Taking some comfort in the weight of iron strapped to her hips, she briefly considered a confrontation but quickly discarded the idea. While she didn't like the idea of being chased to her room, Cap would surely punish her if she started killing civilians because they looked at her the wrong way.

And rightfully so.

If Caleb was surprised that she was already asking for more, he didn't comment, just poured a second, slightly more generous allowance of whiskey into her glass and stashed the precious bottle beneath the bar. Most of his regulars drank gin, which Caleb made himself. The whiskey he was serving her was likely imported. The good stuff came from across the ocean. Because the Americas were under quarantine, whiskey had to be smuggled in through the Scraper cities or the few remaining walled port towns on the coast. Every bottle cost an arm and a leg, but Caleb would bill the fort for whatever she drank. The forts were funded by a tithe from the City-States of America and the CSA had very deep pockets indeed.

"Well, hello there, beautiful." A hand closed over her shoulder and she nearly jumped out of her skin. "Ain't seen you around here before."

She had her hand on her gun, ready to draw, before she realized there was no threat. Civilian, she reminded herself sternly, forcing her muscles to relax. That cowboy had her on edge. She took a sip of the fine and very expensive whiskey before turning her attention to the gangly young fool stupid enough to sneak up on an armed Ranger. And he was young, with smooth skin on his baby cheeks, tousled brown hair and drunk-bright eyes. He'd likely just come of age and was out to prove himself to his friends, which made him both reckless and dangerous. Someone would have to teach him a lesson but it wasn't going to be her.

"I'm not interested."

He tsked. "Not interested in a friendly chat?" Sliding onto the empty stool beside her, he said, "Dale's out telling people about the airship crash. I imagine you're all shook up about it. If you're looking for company—"

"No," she said firmly. "I am most definitely not."

Ignoring the warning in her voice, he leaned in closer, resting his elbow on the bar next to her. His friends settled in too because, of course, his kind tended to run in packs. Surrounded. She could feel the men crowding in behind her. She could smell them. When Lou had grabbed her bags, she'd held on to her rifle. It lay across her lap, useless as a gun in these close quarters, but she could use it as a club if she needed to. And there were always her pistols and the knives.

Caleb hovered, eyes darting nervously around at the men. She *could* possibly take all of them, even alone, but his bar would be damaged and the fort wouldn't pay him for that, not if a Ranger was attacked in his establishment. Caleb ended his head count with a stern look directed at the man now ogling her chest. Lord knew why, not much there to begin with. Her breasts were bound and completely covered by a sweat-stained cotton shirt buttoned to the neck. "Nelson."

This was Nelson?

Her gaze shot to the mirror, searching for the man in the corner, but he was gone. The empty wooden chair was tucked neatly beneath the table. Light from the dirty window reflected off the wet ring where his glass had been.

Nelson spread his hands on the bar. "Me and the lady are just sitting here having a nice conversation. Isn't that right, beautiful?"

Caleb's hands were out of sight behind the bar. Sweat beaded on his forehead. She decided to have mercy on him.

"We're fine here, Caleb. I can handle this."

Still, he hesitated. Nelson had to push it. "You heard the lady, Caleb. Why don't you go fetch us another round?"

Again, Caleb looked to her for direction. She gave him a slight nod. He took a tray and grabbed glasses from the shelf, five a hand, one for each meaty finger.

Grumbling to himself, he poured, keeping a wary eye on them the whole time.

Abby shifted her attention back to Nelson. He was definitely not the type to chase after a too-tall, too-thin woman as hard as an unbroken saddle. But then, some men had a fascination with Rangers. Kids always chased after them when they rode through town, boys asking if they could come along. Maybe Nelson had been one of those bright-eyed kids. The thought kept her from immediately driving the butt of her rifle into his perfectly straight nose.

"I was gone last year when your patrol came through." Nelson's words were mildly slurred. "My fiancée was here though and now she has a little star-marked boy."

"Congratulations."

"Oh, I don't want the money." A hank of hair had torn loose of her braid. He slid the strands between his fingers as if testing the sheen of satin and then slowly coiled them around his finger. When he had purchase, he tugged, pulling her close enough that his gin-soaked breath spilled down her neck to her collarbone. "But I do intend to get paid. Do you understand me, *Ranger?*"

She pushed the barrel of her rifle into his gut and he dropped her hair. His eyes widened, more in surprise than alarm. He wasn't nearly as frightened as he should be.

"Tell your friends to back off."

The ones nearest to her didn't wait to be told. They were only hired hands, not looking for a fight with a Ranger. People didn't pick fights with Rangers—and for good reason. Cap wouldn't have to lift a finger for retribution. All he would have to do is not show up next time the Reapers raided New Providence. Caleb knew it. The ranchers knew it. Only Nelson was too drunk, stupid or proud to let it go…likely all three.

"You're making a mistake, darlin'. I ain't looking for trouble. Just offering you a clean ride from someone who doesn't smell like gun smoke and horseshit."

"Oh, I smell a load of shit. There's no mistaking that." Her finger flirted with the trigger. "As *I'm* not looking for any trouble tonight, I'm going to give you a chance to reconsider your…offer." She gave him her nastiest smile and pointed the gun at his groin. "This is a no-thank-you you're looking at and I suggest you respect it."

One of his friends clapped Nelson on the back. "C'mon, Gallagher. There are other women upstairs, prettier ones and willing."

Nelson slid off his stool. He hesitated for a moment. She could see the calculation in his eyes as he tried to decide if he was fast enough to swat the barrel away before she could pull the trigger. A man like him…a *boy* like him would hate to be made a fool of by anyone, but especially by a woman. She pitied his poor young bride, she sincerely did. Abby settled her finger more firmly upon the trigger, knowing precisely how much pressure it would take to pull it.

For fuck's sake, walk away, kid.

And he did, after making a slight feint meant to startle her. If her nerves had been jumpy or she'd been less familiar with her weapon, he would have died in that moment. Instead, he lived to swagger back to his table for another drink with his buddies. She tracked him with her gun until he sat down. Releasing a shaky breath, she removed her finger from the trigger. When she turned back to face the bar, Caleb was standing directly across from her, white-faced and wide-eyed.

Nelson said something she couldn't quite make out and his friends laughed uproariously. She kept an eye on him through the mirror until Nelson let Maggie lead him upstairs and his friends drifted away to attend to their own business.

Caleb's expression was miserable. "I'm sorry about that."

She shrugged. "Not your fault, really."

"He'll be back down here in a half hour, maybe less. *Probably* less." Caleb tried for a smile and failed. He was stuck in a hard place, she knew it. He couldn't offend the Rangers, but the Gallaghers owned this town.

"I was thinking maybe it would be for the best if I stayed with widow Foster tonight."

May Foster ran a boardinghouse for women at the edge of town. Abby had only stayed there once, as widow Foster had puritanical rules and a watchful eye. It would be worth it for one night if it meant she avoided having to put a bullet in a stupid boy who didn't know when to shut his mouth.

Caleb released a ragged sigh and bobbed his head in agreement. "I am truly sorry, Abby, but I think it might be for the best. If you leave out the back and go through the courtyard, none of Gallagher's men will even know you're gone. I'll send Lou over with your things."

Abby downed the last of her whiskey and stood. "Have Marley ready for me at dawn. I'll be leaving early."

"I'll pack a basket of food to see you on your way to your sister's." He hesitated. "Does Amy still like cherry pie as much as she did when she was little?"

Abby bit back a smile. "She does. Apple too. Never lost her sweet tooth."

"Sally makes the best. I'll send a bottle of gin for Bill too."

Abby touched his hand and he finally met her gaze. "You don't need to buy me off. You've always treated us fairly. I don't need pie and gin to keep my mouth shut."

His smile didn't quite reach his eyes. "Maybe I need to give it to you."

She left out the back as Caleb suggested. She wasn't going to get caught up in the politics here. If slinking out meant less trouble for Caleb, she'd do it—even if it stung her pride.

And it would have been fine too if Nelson, who'd taken considerably less time with Maggie than a half hour, hadn't been coming back from the outhouse at the exact moment that Abby was crossing the courtyard. The sun had just set behind the mountains. The sky above was bruised and starless. One shuddering lantern lit a path to the outhouse but even in the dim light, she recognized Nelson by his swagger. Of all the luck…

"Hey there, beautiful," he said, voice dripping with sarcasm. "Did you have a change of heart?"

She took a step back toward the inn but stopped when a door squealed open behind her. Glancing over her shoulder, she recognized two of Gallagher's friends. Not the hired hands who'd been uncomfortable with the exchange but Nelson's actual friends who would back him up even when he was being an idiot.

The courtyard was framed between the inn and the stables. Caleb had fenced the front for privacy and to keep vagrants from begging at the kitchen doors. Sally, Caleb's wife and the inn's cook, had a small herb garden along the fence line, well away from the outhouse in the back. The smell of basil and lavender mixed freely with the smell of horse and the lye Caleb used to control the stench from the pit. The kitchen was at the rear of the inn and it was dark, Sally having gone up to bed as soon as Abby left. If she yelled for help, one of the stable boys might hear her. It was less certain that they'd come.

And truth be told, she wasn't sure she *wanted* to call anyone else into this fight. Not while there was still a chance to avoid bloodshed.

"Stand aside, Nelson." Sweat trickled from her hatband and slipped down the side of her face. "I'd rather not kill you, but I will shoot if you force my hand."

She lifted her rifle to demonstrate that point, the cold barrel heavy in her palm. She hoped he wouldn't make it necessary. These weren't Reapers. These were the people she was supposed to protect. Cam would tell her not to take any chances, that it was better to shoot first and sort out the bodies later. Lyle, the captain, even Doc would give her that same advice, *had* given her that same advice time and time again. But she'd never had to kill a human before. Someone uninfected with loved ones at home and his whole life ahead of him.

She thought that might break something inside her even if her hand was forced. All the things she told herself about how she was more than just a killer, that she fought for the good of normal people, that her life meant *something* would begin to unravel if she pulled the trigger now.

The two men behind her moved in closer, but she stood her ground. One of them, standing directly behind her, said, "Nelson, step off. You've had your fun."

"Fuck you, Charlie. I ain't done with her yet."

In the next yard over, a dog started barking and Charlie raised his voice. "The last thing we need is to cross a patrol of Rangers."

Nelson ignored his sensible friend and took another step forward. She could have taken her shot then. Unmarked men were so fragile. Even if she only clipped him, infection was almost unavoidable. But before she overcame her reluctance, she heard the soft click of a hammer and a hard weight pressed against her spine.

"Take her rifle. Nelson, you're a fucking idiot." Charlie's breath was hot on her neck, even as Nelson ripped the gun from her hands. He lowered his voice. "There doesn't have to be blood over this, Ranger. We go have a few drinks, a little fun and then we'll go our separate ways."

But helplessness turned some men mean and apparently Nelson was of that breed. While his friend whispered reassurances, Nelson took a step closer, grabbed her chin hard and tilted her face up. When he tried to kiss her, she reacted, pulling him forward and off balance, planting her leg between his to trip him up and then swinging him around as he started to fall. Nelson caught himself on his hands and knees, and Charlie's gun stopped pointing at her as he bent to help his friend. She still had her pistols. Before Charlie aimed the rifle, she could take him. She could kill them all and good riddance.

She began to draw but then caught a glimpse of the terrified expression on the face of the nearest man. He couldn't be more than fifteen. Biting back a curse—directed at herself—she turned and ran.

Darting down a back alley, she shoved her pistol into its holster to free her hands. There were no lit windows on either of the tall buildings hemming her in. The alley smelled like piss and seemed to narrow as she ran toward the unrelieved darkness at the far end. She could hear the thud of boot heels behind her along with Nelson's raised voice. When she reached the end of the alley, her heart sank into her boots. A makeshift wooden fence blocked the outlet. No gate. Too high to climb with what little time she had left.

Behind her, Nelson laughed. "Ain't going nowhere, beautiful, are you now?"

Charlie swore. "You're such a fucking moron, Nelson. I tell you this is the last time I listen to you. What do you think happens when she goes back to her patrol and talks?"

You're dead, that's what, Abby thought without a great deal of sympathy.

"That's right," Charlie said, as if he'd heard the thought. "We're dead."

"Then she doesn't talk."

"I'm going home. I want no part of this. If you think—"

There was the heavy sound of a fist hitting flesh followed by a sharp grunt. She couldn't see the scuffle clearly in the darkness but since they seemed distracted, she decided to attempt the wall. There were a few broken crates along the bottom of the fence and she scrambled up, launching herself toward the top with everything she had. Her fingertips barely caught the roughly sawed edge. Momentum slammed her body into the wall, making it shake. Nelson cried out behind her.

She managed to hook a toe over the top when one of the bastards grabbed her hanging ankle. Kicking out hard, she smiled grimly at the shock of contact that ran up her leg. With one last heave, she threw her leg over and then straddled the fence for a second before swinging down to the other side.

Chickens scattered. She was standing in a small, foul-smelling yard between two houses. The chickens squawked in annoyance as she pushed her way through their domain. There was a gate on the opposite side.

Her palms were scraped all to hell and...*damn it*—she poked her finger through a hole in the back of her pants. Right on the seat. That would be a bitch to patch, if she got out of this alive.

She would get out alive, she thought grimly. Just like she'd survived everything else. If it came down to it, she'd kill Nelson. Charlie too, and anyone else who got in her way. She just didn't want to fucking have to do that.

Ducking her head, she kept to the shadows. She didn't want to give anyone a clean shot if they came at her from the other direction. She had no illusions that Nelson's crew would let her go if they found her. Not now. It had gone too far for that. They'd need her silence and, idiot that he was, even Nelson would recognize that there was only one way to ensure it. When she reached the gate, a hand caught her wrist. Before she could scream, another clamped over her mouth.

She tasted gin and salt until her attacker jerked her back and her lip split against her own teeth, filling her mouth with blood. He was taller than she was by at least half a foot and very strong, hauling her back as if she didn't weigh a thing, every step taking her farther away from the gate and deeper into the shadows.

"Quiet."

She brought her arms up inside his hold and then sharply down, but she couldn't dislodge his grip. When she jerked forward, he moved with her, using his weight to force her off balance. The kick she aimed at his shin barely grazed him before he turned her and pressed her face into the wall, trapping her legs between his own. She landed an elbow to his ribs and he grunted. A low and violent sound that chilled her to the bone.

Maybe she shouldn't have bit his hand.

Up until that point, he'd only been trying to restrain her, but as soon as her teeth broke skin, he pulled her head back sharply, nearly lifting her off her feet. She bit harder but he didn't so much as flinch, only tightened his hold until she gasped. Swearing, he unclamped her teeth from the meaty part of his hand. Stubble from his cheek caught in her hair as he pressed his lips to her ear. "Be still, damn it. I'm not going to hurt you."

Right. But she knew when she was overpowered, knew how to lie still and look for an opening to attack. When she stopped fighting, he loosened his hold just enough for her to drag in a breath.

"You *are* hurting me."

"Your choice to turn this ugly, not mine. The wall won't stop them for long." Even as he said it, she could hear the creak and rattle of the fence.

"Which is why I was headed for the gate," she snapped.

"They sent men around to that side, with horses and orders to take you back to some cabin. They're herding you away from the inn."

"And what? Your conscience get to you?"

"I'm not with those men."

Bullshit. "Who are you then?"

"No time for introductions, sweetheart." His weight lifted from her. "Come on. This way."

He grabbed for her wrist but she swung away, stepping out of reach. In the same motion, she drew her gun and pointed it at his chest. He held up his hands to show he was unarmed but she still couldn't see his face. She wished she could see his face.

A huff of laughter escaped his lips. "You'll shoot me for trying to help you but let that mewling brat put his hands all over you? If you want to stay here and wait for them to come through that gate, you do that. If you want a way out, it's this way."

Ignoring the gun leveled at him, he turned and headed toward the house. A sliver of light seeped from beneath the back door and her breath locked in her throat when he passed in front of it. She recognized the lean silhouette of his body. The creased gray hat and the way his eyes glinted when he turned his head to see if she was coming. The cowboy from the saloon. The dangerous, dirty, unsettling man who'd disappeared like a ghost.

There were three angry men behind her or this one man. Dirt and danger notwithstanding, he seemed to want to help. And she still had her pistols. Jogging to catch up, she followed him toward the house. He didn't lead her inside. Instead, he brought her to a gap between the house and fence. Working his hands into the opening, he tugged at the warped board. The squeal of the nail pulling free made her wince and she heard someone stir inside.

"Hurry." He took her by the arm and propelled her forward. She slipped through without a problem, but it was a tighter fit for her savior. While he worked his way through, she ran ahead, dodging puddles and keeping to the shadows. One look told her the side street was clear. She could run for it but hesitated, unwilling to leave the stranger behind. She *should* run. For all she knew, he was no better than Gallagher. But years of working on a team made her loathe to leave a man behind.

Ignoring the voice in her head calling her a fool, she started back only to draw up short at the sound of splintering wood. Taking aim down the alley to be on the safe side, she lowered her pistol when the cowboy stepped from the darkness. He didn't pause at the sight of her weapon, didn't even blink. Just grabbed her by the elbow to turn her around and pulled her with him down the alley.

"Was that the fence?"

Light flared from the window directly above their heads as the occupants of the house rushed toward the back to see what was happening. Briefly, the light illuminated his face. A glint of stubble, the stark angle of a high cheekbone. Even his black eyes were hard as his gaze met hers. The curve of his mouth was the only soft thing about him and that, too, was disturbing in its own way. "They decided to go around. We need to move fast."

Crossing a side street, they slipped down another alley, turned right at the end and then jumped across a sluggish stream of waste coming from the shacks above. She'd seen the rickety clapboard structures. New to the town. It always amazed her that people came to these border towns on purpose, most of them running from something and ending here as a last stop.

Breath panting out in small gasps, she tried to keep up with the cowboy. She wondered what his story was. Even if they weren't running for their lives, she wouldn't ask. New Providence was the kind of town where nobody had a past. Your new life started the day you walked into town and if you caused trouble, justice was usually swift and final.

A fine way to run a town, really. She should have

considered that before she decided to give Nelson a second chance.

Seeing her lagging, the cowboy grabbed her hand and hauled her up the short hill along a crude gravel path. He had the hands of a hard laborer; the skin on his palm was thick and dry. A grip like a manacle. When he paused inside the mouth of another dark and piss-scented alley, she jerked free.

"That's enough. We've lost them." She stepped back to put some distance between them as he turned around. The alley was dark and his face was in shadow. Only the glitter of his eyes told her she had his attention. "I'm not going any farther until I know who you are."

"I'm the man who saved your ass."

The cowboy didn't make a move for her, possibly because her hand was resting on her pistol. Possibly, he was just biding his time. His posture was relaxed but alert. Nothing in his body language was aggressive, but he still made her nervous. Strange, because Nelson had only made her feel tired and very old.

"You have my thanks, but I can make it on my own from here."

His weight shifted. A subtle change, but threatening all the same. Every damn thing about him was threatening. He jerked his chin toward the road. "I've got a place nearby where we can wait for them to clear out."

She thought about the strength in his long frame when he'd crushed her body to his. Those hands like manacles closing around her wrists. The hard glint to his eyes now. Nothing about him suggested that kindness was one of his governing characteristics. A droplet of sweat slid down the side of her neck and she shivered.

"I don't think so."

The raspy sound that came from his throat might have been laughter. "You think I'm leaving you here alone when there are a half dozen men out there prowling for your blood?"

"What I think is that you don't have a say in the matter."

She peered around the corner of the building to get her bearings. They were on the opposite side of town from the inn, but she could slip along the back of the properties and come at it from the other side. New Providence was no metropolis. Even if she crept from shadow to shadow, it wouldn't take her more than an hour to reach May's. When he touched her shoulder, she nearly jumped out of her skin. Damn it, he was light on his feet.

"I'll follow you if I need to."

She opened her mouth to protest, but a shout drew her attention. The rumble of excited male voices coming their way. The cowboy lifted his head and turned it slightly, listening. To her it sounded like the men were still a ways off, but it was difficult to be sure.

Without warning, the cowboy dragged her farther down the alley. When she hesitated, he picked her up and slammed her against the rough wood. She let out a startled yelp and he smothered the sound with his mouth. His lips were hard on hers but gentled when she tried to pull away.

"They're coming. And I can't take them all. Not without… You just follow my lead, all right?" She nodded and his big hands caught at the backs of her thighs. "Around my waist. There you go."

Shifting his hips forward to pin her to the wall, he widened his stance and flipped the edge of his leather duster down from where it had gotten caught on her boot.

"Can't let them see your trousers." His breath fanned her cheek. "Not when we want them to see just another whore."

"I'm not a whore."

The voices were coming closer and she could see the flicker of orange torchlight creeping down the alley, making shadows bounce along the wood. Even with his big body supporting her, she felt like she was going to fall. She clutched at his shoulders. He leaned hard against her to keep her in place, dropping an arm beside her head and lowering his mouth until it was a hairsbreadth from hers.

"Stop squirming, Abby."

Campfire smoke clung to his clothes and hair, overpowering the smell of horse and sweat. She could almost taste the gin on his breath.

"How do you know my name?"

"The barkeep said it."

She parted her lips to ask another question but he closed the distance between them, silencing her with the slowest, sweetest kiss she'd ever shared. That gentle, almost shy kiss coming from this man made her forget for a minute where she was. Bending his knees, he tipped his hips forward to rub his cock against her. A sharp hunger rose inside her and she wished suddenly that this wasn't an act. That they were alone and free to indulge every filthy desire that sprung to mind. She hadn't been with a man since Mason joined the patrol and she promised his Ranger mother that she'd look out for him. Watching over the boy had made her feel maternal. Doc had teased her mercilessly about her sudden respectability but…well, lovers or not, she'd been lonely for a long time before that.

Now, with this stranger's tongue delicately exploring her mouth and his hard cock insistently rocking against her most sensitive parts, she couldn't help but respond. She wasn't innocent, certainly wasn't a virgin. Her desire to stay childless kept her chaste—it didn't make her a saint. She made a noise back in her throat and he laughed, low and dirty, the sound of it rumbling from his chest right into her body.

"Who's there?"

She flinched. Nelson sounded as if he had every right to be out pestering people. The cowboy didn't acknowledge the question. He stretched an arm behind her back and slammed her into the wall, making old paint flakes fall around them like snow. He was protecting her, this stranger. Hard to remember he was a stranger when his enormously erect cock was riding against her clit. "Make them believe it, Abby."

His fingers knotted in the hair at her nape and he tugged back her head, bending his mouth to her neck and nipping lightly.

She gasped in surprise and he growled. "That's it. Louder. Let them hear you."

"You there. I'm talking to you."

The cowboy lifted his head. "I'm busy."

He made the wall shake again. She could feel him there between her legs. Hot and hard. She was wet. She wondered if he could tell that, tried to decide if she cared.

"We're looking for a woman."

"Find your own. This one's bought and paid for and I mean to enjoy her." The cowboy looked over his shoulder and the scruff on his chin grazed her cheek.

"Let me see her." She could almost see the scowl on Nelson's face.

"I told you this one's mine. Find your own."

"She's a Ranger."

The cowboy laughed. "This ain't a man."

She heard Nelson take a step closer and she eased her gun from her holster. The cowboy didn't say a word, but Abby could feel his body tighten.

"Come on, Nelson." That was Charlie. Apparently, the two friends had reconciled. "It's not her. She could be gone by now. Her horse is back at the inn. She'll have to go back for it. We'll wait there."

She heard a splash as someone stepped into a puddle, followed by a muffled curse. The light dimmed as the men retreated. They meant to kill her. They were likely scared now that things had escalated to this point. Once the Rangers of her patrol learned of this, they'd descend like avenging angels.

As she listened to the men leave, she stared up at her cowboy. Strong jaw, high cheekbones, heavy brows drawn tight together in a frown. He turned back to her as the alley fell abruptly dark.

"They're gone?"

"Almost." He didn't release her immediately and she didn't try to get free. Instead, she tightened her thighs around his hips, placed her palm to the back of his neck and pulled his head down.

One more taste.

When she touched her lips to his, he froze. All the heat seemed to drain out of his body, leaving a statue behind. *Had it been an act for him?* She didn't believe it. There'd been something desperate in his kiss there at the end. A raw and needy hunger like the one welling up inside her. She traced her tongue along his compressed lips, angled her hips so she cradled his still rock-hard erection. Not a statue. Not indifferent anyway.

A shudder ran through his body and his hips rocked forward. His lips parted enough for her to slip her tongue inside and she groaned as he tentatively touched her. She deepened the kiss and he finally responded. Heat flared between them like a spark hitting tinder. His weight pinned her to the wall and his hands came up to cradle her face. He kissed her hard enough to bruise and when his teeth accidentally grazed her lip, she gasped. He sucked at the wound, soothing it with his tongue. Another shudder ran through his body and he pulled back, murmuring an apology as he nuzzled a path down the column of her throat. Moaning, she angled her head to allow him better access.

God, that was good. She closed her eyes to more fully savor the feeling. The soft brush of his lips and the sting from the stubble on his jaw. The smell of him—gun oil, smoke and gin. The way his breathing was as unsteady as hers, though she reckoned he was probably more familiar with a back alley tumble than she was. That thought she shoved aside. She slipped her hands inside his duster, pressing her palms to his waist just above his belt. Heat like a forge. She flexed her fingers, felt the muscles in his abdomen twitch beneath the thin fabric of his shirt. Too skinny. All sinew and bone. They were a pair.

She skated her hands up his body, enjoying the feel of his chest, the thud of his heartbeat beneath her fingertips. He nuzzled at her jaw, his tongue stroking a sensitive spot below her ear. She squirmed and he moved his hands to her thighs, lifting her body and pressing her harder into the wall at the same time.

Her head knocked against the wood and she yelped. It hadn't really hurt. Surprised her more than anything, but the cowboy reacted as though she'd tossed a bucket of cold water over his head. He jerked back and then stared down at her. His expression said he was wondering how she'd managed to sneak up and wrap herself around his body when he wasn't looking. Since she felt some of that herself, she wasn't particularly offended.

She smiled at him, warm and hopeful. "Is it time for that introduction?"

"They're gone, Abby. We can stop this."

His hands tightened and she moved at the pressure, instinctively tipping her hips. Stiff as a rock. She scraped her teeth over the whiskers on his chin, licked at the seam of his narrow lips. "And if I don't want to stop?"

"That's the fight talking." He released a ragged breath and started to untangle her legs. "We need to get you away from here. Find somewhere safe and figure out how to get your horse."

The shock was nearly painful. She couldn't do anything but stare as he stepped away. Her feet dropped to the ground with a thud. At least in the dark, he wouldn't be able to see the blush rising to her cheeks.

He wiped his mouth with the heel of his hand. "I'll check the road."

Numb with disappointment, she watched him walk toward the mouth of the alley. The distance cleared her head, along with the chill air that replaced the heat where his body had been.

He was right, she knew that. This was neither the time nor the place. She didn't know who he was or why he was helping her, and Nelson was still out roaming the streets. The last thing she should be worried about was seducing the pants off a dangerous-looking cowboy in a dark, dank alley behind the tannery. But knowing it was the truth didn't make her feel any less surly.

Scowling at the cowboy's back, she jerked down her shirt and followed. By the time she joined him, she felt, well, not better but at least less likely to pull her gun on him and demand he finish what he'd started. "Did you see which way they went?"

"East." His voice was rough as a rusty hinge.

"I have a bed at widow Foster's. Caleb's already sent my belongings." She glanced down the road. No streetlamps but no movement either. Just shadows and dark windowless shacks. "If I could get my horse, I'd move on tonight."

"I can get to your horse."

"They'll be watching the stables."

He scratched his jaw, not quite looking her in the eye. "Take mine, then. I'll catch up with you outside of town."

She didn't want to do that. She wanted to leave—alone—and not look back. A gust of wind whipped a piece of hair into her mouth. Impatiently, she pushed it away and squinted at him. "Why are you doing this?"

She'd thought he was doing it for a chance to bed a Ranger. Clearly, that wasn't the case or he would have been more willing to finish what he'd started. He looked down the street once more and then put his hand on her back to guide her forward. As soon as she started moving, his hand fell away. "I didn't want to see you get hurt."

"That's it?"

The corner of his mouth turned up. "You don't believe me? Isn't that what Rangers do—protect those who can't protect themselves? Maybe I'm just repaying the favor."

She bristled. "I can protect myself. You saved Nelson from a bullet, not me."

"Ah."

She looked at him sharply, but he was staring down the empty road. He pointed to the right and she followed his direction, onto a path that would take them opposite the inn, behind the general store and blacksmith's. They walked in silence.

Once, he touched her shoulder to stop her and cocked his head like he was listening for some sound she couldn't make out. After a minute, he released her and they started off again, keeping to the shadows, avoiding the runoff from the ditches that trickled along the backs of the houses. For such a big man he moved quietly. Their boots scuffed upon the occasional rock but other than that small noise and the voices coming from the saloon, the night was still.

By the time they'd reached the edge of town, some of her surliness had faded, replaced by regret that she was treating her Good Samaritan so shabbily. If she couldn't take rejection gracefully then she was no better than Nelson.

A faint orange glow reflecting in a puddle up ahead caught her attention and she grabbed hold of the cowboy's hand, pulling him down to crouch behind the wall of the smithy. She pointed and he squeezed her hand to let her know he saw it too. After a moment, a lone man passed, headed in the opposite direction.

Before they moved on, she whispered, "I'm sorry I said that about not needing your help. I don't mean to seem ungrateful. I appreciate you stepping in like you did. It would have come to bloodshed otherwise, Nelson's or mine." She touched his arm. "What I'm trying to say is thank you. I mean it."

He looked startled. Well, if he was to judge by her earlier behavior, he probably thought she had no manners to speak of. But despite her actions and Cap's opinion of her, she did know how to comport herself in civilized society. The cowboy held her gaze and nodded gravely. "You're welcome."

"If the offer of a horse stands, I'll take it. I can pay you, well enough for you to buy another. Caleb will keep Marley until the patrol comes through. I don't need an escort."

He seemed to consider it for a moment. "They'll follow you."

"If they follow me, I will shoot."

"Good." His eyes narrowed. "Why didn't you pull the trigger back at the inn?"

She shrugged, not sure she could explain it herself. She'd given Nelson and his friends a chance and one was all she had in her, especially now that they were after her blood. The Gallaghers didn't want her coming back to town with a band of Rangers at her back. Well, they should have thought of that before putting their dirty hands on her.

"Do we have a deal?"

He sucked at the inside of his cheek, clearly unhappy and she thought she understood the reason why.

"If you're especially attached to this horse. I can find a way to return it to you."

"That's not it," he said. "I still don't like the idea of you leaving on your own."

She smiled at the thought. "Mister, I appreciate the sentiment. But present circumstances notwithstanding, I do actually know how to take care of myself."

He grunted, a noncommittal sound that made her smile widen. If she'd been passing through this town with her patrol, she would have tried harder to seduce him to her bed. Doc had told her several ways to avoid pregnancy and while she didn't employ them often, this man might be worth the risk.

"Do we have a deal?" she repeated.

He angled his head up, eyes glinting from beneath the rim of his hat. "We have a deal."

They passed without incident to May's. She collected her bags while he retrieved his horse. May scowled at her for turning her out of her bed so late in the evening, but Abby signed the note that would compensate her handsomely for a little lost sleep. May also had a few toys in her parlor that she'd recently purchased for her grandson. She was gracious enough to allow Abby to purchase them—for triple the price. Something for the boys, which had been Abby's aim in stopping by New Providence in the first place.

Thirty minutes later, she left to meet her cowboy at the edge of town. He was already waiting, horse saddled and ready, holding the reins in one hand and her rifle in the other.

When he handed it to her, she lifted her brows. "How on earth did you manage to get this back?"

She smoothed her hand over the stock, smiling when her fingers reached the familiar starburst design carved into the wood.

He shrugged. "It's a hanging offense to be in possession of a Ranger firearm. Apparently no one wanted to take the risk. I found it in an alley outside the stables. They were watching or I would have tried for your horse too."

"You weren't followed?"

"No."

She wasn't sure she believed it even though he sounded terribly certain. Best be off. She mounted, pausing for a moment to say her thanks.

It was late, the town was quiet and the nearly full

moon was just now topping the eastern hills. The cowboy stood a few feet away from her, weight balanced slightly on his left foot. She memorized this image of her Good Samaritan in case they ever chanced to meet again. She wanted to remember him so she could thank him properly one day. Truthfully, she didn't know that she could forget him. Faded jeans, creased cotton shirt with the sleeves cuffed back. A worn belt circled his waist, only one gun in his holster. The muscles in his forearm bulged a bit from the weight of the bags he held at his side. He'd already pocketed the money she'd paid him for the horse.

"Don't get it into your head to follow me." She touched the butt of her rifle. "I won't take chances out there."

"Good." He nodded as if to emphasize the point. "You shouldn't take any chances. Goodbye, Abby."

He raised two fingers to his hat before slinging the bag over his shoulder. She watched until the shadows swallowed him and then she turned her back on New Providence.

Chapter Three

TWILIT BLUES AND purples lightened to pink at the horizon as Abby and her newly acquired horse clopped down the road, passing the final distance of their journey accompanied by birdsong and the dry whisper of wind in the grass. She'd stopped after midnight for a brief rest but hadn't managed to fall asleep. She'd been too riled up, too jumpy over what had happened in New Providence to do more than eat a few bites of the dry tack she found at the bottom of her bag and refill her water skin from the creek. After two hours of tossing and turning on the hard ground, she'd given up and saddled the horse.

Just like any nightmare, her fear began to fade with the rising sun. The memory was still there. Nelson and his crew. Her cowboy—dirty and disturbing and hot as hell. The cold press of the gun against her spine and that alley… She still didn't know what the hell she was going to do about it once she got back to her patrol, but she remembered every last detail as if they'd been burned into her mind.

It didn't sit well with her that the entire town would have to pay for Nelson's stupidity. On the other hand, *someone* needed to keep him in check or he'd just go on hurting other people. Maybe if she requested a public whipping for Nelson and let it go at that… Such a mess. Not for the first time, she cursed the momentary sentimentality that had made her hesitate to pull the trigger.

For now, she pushed it aside. It wasn't a decision she needed to make this morning. Better to wait until she was rested and thinking clearly. Right now, it was enough that she was alive to enjoy the new day. The sparkle of dew on the grass, the cool breeze stirring her hair and the familiar landmarks telling her that she was almost home.

Up ahead, she could see the old oak that marked the southwest corner of Amy's property. Lightning-split and leafless, it formed a stark outline against the early morning sky. Abby had always liked that tree. They'd often picnicked under its spreading branches. There'd been a spot near the top where she would perch when company was expected, pretending she was in the crow's nest of a pirate ship.

The storm that killed it happened the month before she left for the fort. Her mother had died a year earlier, which was a mercy. Beatrice Clark had lived in dread of the day when Rangers would come for her eldest daughter. When Abby was barely two, her mother—in one of her fits—had tried to burn the mark from her shoulder. Unheard of, that. Most people viewed the birth of a star-marked child as a gift sent direct from the Creator himself. Aside from bragging rights, a star-marked child meant your family would never starve and there was a good chance you'd be able to save enough from the child-price to move into the foothills and higher up to safety.

Her mother hadn't wanted her to be a Ranger. Abby's ambivalence about her place at the fort likely owed something to her mother's fear and hatred. To be fair, her mother had been heartbroken at the time and crazed with grief. Abby had no recollection of the event, only the puckered scar that was evidence of it. And her mother—a strong woman—had eventually recovered from that temporary madness, remarried and moved on.

Abby was one of the few Rangers who knew who her father was. He'd grown up on the next ranch over and had fallen in love with Beatrice while they were still children. By rights, he should have been transferred to a different patrol. It was against the rules for Rangers to form permanent attachments, but sometimes it happened.

Never ended well.

Amy and Bill shared a similar tale—neighboring farms, young love. But their story had a happier ending. Bill came from a ranching family and had married Amy for the water rights. Well, that wasn't the only reason, but it was what made his wealthier family approve of the love match. Abby was pleased to see that they seemed to be doing well. The year after the wedding, they'd switched the focus of the farm from agriculture to ranching in order to meet the demand for beef from the cities. Roland, her stepda, hadn't kept livestock beyond a few cows for milk, chickens and a small flock of sheep. When the buffalo roamed close, they had meat. Otherwise, they made do with what game they could catch.

It was risky work, ranching so close to the border,

but if you were careful and lucky, the money was decent. The place looked good, neat and well-ordered. It warmed her heart to see her family doing well.

The big black horse Abby had bought from the cowboy lifted his head and snorted, steam puffing from his nostrils in the cool morning air. Still skittish with his new rider. As loathe as she'd been to leave Marley behind, if she *had* to ride an unfamiliar horse, this one wasn't so bad. Sturdy and even-tempered. Not as fast or smart as Marley, but he had a clean smooth gait. When she'd retrieved her bags, she'd made arrangements with widow Foster to have Caleb deliver Marley to the fort once things settled down. Caleb owed her that much, at least.

The horse startled when a rabbit shot out of the ditch and across his path. When she patted him on the shoulder and murmured reassurance, he quickly settled.

"Not battle trained, are you?" He twitched a fly from his ear, but it gave the impression that he was shaking his head. She smiled. "I don't blame you. The good news is your master won't be riding you anywhere near Reapers once he comes to claim you. You should try to grow accustomed to rabbits though."

Her stomach grumbled. Hopefully, Amy would have coffee ready and breakfast on the table. The timing was right.

"I thought the boys might like to name you. You'll like them." They would like *him*, anyway. Overly enamored of horses and guns, her nephews.

The breeze passed a shiver through her and Abby pulled her coat closed. Strange. She didn't see any smoke rising from the chimney. Amy should be up by now. Bill should already be out seeing to the morning chores. Straightening in the saddle, her hand reached instinctively for her rifle.

It was too quiet.

By now, someone should have heard her. The kids should be running down the lane, shouting her name. A cold finger of dread slipped down her spine and knotted her gut. No use jumping to conclusions. She could see cattle in the pen behind the house so this wouldn't be a Reaper attack. Even if Reapers had managed to push so far north without the Rangers knowing about it, they surely wouldn't leave behind live cattle.

She got close enough to see the open door, to hear the plaintive lowing from a cow that had missed at least one milking. Chickens pecked in the dirt out front and fussed as she passed through. But other than the noise from the animals it was eerily quiet. The hiss of wind through the grass, the crunch of gravel beneath the horse's hooves sounded loud and unnatural. There were no birds singing from the boughs of the apple tree in the side yard.

Throat so tight she could barely swallow, Abby dismounted and slipped the reins over the front post. Her sweating palms made her grip on the rifle slippery and she flexed her hands as she mounted the porch steps to stare at the cracked door.

Wrong. Wrong. Wrong. Amy hollered like a banshee when the kids forgot to close the door.

The squeal of a swinging gate made Abby jump and spin with her rifle raised. She cursed when she realized it was just the wind. Dread threatened to lock her in place but she forced herself to turn and, heaving a deep breath, stepped inside.

Empty. Cold. Silent. Echoingly devoid of life.

Her gaze swept the big front room before lifting to the loft. Three steps took her into the only other room in the house, where Bill and Amy had their bed. The blankets were rumpled but the room was empty. Dust hung in the light streaming in through the open window. Footsteps echoing, she walked slowly back into the main room and then froze.

The pool of blood had been hidden from her view by the table. It was only about the size of a large plate and it looked like it had been there for a while. She knelt, tucking the rifle against her belly, and reached out a trembling finger to feel it. Tacky, but not completely dry. And just this one small spill.

This didn't have the markings of a Reaper attack. The animals alive. The cabin relatively untouched. She crouched on the floor staring into space with her fingers coated with blood until a fly landed on her knuckle. Shaking it off, she stood.

Right, then. She wasn't going to panic. Outside.

She didn't find any bodies in the barn or pens. She didn't see any more blood. But the horses were gone and there was a path cutting a straight line through the north field toward Fort Hill. She crouched at the edge of the trail. She could see the imprint from the horses' hooves, but the trail was wider than it should have been. Her family wouldn't ride shoulder to shoulder like that.

Rising, she walked several feet along the edge, not liking what she saw.

The ground had been trampled by human feet. Bare, because Reapers hadn't the sense to wear clothes. If she'd been on patrol, she'd have reported a small troop of about a dozen. But the horses… Someone had gotten out. Injured maybe, but alive. And it explained the state of the house too. Reapers had a macabre preference for human meat. If they'd caught the scent of human blood, they might have given chase before doubling back for the livestock. Which hopefully meant her family was still out there.

Abby squinted at the sun, now a hand's span above the horizon, and took off her hat to wipe the sweat from her forehead.

Passing through the house once more, she gathered up food she could eat in the saddle—a not-quite-stale loaf of bread, some dried plums she found in the pantry along with a thin wedge of cheese. She dropped the bulky toys she'd brought for the kids in the dirt and replaced them with a sheet pulled from the bed. That blood…they'd need something for bandages. Gripping the saddle horn with one hand, she shoved her foot in the stirrup. But then her gaze caught on the sad bundle of toys and she froze. With a muttered curse, she dropped to the ground and grabbed the bag, jogging up to the house with it clutched to her chest. Setting the toys down on the kitchen table, she latched the door behind her.

They were coming back.

Protocol said she should go back into town to raise a

warning. At the very least, she should ride to the nearest farm and have them dispatch messages to her patrol and the fort. But that would be nearly a day lost, leaving Amy and the kids to fend for themselves.

Abby set herself on the trampled path leading north and prayed to the fickle God who watched over the borderlands that she'd catch them in time.

FIVE HOURS LATER she slouched in the saddle, letting Harvey pick the pace to give him a brief rest. There was an ache in her lower back that just wouldn't go away no matter how she adjusted her seat. Her clothes were still damp from a patch of rain showers she'd run into about noon and she'd have to stop again soon to water the horse. Harvey. It had seemed rude not to name a horse you were asking to perform heroic feats. She'd picked Harvey after a Ranger who'd come to the fort the same year she had. He'd died on their first patrol, saving the life of a little boy a Reaper had cornered beneath a wagon. Harvey had been a fine young man. And Harvey the horse was a good horse, stouthearted and easy tempered. She wanted him to survive this and hoped she hadn't jinxed him with the name. She was pushing him hard, but even if it killed him, she couldn't do more than steal these quick rests along the way.

"A nice brush and a bag of oats," she promised, patting his neck. "A new pair of shoes." Did horses like new shoes? She surely wouldn't if they were nailed on to her feet.

They'd come across one of Amy's horses a few miles back, dead and looking like it had been gnawed on for a while *before* the vultures got to it. She'd scattered the vultures and gotten close enough to make sure it was only a horse. And then she'd stumbled away, trembling legs collapsing beneath her as her stomach cramped. Not disgust—she'd seen far worse than a poor dead horse—it was relief that had her heaving into the grass. She'd been so afraid. Shaking her head, she straightened her spine. Best not to think on it.

The sound of gunfire made her jerk upright. She squinted in the direction from which it had come. Straight ahead, maybe five miles distant. The rolling echo swept over her and she kicked Harvey into a run.

For a second, she thought he might revolt. A shudder passed through him, right down his spine. But then he threw himself forward with such a mighty heave that it seemed to Abby momentum would see them the rest of the way there. Gripping her rifle, she bent over his neck.

Please, God, don't let it be too late.

It seemed to take forever to cross the distance and there was a time there at the end when she thought Harvey would give out. But he made it, and she slipped out of the saddle at a dead run, only slowing when she realized she'd come up behind the Reapers. Her family was alive—thank God—but they were pinned in a blind alley, hunkered down in a little knot behind a fall of boulders. She hoped they were all there. Amy certainly was, impossible to miss with that fiery red hair. From here, it appeared that her arms were wrapped tight around the squirming little ones, shielding them with her body. *Good. Stay there.* Abby started to circle around, trying to get a count on how many Reapers she was dealing with.

Four, six…no, three more up on the ridge. Bill had taken out a pair and the others were holding back for now, knowing his ammunition wouldn't last. Not when, eventually, their bodies would heal from even mortal wounds. The only way to kill a Reaper was to sever the spinal cord. Decapitation worked best after you disabled them with a gunshot wound to the chest or head. Reapers weren't stupid, which surprised most people who regarded them as little more than ravening beasts. They hunted like a wolf pack, had sharply honed predatory instincts, animal cunning and reflexes no human could match.

She'd need Bill's help if she wanted to kill them all. The one on the ridge dropped down just a few feet away from the kids and lunged across the distance going for Bill's gun. Amy screamed and Bill swung around an instant before the Reaper grabbed the barrel. Its brains splattered against the sandy rock. Abby ran for higher ground. If she positioned herself beside that scrub tree, she'd be able to pick off the Reapers Bill couldn't see.

This felt good. Blood pumping through her veins, the flex and stretch of her muscles, the gun in her hand. A grin pulled at her mouth and she set her gun on a ledge above her head so she could climb up. She froze momentarily when she heard gunfire from the left but then kept going. It might be a trick of the ear—sound bounced strangely off these canyon walls. Or it might mean that more help had come, which was welcome. Either way, Reapers didn't use firearms. Claws, teeth and inhuman strength, not Winchesters.

She heaved herself up and took another look around.

Bill, Amy and the boys, all still alive and apparently unharmed. The glint of sunlight on metal across the canyon told her where the other shooter lay, although she couldn't make out anything more than his position.

She sprawled in the dirt and took aim at the one she thought was the leader. He hung back and seemed to be driving the smaller Reapers toward Bill. She clipped the big one's shoulder, but the other gunman seemed to have had the same thought. His shot blasted the Reaper's ear clear off, along with a good chunk of his skull. She worked methodically, taking out the closest to the civilians first before aiming for the outliers.

Within twenty minutes, the remaining Reapers were no longer trying to get to Amy, Bill and the kids. They were looking for a way out and there were only three of them left. Abby could hear the frustration in their snarls and howls as they backed down the narrow ravine. She hated to let them go, but she'd have to. The most important thing was making sure her family was safe and then cleaning up the Reapers they'd already shot before they started to reanimate.

She stood, looking for the man holed up across the way, but he'd already moved and she didn't have the time to track him down.

Placing a hand to her mouth, she yelled down, "Do you have a hunting knife down there, Bill?"

He raised his head from behind the boulder. "Abigail, my girl, you are a sight for sore eyes."

The boys jumped up waving their arms, hooting and hollering and she waved back. Amy grabbed their collars to keep them close.

"We've got an ax," Amy shouted above the din.

Grinning, Abby cast around for the best way down. "That's even better."

Chapter Four

AMY WAS MULISH, shaking her head for the umpteenth time when Abby tried to convince her to go to Fort Hill. The kids were sleeping, Robby's head resting on her thigh and Tom was slung across his dad's chest. Bill leaned against a boulder, his big legs stretched out in front of him, hand splayed on his son's back. Strips of bed linen formed a bandage around his forearm where he'd cut himself back at the cabin. Barbed wire. He'd come back to the house to clean it when they'd been attacked. The smell of blood was probably what drew the Reapers in the first place. How a band that size had slipped so far north was still a mystery.

"There's the ranch to consider," Amy argued. "We'll have lost at least some of the herd and winter's coming."

"You could have lost more than the herd."

Amy combed her fingers through her son's tousled hair, which was nearly as bright as her own. "That's always a risk and you know it." Her gaze angled up. "You said you didn't run into any others on your way here."

"They shouldn't have been this far north in the first place. My patrol is a good twenty miles south, but someone from Fort Hill should have raised an alarm before now."

"You would know better than I," was Amy's polite

way of pointing out that the Rangers had fucked up. Abby didn't deny it, which was exactly why she wanted Amy to come with her to find out what had gone wrong.

A log popped on the fire and Abby jumped, glancing over her shoulder before returning her attention to her stubborn-as-hell younger sister. "There are still some of them out there. We didn't kill them all."

The other gunman had never come back. Abby had followed his tracks a few miles out when he didn't return. He'd been chasing the pair of Reapers who escaped. When it got dark, she turned back. They hadn't heard any gunshots and she could only assume that the Reapers had claimed him. She felt badly for that.

"There were only two that got away," Amy said.

"You don't know that there aren't more." The gunman for one…if he survived the initial infection.

"We'll be vigilant and we'll stop by the Mortons' place. They can send one of their boys into town to raise the alarm. These are our neighbors and friends. You go to Fort Hill and come back with the patrol. You have a job to do, I understand that, but we'll be fine from here on out. We don't expect you to come with us."

Abby *wanted* to go with them and she could see that understanding in Amy's eyes. They'd always been close though they looked nothing alike. For one thing, no one would ever mistake Amy for a man. She wore dresses and always managed to smell faintly of lavender. Even now, after staving off a pack of Reapers, she looked as sweetly rumpled as if she'd spent the afternoon at a picnic. Amy reached over to pat Abby's knee. "It wasn't your fault the Reapers broke through and it's not your fault he didn't come back."

"I know that," she snapped. She'd never even seen his face. Stupid for an unmarked man to chase after Reapers.

"Do you?" Amy asked gently.

Abby stared at the fire, tossed the piece of scrub grass into it that she'd been twisting around her fingers. "Okay, then, but you be careful." She fixed Amy with a hard look. "I mean it, Amy. I'll be back through in a few days."

At least this gave her a reason to ignore Cap's order to wait for him at Fort Hill. She'd deliver the news to the fort but then insist on running the message about the attack personally to her patrol. She could see no reason why they'd refuse her, and this time around she'd swing wide of New Providence.

IN THE MORNING, Abby kissed her family goodbye and watched until they disappeared from sight. Bill and Amy walked while the boys rode double. They'd lost two horses during their flight. More money would be lost by their absence, so Abby could understand their anxiety to return home. But she hated the necessity of leaving them. Little Robby had twisted around in the saddle before they rode off to ask about the licorice she'd promised him on her last visit.

"It's waiting for you at the house," she'd said and his answering grin told her that he'd already put yesterday's terror behind him. She wished she could as easily do the same.

They'd camped about five miles from the site of the attack and Abby briefly considered just leaving the bodies behind. It would take her at least two hours of hard and bloody labor to run cleanup on her own. The Reapers were decapitated. They wouldn't reanimate, and anyone who stumbled across a dead man and got infected blood on him probably deserved what would happen anyway. In the end, she turned back, leaving Harvey to graze above the canyon and dropping down to find a likely spot to start the fire.

If they'd been human corpses, she wouldn't have been able to leave them alone for this long. Coyotes and vultures would have begun the work of destroying the bodies for her, but even scavengers avoided Reaper flesh. The corpses would slowly rot in the sun unless another pack of Reapers stumbled across them. While they preferred live human flesh, Reapers were essentially opportunistic hunters. They often ate their own dead.

For several seconds, she stared down at the first body. Male, because women never turned, they just died. He was nude and caked with dirt and blood. Layers of old blood. This one had been a Reaper for a long time. Yesterday she'd kicked the head a few feet away from the body—out of suspicion more than necessity—and she went to fetch it now. Pulling on her thick leather gloves, she bent and grabbed it by the hair. Her training said it was enough to simply sever the spinal cord but no one ever left the heads too close to the bodies. Pointedly avoiding looking at the face, she dropped the head near the Reaper's feet and cast around her for the next one.

Bile rose in her throat and she swallowed it down. *Should have left this fucking mess behind.* She hated this. *Think of something else.* Anything. The fact that Amy and the kids were alive. The stranger she'd never get to thank for helping her save them. Her patrol and how she was going to get Cap off her back once he got to Fort Hill. She didn't want to stay at a place like Fort Hill, no matter how safe it was. It made her skin crawl just thinking about it.

She let her mind wander, forcing it away from the task at hand. By the time she'd grabbed on to the heels of the fourth body to drag it toward the pile, she was mentally counting bullets and wondering if she should have picked up extra ammunition while in New Providence. New Providence made her think of Nelson, which made her wonder if she could confide in Lyle about what had happened. Passing into the shadow cast by the canyon wall, she paused to stretch her back.

He came at her from behind, dropping from the ledge on silent feet. If not for a single loose pebble that followed him down, she wouldn't have had any warning at all. She whirled, instinctively drawing her pistol from its holster. But before she could pull the trigger, he stepped forward and swatted her arm aside, causing her shot to go wild and ricocheting bits of rock against her shins. Shards sliced through her trousers above the boot and she lost her gun.

Hand numb, arm stinging where he'd hit her, she scrambled back, shouting for help even though there wasn't anyone close enough to hear her scream. When she realized what she'd done, she clamped her teeth together. There was no one she *wanted* to hear her scream, or hear a gunshot and come running. Hopefully, her family was far enough away by now that they hadn't heard anything.

A Reaper. He couldn't infect her, but he could rape and kill her. If God was truly merciful, the Reaper would kill first and feed later. Now that he'd disarmed her, the creature seemed to enjoy her panic. Standing above her, he drew himself up as a slow, cruel smile spread across his dirty face. He tipped his head back to scent the air—to scent her—though how he could smell anything over his own stench was beyond her.

He was tall and stocky, with thick shoulders and a great shaggy head of blond hair that looked like it had been trimmed by a demented goat. His clothing was torn in places, and a black stain she strongly suspected was blood ran from his armpit to his waist on his left side.

Newly turned, then. Eventually the tatters of clothing from their human lives rotted from their bodies. He moved forward and the part of her that recognized she was prey took over. She rolled, scrambling to get her feet under her. He lunged forward and, with a bone-jolting thud, she dropped to her knees to dodge beneath his arm. When he changed direction, she threw herself back toward the rock wall.

The Reaper was fast. So fast. It had been years since she'd let one get this close. She lunged for the edge of the cliff. Silly really. There was nowhere for her to go, but the instinct to run was overpowering. He grabbed her from behind, wrapping his beefy arms around her chest and plucking her from the rock like a hawk scooping up a juicy mouse. He nuzzled his face into her neck and she felt wetness there. That spreading warmth was probably blood and she braced for the pain to hit.

He growled against her skin, a low warning vibration that made her muscles go slack. She began to shake. Long, violent tremors that made her teeth rattle. She clenched her jaw. Her hands scrabbled for purchase, fingernails tearing against the limestone. He dragged her from the shadows into the sunlight. Reapers liked the sun, the warmth, which seemed particularly obscene to her just now.

She kicked her heels into his shins, but he didn't even flinch. His hands came up to her neck, nails breaking the skin. He must not have bitten her before because, while the sharp splintering pain of a bite never came, she could feel the scratch and scrabble of his claws perfectly well. He forced her head down, kicked her legs out from beneath her and let their combined weight drive her into the ground. Her hands didn't come up fast enough to break her fall and she hit her head hard against the rock.

Despite the pain radiating out from her temple and the crushing weight that fell on top of her, she tried to roll. She bent her knee, drawing it up high enough that she could reach the knife tucked into her boot. Cam had insisted she learn how to use a knife even while warning her that if she let a Reaper get close enough to stab, she'd already lost the fight.

A hysterical laugh bubbled up in her throat as she twisted her hips enough to drive the blade into his thigh. The Reaper's body jerked and he howled with pain, but it didn't matter. Even as she tried to dislodge the knife, he drew her back and slammed her head into the rock again. Shock, regret, anger. The last thing she saw was the ground approaching at a horrifying speed and then everything went black.

Chapter Five

ABBY OPENED HER eyes to darkness, the kind of still and heavy darkness that meant she was underground. She blinked several times until she was sure that, yes, her eyes actually were open, though she couldn't see a damned thing. There was a bright throbbing pain in her temple and she could taste blood in her mouth. When she drew in a sharp breath, the sound of it echoed strangely and she reached up to touch stone, less than a foot away, directly above her. She winced at the contact and let her hand fall away.

Where the hell am I?

For a second, she drew a blank. All she could grab on to was an overwhelming sense of fear that screamed at her to run. But where? *And why?*

There didn't seem to be any immediate danger. Slowly, she turned her head and bit her lip to hold back a whimper of pain. This place…it had to be some kind of cave or old mineshaft. Pitch-black. The air stale and damp. Trying to get a better sense of her surroundings, she stretched out her hands. The right swung into open air, but her left hand jolted against a wall of rock only a few inches away. Right, then. Rolling onto her side, she slid her fingertips across the gritty, uneven floor.

Distantly, she could hear the sound of water dripping and, closer—heart-stoppingly, blood-chillingly closer—the scuff of a boot heel on stone. She froze, but the sound didn't come again. That annoying drip. The sound of her own breath and the rush of blood through her veins. It might have been a rock falling, her imagination or some rodent scurrying around. Cautiously, she stretched out her hand again but then stopped because, suddenly, like flipping through the pages of a picture book, it all came back to her.

The Reaper. Her head slamming against the rock. A heavy weight against her back and a sharp, ripping pain. Beyond that there was a great gaping void in her memory. Was she even still alive? Maybe this was what hell was, not fire and brimstone, but a cold dark tomb. Quiet and eternal solitude. A shiver racked her body, but she pushed herself forward anyway. Stupid to wallow in that fear. Stupid and useless. She was alive and the first step in making sure she stayed that way was figuring out where she was.

The idea that a Reaper might have dragged her back to his lair flashed through her mind like cannon fire. Fear clutched at her throat, stealing her breath, but she made it onto her hands and knees. The ceiling must be higher here. Feeling her way forward with her fingertips, she crawled, every muscle in her body screaming in protest.

A weapon. She needed a weapon.

Sitting back on her ankles, she checked her holsters, the sheath at her waist and in her boot. She'd lost her gun and one of her knives in the fight but couldn't account for the rest. Cursing under her breath, she turned to search the spot where she'd been stretched out, thinking that maybe something had fallen. There wasn't even a good-size rock within range of the sweep of her hands.

Okay. It would be all right. Somehow she had gotten in here. There had to be a way out. A Reaper would eat her flesh down to the bones. He wouldn't drop her down a hole and then seal her in to die. Lots of bad things you could say about Reapers, but they didn't generally play with their food.

At the sound of striking flint, she flinched. Golden light flooded the cave and danced wildly over the uneven walls of a cavern before steadying to an even glow. Blinking rapidly, she willed her eyes to adjust as she attempted to get a sense of her surroundings. She was still wedged in a crevice. Black rock with a thick vein of quartz slanted mere inches above her head. Ahead of her, in the direction she'd begun to crawl, the cave opened up so the roof was high enough to accommodate even a tall man's height.

And a man was there, crouched beside a rusted-out lantern near a split in the rock face. His back was to her, but he wore the clothes of a working man—a faded cotton shirt that might once have been red, stained denim pants and worn boots.

The lantern rattled as he set it aside and then, standing smoothly, he turned to face her. Wide mouth, black-stubbled jaw, tall frame and trim body. His dark eyes fixed on her and her heart faltered as recognition hit. The cowboy from New Providence, the one who'd helped her to escape Nelson and his marauding band of rapists. He took a step in her direction and everything started working again, her heart and lungs and finally her feet. She rolled out of the crevice and scrambled up, keeping her back to the wall for support.

"You." The word scraped out of her raw throat like a razor blade.

"Easy now." His voice was deep but gentle. The tone you'd use on a skittish horse. A tangle of emotion roped around her, holding her in place—fear, relief, a strange sort of joy, fear again. The fear was definitely winning out no matter how hard she tried to beat it back.

Touching the knot on her temple, she pressed back against the wall. Only one entrance to the cave and he was standing right between her and it. A gun strapped to his leg. Even without it, she was no match for him. Weak and injured, she didn't even have a knife.

"Just settle down. You know me."

"I don't know you."

"You know I won't hurt you."

She didn't trust that, didn't trust him. She hadn't, even in New Providence. She trusted him even less now that she was alone and unarmed.

"The Reaper's dead," he said. "Dead and gone."

He didn't move any closer and she realized that he was waiting for her, patiently, to get a grip on her panic. Mouth dry and throat swollen, she had to swallow twice before she could speak. "You followed me."

His expression didn't change. "Not exactly."

"How then, *exactly?* What are you doing here?"

He didn't answer immediately. Instead, he regarded her head to toe before shaking his head. He wasn't wearing a hat and looked younger without it. "Sit down before you fall over."

"I'll sit after you tell me what the hell you're doing here. And the Reaper...what happened to the Reaper?"

"I killed it."

"Did you take its head?"

"I did, and then burned what was left. Do you want to poke around in the ashes?"

She gave him a quelling look and he blew out a frustrated breath. "Just sit and I'll tell you what happened, what I saw anyway. I didn't save your life just to watch you crack your head open on a rock when your legs give out. My name is Jake, by the way."

Jake. She hadn't asked his name in New Providence. Strangely, it had seemed too personal at the time. But he'd known hers, she remembered.

Jake sat on a low stone outcrop and leaned forward so his arms rested on his thighs. Letting his hands dangle loose and empty between his knees, he regarded her calmly. She thought he might be trying to look harmless. At any other time, that would have amused her greatly. He was possibly the least harmless-looking man she'd ever stumbled across. She glanced at the opening to the cave.

"Don't. You're in no shape for it and you've no cause to run from me. I won't hurt you. You've been out for almost an hour. If I'd wanted to hurt you, I would have done it by now."

Hard to argue with that logic. When he made no move to come after her, her panic began to fade. Her legs were trembling and she didn't think they'd hold her up if she tried to run. Every muscle in her body ached. Her head felt like…well, like someone had just slammed it against a boulder. But it was her throat that was clamoring for attention. She sank down to the ground cross-legged.

"Do you have any water?"

He rose to fetch a skin from the small pile of his belongings beside the lantern. There was a bedroll there—just one—and an old saddlebag. This time, he came in closer and tossed the skin across the remaining distance. She caught it and drank greedily. A trickle of water slipped down her jaw to her neck. She tugged a handkerchief free and wet it to press to the lump on her head. She hissed at the sting, but the cowboy's expression didn't change. Quiet, like a closed-up house with the windows shuttered and a bar over the door. She wished she could read him better.

"Keep the water. Your throat has to be raw." He touched his neck and then his temple. "I worried he broke something but other than a few bumps and bruises, I didn't feel any fractures." Something flickered in his eyes too fast for her to interpret. "He didn't break the skin…with his teeth anyway, but I suppose with you being a Ranger that wouldn't be as much of an issue. He didn't rape you."

He held her gaze as he said that. She appreciated his blunt honesty. Nodding her thanks, she took another, smaller sip from the skin. It somewhat eased the ache in her throat. "How did you manage to kill him?"

His brows drew together in a frown. "He was distracted. It let me get close enough for a clean shot. That blood—" He lifted his chin to indicate her stained clothing. "That's his, not yours. I don't have a spare shirt."

She leaned against the wall and touched the goose egg protruding from her forehead. It was sore to the touch, the skin around scraped raw. Painful, but not as bad as it could have been. As it should have been. "I have a change of clothes in my saddlebag," she said. "Did you find Harvey?"

"The horse?" He nodded. "I thought you'd be safer in here than out in the open while I caught your horse. *My* horse. Harvey—is that what you're calling him now?"

Her mouth curved. "You never told me his name, so I took the liberty of picking one. I didn't… I never thought to see you again. What are you doing here?"

"I followed you from New Providence, saw the cabin and that trail. I thought you might be in trouble again. That you could use some help, anyway. I didn't catch up to you until the fight yesterday."

Realization made her skin tingle. "You were the other gunman."

He nodded and the last of the tension left her body, all her energy slipping away with the fear. He'd saved her life twice now, had helped to save her family too. Whoever he was, whatever his interest in her, there was no reason to think he meant her any harm. She owed him a debt.

"I thought the Reapers got you. It was stupid to go after them like that, you could've been bitten."

"I didn't consider it at the time."

"I was worried when you didn't come back." He looked up and she smiled, shrugging. "I didn't know it was you, of course. But I was worried about the man who'd helped us. That was my family and they might not have made it if not for you."

"You were managing well enough on your own."

"Thank you." She meant it and waited for him to nod before leaning back against the wall. "So is this what you do—wander around the countryside playing hero?"

He snorted. "I'd stopped in New Providence for a drink, but Fort Hill was always my aim. You'll remember I did offer myself as escort."

He paused just long enough that she knew he was thinking of that dark alley, which made her think of it too. His tongue and his heat. His hard hands cupping her ass while his hips ground against her. How easily he'd walked away.

She took a sip of water before she said something she'd regret and he continued, "When you made it clear you weren't interested in company, I thought I'd stick around to be sure Nelson and his gang didn't give chase."

She tried to ignore the flare of heat that blossomed in her chest at the thought of him watching her back. On patrol, she was surrounded by men who would take a bullet for her if need be. She didn't know why his concern should affect her. "What business do you have at the fort?"

"I'm looking for work."

"They won't have any work there for an unmarked man," she said. "The transport jobs are hard to come by, and you don't want to get caught up in any of their experiments no matter how much they offer to pay you."

His gaze dropped to his hands and he fell silent. She stared at his profile. He had native blood in him, she'd swear to it. You could see it in the crow-black hair and stark angles of his face. You didn't see that often except in small, isolated pockets of survivors. The native tribes had been among the first infected, herded south from their northern lands at gunpoint by the colonial militia. When he looked up again, her face heated like a schoolgirl caught staring.

"When I get to the fort, I'll see what I can do about getting you on one of the wagon crews, if that's what you really want."

"What if I want something else?"

A warm feeling tickled her belly, but she did her best to ignore the sensation. Even if he was interested in picking up where they'd left off, she was in no condition to do anything about it tonight. "If there's something else I can do for you, all you have to do is name it."

"I want to see your mark."

She paused with the skin half raised to her lips. Slowly, she lowered it to the ground. No mistaking what he meant. Every child was tested with a serum that formed a starburst-shaped scar at the injection site in the immune. The star-marked became Rangers, whether they wanted to be or not. "And why would you want to do that, Jake?"

She thought she already knew the answer. Some people, like Nelson, developed a strange fascination for Rangers. Though generally they were more reverent than lecherous. She wouldn't have pegged Jake as a camp follower, but it would explain all his actions so far—his protectiveness, his willingness to help, his desire to work at the fort. His concern for her—which had been all about the blood in her veins and the mark on her arm after all.

"I saved your life," he said again, as if she needed a reminder. "It's not asking for much of a reward. I've never seen a star-mark before and I've always wondered what they look like."

It wasn't strange, not really. She heard women make the same request of male Rangers all the time. There was no lust in Jake's eyes. He looked curious, intently so, and far too attractive for her peace of mind. But where was the harm?

"It's not…well, I'll let you see for yourself." She undid the top three buttons of her shirt and slipped it down over her shoulder, twisting so he could see the star—the edge of it that was left anyway. He got up and moved closer, crouching behind her so that he could see it.

"It's a scar."

"Under the scar." She held her shirt up with one hand and reached back with the other to push her hair aside.

"Come here. I can't see."

He took her arm and pulled her up, turning her toward the light. He brushed his fingertips over the flesh. His skin was roughly calloused, but his touch was gentle. The way he touched her—soft, hesitant, respectful—reminded her of that kiss they'd shared. A warm throb started low in her belly. She could feel the heat of his breath against her skin when she turned her head.

He glanced up, his expression troubled. "I'm sorry."

Before she could ask him what for, he pressed his lips to her shoulder and then sank his teeth in deep.

ABBY'S BODY JERKED and Jake closed his eyes, suppressing the growl that rose in his throat. When her legs buckled, he snaked an arm around her waist to keep her from falling and tried to ignore the richness of her scent filling his nose and spilling into his mouth.

Like sunshine, like a feast after years of starvation, like sex and…

The rider leaped up inside him and started to rattle its cage. Control. He needed to remain in control.

She was weak. Of course, she was weak. Ranger or no, she was only human and he needed to be careful. He couldn't afford to break her. Her blood touched his tongue, slick and warm, and his whole body tightened. When she tried to get away, he bound an arm across her small breasts, locking her body in place so that he could gently disengage his teeth without tearing her flesh. Her warm body flush to his, tucked tight against him like a promise. A different kind of temptation than the blood but just as powerful. His cock was hard, straining at the denim. She bucked back and must have felt it because she made a soft choking noise and fought him harder.

As soon as he released her, she shot to the far side of the cave and he let her go. There was nowhere for her to escape. Even if she somehow made it out of this cave and onto her horse, he'd be able to track her down before she reached any kind of civilization. He'd picked this spot for that reason.

She stumbled and cried out as she fell, but before he

could even think about whether to help her up, she'd regained her feet. Throwing her back to the far wall, she glared at him. At the moment, he was incapable of answering the question in her eyes. Her fear rolled off her in waves, calling him in for another bite. Her blood was in his mouth. The feel of her still imprinted on his skin. And he was dangerously close to losing it, so he let her get as far away from him as the small space allowed.

"What are you?" Her voice was shaky and he could tell by the look in her eyes that she already knew the answer.

"You know what I am."

He studied her. Women who were bitten usually went into seizure within seconds of the parasite entering the bloodstream. A trickle of blood slipped down her arm, curving gently toward her inner elbow. She was scared and shocked and definitely repulsed, but she wasn't dying.

"I had to be sure you were immune."

Her eyes widened. "So you *bit* me?"

Of course. It was the only way. She cringed against the wall when he stepped closer, pulling at her half-undone shirt to cover herself. Her eyes were wide and unblinking, and she'd wedged herself against the wall as if she thought it might protect her. He could still hear the tight, steady beat of her heart. It was arousing as hell. His own pulse kicked up a notch in response. Fear roused the rider. Fear, anger, lust—all the most primal emotions. That was where the rider was bound most tightly to him and where he had to fight the hardest to stay in control.

It had taken him nearly two centuries to get to this point. Two centuries of being ridden like a dumb beast by a ravenous inhuman creature that cared only for its own survival. His memory was a hazy mess of blood and pain and hunger. He remembered the time before. And then there was now. This dark pit and the woman hunched and trembling against the wall, stinking of stale sweat and fear.

Another shudder passed through him and he rode it out, letting the pain pull at his muscles and seize his heart. No matter how bad it hurt, the thing living inside him wouldn't actually kill him. It couldn't, not without killing itself.

"I'm not going to hurt you," he said, reminding himself as much as reassuring her.

"You *bit* me."

If she understood the hunger that clawed at his mind, she wouldn't keep reminding him of that. "I need a Ranger and I had to make sure that you truly were one."

"You need a Ranger," she echoed, voice breaking. "What the hell for? What are you going to do with me?"

One hand came up to her neck. The skin there was bruising already, angry red marks starting to turn purple at the edges. She'd looked so strong in New Providence. Her body was all long, lean lines and bony angles, her face narrow and severe. Slashing brows over lovely eyes, a pure pale blue now shadowed to gray. He'd been making his way toward her patrol when he'd stopped in that piss-poor excuse for a town for supplies and news.

And then Abby… Well, Abby had practically fallen into his lap.

That she was female made her more desirable for his purposes even if it would make the next few days a living hell. *More* of a living hell for him than it already was. When she'd gulped down the water, letting it trail down her neck, he'd wanted to lick it off her skin. When she'd bared her shoulder to him…well, he'd been fourteen when he'd been changed and he'd never seen a woman willingly undress. Only three small buttons. It shouldn't have made his mouth dry. It shouldn't have hardened him.

He was still hard now, still hungry, and she was shaking so violently it was a wonder she could still stand. Nothing he could say right now would reassure her. Stripping off his coat, he tossed it to her. She let it land at her feet, staring at the pile of dusty leather as if it was a creature that might attack. He didn't have any food to give her, though he doubted she'd accept it even if he had it to offer.

"It's clean enough," he said. "Just a coat, no blood in the lining or eyeballs rolling around in the pockets. I bought it at the mercantile store in Logan. Get some sleep and we'll talk in the morning." She simply stared at him in horror, a healthy dose of shock mixed in for good measure. He'd seen that look before, knew down deep in his bones that he deserved it. "And Abby—" She flinched but bravely held his gaze. "Just to save you the time and trouble. There's only one exit and I'll be waiting outside."

Chapter Six

SHE FOUND A ROCK, heavy enough to brain him with but not so heavy that it would slow her down. He'd taken her weapons and hadn't even left behind the lantern last night. Her palms were sweating and she readjusted her grip, easing her way a few more feet down the black, uneven tunnel. The glow of daylight up ahead was enough to serve as a beacon but did little to illuminate her surroundings. Just as well. She smelled bat and didn't wish to see the dank hole the Reaper lived in too clearly.

She'd spent the night shivering and awake, staring into darkness so thick that Jake could have sat down beside her and she wouldn't have known it. That thought alone had kept her up for hours. If Jake did creep back inside, he never revealed himself. By dawn, her panic had faded, replaced by cold determination to make it out alive. She was scared, more scared than she'd ever been in her entire life, but she sure as hell wasn't going to give up now.

When she came to the mouth of the cave, she held back for a minute, letting her eyes adjust to the light and listening to get a fix on his location. Close. He had to be standing almost directly outside the cave just like he'd promised and by the sound of things he was saddling the horses. Good.

She stepped out silently. She knew she hadn't made a sound, she wasn't even breathing. But still he turned, one hand lingering on Marley's neck, his dark eyes fixing immediately on the rock in her hand. She didn't hesitate, but neither did he. Before she took her first step, before the rock was fully raised, he was right in front of her. She barely saw him move, but his left hand clamped over her wrist before she could bring the rock down.

His right hand fisted in her shirt and he jerked her forward, knocking her off balance and pinning her flush to his body while he gently wrested the rock from her hand. With her free fist, she clocked him in the jaw. She didn't have enough leverage to put much weight behind it, but it turned his head. He grunted and she slammed the heel of her boot down on his instep.

She had somewhat of an advantage because, for his own reasons, he was not trying to hurt her while she was doing her damnedest to maim him. If she'd been a smidge faster on that shot to his groin, she might have had a chance. But he twisted at the last minute and kicked her leg out from under her. His reflexes were faster, he was stronger than she was and he dropped on top of her like a ton of bricks, pinning her hands to the ground and wedging his legs in between hers. At first she thought he did it to keep her from kicking out, but then she felt his erection like a length of iron lodged between them.

He was excited by this. *Damn him.*

He glared down at her. "Now, Abby—"

She head-butted him—hard—the way Lyle had taught her. A quick snap of her head, using her skull like a hammer and aiming for his nose.

His head jerked back and she tried to roll, but his head was the only thing that moved. Everything else stayed fixed in place, solid and hard as the rock she was lying on. He dipped his head to look at her again and blood from his broken nose dripped onto her cheek. It slid down behind her ear in a warm wet tickle.

"I'm trying not to hurt you."

"I can see that."

He grit his teeth as she squirmed. "I wasn't planning on tying you up."

"To ease your conscience? Whether I'm bound or not, this is abduction plain and simple."

He caught her arms and forced them up, pinning her wrists to the ground on either side of her head. Panic welled in her chest, but she beat it back. Reapers liked fear. She needed to keep a tight rein on hers, especially now.

"You're mistaken if you think I've got a conscience. You'll behave yourself or I'll strap you to the horse. It's your choice."

Part of her wanted to spit in his face and call his bluff, but looking at him now, with his eyes slit and his jaw set hard, she didn't actually think he was bluffing. And he'd stopped bleeding. That was the kicker. She'd gotten him good. Her poor sore head ached with the impact and she'd heard the crunch of broken bone. But he wasn't bleeding on her anymore and while his first words had been muffled because he wasn't using his nose, his last had come out crystal clear. Despite his speed and his strength, she'd still held out a small hope that it might all be a lie.

Maybe she hadn't hit him as hard as she thought. Or maybe the blood was draining down his throat instead. Maybe.

"You *can't* be a Reaper."

"Is that why you thought you could come at me with a fucking rock? I'm a Reaper, sweetheart. Don't push me to prove it to you." His face pinched, as if it hurt to move as he shifted his weight. "I'm going to let you up. You can either sit and eat the breakfast I caught or I get the rope. Do you want to know which one sounds more appealing to me?"

"Let me up."

She shifted her butt, ready to get up, but the movement dragged the front of her jeans across his crotch. Not her best idea when she knew he was aroused, but she didn't consider it until his hips jerked back as if he'd been burned. His hands released her wrists and he pushed himself up.

Seeing an opening, she surged up before he straightened completely and grabbed his gun, rolling to free it of the holster and swinging it up as she landed hard on her shoulder. His eyes narrowed. "Don't you dare."

She pulled the trigger.

It was a bad angle and the kick stung her wrists, nearly causing her to drop the gun. She held on…or she would have if Jake had acted like any normal man and dropped to the ground screaming in agony when she shot him at close range.

He didn't. She could see the wound in his thigh. The tear in his trousers, the raw flesh, the blood blackening the fabric. But he kept walking on his mangled leg. Two steps and before she was able to take another shot, he'd grabbed hold of the barrel. She pulled the trigger anyway, but he forced the shot wide. The gun kicked in her hand. He lost his grip and she tried to jerk it away from him. With a growl that raised every hair on her body, he wrenched the gun free, nearly breaking several of her fingers in the process.

"You fucking shot me."

He didn't so much as glance at the wound. Just holstered his gun and glared murder at her. He clenched his jaw so tight it was a wonder his teeth didn't shatter.

Twenty seconds and she'd know for sure. That's how long it took for wounds to begin to heal. With as much dignity as she could muster, she sat up and slid back a few feet to put some distance between them.

"You bit me," she reminded him.

"So now we're even?" The corner of his mouth lifted, but that wasn't a smile. She didn't know what the hell it was. Nothing friendly.

Ten more seconds… She glanced at his leg and everything stopped. There was her proof. His skin stretched and squirmed, reknitting itself before her eyes.

I am so fucked.

She jerked her gaze up. Into black eyes and the face of a man clearly at the end of his rope. "You didn't shoot Nelson after what he tried in New Providence, but with me you don't even hesitate."

He bent to pick up his hat, slapped it hard to shake off the dirt and then jammed it on top of his head.

"You're a Reaper."

"Oh? You believe me now?"

"I had to be sure."

He did, finally, look at the wound, but then all he did was mutter, "You ruined my trousers," and shot her another glare.

Was he expecting an apology? An offer to mend the hole? Because that sure as hell wasn't happening. She waited for him to retaliate, braced herself for it, keeping her eyes fixed on him while her fingers cast around for a rock. There was nothing. When he saw what she was doing, his expression changed. The scowl stayed, but the anger in his eyes cooled. After a moment, he jerked his head toward the small fire burned down nearly to embers.

"Go eat." When she didn't move, he growled. "I mean it. We've got a hard ride ahead of us and you need the food. Go eat or I shove it down your throat."

She sure as hell didn't want his hands on her again. Pushing herself to her feet, she limped over to the fire, feeling his eyes on her back following every step. The hair lifted on the back of her neck, but at least she was walking away from him. She found a whole fish at the fire pit, spitted and already cooked, propped on some rocks so it warmed over the coals. She stared at it. She didn't know what she'd expected when he'd said breakfast. A human foot or raw meat, maybe. Not fish. Her stomach growled as she sat, positioning herself so that she could watch him work.

Jake resumed where he'd left off, showing no sign that the gunshot bothered him at all. He righted the saddle, which had begun to slide, and tightened the cinch. His back was to her but she didn't make the mistake of thinking that meant he wasn't paying attention. Trying to decide whether it was really safe to eat anything a Reaper gave to her, she pulled the fish from the coals and wondered how she might use that sharpened stick as a weapon. Flimsy and pathetic weapon, a stick. Especially against someone…*something* like Jake.

The fish stung her fingertips when she broke off a piece to put in her mouth. She chewed slowly, not hungry but knowing she needed to regain her strength if she had any hope of getting out of this.

"You're not like the others, you have to know that," she said. "You look and act like a man. You wear clothes. You can reason and talk."

He ignored her, going back to work on Harvey. He'd put her saddle on Marley, for which she was grateful. In a flat race, Marley was faster. If Abby got a break and some open ground, she'd have a good chance of outrunning him.

"Are you some kind of new breed of monster? Smarter. Stronger. Able to blend in better with your prey." A shiver took her as she considered the implications of such a thing. "The scientists have a name for it…"

"A mutation," he said, surprising her when he answered. "And no, I'm not."

He grabbed his flask and stepped away from Harvey to rinse the blood from his mouth. He spat into the bushes and then started toward her. She forced herself to remain sitting even though every instinct screamed at her to run. When he held out his flask, she flinched and then slowly shook her head.

"It's fresh from the stream and cold. If you wet that cloth around your neck and hold it to the bruise it will help with the swelling." He paused. "You'll need to wash away the blood too."

She opened her mouth to mock him for pretending to care and then snapped it closed. She'd seen Reapers frenzy at the sight of blood. He wasn't playing nursemaid, he was trying not to kill her. Which was ridiculous because he was a fucking Reaper. And Reapers killed. That's what they did.

"I'm not sharing water with you."

The edge of his mouth curled. "Don't you remember New Providence? You sucked on my tongue, sweetheart. A little spit isn't going to harm you now."

She still wouldn't accept the flask and after a moment, he withdrew his hand and walked back to his horse to reattach it to the saddle. Ripping off a small bite of the fish with her teeth, she watched him warily while forcing herself to choke down the food. Her throat was still raw from when the other Reaper, the normal one, had tried to choke her. It probably wasn't wise to provoke Jake, but if he was some kind of mutant who was to say she was still immune? She'd rather die than turn.

Jake unhooked her flask from Marley's saddle. Her traitorous horse nuzzled his arm before bending her head to rip at a small patch of grass sprouting from a crack between the rocks. That gave her pause. Marley could usually sense when Reapers were near before Abby could. Her eyes would roll white and her whole body would tense to run. But here she was, calm and easy beneath a Reaper's hand.

Jake gave Marley's shoulder a familiar pat before returning to Abby and wordlessly handing her the flask. This time she took it.

With a sigh, he propped himself against a slab of rock, crossed his arms and watched as she set the flask aside to strip the bandana from her neck.

"We can't linger here," he said, "but I'll do my best to answer your questions if it will set your mind at ease. Your fear is…it's going to be a problem for me."

Not even wanting to consider what he meant by that, she looked down at her lap. The bandana was snarled at one end and she started to unknot it as she gathered her thoughts. Her hand slipped. One of her ragged nails tore to the quick and she yelped, sticking her finger in her mouth and sucking at the wound. Bleeding. When she looked up, Jake's body was as rigid as the stone he leaned against. His burning gaze fixed on her mouth. The morning stilled. Even the pair of birds twittering in the bush beside them fell abruptly silent.

Shit.

Every instinct screamed at her to run, but she knew she wouldn't be able to escape. Not without a plan, a weapon and a lot of luck. When the blood slowed, she withdrew her finger from her mouth and lowered her gaze to the bandana again, focused on folding it into a small pad that she drenched with water. When she dared to look at Jake again, his head was bent and his eyes were closed.

"Are you the only one?"

He took a deep breath before raising his head. The blank look on his face told her he'd missed the question.

"Are there others like you?"

"Not many, but a few." He shifted, bending the leg she'd shot so she got a good look through the ripped and bloodstained denim to the perfectly healed skin beneath. Even the hair on his leg had grown back, black and springy and perfect. "I'm older than the Reapers you're used to seeing. You fight younglings in the first stage of infection, when the parasite is holding the reins. I'm old enough to be in control of my appetites." He caught her gaze and held it. "That said, it's not a good idea for you to deliberately test my patience. If you're thinking about trying to escape, you can put that right out of your head. I'll be as easy on you as you let me be."

"Don't make you hurt me, is that it?"

He smiled faintly but didn't touch the question. "I'm not any happier with this than you are."

"Oh, I doubt that."

She cocked her head to the side as she considered him. He appeared to be about her own age, twenty-seven. "How old *are* you?"

"One hundred and eighty-six."

"And you used to be like the rest of them?"

A slow nod. "For longer than I like to consider."

She started to wipe the blood and dirt from her face, and he turned his head to stare at the fire. His throat moved as he swallowed and goose bumps rose over her skin. She poured more water on the cloth and scrubbed a little harder at her face. When Jake spoke again, there was a rasp to his voice that hadn't been there a moment ago.

"It takes a long time to fight free of the rider, the parasite. I became sentient about fifty years ago and I was among the first infected."

"I've never seen anything like you."

"When do you ever see us except when you're aiming down the barrel of your gun?"

Never. "I've never met a Reaper who wasn't after my blood."

If she hadn't been staring straight at him, she would have missed the flinch at the corners of his eyes. "I'm not a threat to you," he said. "You're a Ranger. You can't be infected. I proved that if nothing else."

"That's not the only way you're dangerous to me. Don't try to convince me I'm safe with you because I know better. I've watched too many friends get mauled by your kind. I lost my hand—"

"And then sliced a new one from a boy who couldn't control himself. Who was terrified and locked inside his own head, half-crazed trying to get out."

"Then I put him out of his misery," she said fiercely. "And I will not regret it."

He was quiet for a time. "We're infected. That's all that we are. Infected by a sentient parasite that fights us for control of our own bodies. But we were all people first, with lives and families of our own. Some of us still remember that."

"Maybe the lucky ones."

"No," he said quietly. "That's where you're wrong."

That silenced her momentarily, but she shook off her pity. She wouldn't be suckered into feeling sorry for a fucking Reaper. "All right, then. Let's say for the sake of argument that I believe you. Why—"

"If you believe me?" His eyes narrowed and his stance changed. Suddenly, he straightened from the rock and her heart started beating faster. He loomed over her. "I'm not playing games here. I answered those questions in good faith with honest answers your scientists would kill for. I'm doing my best to be civil, but if you're determined not to believe me then we're wasting time."

He kicked sand over the fire. When he held out his hand to help her up, she instinctively recoiled. The thought of touching him made her skin crawl.

"You're done eating and we need to go."

Stiffly, she climbed to her feet on her own. "Go where?"

But Jake was done answering questions. He turned and started walking away from her.

"Jake," she shouted at his back. "Why did you follow me from New Providence?"

"Get on the horse or I'll toss you up there myself. Believe me, it's in both our best interests if I touch you as little as possible."

Careful not to brush against him, she moved toward the horses. Marley nickered a soft welcome and nuzzled at her hand, searching for a treat. In a single fluid movement, Jake mounted and waited impatiently for her to do the same. The sun was behind him, casting his face in shadow. Big and strong, he had lightning-fast reflexes and extraordinary senses. He would be the devil to escape, but she was going to find a way.

"At least tell me where we're going."

"I told you last night. We're going to Fort Hill."

Chapter Seven

HARVEY'S EAR TWITCHED and the fly that had been pestering him for the past half hour lifted into the air. The buzz sounded abominably loud in the quiet wood. Jake was used to the stillness. Animals tended to sense his presence and make themselves scarce, birds too. Even insects generally left him alone. This one was only making a nuisance of itself because it was after the horse, drawn to the smell of sweat and warm blood. An impulse to which Jake could unfortunately relate.

He shot his hand out, caught the fly in his fist and then brushed off the remains on his denim. Abby's shoulders tightened at his sudden movement and she glanced back. He met her gaze and she held it just to prove to him that she wasn't scared before returning her attention to the deer path they followed. When her back was to him again, he allowed himself a small smile.

She was scared—he could scent it on her, taste it in the air, hear it in her pulse. But she was also testing him. Seeing how far she could drift away before he called her back. Checking her saddlebag for her knife when she thought he was distracted. She was scared, but there was no quit in her. Even injured and too weak to walk in a straight line, she'd fought him. He still couldn't believe she'd shot him.

Abby glanced over her shoulder and although she flinched when her gaze met his, she didn't turn away. "It's shallow here. Do we cross or follow the river?"

"Cross," he said and lifted his face. The wind coming off the water smelled clean and sweet. There was no trace of a threat but still Harvey sidestepped restlessly. Jake held him back with a soft word as he watched Abby push Marley through the scrub brush toward the water. Even though the slope was negligible, she went slowly for the horse's sake, a frown of concentration on her face.

The afternoon sun slanted through the trees across the river, making the water sparkle and lighting a swarm of gnats ahead of him. Abby hadn't uttered a word of complaint during the course of the day, but she looked haggard. Beneath the dirt and grime, her face was very pale. The knot on her forehead wasn't as pronounced, but the skin had bruised an ugly purple color that matched the color beneath her eyes.

When she reached the water, she paused for a second, reading the currents. It was late in the season and there'd been no rain for weeks. The river was low but still wide, moss-coated rocks peaked above the surface and stirred the quick-moving water into little eddies. He waited for her to start moving before urging Harvey forward, down the bank. He let the horse pick his way, keeping his eyes fixed on Abby.

He'd watched her enough to recognize the change in her posture. Her spine was a little straighter and when she turned her head, the angle of it disturbed him. She studied the opposite bank upstream and down. He knew the exact moment she decided to make a break for it.

She didn't look back, because she was smart and didn't want to alert him to her intentions. She simply picked up her pace, aiming for a spot on the other side of the river that opened onto a flat grassy plain. Her horse was faster than his, he knew that, and she was a lighter load. Tightening his thighs to urge Harvey faster, he angled upstream of her, forcing his horse through deeper water in order to cut her off. Her head turned at the splash as Harvey heaved up out of a dip. Her mouth tightened and eyes as gray as a thunderhead briefly flicked up to meet his.

She adjusted course smoothly, making room for Harvey. The only sign that she was upset was when she reached out a hand to touch Marley's neck. He'd seen her do that many times during the course of the day, as if she drew some comfort from the contact. The set of her shoulders sagged as she leaned forward, but he didn't make the mistake of thinking that he was looking at defeat. She'd pick another spot to test him and he'd be ready to stop her again when she did.

He forced her onto the bank at a spot where she was caged in. A tangle of blackberry bush to her left, clean picked over except for the thorns. They passed beneath the shade of an old black willow whose leaves were beginning to yellow. A gust of wind caught the upper branches making the leaves dance and shiver, the sound as soothing as that of water passing over the rocks beside them.

"We can rest here."

"Can't we stop for the night?" She looked past him toward that open stretch of plain when she said it. He knew exactly what she was thinking. "We won't be able to ride much farther without risking the horses."

He shook his head. "I have another place in mind." A bend in the river, hemmed in by trees. Well off the road so they wouldn't be spotted and with no easy route of escape. "We need another hour or two before we make camp. But if you need to close your eyes, we can stop here awhile."

"I'm good."

Like hell she was. She was swaying in the saddle, and her eyes were alarmingly unfocused. Shock, that's what the doctors called it. He was having trouble guessing at her limits. "You can ride with me. Harvey can carry us both."

Her eyes narrowed to slits and he laughed. "I'm not going to molest you on a horse."

She shifted her weight to start Marley off. "I said I'm fine. Let's get someplace we can make camp."

They traveled north along the river, not reaching the site until the sun was nearly set. When he told her they were stopping, Abby nearly fell off her horse. Jake resisted the urge to help her. She didn't want his help, didn't want him anywhere near her. Rightfully so. He watched her lean against Marley and then gather herself up to tug at the strap securing her saddlebags.

"I can take care of the horses," he told her and she nodded gratefully. "Grab a blanket and go rest over there."

He pointed to a thick patch of moss, thinking that it

looked like the most comfortable place. He'd bring her fresh water, find food. Strange to think about caring for anyone's needs but his own. Abby dropped her bedroll on a mound of dried pine needles instead and he smiled to himself as he lifted the saddle from Harvey's back.

She turned around with her hands on her hips. "I have to…" She pointed toward the trees and it took him a minute to realize what she was saying.

He nodded. "I won't follow you unless you run."

She turned around when he called her name. Her eyes were wary, her face pinched with pain, but she still stood there like she was ready to fight. He gave her his hardest look and was not remotely pleased when he saw her shiver.

"Don't run."

He didn't want to have to chase her down. Right now, the Reaper had retreated to a dark corner of his mind. Always there, like a canker. The hunger never left him completely, or the pain, but for the moment it was bearable. He didn't know what would happen if he was forced to hunt her. He didn't particularly want to find out.

While she tended to her needs, he dug a shallow pit for a fire and ripped off a few dry branches from a nearby deadfall to get them started. Shaking out her bedroll, he spread it next to the fire and stood as she returned to the clearing. When she stumbled, he was halfway to her before he thought it through. Swatting aside the hand she raised, he lifted her up and strode toward the fire.

"Put me down." Her body was stiff as a board, vibrating with tension. He couldn't help but remember the last time she was in his arms—willing, warm and pliant. All heat and clutching hands, her sleek mouth and strong thighs tight around his hips.

"You might as well relax."

She made a choking noise and he checked a smile. "I'm not going to eat you. Not tonight."

He dumped her near her blankets and she jerked back, one hand reaching for her empty holster. When she realized it, she checked the motion, squaring her shoulders as if she'd take him on with her fists instead. "Don't ever touch me again."

He nearly reminded her that she'd begged for his touch only a few days ago. That she was only alive now at his mercy and if he lifted her into his arms again, there was nothing she could do to stop him. The words were on the tip of his tongue.

"Go to sleep, Abby," he said gently. "There's no food left, but I'll find you something in the morning."

She stood there glaring at him, all fire and spite, but her scent said fear. It wasn't until he turned away to tend to the horses that she began to relax. He listened to her move about the camp as she prepared for sleep. The snap of the blankets as she shook them out again. The pained sigh as she lay down. It was an hour before he was able to join her, and she was still awake, watching him.

He tossed another log onto the fire, and then stretched himself out a few feet away, turning his back to set her at ease. He had time to be patient. Dawn was still a long way off and this was nice, resting here in the quiet dark as the river passed by. It had been a long time since he'd enjoyed such a thing. The clouds began to part, and he could pick out the constellations. Somehow not being alone while he did it made a difference. He'd spent his childhood sleeping under the stars, or tucked inside with his mother and sister beside him. Then the plague. And then he'd had to be alone. Alone or with other Reapers like himself.

He pretended to sleep. The stars moved across the sky and the moon slowly rose. He listened to the sound of Abby's breathing and the steady beat of her heart. After a time, when he was certain that she was asleep, he stood.

Her braid was beginning to come undone. A tendril of golden brown hair had slipped free to curl across her cheek. Her hair was very fine and, even dirty as it was now, had the sheen of satin. Her hand lay beneath her cheek, fingers curled. Long legs twisted in the blankets. She wasn't a pretty woman. Her sunburned cheeks and the lines at the corners of her eyes made her look older than she was. Too rangy. Too hard. Before she learned what he was, she'd smiled at him and it had softened her features, made her eyes crinkle into little half-moons. The smile had made her pretty. Not that he was likely to see it again.

He moved toward her, his booted feet not making a sound on the soft earth. He likely needn't have bothered for stealth. She didn't stir. Her body needed sleep to heal and once she'd let go, she'd fallen hard and fast. Her breathing was deep, her eyes behind her closed lids still. He knelt beside her.

The top button on her shirt was undone and he eased the next two free without disturbing her. Gently, he pushed the fabric aside. Her breath hitched and he froze, waiting for her eyes to open, ready to subdue her if she tried to fight. She would fight him if she woke to find him looming over her, he didn't doubt that. She'd never truly stopped.

But her breathing evened out again and he bent his head to examine the wound. It was on the crest of her shoulder. Not swollen and red as he'd feared. The puncture wounds left by his teeth had scabbed over and the skin surrounding the area was bruised a deep dark blue. No sign of infection—that's what he'd been worried about. Not Reaper infection, the regular kind that could be just as deadly to a fragile human.

This wound seemed to be healing faster than her others thanks to the parasite in his saliva. Maybe the only good thing that had ever come of it. He wondered if it would leave a scar. The thought twisted in his gut—regret, a sick sort of longing, lust. The lust hooked deepest.

Abby stirred, her soft moan drawing his attention away from damaged flesh to her face. There was a frown line between her brows and as he watched, one hand curled into a small fist. He wondered if she was dreaming about him. *Dream.* He smiled. *More like a nightmare.* She rolled onto her back and her leg kicked out, the weight of the blanket outlining the V between her legs. He inhaled sharply, which was a mistake. Her scent filled him, warm and female.

His cock began to swell. He was attracted to Abby,

admired her, might even have liked her if he'd been capable of such a thing. But arousal had never been simple for him, never clean or easy. His reaction woke up the rider and the creature struck fast, sinking its needle claws into his brain. The pain splitting his skull was so sudden and pure, it momentarily blinded him. His hand moved, reaching for Abby, and for the life of him, he couldn't pull it back.

He fought hard, aiming straight into the heart of that fire, feeling pieces of his soul shred away as he grappled with the thing living inside of him. No reasoning with it. Jake had never seen evidence that the parasite was even aware of itself as a separate entity. It was hunger. It was cruel. And it was very, very strong.

With immense effort, he wrenched back control, curling his hand into a fist and driving it into the dirt beside Abby's bedroll. It took him a moment longer to come fully back to himself. Cold sweat coated his skin and his arms were shaking. His stomach lurched. If he'd eaten anything that day, he'd likely have lost it. His erection was gone, his cock shriveled and cold. When he opened his stinging eyes, he expected to find Abby staring up at him in horror, or gone. Either would have been fine, and far better than a corpse.

Nothing had changed. He still knelt beside Abby. She still slept like an innocent babe. Her exposed neck was only inches away. Her heart beat steadily beneath the skin, the throb of it echoing inside him like a drumbeat.

Shaken, he rose and stepped away.

She turned in her sleep, tossing a slender arm above her head and arching her back. The wind picked up, sighing through the trees, but the cicadas had gone silent. When she settled again into deeper slumber, he laid his blanket over her and then slipped into the night to hunt.

ABBY WOKE EARLY from a fitful sleep to find food waiting for her. Rabbit this time, cooked and still warm. She didn't see Jake at first and scrambled to her feet, ready to run. She cast around for the horses but didn't see them either, which made her hesitate. Idiotic to attempt to escape on foot.

Still, she couldn't afford to waste any chances. Ignoring the ache in her belly as she passed by the food, she went directly to the saddlebags. Her stomach sank as she rifled through her belongings and then his. It was strangely intimate, that. He didn't have much. A pair of socks, much mended. A small bag of coins. Bullets but no gun. A soft handkerchief with someone's initials neatly stitched in the corner. *LBK.* She wondered who he'd stolen that from and why he kept it. There was nothing in the bag she could use as a weapon. He'd taken her guns with him and even her dinner knife was missing.

Bastard.

A sound behind her spun her around. Horses moving through the brush. He was coming back. For a moment, she stood torn. Her instincts told her to run. He wouldn't shoot. For some reason he refused to share, he wanted her alive. But he was fast and she was hurt. There would be a better chance, there had to be.

The bushes stirred a moment before she saw the top

of his hat. He passed through a gap in the trees leading the horses and his gaze immediately locked on her. She scowled and tossed the useless bag into the dirt, not bothering to hide what she'd been doing.

One corner of his mouth turned up and he returned his attention to the horses. He'd known she was going to run, of course he had. The thought of chasing her down had probably turned him on. Reapers liked it when their prey ran. It was one of the first lessons she'd learned as a young recruit—how to stand your ground. She was trying to stand her ground with Jake but it was hard, especially when she didn't know why he'd taken her.

"How is your head?"

"It hurts," she said, not seeing any reason to lie. "Everything hurts."

"I could rub out your muscles."

"You're joking." The look he gave her was dead serious. If a normal man had said that, she'd think he was after something else, but she was pretty sure that if Jake decided to fuck her, he wasn't going to offer a massage first. "*It's in both of our interests that you don't touch me*, isn't that what you said?"

"Maybe I've reconsidered." He paused, looked as if he was wrestling with himself and then said, "I'm not trying to be cruel by pushing you so hard. If there's something I can do to make it easier on you, I'll do it. If that means touching you, I can stand it."

"You can stand it?" She smiled grimly. "Just like you had to *force* yourself to touch me back in New Providence."

A muscle in his jaw jumped. "Exactly like that."

He was lying. He knew it and she did. He hadn't been faking anything in that alley. She didn't know if he was lying to her or himself but whichever it was, she sure as hell wasn't calling that bluff. "Thank you, but I'll find a way to manage."

"Abby..."

"The thought of you touching me makes my skin crawl."

He didn't argue, just regarded her calmly for a moment before setting to work readying the horses. Dismissing her as if she were no threat whatsoever. She stepped forward.

"What would help me is if you told me what the hell is going on, why you took me and why you're dragging me to Fort Hill when I was on my way there anyway. Do you know what they'll do to you there?"

That brought a sliver of a smile to his face. "Concerned for my welfare, are you?"

"Hell no," she snapped. "But you...none of this makes a damn bit of sense."

"If you still expect the world to make sense, you're younger than I thought."

"I'm twenty-seven."

"Ancient." He grabbed the saddlebag she'd rifled through and swung it onto Harvey's back before turning to face her again. "Why were you on your way to Fort Hill? I've never seen a Ranger wander more than a mile or two from their patrol. Rangers usually use unmarked messengers between forts, don't they?"

"We do." She shifted uneasily. Again, she couldn't see any reason not to tell him. Maybe if she answered his questions, then he'd start answering hers. "I'm a woman and there aren't many female Rangers. The scientists say it's for the same reason that women don't turn Reaper, but they don't understand exactly how it works. There are people who think I shouldn't be out riding patrol. That I should be locked up behind the fort walls popping out baby Rangers. My captain is one of them. He got it into his thick, *stubborn* head that if I spent some time at Fort Hill I might come to like it there and decide to stay."

Jake rested one hand on Harvey's shoulder and tilted his head as he considered her. It wasn't right for a Reaper to be so attractive. Even scruffy and covered with dust from the road, Jake was a fine-looking man. Except that he wasn't a man. She shouldn't be attracted to him at all. Of course, there was the fact that he was repulsed by her, that he wasn't sure he could stand to touch her even if it meant keeping her alive for whatever he needed her for. Helpful to remember that.

"He wants you to take a mate."

"One mate…two." She smiled bitterly. "I could take the whole fort if I wanted to. He just needs more men and now that I'm getting to be so *ancient*, he's been pushing harder."

"Ah."

She glared at him. "What?"

"That explains why you were on your way to Fort Hill." He lifted his hand. "Eat your breakfast. We need to be on our way."

She picked up a piece of meat. "Are you going to tell me what this is really all about before we get there?"

"It will be easier just to show you. You've had enough trouble swallowing the fact that I'm a Reaper. Better if I have the proof in my hands. It's only a few hours." She made a rude sound and he smiled. "I forgot how impatient people can be."

"Mortality will do that to you."

He turned his back, signaling an end to the conversation. Though she was tempted to push him further, she decided it was better to wait. They were traveling in the direction of Fort Hill and—for her at least—that way lay safety. He hadn't done anything to hurt her. Yet. And she needed to regain her strength if she wanted a chance at taking him out.

Squatting beside the fire, she ate, not even tasting the food, just choking it down for sustenance. She ignored the critical way Jake looked at her, as if she was a horse that had turned up lame and he was trying to decide whether or not to put a bullet in her head. He spoke her name when he was finished packing away their remaining things. When she looked up, he asked, "Do you need anything else?"

"Not unless you have a vat of coffee I can dunk my head in?"

He shook his head and pointed toward Marley. "There's fresh water in your canteen."

That was the last she heard from him for hours afterward. At first, she was nearly grateful for that. It gave her time to think, to get a hold of her fear. And it gave her a chance to study him. But six hours later, she still had no plan. Still didn't know anything about him save the fact that he never tired, his attention never wavered and he was determined to keep her alive.

As the afternoon passed into evening, his silence only emphasized the preternatural quiet of the summer day. A cold feeling settled over her when she realized that she hadn't seen any birds for miles. Not only the birds were mute, but all the animals seemed to have disappeared or gone into hiding.

It was too early in the day for deer to be out but there should have been small animals scampering around. In general, the land was pretty barren around Fort Hill but the spot they passed through now was hospitable enough. In fact, Abby was surprised that no one had claimed it. There was a good-size creek threading through the hills, enough vegetation to suggest that the soil was fertile and a grove of old hickory and oak that would have provided enough wood to build five cabins. No squirrels though. No sparrows flitting through the trees. The silence pressed in on her. Marley sidestepped nervously when a dry leaf blew across the path.

Jake glanced her way and Abby ignored his questioning look. They were close now. She'd know within the hour if he truly meant to bring her to Fort Hill.

As soon as she told the Rangers that Jake was a Reaper, they'd kill him or use him in one of their experiments. And she *would* tell them what he was. She had to.

"They'll kill you, you know that right? I'd think that the parasite mangled your brain if there wasn't evidence to the contrary."

The corner of his mouth tucked up. "Why, Abby, is that a compliment?"

She snorted.

Jake stretched his hand and wiped his palm dry on the leg of his jeans. "You've noticed how quiet it is."

It hadn't really been a question, but she nodded anyway.

"Fort Hill was raided last week. Reapers…younglings driven up here like cattle to attack the fort. They avoided the border towns, so an alarm never went up." Dark eyes fixed on her briefly. "The quiet means the Reapers who attacked are still in the area. I thought they'd have moved on by now or else I wouldn't have risked bringing you this way. With the Reapers still here, I'll have to stash you somewhere safe and go on alone."

"A safe place? With packs of Reapers roaming the countryside?"

He inclined his head in a slight nod. "Reasonably safe."

She shook her head. "You're not going to tie me up out here, not if there are Reapers around. That's a death sentence and you know it."

He frowned. "Do you think I brought you all this way to set you out like a sacrificial lamb? You'll be safe, I'll make sure of it."

"You're lying about the fort." He had to be. The fort walls were twenty feet high and there were regular patrols going in and out on a weekly basis. Her patrol would have been there if not for that unexpected group of Reapers they'd run into and the airship crash. Reapers avoided the forts, they didn't attack them. They might be as cunning as animals but they weren't that organized.

Jake was silent.

"We would have heard about something like that happening," she insisted.

"This area's sparsely populated. I'm not surprised word hasn't gotten out. I doubt there have been any survivors."

She thought of Amy and the kids and her blood chilled. "How many?"

When he frowned at her, she demanded, "How many Reapers are we talking about?"

"About a hundred. There won't be that many—"

She pulled back on the reins, intending to turn Marley, but he blocked her. "Where do you think you're going?"

"My family is between here and the border. If there are Reapers—"

"Most of the Reapers are already gone," he said calmly. "They'll have split into smaller packs. Your family will be more careful after what happened. I can't let you go. There's more at stake here than the lives of four people."

Her hands tightened and she thought about running anyway. She was unarmed in a territory swarming with Reapers. She could outrun Jake for a while, but she'd have to rest eventually, as would Marley. Jake…he could keep running long after Harvey dropped.

He watched her face as if reading her thoughts, looking ready to leap on her if she so much as twitched.

"Trust me, sweetheart, you don't want those kids along for this ride."

After a moment, she nodded. "I want to see the fort."

She expected him to argue but he didn't, just waited for her to start moving again.

Once past the shade of the trees, the sun beat down on them again and she adjusted the angle of her hat. In the distance, she could see an airship, one of the slow, bloated cargo ships that hung low to the ground when full. Probably hauling cattle. All the slaughterhouses were in the foothills near Koln, miles west of here and relatively safe from the Reapers. In Canada, they used trains for transport but down here all the tracks were rusted and half-buried, crisscrossing the land like old scars. Years ago when there'd been enough Rangers to guard the border farther south, a team of investors had hired hundreds of groundlings to lay track, but the sleek passenger trains that were supposed to be able to outrun the Reapers hadn't been quite fast enough.

That, too, was when they discovered the Reapers had an astonishing aptitude for ambush. That left the big cargo ships as the only means to transport the food produced on the plains up to the people nestled safely in their mountain fortresses. Strange how the sight of that ship and the occasional reflective flash coming from the cities could make her feel so very alone.

"We're almost there," Jake said, drawing her attention from the ship. "Can I trust you with a pistol?"

"Are you asking if I'll shoot you again?"

"Point-blank range, you couldn't kill me before I disarmed you. But if you're attacked by younglings, it might buy you enough time to run."

That sobered her and, taking her silence for an answer, Jake leaned across the distance separating them to slap the cold weight of metal into her palm. As her fingers closed around it, she considered putting a bullet in his head. It's where she should have aimed the first time. The look he gave her said he knew what she was thinking and his smirk almost dared her to do it. Instead, she turned away and slipped the gun into her holster. They'd be able to see Fort Hill any minute now and she'd make her decision then about whether or not to pull that trigger.

"Where?"

"There's a river to the west of the fort with a small island set midway between the banks. Younglings won't cross running water if they can avoid it, and that particular river comes down from the mountains."

"Which means?"

The corner of his mouth tucked up. "That they'll avoid it. You'll be able to see the fort from the top of this hill. We'll drop down behind it and you'll head for that island. If you're attacked, cross the river and run for the hills to the highest point you can get to."

"And then what?"

"Keep the pistol ready and pray that I manage to track you down before the younglings do."

She stared at him for a few seconds and then shook her head in disbelief. "That is the worst plan I've ever heard—and my last captain was a drunkard."

"I won't be long. So long as you stay quiet on that island you'll be fine."

She opened her mouth to argue, but just then the

wind shifted and something in his posture changed. He came suddenly alert and his attention shifted away from her. Smoke…she smelled smoke. She scanned the horizon and sure enough, there to the west—a pale gray thread of smoke spiraled into the clear blue sky.

"Idiots," Jake snarled and kicked Harvey forward. She followed, reluctantly, with a catch in her throat. When she crested the hill, the sight that met her eyes made her blood run cold. She pulled back hard on the reins, her heart stopping for a tick before trying to pound its way out of her chest.

My God.

The great ironbound gates were split, what was left of them hung from warped hinges. Dynamite. She'd never heard of Reapers using explosives and didn't want to consider the repercussions of that. The fire was newly lit, oily black smoke coiling up into the exquisitely blue September sky. The earth surrounding the fort was churned and the dirt was black with blood. There were no bodies—that was the most disturbing thing. Everywhere was ruin, but there weren't any dead. Shreds of clothing. Shreds of *meat.* Discarded weaponry everywhere, bright metal glinting in the sun. No bodies. Her stomach churned and she swallowed down bile.

Her knuckles stretched and popped, and she forced her fingers to ease their death grip on the reins before she caused Marley to panic. She'd never…she hadn't really believed. Her eyes shot to Jake, already several lengths ahead of her. He was yelling something at her but the sounds all blended together in her numb mind—hoofbeats and the thundering of her heart, Jake's voice which she couldn't make sense of just then.

She saw movement below and wheeled Marley around. *Reapers.* She took one last look at Jake's face and could tell by the shape of the words forming on his lips that he was cussing her out. But he didn't turn around to give chase. Instead, he bent down over Harvey's neck and, if anything, rode faster away from her. She sped away just as quickly in the opposite direction. No way in hell was she following him there. Now was her chance.

She had to get back to New Providence and raise an alarm. Get back to her patrol and drop this in the captain's lap. Get back to her sister's ranch. She swiped at the sticky wet road dust tracking down her cheeks. What the hell was she supposed to do alone even if there was anyone left alive down there?

There wasn't, she knew that. No one had survived *that.* Guilt and grief and anger twisted in her gut and she fought to remain calm. She'd escaped from Jake. She needed to avoid the Reapers he said were still about and then she needed to get out a warning.

She ran, as fast as Marley could take her, which was pretty damned fast. But the poor horse had already been pushed to the edge of her endurance and couldn't manage a flat-out run for very long. Marley jumped a dry streambed and landed shy of where she should have, not enough to take them down but enough for her step to falter. That jarred Abby to her senses. She slowed them to a walk, letting Marley catch her breath while she caught hers. Glancing back, she expected to see a horde of Reapers pouring down the hillside after them, but there was no one. It was as silent as a grave. Nothing behind her but smoke. She imagined she could smell the battlefield stench, but that wasn't impossible from this distance, was it?

And Jake—*damn him*—he'd been telling her the truth all along.

Chapter Eight

THE FIRE WAS too far gone. Whatever papers and samples Josiah had managed to secret away before the Reapers blasted through the gates were lost.

Fuck.

Jake growled out a low warning before kicking the youngling out of his path. The smoldering ruin reeked of blood and death, and he needed to get the hell out as quickly as possible. One part of his mind knew that what remained of the rotting body the youngling dragged behind him *should* repulse him. Another part simply didn't care. Sweat beaded on his brow even as his mouth began to water. Before he tracked down Abby, he needed to eat. He'd tried to stop her from bolting, yelling at her to get to the island, but he'd seen the white-rimmed look of panic in her eyes and knew she hadn't heeded his warning. She'd fled as if a pack of demons were on her heels, which was close enough to the truth. And with the fire, he'd had to let her go.

It had been for nothing. All of the research, all of the paperwork, everything was gone.

Few Reapers remained at the fort…what was left of it. The gates were gone and while the outer walls and the barracks were mostly intact, all of the research buildings had been destroyed. The food supply was exhausted and most of the younglings had already left, in small packs of ten-to-twenty men. They'd hunt in an expanding circle of destruction until they were stopped. For Abby's sake, he hoped the Rangers of her patrol reached her family's ranch before the younglings did. As for Abby…if night fell before she managed to put some distance between her and this place, she didn't stand a chance. Not unless he found her first.

"Jake," a familiar voice called out from behind him and he turned slowly.

Shit.

Standing a cautious dozen feet distant, Marston regarded him through narrowed eyes. He was short and wiry with straight blond hair that he normally kept tied back in a queue. When he ran the border, he left it loose and tangled as it was now to blend in with the younglings. Jake had seen him during the fight—nude to the waist, hands, face and chest dripping with blood. Marston had personally killed the captain of the fort as the man begged for mercy. At the time, Jake had been grateful for the distraction, which had given him enough time to help Josiah escape. Now, he'd give just about anything for another distraction that would allow him to avoid this confrontation.

"Where have you been?"

Jake scrubbed the dust from his hair and flipped back the edge of his coat for access to his gun. "I was feeding."

Marston's mouth flattened. "There was food here, plenty of it. I thought we'd lost you."

He walked toward Marston, noted the dark stains in

the creases of the other man's skin. He stopped when he was close enough to smell the blood. "I wasn't lost. I needed to hunt and I was hungry for more than just food. Twelve years is a long time to be locked up." He lifted his chin toward the gate. "You'd be sick of these walls too."

Marston, whose appetites were depraved even for a Reaper, accepted that without blinking. In fact, Jake's answer seemed to reassure him. He took a step closer. "I'm surprised you came back at all. If I'd been caged here for twelve years, I'd have killed every scientist I could get my hands on and then gone after the witnesses."

"I don't care about revenge." Not against the scientists, not against the "friends" who'd left him here to rot. "I came back for answers. Why the fire?"

Marston shrugged. "It was the quickest way to clear out the younglings and destroy the evidence. Tomas wants the humans to believe this was just a run of hungry younglings and unlike you, they won't know any better."

"Was everything destroyed, then? All of the papers?"

"Every last scrap. If I'd known you wanted to look around, I would have waited. You *should* have stayed. I needed you to identify Dr. Welks before the younglings got to him."

"I killed Welks myself," Jake lied. Marston nodded, a subtle easing of the muscles in his shoulders signaling his relief.

"Good. Tomas will be pleased." Leaning against a smoke-blackened post, he crossed his arms over his chest and regarded Jake curiously. "After what they did to you, why do you care about the research?"

"I wanted to know if the rumors were true." The expression on Marston's face said it all but Jake wanted to hear the words. "I thought not, but this attack suggests otherwise. That's why you came, isn't it? You heard about the cure."

"One of the ships they send to keep watch passed over the city and dropped a message directly into the throne room." Marston's eyes glinted with amusement. "You should have seen Tomas's face. Furious they knew about his little den. Julian thought it was a trap. But trap, or no, there wasn't anything to lose by investigating the report except for a few younglings."

And the Rangers guarding the fort, all of the ranches and towns that would be hit by the horde Marston had driven up from the south. "Why would humans deliver that message?"

"They called it 'protecting a mutual interest.'" The corner of Marston's mouth turned up in a smile. "And you wonder why I'd rather forget I was ever one of them."

Who? Who sent the message? Jake couldn't ask that question without making Marston curious. The last thing he wanted was a curious Marston. He feigned indifference, letting his gaze drift over the plains. "I suppose there are humans as hungry as any rider and plenty of them with a vested interest in keeping things exactly the way they are now. The alliance is a bad idea. The humans who live in the mountains have their own agenda."

"That is surely true," Marston said, casting him a speculative look. "I'm just not so sure anymore that you don't have one, as well."

Jake opened his mouth and then hesitated, picking his lie, but Marston saved him the trouble.

"Look, Jake, I don't care what it is. You want to play at being human, you go right on ahead. But don't get in Tomas's way. He's consolidated his power while you were gone, killed Sebastian outright and has Jamie cornered in that strip of jungle with the mountains at his back. If you do return to the city, you'll need to convince Tomas that you're not going to stir up trouble for him."

Jake raised his brows. "Is this a friendly warning?"

"A warning, at least."

"And what exactly is it that Tomas wants?"

"Everything." Marston grimaced. "He wants it all. The demented bastard's calling himself a god these days."

"He plans to move north then."

Marston laughed. "You think he'd destroy a self-replenishing food source? No. He's not that crazy. Not yet. But he won't let anyone find a cure either."

Jake fell silent as he considered that. Tomas had always been dangerous. Territorial. Ambitious. With no interest in preserving anything about human culture. He wouldn't be content to let things continue on as they were. As the sentient grew in numbers, he would move north. Marston would serve him so long as it entertained him to do so, and there was no point in killing Tomas. Jake had killed Tomas's predecessor and it hadn't changed a damned thing. There was always another Tomas waiting to climb the bloody heap of bodies and call himself king. Another Marston to swim in the blood. Jake swept his gaze over the now-empty courtyard, the smoldering building, the sinking sun. "You're leaving tonight?"

"Heading south to make my report. Most of the younglings have already scattered, but the ones still here will keep the Rangers busy for a few weeks. You're welcome to join me. You can even ride your horse if you can't keep pace—" he grinned as if greatly amused, "—unless, of course, you've developed a taste for them. That's what they fed you, isn't it? Rotting horseflesh?"

Jake ignored the taunt. "I'm staying up here, at least for a while."

"Tomas won't like that. He'll want to know where you stand."

"Fuck what Tomas likes."

Marston snorted. "I'll pass that along."

Jake was sure he would. He could almost see the wheels turning in Marston's head. He thought Jake was afraid. That captivity had weakened him and the city was no place for the weak. Marston was quietly calculating whether he could take Jake out himself and, more importantly, how much his position would improve by the conquest. Jake waited for him to make a decision, part of him hoping that Marston would try it. It might—just—take the edge off the hunger roiling in his belly.

But Marston looked away, lifting his chin toward the road. "Simon caught something."

Jake turned his body rather than his head so that

he could keep an eye on Marston. "Simon? A protégé of yours?"

"He's teetering on the edge of sentience, but I think… Jake?"

Fuck. He'd taken five steps toward the road before Marston caught up with him.

"Still starving?"

Jake didn't answer. She was still alive. He could see her struggling.

Marston tsked. "It's impolite to steal food from younglings."

A growl rose up in Jake's throat unbidden at the challenge. It was all he could do not to break into a full run. That would change Marston's mind. He would read it as impatience and loss of control. Not only would killing Jake add to his reputation, it would bring him one step closer to the throne…or godhead, or whatever complicated political games the others were playing at this century.

Marston kept pace. "Right, then. Let's see what they've got."

The younglings changed course as Jake and Marston approached, or they tried to, anyway. They nearly split Abby in two when they attempted to scatter in opposite directions.

"Drop her," Jake demanded, alarmed at the feral sound of his own voice. One youngling, the smallest, obeyed immediately, yelping and scuttling back. The others stood their ground.

"Her," Marston murmured, a touch of amusement shading his voice. "It."

Jake leaped onto the larger Reaper, Simon, the one old enough to attempt to drag Abby away from the younglings who would have shredded her flesh where she stood. He crushed Simon's windpipe with a sharp chop to the neck, hoping that Marston wasn't too attached to his protégé. Probably not—Marston was rarely sentimental.

It was…unpleasant to be this close to a youngling. The smell, the frenzied movement, the terror of awareness that shadowed their eyes. Jake didn't look Simon in the eyes. He struck again, breaking the youngling's wrist so Abby could pull free. Simon clutched at his neck with his working hand and stumbled back. Jake let him go. Marston hadn't been as merciful. He'd slaughtered the other youngling and judging by the expression on Abby's face as she backed away, she'd watched him do it. Keeping his gaze fixed on his true prey, Marston licked the blood from his hand and grabbed hold of Abby's ankle to haul her back.

He shot Jake a grin. "This is what you wanted? Her screams will frenzy the younglings. Watch my back?"

"I want her."

Abby jerked, but Jake paid her no mind. Couldn't just then, fixated as he was on Marston, who had his hands on her body. Who could kill her between one beat of her stuttering heart and the next.

"She's a Ranger," Marston whispered in wonder.

Jake ground his teeth but answered. "Yes."

Marston knelt down to gently cradle her jaw. He was always gentle at first. It seemed to scare them more, knowing what he was. Jake considered his options.

Abby wasn't in danger yet and Marston would be difficult to kill, even for him. And they were surrounded by younglings. He could see the reflective glint of their eyes as they crouched at the edges of the clearing in the gathering dusk. The only thing keeping them there was fear of him and of Marston. If they sensed an opportunity to attack, they would.

Marston rasped his fingernails across Abby's fair skin, leaving angry red tracks on her cheek. She whimpered, a broken sound that wrenched Jake's gut. He could smell Marston's arousal and it roused his own.

Softly, almost reverently, Marston whispered, "A female Ranger. We could keep this one alive for a very, very long time."

Jake hoped to God that Abby didn't comprehend what Marston intended for her. But he sensed the spike of fear that sharpened her sweat and, judging by the way his smile widened, so did Marston. He needed to get Marston's hands off her, and get away from the younglings hoping they'd be able to clean up the scraps left behind.

"Let's take her and get out of here," Jake said. "Before the smoke draws Rangers to investigate. We can find someplace safe and remote to entertain ourselves."

Abby's head snapped to stare at him, but he ignored her.

"We have time enough," Marston said. "There's no one alive to report the smoke for miles around. No Rangers within more than a two-day ride save this one." His open hand slid down her delicate neck. "What are you doing here all alone, pretty?"

Jake trembled with the effort it took not to lunge across the distance. Aside from the fact that any sudden movement on his part might frenzy the younglings, Marston was apt to close his fist and snap her neck for the sheer perversity of it. Even if he didn't, Jake wasn't completely sure he'd win in a fair fight against Marston.

Abby's breath came in short, choppy gasps as her muscles tightened. Her eyes were round as saucers and sweat dampened her shirt. Her boots scrabbled at the rocky ground trying to find some purchase as Marston drew her close. Frantically, her gaze darted from Marston to him, pleading. *Fuck.* Why hadn't she done as he'd asked? She would have been safe on that island.

Marston's lips pressed to hers in an ugly parody of a kiss. His hand remained locked around her neck, holding her in place. His teeth drew blood and whimpering moans from Abby, who squirmed in his grip. Despite himself, Jake grew hard, his mouth watered and his fingers flexed. A tremor ran down all his limbs…a fucked-up mix of horror, outrage and greedy hunger.

It was always at this point that he wondered why he fought. Marston, at least, was comfortable in his skin. He'd long ago made peace with what he was. Jake… he was almost more of a monster for the knowledge that he *shouldn't* be this way. It would be easier not to know. Easier to forget. Pure delusion to cling to his humanity at this point. He hadn't been human for a very long time.

Just as he took a step forward thinking that it would be more merciful to stop this even if it meant her death, Abby struck. Clever and quick, she'd found Marston's knife. When his hand moved from her neck to clutch at her breast, the blade flashed up, caught the last orange light of the setting sun and plunged deep into the vulnerable skin at the back of Marston's neck. The angle was off. Her position beneath Marston and his reflexes saved him or she might actually have managed to sever his spine.

Marston roared and his face lost all trace of humanity as he let the rider have free rein. Jake moved forward, kicking him in the side of the head with enough force to split open a melon. Marston lurched to the side but managed to hold on to Abby's shoulder, pulling her with him so she lay sprawled across his chest.

The dent in his skull barely slowed him down. His grip on Abby held no matter how hard she tried to break free. Jake could tear her loose, but she'd lose an arm. She cast a fistful of sand into Marston's eyes and he hissed. Using his distraction, she managed to transfer the knife into her free hand and drove it again into Marston's neck.

Marston twisted, managing somehow to dodge that killing blow. Jake crouched, waiting for his chance. The younglings shifted restlessly behind him, some animal sense of self-preservation holding them back. It would be easier if Abby would be still, but she didn't have any quit in her. Marston slammed her to the ground and even though it knocked the wind out of her, she brought her knee up with a hard direct hit to his balls.

It was enough. Jake moved, wrapping an arm around Marston's neck and drawing his head back. The hands holding Abby opened and she scurried back like a crab while Jake did his best to break Marston's neck. Marston ducked away and Jake couldn't follow without abandoning Abby to the younglings. Instead, he reached down, took hold of her biceps and hauled her to her feet. She slashed at his arm, splitting through his leather coat and slicing open his flesh. Warm blood slicked down his skin, but he didn't release her. "I'm your only way out of this."

Teeth clamped tightly together, lips pulled back in a snarl, her entire body shaking with a mix of rage and fear, she glared murder at him. But she didn't strike again, which was good because Marston had already recovered enough to roll to his feet. He cracked his neck and started walking in their direction.

"I would have shared," he growled. "Eventually."

Marston stopped short when Jake shoved Abby behind him. The thought briefly crossed his mind that she might decide to drive that knife into the back of his neck, twist it to pop the vertebrae and slice right through his spinal cord. But instead, she turned around, her back brushing against his as she faced the younglings. Marston's eyes narrowed.

"This is why you were so riled. You knew she was a Ranger. She came here with you and you were pissed the younglings pried her out of whatever hole you stashed her in. Don't bother to deny it, your scent is on her. I could taste it."

A shudder ran through Abby.

"I claimed her first."

"Then why come back here with her? That's not idle curiosity. You're saving her for something." He barked out a sharp laugh. "My God. I thought you'd given up on that. They tortured you for what? Ten? Twenty years? And you come right back for more."

Too clever by far. The rest wasn't much of a leap from that point. Jake could already see Marston making the connections in his mind. He lunged, separating himself from Abby and driving Marston back. She'd have to stand her ground for a time without him. His arms wrapped around Marston's waist and he plowed him to the ground, the impact jolting them both for a moment. Marston grabbed for his throat and Jake dropped an elbow to his nose breaking bone and cartilage. Blood sprayed into his face, momentarily blinding him, so he felt more than saw Marston's fist driving toward his temple. He managed to turn just enough that it was only a glancing blow.

Marston rolled back, using his knees to skew Jake's body to the side and forcing him to lose his balance. They always had been evenly matched, in strength and skill. Partners of a sort, friends as much as one could be friends with another Reaper and a rival at that.

At his best, it would have been a hard fight for Jake to win. But he wasn't at his best. He'd been imprisoned for twelve years, eating dead animals and suffering the myriad of tests and experiments the Fort Hill scientists had inflicted upon him. He'd lied to Marston too. He hadn't had the time or the stomach to go hunting after his release. He'd stashed Josiah and Karlson, located a Ranger as they'd requested and then returned to find the papers and vials Josiah had hidden away before their escape, all of them lost now. Marston was in peak form, rested and well fed. Add rage and lust to that combination and Jake never stood a chance.

Marston straddled his chest, knees digging into Jake's biceps. Like being pinned by an elephant. Jake jacked his body to the side but Marston only laughed, locking his arms around Jake's head.

"Why are you still fighting, Jake? I'm just helping you out with your little death wish."

He didn't have a death wish. He wanted a life, very badly. But no matter how he struggled, he couldn't break Marston's hold. Then, just as Jake felt the bones in his neck begin to separate, there was a deafening explosion. A flash of searing white light. Marston's body jerked and then the muscles in his arm went slack. Jake wrenched himself free. When he looked up, Abby was standing above him holding a smoking gun. *His* gun. She must have drawn it from his holster when he pushed her behind him.

"Are you all right?"

Stunned, he couldn't do more than nod.

"Then get up," she snarled. "I need you. This place is crawling with Reapers."

Marston's sagging body crumpled to the ground as Jake climbed to his feet. The younglings were still there, closer now and prowling the edge of what they considered a safe distance. At least a dozen of them. Aroused by the smell of blood and violence, their movements were fast and jerky.

Jake reached out, hooked two fingers in Abby's collar and pulled her back against him. "My horse is this way. With you here, they haven't bothered with him yet. We're going to move slowly and you're going to stay close."

He thought she might argue but she only swiped her forehead, streaking blood across her pale skin. Her thin lips trembled when they parted. "Marley's dead. They killed her. They—"

"Come on." He gripped her shoulder and pulled her back. "This way."

The younglings hung back, parting as he led the way toward the forgotten but nearly frantic horse. If he could get Abby in the saddle, he could keep pace for a few miles and take care of anyone who decided to pursue them.

"If we're separated, make a run for the river. Then north as far and as fast as the horse will take you. The highest point you can find."

Harvey quieted beneath the soft touch of her hand. While Abby murmured gentle nonsense to the terrified animal, Jake reached for the tether, keeping one eye always on the circling Reapers. He'd tied Harvey to a locust tree knowing the younglings would avoid it. Something on the long slender thorns that grew from the branches made the cuts fester. It wouldn't keep them away forever, but he hadn't planned to stay here for as long as he had.

With every passing second, the circle drew tighter. "Go on. Get up now. You run like the devil's on your heels on my say-so."

She mounted and gathered the reins. "He can carry us both."

Startled, Jake glanced up. Her brows were drawn

with fear, yes, and pain too, but what knocked him off balance was the worry there. Worry for *him*.

He caught a flash of movement out of the corner of his eye and slapped Harvey. "Go."

Harvey surged forward, clearing the younglings by a hairsbreadth and then only because Jake used his attacker's momentum to lift him up and over his head, hurling the body into the pack trying to block Abby's escape. Harvey leaped over the pile, stumbling as he came down on the far side. But he found his footing quickly and Jake listened to the staccato beat of fleeing hoofbeats with relief before turning to fight his own way out of the pack.

Chapter Nine

Abby considered heading south after she crossed the river. If Jake was right about running water affording her some protection—and why shouldn't he be?—then she could follow the western bank where the river ran past Black Rock. She could warn the town there and meet up with her patrol, which should be heading north within the next day or two.

It wasn't safe to travel at night. Reapers actually preferred to hunt during the daylight hours but she couldn't see well enough to ride, let alone shoot when it was this dark. She needed to find a place to hole up until daybreak. Harvey could rest and then they'd make a run for it at first light. She ran Harvey for as long as she could and then held him to a steady walk, aiming toward a hill that poked up a good hundred feet above the rest. Reapers avoided higher elevations and it would give her a good view of the surrounding countryside.

It took nearly two hours to reach her destination. Two hours that had her jumping at every rustle in the grass and twisting around in her saddle every hundred feet or so. She bound the cut on her arm in the saddle, drank a good portion of Jake's remaining water and tried to make sense of the attack on Fort Hill.

Except none of it made any sense.

Reapers were ravening beasts as like to turn on their own pack members as not. They were ghouls who hungered for human flesh. Appetite without the ability to plan or organize. An image flashed in her mind of Jake and she shook her head. She'd never met anyone with his terrifyingly intense kind of self-control. He wasn't stupid and he was here for a reason that somehow involved her. He turned everything she'd ever learned about Reapers on its head and made her question all of her training. He made her question *everything.*

He hadn't taken her for the usual reasons, that was for certain. He'd had plenty of opportunities to kill her. She didn't have the strength to take him without her weapons. Her thoughts kept circling back to Marston's words about keeping her alive for a long time, but she couldn't make them fit with what she knew of Jake.

Which was nothing, she reminded herself. He was a Reaper and she was a fool for placing any kind of trust in him.

She hit on a deer path that twisted through the trees and followed it, taking every turn that led toward higher ground. After another hour or so, she came to a likely spot to camp for the night. Harvey couldn't make it much farther and neither could she. After brushing down the trembling horse, she found a ledge overlooking the surrounding area and sat waiting. There was a sharp chill in the air and tonight she didn't have Jake's coat to keep her warm. She couldn't risk a fire that would be visible to anyone on the plains below. The moon was up, half-full and partially covered by tendrils of clouds skating across the sky. The trees swayed beneath the stiff wind and she flinched every time the branches creaked together.

She was safe here, she reminded herself, struggling to settle her nerves. The elevation should keep her safe, along with the chill in the air. It was unlikely that even Jake would find her tonight. Cold made Reapers sluggish. Even knowing where she was, he'd likely have to find a warm hollow to curl up in until morning. Still, it was a long time before her muscles began to relax. The moon passed slowly overhead and her thoughts began to drift, from worry over her family to wondering what Lyle and Cam would think when they arrived at Fort Hill. They'd probably think she was dead. She imagined they'd feel guilty, which served them right for sending her off as a messenger. *For her own good.* Yeah, she snorted, pretty great fucking plan.

She'd just started to drowse off when the sound of a twig snapping jerked her awake. Harvey's soft whinny brought her to her feet. A shadow separated itself from the darkness. She released a shaky breath when Jake stepped into the filtered moonlight. His eyes immediately fixed on her with the arrested intensity that had become familiar to her. Relief flared in her chest and she cursed herself twenty times a fool as she tamped it down. He wasn't her friend. He might not plan to hurt her *tonight*, but she still didn't know why he'd taken her. He was a guard recapturing his escaped prisoner.

Still, better him than a pack of Reapers.

His face was hidden within the shadow of his hat but there was something in his stance that told her to keep her distance.

"I smell blood," he said, lifting his nose to the wind. "Yours."

There was a gash on her knee. She'd stumbled in the dark and had fallen hard on a sharp rock. Her pants were torn and her leg scraped. It had been too dark and she'd been too exhausted to do more than dab at it with her sleeve to wipe the worst of the debris from the cut. The other Reapers had drawn blood too, but she was trying very hard to forget about that. "I tripped. It's nothing serious."

"Get rid of it." He took a step back. "I'll fetch wood for the fire. It's freezing."

She could hear the rattle in his teeth and wondered if he was hurt. It was chilly but not *that* cold. "Is it safe to start a fire?"

"It is now." And he was gone.

There was nothing to do but follow him back to the clearing where she'd settled Harvey. The small campsite was surrounded by pine trees that blocked out most of the wind. Kneeling, he started to build a fire with the few sticks she'd gathered before stopping to watch for him. She watched until it became apparent that he didn't want to talk about what had happened at Fort Hill.

She went to the creek first. *Get rid of it*, he'd said. The blood. Her blood needed to be washed off. The water was freezing, a trickle of runoff from a spring uphill. She managed to get most of what was on her skin off. Nothing she could do tonight about the blood that had soaked into her clothing. She bandaged her wounds in the dark, refilled the water skin and thought vaguely about running again.

It was more habit than intention. She wasn't running anywhere. Not tonight. Not until she knew the truth about what had happened at Fort Hill. Jake was the only one who could answer that question.

She gathered wood on the climb back to the clearing. Jake was seated in exactly the same place as she'd left him, staring into the flames. He didn't look up when she dropped the wood beside the fire.

"Are you hurt?"

"A bullet to the gut." His voice was flat. "One of them got a hold of your rifle. I'll be fine by morning."

He'd been shot? He shifted, moving back to sit on the stump of a downed tree and she saw that his shirt was soaked with blood. "Let me see it. Is the bullet still in there?"

"I think so. I don't know."

Crouching before him, she tried to get a better look at the wound. Maybe she could put all that time she'd spent in medical to use.

"But if I take it out, it'll heal faster, right?"

"There's nothing you need to do."

She touched the hand hanging limp between his knees, intending to move it aside, but froze when she realized what she was doing. Froze, too, because he felt so incredibly human. His fingers were cold and there was a faint tremor running just beneath his skin. It almost surprised her when he didn't pull away. He always kept his distance. Always flinched when they accidentally brushed up against each other. This time, he turned his hand and enclosed her fingers with his.

Her mouth went dry and she looked up, but he was

staring down at their joined hands. His sleeves were wet to the elbow, as if he'd washed himself in the river before coming to find her. *Washing off the blood.* She pushed the thought aside.

"There's no food," he said. "I didn't have time to find anything for you."

"I'm not hungry. When you said we're safe here, what did you mean by that? Are they all dead?"

"The ones that tried to follow, yes."

"You can't be upset about that."

"Can't I? It weakens my control." He looked up then, but she almost wished he hadn't. The blank expression was gone, but what had replaced it made every hair on her body stand on end. His fingers flexed when she tried to withdraw her hand. "I didn't… I didn't feed on them."

She swallowed hard. "Good. That's good, Jake."

"I thought I could handle this…" His eyes dilated, the pupils withdrawing to tight round specks. The light from the fire made it look like there was something moving beneath the glassy surface. "You. I should have stayed down there tonight, but I wanted to make sure you were safe."

His grip eased and she carefully withdrew her hand, sliding it down her thigh toward her gun. Before she was able to draw, he grabbed her forearm and pulled her forward, off balance. Her fingers caught in his shirt. The fabric was damp and clammy cold from his dousing in the river. Beneath it she could feel the shape of his body. Skin and bone, solid flesh that moved beneath her hands as he inhaled.

“I killed for you and you’re going to thank me with a bullet?”

“You’re a Reaper,” she said. “That’s why you kill. It has nothing to do with me. I’m a bone and you’re the dog who won the fight. Don’t pretend different.”

He made a rough sound of denial. “You don’t understand shit.”

“Let me go, Jake.”

He did. He released her arm anyway, but then he lifted his hands to her face. His fingers sank into her hair and clutched at her scalp, thumbs settling below her jaw as he angled her head back so he could take her mouth.

Hard, hungry. This was no gentle kiss like the one in New Providence, nothing shy or tentative about it. His teeth knocked into hers and his tongue filled her mouth. He devoured her, stealing away her breath as he pulled her in closer. It was the kind of kiss a man gave when he was riding the hard edge of climax, about to lose control. Heat pulsed through her body, gathered low in her belly. Her nipples tightened. For a second, she froze, stunned that he’d actually made a grab for her, stunned by her response. Then disgust filled her, a black self-loathing that brought her to her senses. She pulled her gun from the holster.

When she shoved the muzzle against his chest, he lifted his head only slightly. “You won’t do it.”

“Try me.”

His black eyes glittered. “You want this too.”

“I don’t.”

“I see the way you look at me.” His voice sounded

strange, hollow and gruff. The hard edges of the words too soft. "I can smell it on you. The way your body gets wet whenever I stand too close. The way you twist in your sleep and whisper my name. I can taste it on your tongue now."

Her hand was shaking. It didn't matter if he felt it. No way could she miss at this range and while the first shot wouldn't kill him, it would buy her enough time to take another. "All I taste on you is blood."

"Blood." He stilled and she watched as something shifted in his eyes, like something swimming up to the surface of a thick, dark pond. "Did I bite you?"

"No." When she pulled away, his fingers tightened, tugging at her hair and making her scalp sting. Not hard enough to stop her though. She jerked back harder and he let her go, his hands falling into his lap and curling into fists. She rose to her feet and took another step back just to be on the safe side. Her hands were shaking and she had to use both of them to steady the gun. "You're dead wrong. I do not want you. That's a lie, Jake, and you know it."

He didn't argue the point, just watched her to see what she'd do. He wasn't frightened of the gun. At first, she'd thought his lack of fear was because he could heal so quickly, but she was beginning to think that he simply didn't care much either way if he survived the shot.

"Try anything like that again and I will put you down just like I did your friend."

She meant it, damn it. Nelson was one thing. An arrogant, spoiled turd of a man—but at least he was human. Jake was a Reaper. Fair game. She'd already shot him once and she could do it again.

Jake studied her face for a long moment before looking down at his hands.

"Good." His voice was hoarse, but he sounded more like himself. "You should. How's your aim?"

"Just fine."

A flicker in his dark eyes. He nodded. "Don't fall asleep tonight, Abby."

With those chilling words, he wrapped himself in his coat and lay down, grunting with pain as he jostled the wound in his side. She withdrew to the far side of the fire and hugged her knees to her chest, gun in hand and gaze fixed on Jake. His back was to her. After a time, his breathing evened out and then he began to snore. A faint sound. Lyle was loud as a freight train. That thought made her feel homesick, lost and alone.

As she watched, Jake groaned and curled into a ball. His leg twitched. The muscle in his thigh flexed. The straining bulge of it visible even through the denim of his trousers. All bone and muscle. Skinny as a half-starved dog.

She moved to the right so she'd have a better angle if she needed to shoot. Leaning back against a boulder, she stretched her legs out and checked the chamber on her gun. She should kill him and try to make it back to her patrol.

It would be the smart thing to do.

Far more merciful to simply put a bullet in his head. Or her own.

Chapter Ten

BURROWING HER NOSE beneath the fabric, Abby blinked open her eyes. She could smell Jake on the cloth—campfire and pine underlain by a wild scent that reminded her of quiet December nights and the sound of wolf calls lifting into darkness. She sat up stiffly, her arms tangling beneath the weight of the leather. She'd fallen asleep after all, but it was daylight now and she was still alive.

A few feet away, Jake sat on an old log watching her with an unsettling mix of cold hunger and iron-hard determination. He'd given her his coat while she slept and apparently he'd been awake for some time already. He looked clean, rested and ready to go. His damp hair curled at the collar of a clean shirt. His sleeves were rolled back to reveal sun-browned forearms dusted with dark hair. Not a speck of blood in sight.

"Bad dream?"

Squinting at the sun through the branches, she shook her head. She barely remembered her dream.

"Were you watching me sleep?"

"Trying to decide whether to eat you for breakfast or not."

She looked up sharply, saw his faint smile and lifted

her brows. "Is that your idea of a joke? I didn't know you were capable of such a thing."

"For that, I *should* bite you." And then, astonishing her, he grinned. "Again."

It was a real smile, fleeting but genuine. It hit her hard, right in the chest. She straightened the coat so that it draped across her lap and lifted the edge. "Thanks for this."

Nodding, he picked up a tin cup that looked tiny in his big hands. Coffee. It was strong enough that she could smell it across the distance that separated them.

"How on God's green earth did you manage to find coffee?"

The cup paused on its way to his lips when he noted her interest. "I can be resourceful when called to it. You said you missed coffee. I found coffee. Here, I only have the one cup. Take it."

She shook her head. "I can wait."

His arm didn't move. "I insist."

Despite his strength, his ability to heal and his own insistence that he was a Reaper, up until yesterday it hadn't really sunk in. Her doubt along with his protectiveness was what had made her willing to accept him as a companion with some degree of composure. That doubt was gone this morning. Still, as troubling as that was—and it was awfully troubling—she couldn't make herself refuse a hot cup of coffee.

He cleared his throat. "Were you injured?"

Her mouth was still a raw mess of tiny stinging cuts courtesy of his demented friend. But otherwise…

"There's a scrape on my arm and another on my

leg. Both are wrapped but I'll need to clean them before we go."

"I have alcohol in my pack."

She frowned. "It doesn't hurt *that* badly."

"To pour on the wounds to keep them from getting infected." He must have seen some of her panic because he quickly added, "A regular infection, not a Reaper bite. It's a trick I picked up from the good doctors at the fort."

The way his mouth twisted around those last words caught her curiosity, but she didn't press. "I'll try it then and…thank you. You've healed?"

He shrugged. "The bullet will take a few days to work itself out, but it won't slow me down."

"Good." Or possibly bad depending on how the rest of this conversation went. Drawing a deep breath to steady her nerves, she looked him dead in the eye. "Then it's time we lay our cards on the table."

He raised his brows.

"I need the truth. About what you're doing here, why you've taken me, what the hell happened at Fort Hill."

"You saw what happened at Fort Hill." She could tell by his frown that he didn't like the turn in the conversation.

Too bad.

"I saw it," she said, "but I don't understand. Why would Reapers attack Hill? You know as well as I do that Reapers don't come this far north. They don't organize like that and they sure as hell don't raid the forts. If I had any doubts about this being random, your presence and that friend of yours would have laid them to rest."

His gaze dropped to her hand, which was shaking so badly a drop of coffee spilled over the rim and splashed to the ground. *Damn, damn it.* She needed to get a hold of herself. Lowering the cup to her lap, she wrapped both hands around it and took a deep breath. "You dragged me into this. I deserve an explanation."

He scowled. "I don't owe you anything."

"I could have killed you last night while you slept."

"I could kill you now. Does that mean you owe me something?" He paused and a strange expression flickered behind his eyes. "Why *didn't* you pull the trigger?"

"Because I wanted answers." It was the truth, but only part of it. She'd thought about it a lot last night, sitting in the cold dark watching him twitch and moan. She still wasn't completely comfortable with the decision she'd made, but there was no turning back now. "Why did they raid Fort Hill?"

He considered her for a long moment and then cussed under his breath. "Do you know what kind of research they were doing there?"

No one did exactly, but the rumors about the experiments were the stuff of nightmares. "From what I understand they dabbled in everything—medicines, preventatives, weapons."

He inclined his head. "There was a story passing through the fort that one of the doctors discovered a cure. Four weeks ago was the first I heard about it and last week Fort Hill was destroyed. Whether there's any truth to the rumor or not, the attack happened because it got out."

"That's a hell of a leap. How would Reapers get hold of a rumor like that?" Ice slid down her spine. "*You* told them."

He shook his head. "Not me. I was a prisoner at Fort Hill. I'm trying to find out who called for the attack and if there was any truth to the claim in the first place."

A cure. Everyone prayed for one, but Abby had never really expected the scientists to find it. The rumor was unlikely to be true, not that they'd ever know now.

Her mind stuck on the revelation that Jake had been a prisoner at Fort Hill. A strange mix of pity and outrage stirred in her chest, both misplaced. There was a constant demand for live specimens but Cap didn't like to transport Reapers, and their patrol rarely took them all the way to Fort Hill anyway. Truth was, she'd never thought much about what happened to the Reapers once they released them to the scientists. Now, she couldn't help but wonder.

"How long were you a captive at Fort Hill?"

"Twelve years."

Twelve years. That was longer than she'd been a Ranger. "You made it longer than most, then."

"I did."

"What'd they do to you while you were there?"

"Don't look at me like that, sweetheart. I could have escaped if I'd wanted to."

"Why didn't you?"

The wind stirred in the trees. He was sitting under an old oak that still had most of its leaves, all shades of orange and gold. The dappled light picked up the same colors in his hair. In the sun, his hair was actually a rich dark brown and not black after all. Shadows danced over his skin, but he was still as a rock. His gaze never wavered. "They were working on a cure and I wanted to know if they could do it. Twelve years might seem like a long time to you but it's nothing to me."

"And you *let* them experiment on you?"

"The experiments were...unpleasant but not unbearable." He shrugged. "Dr. Karlson and I had an understanding about how much I was willing to take. Four weeks before the attack, Josiah Welks started talking about a serum. I don't know if he was telling the truth. So far as I know, no one does. The test subject he was working on seemed to turn back to human, but he was...damaged."

"Damaged?"

"By another experiment. Edward had been there for a time and Josiah wasn't the first to use him. He wasn't remotely sane but, Reaper or human, that's understandable considering what he'd been through. Josiah said Edward's inability to heal was proof the serum worked. Most of the other scientists were doubtful of the claim, but..." He paused for a moment and Abby had the feeling that he was sifting through the facts to decide which morsels to throw her. When he spoke again, it was as carefully as if he were tiptoeing through a nest of rattlers.

"Josiah was a difficult man to work with. He was young and had only been at Fort Hill for seven months. It would have been an embarrassment to the others for him to have discovered a cure so quickly when they'd been working on it for decades. I could never be sure if their distrust of his results was personal or professional." His voice turned gruff. "Someone sure as hell believed him."

His tone of voice raised the fine hairs on her arms. "What do you mean by that?"

But he didn't answer. Instead, he leaned forward to empty the pot of boiled water onto the smoldering fire. Apparently, he'd decided the conversation was over. Just like that. He stood, his long body unfolding in a single fluid movement that was eerily graceful. She supposed that now that she knew what he was, there was no reason for him to bother trying to hide it. She didn't like the way he towered over her so she stood up too, flicking her wrist to empty the cup and passing it to him when he held out his hand.

"Jake," she insisted. "What do you mean 'someone believed him'?"

"That's enough. The scientists at Fort Hill announced they had a cure and the Reapers moved to destroy it. Successfully. You have your answers and we need to move on."

She didn't believe for a second that Fort Hill was destroyed because of a stupid rumor. There were a dozen like it a year.

"If you expect my cooperation, you can't keep me in the dark. I want all the details, not only what you know but what you suspect too. For starters, I need to know where you're taking me." She had dozens of questions pressing at her mind. Like...how the hell did the Reapers find out about the supposed cure? Was Jake some kind of spy and, if so, how had he passed information from the fort? But the question that fell from her lips was far more important to her personally. "Where do I come into all this?"

His eyes narrowed and, even though her stomach twisted, she stood her ground and waited him out. He studied her face, weighing her, before giving a short, tight nod. "You're here because you're a Ranger and I need your help."

"*My* help?"

"Your help, Abby. Come on. I'll explain it on the way. The river's only about a mile that way. You ride Harvey. I can keep up at a run until we find another horse to replace Marley."

She felt a sharp stab of grief and then a sharper jab of anger when she realized he was using Marley's death as a distraction. She'd started to follow him meekly toward the horse and when she realized it, she stopped in her tracks. Balling up his coat in her hands, she tried to decide what to do.

She should have shot him in the head and run while she'd had the chance. Her curiosity…her need to know what had happened at Fort Hill had kept her from pulling the trigger last night and that need still boiled in her blood now. Harvey was already saddled, the bags packed, aside from the tin and that one small pan Jake had used to boil water.

"Jake," she called out, ashamed of the plea in her voice but unable to control it.

His shoulders stiffened but he didn't turn around.

"I need you to tell me the truth."

He tightened the flaps on the sidebag and cursed softly before turning to face her. "I have been telling you the truth. You're the one who hasn't wanted to hear any of it."

"I'm listening now. I want all of it, not the bits and pieces you've been doling out."

"We're leaving."

She shook her head. "I'm not going anywhere until I have some answers."

He snorted as he shoved his hat onto his head. He ran a dispassionate gaze over her body, lingering for a moment on her wounded arm before lifting to her face. "What gave you the impression you have a choice?"

"This is me willing," she said in a low voice. "You have no idea what I'm capable of. I've been killing Reapers for more years than I can count."

"Mindless, ravening infants. You've never faced anyone like me, sweetheart. I let you keep your gun and your distance. Don't think that means you have a chance at running or at taking me out."

"You think I don't want to help after what I saw yesterday? That was a massacre and if you're working to keep that from happening again, then I'm in. Reaper or not, I will help you."

He stared at her hard before shaking his head. "I'm not looking for a partner."

"That's too bad, you got one. And your partner needs answers."

A hard smile curved his lips. "My partner needs to mount up. You don't want my hands on you."

"I'm not afraid of you."

His eyes flickered down, rested briefly on her breasts. "Yeah? You have a change of heart since last night?"

Warmth flushed her skin. Control –that grim, icy silent reserve he wrapped around himself to keep the world out. He would hate to lose that control. It might very well be her only advantage and his only weakness. The truth she'd been hiding from since she'd woken up that morning was that he was a Reaper and she, for whatever purpose, was his captive. He'd saved her, sure, but it was only because she was useful to him in some way. She couldn't afford to trust him.

She needed answers. Not only because of her own curiosity but so that she could pass that information on to the other Rangers if she was able to make it out of this alive.

So she could make sure that what had happened at Fort Hill didn't happen anywhere else.

"No change of heart," she said. "But I'm done listening to your bullshit threats. I could stand here naked as the day I was born and you wouldn't touch me unless I said so." Letting his coat fall to the ground, she drew a blade from its sheath on her thigh and held it up, turning it so that it caught the gentle morning light. "I could slide this right across my arm and you'd only offer to help me wrap the wound."

He gave her a dark look. "This isn't a game, Abby. Put down the fucking knife."

She did, tossing the blade atop his coat and her hat too. Then, she flipped her buckle loose to let her belt slide down her hips. When she released the top button on her shirt. Jake's eyes fixed on that sliver of bare skin and he went utterly still. Dragging in a deep breath, he forced his gaze up to her face. "Don't."

She caught the wooden edge of the button with her thumb and slipped it neatly through the hole. He flinched. "I don't want to hurt you. Is that what you want to hear?"

"I want to hear where you're taking me. If you don't intend me harm, I don't see what the problem is. And if you do intend me harm, I'd rather have it out now."

Two more buttons. The breeze stirred her collar, slipped inside the rough cotton and raised goose bumps all over her skin. Her nipples drew tight and, by the way Jake's scowl deepened, he noticed it too.

"And if you're wrong?" he asked softly. "If you think you can take me out like you did Marston, think again, sweetheart. You got lucky. It had nothing to do with the rider being in control. That won't weaken me, it'll only make me vicious."

"Maybe, maybe not. I saw his eyes." There'd been no reason in Marston's eyes at the end, only hunger. As scary as that had been, it's what had given her an edge, the chance to slide her knife into his neck.

"Marston underestimated you." Jake's color was high. His nostrils flared and his mouth set in a grim line. He was glaring murder at her and damn if she didn't think she deserved it. But she wasn't taking another blind step without a fight, even if she had to fight dirty.

Her chances of escape dwindled with every step she took and it was time to make a decision. She *would* fight Jake if he didn't talk, she'd kill him if she could and she wouldn't lose any sleep over it. But Jake… He was smart, disciplined and human enough to be aware of her weaknesses. And damn it, she *liked* him, which made her twenty kinds of stupid.

She didn't like feeling stupid.

He took a step toward her and stopped abruptly. "Abby, you don't know…you can't understand how hard this is, how easy it would be for me to hurt you."

"Then talk to me, Jake. As a partner. If I take another step with you, it won't be as your prisoner."

"Fuck." He ran a shaking hand through his hair. "Do you want to die?"

"No," she said quietly, watching the struggle in his eyes. "But I need to know. Sentient Reapers, Fort Hill destroyed and…you hauling me off to God knows where. Did you think I'd keep following along like a lamb to slaughter?"

"If I wanted you dead, you'd be dead."

The simple truth and they both knew it. But he didn't want her dead and this was her only advantage. Her body. His hunger for her and his desire to keep her alive. "That's exactly the point. You'd cut off your own arm before you hurt me. Throw yourself in front of a pack of Reapers to save my life. I don't pretend to understand that but I know it's the truth."

He took another step, closing the distance between them. Trembling, she held her ground, tipping her head back to look him in the eyes. His scent folded around her, coffee and leather, sweat and old smoke. It was strangely reassuring considering the wild look in his eyes. Gently, he pulled the edges of her shirt together.

"This was a damned stupid thing to do." His voice had deepened nearly to a growl and his hands were shaking. "Just because I don't want to hurt you doesn't mean I won't."

She touched the back of his hand. "You left me no other choice, Jake. I need answers."

He closed his eyes for a beat, taking a deep breath. When he opened them again to look at her, he seemed more in control of himself—not happy—but not quite as on edge.

"Three people survived the massacre at Fort Hill," he said quietly. "Two of them scientists. One is Dr. Josiah Welks, the man who found the cure."

Her lips parted and his eyes fixed briefly on her mouth before lifting to meet her gaze. Heat. Desire. Barely checked violence. She fought the urge to run and he looked down at his hands, still tangled in the cloth of her shirt. Slowly, he opened his hands and let them drop to his sides. She released her pent-up breath.

"I was only able to save three. No one. *No one* can know they're still alive. Right now they're the most dangerous and the most endangered men on the plains. I got them out but we had to leave everything behind."

"You're saying it wasn't just a rumor." She felt a little dazed by the possibility. "You think they really found the cure."

"I believe so."

"And you saved the scientists who know how to make it."

"Josiah was secretive. He kept his research and samples locked up in his lab. Unfortunately, we weren't inside his lab when the Reapers attacked and we weren't able to get there before the gates were blown. I got the scientists out, stashed them someplace safe and went back for the research."

"You didn't get it," she said slowly. "That's why you raced into the fort when you saw the fire."

"It was already gone. But Josiah promised me he'd be able to recreate the serum if I brought him back a Ranger."

"Why?"

His expression was flat and utterly unreadable. "They need your blood."

She lifted her hand to her neck and he followed the motion with his eyes. "If I thought that would work, I'd drain you myself. Reapers have been drinking Ranger blood for decades. Your blood isn't the cure, but there's something in it that's lethal to the organism. Between the two of us, he says he can re-create his cure."

She shook her head. No wonder he'd tried to keep the truth from her as long as possible. He planned to turn her over to those scientists to use in their experiments. It was a god-awful plan.

"Okay." She could deal with this. "Okay, so we bring the scientists back to Fort Dougan. We'll be able to protect them there." And she'd be protected too.

"Best that everyone continues to believe they're dead."

"Why? We need to keep them safe from the Reapers and we need to get that cure. There are plenty of Rangers at Dougan. You and your bloodthirsty scientists can have all the *samples* they want."

When she started to walk away, he grabbed her arm. "You saw what they did to Fort Hill. You really want to bring that to your friends?"

"If you're worried, I can make sure they don't hurt you."

A sharp bark of laughter. "You'll be my personal bodyguard? Protect me with that sweet little body when the big bad Rangers come after me? I'm not worried about your people, I'm worried about mine."

"That's the point," she snapped. "If we go to the fort, we'll be able to protect the scientists from your people. The Reapers don't know the scientists survived, there's no extra danger to them or us."

"The Reapers found out about Fort Hill," he said. "I don't trust your people to keep their mouths shut and I don't want to see the same thing happen again. No one can know about the scientists until we find out who wants them dead."

Abby rolled her eyes. "The Reapers want them dead."

"But how did they know to target Fort Hill? How did sentient Reapers living hundreds of miles south of here hear that a cure had been found?"

"Maybe one of your kind escaped. You were a prisoner there, you can't know everything that happened."

"Trust me that I know better than you."

Like hell. "You can't possibly mean to suggest that someone from the fort told Reapers about the cure."

"Can't I? Marston told me that much before you got yourself dragged back into camp."

She was shaking her head, so stunned she couldn't even form the words to argue.

Jake regarded her with a resigned expression as he continued, "Think about it. You inject a new Reaper fast enough and they don't change, they don't infect anyone else and our numbers start to diminish. Eventually, people start to reclaim the plains. The people who've built their fortunes on airships and leasing land rights in the mountains lose in that equation."

"No one would do that," she whispered.

The hint of amusement in his eyes made her feel five years old. "Oh, darlin', you're just a babe, aren't you?"

"Fuck you, Jake. No one else even knows about sentient Reapers, let alone how to contact you."

Jake's eyes were hard but his expression gave nothing away. "The scientists at Fort Hill knew. They knew all about me—inside and out. I can't say for certain why they didn't pass that information on to the Rangers but I can guess."

She almost accused him of lying again but just like Fort Hill, she couldn't see why he'd do such a thing. He had no proof. He was only playing on all her worst fears and prejudices and there was no point arguing. She started to turn away, but he wasn't done. He slid his hand into her hair and turned her head back to face him.

"They made contact twenty years ago. A delegation of Scrapers came south wanting to negotiate for territory, but they had nothing to offer. Why would we give a fuck for their silver when we can take what we want? We sent back a ship full of bones for an answer."

"You were there?"

"I saw it. And then came north to find out if what they said about looking for a cure was true."

Of course it was true. Of course they were looking for a cure. They had been for centuries. She moved to shake her head but her hair pulled and his fingers tightened, holding her in place, forcing her to hear him out.

"Some of the Scrapers want a cure," he said. "They want to own it and control who gets it. Some of them know a cure would ruin their fortunes. You think of them as moving with one purpose but they're not like that. They're out for their own good, fighting for the top of the pile and stabbing each other in the back to get there."

"Just like Reapers. No wonder you understand them so well."

She'd meant it as an insult, but the fool man smiled. "You're a small cog in a big machine, Abby. You didn't know you were only slaughtering our younglings because you're only looking down the barrel of a gun at us, seeing the small part that's right in front of your face."

There was plenty of fighting between the Scraper cities, each with its own separate laws, interests and elected officials. But he wasn't talking about politics.

"No human would align themselves with a Reaper."

"You did."

She jerked free of his hold, losing a few strands of hair in the process. "And Fort Hill was a Ranger facility, not a Scraper one."

"It's common for scientists to have benefactors in the cities. Only good business sense for them to stay informed on what was happening there. There was no such thing as a secret at Fort Hill. Someone who knew about the sentient and who didn't want a cure getting out sent word south…and quickly. That's Eyrion, Ballonet or Stormking. Oro wouldn't care. Blowdown and Koln don't have the means. Tell me I'm wrong."

She glared at him, wanting to argue but unable to come up with the words. Eyrion was the bright shining capital where all the political games played out. Ballonet was a merchant city where most of the airship families lived. Stormking…well, she wouldn't put anything past the residents of Stormking. What he said made an awful kind of sense. At least, it would make sense if you were only interested in power and didn't care what you had to do to keep it. She felt sick.

"There has to be another explanation."

She could tell by the look on his face that he disagreed. "When you come up with something better, you let me know." His expression darkened. "And don't ever push me like that again. I'm fighting it now but until we have that cure, don't make the mistake of thinking you're safe with me."

"You'll accept the cure?"

"Gladly."

And that hungry glint in his eyes would be gone. He would be gone, out of her life forever. Good. It was a good thing. "I want to talk to these scientists of yours before I agree to anything."

"Of course."

"I'm keeping my guns. Anything suspicious and I shoot first ask questions later. I'm nobody's canary."

A muscle along his jaw tensed. "I won't let them hurt you."

"You're going to let them slice me up to see how I tick," she snapped. "I don't heal like you do."

He touched her restored hand, bigger than her other. "Don't you?"

She flinched, both because she didn't like to be reminded of her deformity and because it made her skin crawl to have him touch her.

"I've seen what can happen to the people who are taken for testing," she said. "To those scientists, I'm dispensable. You're dispensable. They're after knowledge and glory, and pity to anyone who gets in their way. I reckon the ones willing to work for you are the worst of the lot."

"The best, Abby. They're the best and the brightest."

She grunted. To her mind, that only made them more dangerous.

Chapter Eleven

JAKE TOOK HIS time catching dinner, standing in the icy water and waiting for the fish to swim right into his hands before tossing them onto the bank. It was soothing, feeling the little swirls of water pass between his fingers, the tickle on his palm that meant food. Water soaked his pants all the way to his hips, but he didn't care. As a Reaper, cold was one of his few weaknesses. The parasite didn't like it, which is why Reapers avoided the mountains and retreated south as soon as frost touched the plains. If he could ride out the urge to retreat, then his lowered body temperature would repress the parasite for a time.

Abby had been silent for most of the day, lost in her own thoughts, which suited him fine. He didn't like having to explain himself and she was too damned ornery to come meekly. She'd almost gotten herself killed earlier forcing his hand and he hadn't forgiven her yet for winning that round. His lips twitched into a smile. In twelve years, the scientists hadn't figured out a way to coerce him into anything. It took Abby less than a week and already she was leading him around by the balls. She scared the hell out of him. Not that she might somehow manage to kill him. He'd long ago lost his fear of death, but he could *hurt* her. So easily. One slip is all it would take.

His own death he could face, but he wouldn't easily recover from knowing that he'd caused Abby's. Not because he liked her, but because she was his responsibility. For his mother's people, honor was important. She'd instilled that value in her bastard white-blooded child from his earliest days and even now, over a century later, he couldn't quite shake the burden of it.

By the time he strung up his catch and decided to head back, it was nearly dark. He'd prepare the food and they'd eat, sleep and then wake before dawn to ride for one last long day. They'd have to camp for one more night before reaching the abandoned ranch where he'd stashed the scientists. He'd locked them in a root cellar with enough food and water to keep them alive for a month if they rationed it, but he'd stopped expecting people to show good sense a long time ago. What he expected was to find them gnawing on each other's bones when he returned. So long as Josiah survived, that would be all right.

Of all of them, a snake like Josiah would be the one to make it out alive.

They hadn't made it as far as Jake would have liked today, but he didn't want to push Abby too far or too hard. It had been so long since he'd traveled with a human, he couldn't begin to guess at her limits and couldn't afford to lose her now, especially without the papers and samples he'd hoped to recover from the fort. It would take him weeks to find another Ranger and Abby was perfect—female so she didn't rouse his territorial instincts quite as violently, smart enough to consider that he might be telling her the truth and sensible enough not to kill herself against the bars of captivity. Back at the fort, he'd seen that happen more times than he could count and would hate to witness it with her.

He didn't make the mistake of thinking she'd given up on escape. At least for the time being, she was a willing companion. Abby was curious and softhearted. She wanted to see for herself if he was telling her the truth about the scientists. She likely thought it her duty to attempt a rescue. By the time she realized they didn't want or need to be saved, it would be too late for her.

Ever since their confrontation, she'd been more wary of him than ever. Watching him, as though he might snap at any minute and come after her. It wouldn't happen. His control over the rider was better than that. *Fuck.* She'd practically had sex with him in that alley and he'd let her walk away. Difficult, but he'd managed it. Two nights on the road with her wasn't going to do him in. On the other hand, if she spent those two days scared shitless that was fine too. He didn't need her trust or her friendship. He needed her blood. And if she gave it willingly that would be one less sin on his head.

In New Providence, she'd trusted him in a way. She'd smiled at him and it had made her pretty, even with a streak of dirt on her chin and her sweaty hair stuffed beneath the wide-brimmed hat she wore. She'd let him press his hungry cock against her heat, had dug her nails into his shoulders and sucked on his tongue as if it was a delicacy. As if she was as starved as he was. That was before she knew what he was.

Bowing his head, Jake stopped walking to let the hot wave of lust roll through him. He waited until it settled and then focused on slowing his pulse. He shoved the rider into the darkest corner of his mind, slammed the door closed on that part of himself and fixed his mind on the here and now. The ache in his back. The cold weight of the denim clinging to his legs. The soft caress of the breeze on his face, carrying with it the scent of apples from the orchard to the north. The cicadas were noisy tonight, all but drowning out the slithery sound of wind blowing through the dry grass. He let the solemn quiet of twilight soothe his raw nerves and then, once the Reaper stilled, he started walking again. Two days and they'd be back at the ranch. The scientists would know what safeguards were necessary to protect Abby from him. And before long, hopefully, they'd have their cure.

As he stepped into their camp, Harvey lifted his head and offered a soft huff of welcome. Abby's back was to him but at the noise she stood and looked around uneasily. Her wide eyes and uncertain stance reminded him that it was too dark for her to see clearly.

"It's only me," he called out, not liking to see her anxious. Not liking to be the cause of it.

That earned him a nod, but she didn't truly relax her guard. Keeping his distance, he set to skewering the fish he'd cleaned in the river.

As he walked to the fire, he could feel her watching. Always, she kept at least one eye on him, except when she was sleeping. When she was sleeping, her face and body relaxed and he could stare at her for as long as he liked, imagining another life without scaring the hell out of her.

The blaze had the fish sizzling in no time and the heat drew steam from his pants. If he'd been alone, he'd have stripped off the wet fabric and set it aside to dry. If he'd been alone, he wouldn't have bothered to cook the fish. Abby drew her knees up to her chin and wrapped her arms around her legs. Cold. He shrugged out of his coat.

"You don't have to hand me your coat every time I shiver." But she took it when he held it out to her.

"You don't have to keep looking at me like I'm going to eat you. I thought you trusted me that far." He didn't know why it was important to him to hear her say it.

"I don't think you're going to eat me." Her eyes glinted as she looked up from the fire. "Because you need me. I've been wondering something..."

He raised his brows, waiting for her to continue. She cocked her head to one side. "Why didn't you go back for the papers first? Unless you have no sense of direction at all, you would have had to pass the fort to get to me."

"I didn't want the Reapers to know I made it out. Especially not Marston. Whoever was behind the massacre, he was in charge of it." A shadow crossed behind her eyes and he said, "It's just as well that you killed him. He was suspicious. He probably would have followed us. I thought the pack would be long gone by the time I returned to Fort Hill and I sure as hell didn't think they'd burn it. Josiah seemed to think his hiding place was secure. I had no reason to believe otherwise."

Abby shivered again and he was uncomfortably aware of the concern for her that welled up inside of him. She had his coat, the fire. The only thing left that he could do to warm her was share the heat of his body. He couldn't offer that—she wouldn't take him up on it if he did. He turned the skewer and oil slipped into the fire to sizzle atop the wood.

"I dream about him." Her voice was a bare whisper. She rested her chin on her knees as she stared into the fire.

"Marston?"

She looked at him, gave a wry smile and shrugged. "That he's still alive. That he's out there waiting somewhere. With half his head blown away but that smile still on his face. You know the one?"

He knew the one. "He's dead. Don't worry about him. I told you, I'll keep you safe. I'm getting good at saving you. It's a new hobby of mine."

She smiled, a real smile, not one of those bitter twists, and it warmed him clear through. The rider didn't stir, so it wasn't lust. He didn't know what the hell it was.

"I just stumbled right into your path in New Providence, didn't I?"

He lifted one of the skewers and passed it to her. "Providence of the divine kind." Her eyes narrowed as if she thought he might be mocking her, though he was doing nothing of the sort. "A gift from whatever dark god watches over the plains."

Another smile, this one accompanied by a short laugh. "There's not a god out there who'd have anything to do with Reapers."

"Which is why we make our own." He set his hat aside and ran a hand through his hair, scratching at his scalp. "When I saw you in that saloon and heard you tell the barkeep you were headed to Hill, it seemed like a gift. Easy as pie to follow you to the fort. Didn't count on Nelson or that trouble with your family. I didn't expect it would be so hard to keep you alive. You attract trouble like blood draws flies."

She touched the fish and jerked her fingers away, licking each one and then blowing on them to ease the sting. She glanced up to catch him staring and he did his best to look innocent, as if he hadn't been imagining that pretty mouth wrapped around his cock. *That* thought riled the parasite and he shoved the damn thing back in its cage.

"What would you have done otherwise?"

"I'd have taken someone from the patrol."

She shook her head. "You never would have managed that and even if you had they'd have tracked and killed you before dawn."

Not a chance. "This way turned out for the best," he agreed. "By the time your patrol reaches Fort Hill, they'll think you died in the raid too. And it was just plain good luck that they sent you."

She bristled, lowering the food from her mouth and narrowing her eyes at him. "What do you mean?"

He meant that whatever happened, he was happy to have known her. Better for it. Cleaner. "The parasite views a human man as either food or a rival, but you're female."

"So you don't think I'm a threat."

"You trigger other urges."

Her eyes widened and a delicate flush crept up her neck to warm her cheeks. "And these other urges," she said. "You're able to control those too?"

An image flashed in his head—creamy skin and a trickle of sweat disappearing into cleavage as she unbuttoned her shirt. "So far so good. Provided you don't pull another stunt like you tried earlier."

"You're still mad at me for calling your bluff? I needed answers. If you'd attacked me, I'd have had all the answer I needed."

"You'd have been dead," he said in a calm voice completely at odds with the fear and regret churning in his gut. For all that she feared him now, she didn't truly know what he was capable of. He wished like hell that *he* didn't know the horrors he was capable of inflicting on her sweet, smooth flesh.

As if she could read the drift of his thoughts, Abby pulled the coat tighter around her shoulders. There was very definite fear there, although she hid it fairly well. A human man might not have noticed she was anything other than the tough as nails bitch she pretended to be. He could sense it in a hundred tiny details—the scent of her sweat, the speed of her heart, the dilation of her eyes, the slight forward hunch of her shoulders. He could sense her vulnerability, her curiosity and—*damn her*—the faint trace of arousal that seemed to cling to her skin regardless of what passed between them.

"Don't worry, Abby." Firelight flickered over her

face, shadowing the hollows of her cheeks and making her eyes uncommonly bright. "I'm not going to eat you tonight. I'm not going to fuck you either."

He'd sooner kill himself than see her hurt. The muscles around her eyes tightened. Wariness on both their parts might just see them through this alive. He wiped his fingers on a rag and tossed it to her.

"You have grease, there." He pointed to the corner of his mouth and she tested the spot with her tongue. His body stiffened. She noticed, because she suddenly clamped her mouth shut to dab at her cheek with the rag instead.

They fell silent for a time as she finished eating and he stared at the fire. Two more days to the abandoned ranch where he'd locked the scientists. It would be easier to keep his distance from her there. Josiah would want to collar him as a precaution and damned if he didn't think that was a good idea.

Abby drank from the water skin. He watched the way her throat moved. That pale stretch of skin, so undeniably feminine. He would taste her there first if given the chance, press his mouth to the juncture of neck and shoulder and draw her scent into his body.

Setting aside the water, she drew her knees up and hugged them tight to her body. "I'm surprised that you eat fish."

He lowered the skewer from his mouth. "I eat what you eat."

More of it—and he liked to catch his dinner with his own hands—but he didn't eat human flesh, not once since he'd regained control of his body.

She looked as if she was going to ask him another question but changed her mind and went back to cleaning off her hands. After a minute, she looked up.

"Jake? How'd it happen to you? How were you bitten?"

A shudder passed through his body, but he covered his reaction by tossing the skewer into the fire and then wiping the grease from his hands. "I wasn't bitten," he told her. "I was infected by befouled water."

Judging by her expression, she hadn't realized it was possible to become infected that way. He supposed that made sense. Who beside him and a handful of others remembered those days? Marston. Tomas. Julian and Jamie. "That's within our territory. East of Natchitoches. You'd have to travel more than a hundred miles south to become infected that way and you'd never make it past the younglings."

"The water…" Her eyes went unfocused as she stared at the fire. After a moment, she looked up and gave him a lopsided smile. "Doc told me a story once about where Reapers came from. He called it the fountain of youth. Said it was a poison that made you immortal at the cost of your soul. I never believed that one."

"What did you think?"

"I don't know that I ever believed one theory over another. The fountain of youth. Wrath of God. I've always liked Cam's way of thinking with his 'shit happens' philosophy. But I hope to get the chance to tell Doc he was right. He'll like that."

"You'll tell him," he said and then wished back the

words. He couldn't make promises like that, but Abby didn't call him on it.

Instead, she tipped her head to the side and said, "Natchitoches. I don't recognize that name."

"There are very few people left who would."

"So that's what happened to you? You woke up one morning, drank from the wrong creek and that was it?"

"We heard rumors of the sickness less than a week before it hit. Our water was contaminated, but we didn't figure that out until…after." His mother had died instantly. He'd managed to keep Saku alive for several weeks, carrying her on his back as they ran north. The worst part was that he didn't know what had happened to his little sister. Well, he *knew*, but he couldn't remember… He wrenched his thoughts back to the here and now. To the woman regarding him curiously from across the fire. "It was a bad summer. The days were clear but it stormed nearly every night. The hurricanes, two of them back-to-back, caused most of the flooding and poisoned the wells. It started near the coast. Most of the Reapers who are sentient now were among the first to be infected, either from the water or because they were bitten early."

He stretched out on his back. She relaxed more when he wasn't looking directly at her. Not that it made a difference. He could kill her before she could blink. Reapers hunted more by scent than sight. Though they craved the warmth from the sun, they often would hunt at night because their prey was at a disadvantage. None of this he thought would reassure her, so he kept it to himself.

"Were all the wells poisoned?" By the sound of it, she was stretching herself out too close to the fire again. There was a new burn mark on the shoulder of his coat from a stray spark that had drifted there as she slept.

"No." He paused. "Maybe. I don't know."

It was a clear night and there was a blaze of stars. If not for the earth holding him so tight, it felt like he could drop into that velvet sky. "You have to understand, no one knew what was happening at first. The water held eggs and it took months for the parasite to grow large enough for the first symptoms to appear."

"There had to be a point when you knew something was wrong. When there were few enough infected that you could have killed them off and ended this."

It had been an awful time. They hadn't understood anything—what was happening, how the parasite was passed, how to kill the Reapers so they didn't rise from the dead. They'd thought it was a plague. They'd thought it was the end times. The dead rising. Blood everywhere. At that time, there'd been no sentient to police the younglings, to force them to the very edge of their territory, to curb their excesses. "We quarantined the sick. We thought that we could find out what was wrong and heal them, but they managed to escape."

Abby rolled onto her side. She liked to sleep that way, with one hand tucked beneath her cheek. She looked soft, vulnerable and young when she slept. She didn't sound any of those things now. "What about you, Jake?"

"I was fourteen and my tribe was miles from the coast when we first heard the stories. We moved north...just not fast enough."

"I'm sorry." It sounded sincere. She must have thought so too, because when next she spoke, she sounded angry again. "Why are you telling me this anyway?"

Hell if he knew. It had been decades since he'd even thought about that time. "You asked."

Silence stretched between them. The breeze had died off. He could hear the scamper of tiny feet in the brush and far off the call of a coyote. When she fell asleep, he would need to hunt again, make sure that they weren't being followed and that the way ahead was still clear.

"What's it like? Being a Reaper."

"You don't want to hear this." And he didn't want to tell her.

"If I don't hold what you are in my head, it slips away. I don't want to forget it. Remind me for both of our sakes, Jake. Does it hurt?"

The night seemed to hold its breath waiting for his answer. He didn't need to give her one. He could lie and she'd never know the difference. His voice sounded loud when he spoke even though it was barely a whisper. "It hurts...when it first attacks your body and then whenever you fight it."

Like now. Being around Abby was like having a burning poker thrust into the base of his skull every time she smiled at him. Maybe she was right. Maybe he needed to be reminded about what he was too. "Those first years…I have very few memories of the things the rider did when it was in control."

A mercy, that. Those memories were blurred, seen through a thick red fog, as if he was only witnessing the pain rather than causing it. Reveling in it. The nightmares were another story but, mercifully, he required very little sleep.

"So you could wake up with my blood in your mouth and not even know what happened?"

"That won't happen."

He gave her a moment to let that sink in, waited for her to argue it. Hoped that she would fall asleep soon. Unlike him, she needed to rest. Her legs moved, one thigh sliding over the other and he closed his eyes.

"Why are you doing this? You don't get sick, you won't die. Whatever the rider has done to you, you're in control now. Why are you looking for a cure?"

He almost didn't answer. But he'd ripped her away from her family, planned to sacrifice her for the cure, and she deserved an explanation. "Because I was one of the people who started this," he told her. "I was there in the beginning and it's my responsibility to see it ended."

He could feel the weight of her gaze. "That's what this is about? Guilt?"

Not all of it, no. He tried again to make her understand. "This is no way to live."

"Do you want to die?"

The same thing Marston had asked. What did people see in him that made them wonder? There was no judgment in her voice, and he could have left it at that.

He didn't need her sympathy, didn't want it. He didn't care what she thought of him.

"I want a life."

He wanted back what had been stolen from him, but first he had to make things right.

Chapter Twelve

ABBY HAD NEVER taken this road and for a time she allowed the novelty of the terrain to distract her from her troubles. For the past dozen years she'd traveled the same circuit of towns over and over again. She knew the landmarks—every tree, stone and curve of the land. The territory they were passing through now was similar to what she was accustomed to, with rolling hills and hip-high grass, scrub oak and pine, but it was also different enough to be interesting.

For one thing, the mountains were closer. When they stopped to rest the horses and she stood on the rocky ground, the vibration beneath her feet told her exactly how close they were to the cities. It was amazing that even down here she could feel the shudder and thump of the great machines carving out homes from the solid rock. She'd fallen asleep to that sound when she'd gone up to the capital but had never imagined that you'd be able to hear it from such a distance. Maybe she *wasn't* actually hearing it. Maybe it was just a memory stirred by standing in the shadow of the mountain range, where the elite of society lived far above the refuse on the plains.

She'd always been one of the disposable people. Breeders and feeders—the farmers who fed the wealthy and the breeders who created the next generation of Rangers. All of them working their fingers to the bone to move up in the world. As much as she disliked and distrusted the people who lived in the cities, she never would have imagined that any of them had a hand in the massacre at Fort Hill.

Even with Jake's insistence and her own questions regarding how the Reapers had found out about the cure, she couldn't credit it. Scrapers were frivolous, soft…selfish. She frowned at the mountains. Sunlight glinted off the metallic beams supporting the weight of the multitiered city miles above them. Koln, lowest of the seven cities on the western range and the poorest. The slaughterhouses were there and not much else. From here, you couldn't see any details—just the reflection of metal and glass, movement of the suspended cars that transported people between levels. *Why* would anyone up there have done such a thing?

"How did you lose your hand?"

Jake's question startled her from the bitter turn of her thoughts and she jerked her gaze down to where he walked beside the horse. Instinctively, her fingers began to curl but she straightened them. She wouldn't hide, no matter what he thought about it.

"Do you even need to ask?" He knew… *And then you sliced a new one from a boy who couldn't control himself. Who was terrified and locked inside his own head, half-crazed trying to get out.*

He turned his head, squinting as he looked up. "You shouldn't be out here fighting Reapers."

"Spoken like a man."

"You're in more danger than you know. Most Reapers would react to you exactly like Marston did. They'd catch you. They'd fuck you until you died—and with you being a Ranger, that would take a good long while."

"I die like any other human." *Unlike you.*

"With all the parasite-infested fluid they'd be pumping into your body? Even if you can't be infected, it would still work to heal you. The best you could hope for is a quick death at the hands of a youngling too out of control to pace himself. Either way, it would be an ugly way to go."

Her hands were clammy on the reins, but she wouldn't let him know how badly that horrific image affected her. "I'm a Ranger. I can ride patrol killing Reapers or I can let them pen me up in a fort as a broodmare, which one would you choose?"

He didn't answer right away, just studied her face for a moment before turning back to the road. It wasn't really even a road, just an old buffalo trail winding through scrub brush. He reached out a hand and plucked a long piece of grass. Snapping it, he stuck the wet end in his mouth and chewed thoughtfully for another mile before he spoke.

"I saw you with your sister's kids. You care about them. Not that it necessarily means you want your own, but...you didn't have the attitude of a woman who dislikes children. It seems to me that you'd make a fine mother. Is it the kids you don't want or the husband?"

If there'd been even a trace of judgment in the question she wouldn't have answered it, but she heard only a sort of idle curiosity. He was just passing the time and it was a distraction from what lay at the end of this road.

"My kids would be immune."

"That's a good thing, isn't it?"

"I wouldn't have to worry about them being turned, but they'd all grow up to be Rangers. Riding patrol until a Reaper got hold of them or else locked up in the fort. I won't have them live like that."

"Ah."

"Ah?" she mocked.

"I can't blame you for that. And I was right…you would make a good mother."

The flush of warmth that blossomed in her chest irritated her more than the smug look on his face. "Well, since it's not going to happen I'll just have to take your word on that, won't I?"

He glanced at her, black eyes lit with humor. "You just closed the door on all of it then? No sweethearts, no kids, no pretty dresses. Nothing to call to anyone's mind that there's a woman inside this costume." He rapped on her boot with his knuckle.

When she didn't answer, he laughed softly. "That's likely why you were so hungry when I had you up against the wall in New Providence. I've seen younglings with more willpower than you had that night. You made it damn hard to walk away. I thought you were going to—"

"I lost my hand on my third patrol," she said brusquely.

His lips twitched again and she resisted the urge to kick him in the head.

"We were out by Jasper. You know it?"

He shook his head.

"About twenty miles southeast of New Providence. It's a tiny little place at the edge of our territory. Only five or six houses are still standing there now. Cap keeps trying to get them to settle elsewhere, but they're old and dug in."

"Well, it's their home," he said and she was surprised to hear a trace of longing in his voice. She peered down at him but he'd turned his head and his hat blocked her view of his face.

"Ten years ago it was bigger. They had a saloon and a whorehouse. A small general store. They called themselves the last post on the border, so they drew in a lot of idiot young Scrapers who wanted to brag to their friends that they'd crossed into Reaper territory."

Jake laughed and she shook her head. "I'm serious. They do that, you know. Make expeditions here on their airships and stuff their pockets full of rocks and dirt to bring back as proof. They sold bones and rings in the general store they said came from abandoned Reaper dens."

"Sounds like good business. What happened?"

Her smile faded and she wiped the sweat from her forehead. "There was an attack. A big pack hit it with no warning. It took us too long to get there and half the town was dead or infected by then."

She paused, the story bringing her back to that sweltering summer day. The creaking door of the old barn. The heat. The smell… She'd been looking for survivors and the young man had reminded her of Cam—blond and handsome. About her age. At first, she'd thought he was hiding from Reapers in the cool dark, half-buried in hay. Newly bitten, he hadn't looked as ragged as the Reapers she'd seen up to that point. He'd come at her so fast when she lowered her gun.

"I lost my hand because I was stupid."

"You're not stupid, Abby," Jake said, the rasp in his voice more pronounced than normal. He tossed the piece of grass aside. "You can't be on your guard all the time. People make mistakes. At least this one could be fixed."

"*You* have to be on guard all the time."

"Only when I'm surrounded by humans. And it's not the same. I'm a Reaper, not really a person at all, isn't that right?"

He *was* a Reaper and here she was sharing a story she'd never told anyone before. Rangers didn't comment on scars. They simply weren't talked about, ever. The townspeople she met on patrol might be morbidly fascinated by her injury but they wouldn't really understand. Jake understood though. His scars went even deeper than hers.

His face lifted toward the mountains. A crow circled overhead, higher than the airships ever reached, larger than a natural animal would ever grow. She caught the glimmer of reflected light and said, "Drone."

At his curious look, she said, "A new Scraper invention. I saw a demonstration for it last month. They're made up of brass and crystal, meant to replace the need for carrier pigeons. The crystals are supposed to record images to bring back to their masters. They're fairly reliable as messengers, but they haven't perfected the rest."

"Ah," he said, a distracted look on his face as he examined the bird, now winging south. "Is it recording us, do you think?"

"Possibly," she said, though there wasn't much of a chance. Who would be looking for them specifically? It was unlikely that her patrol had reached Hill yet and even if Jake's Scraper traitor was searching for Hill survivors, there was nothing to identify them. And… the birds were like the airships—remote and watchful, but not useful or dangerous to the people on the ground. Pretty little playthings for the rich and bored. "They like to keep an eye on things down here. You get used to it."

He was still tracking the movement of the bird. "Maybe you've gotten too used to it."

She smiled at his dire tone. "Has anyone ever told you that you're a paranoid son of a bitch?"

He flicked an annoyed glance her way. "You don't think Scrapers had anything to do with Hill? Why? Because they're human so they can't kill their own kind?"

"Because they're Scrapers. Fat. Lazy. They don't care about anything but their own pleasure. They watch because it's entertaining not because they give a shit about what happens down here."

"You're wrong about that." The drone shifted direction, gliding off to the west and Jake's attention turned with it. She followed his gaze to the glimmer of reflected light a few miles beneath the snowcap.

"Are your cities like the ones up there?"

He looked back at her. “What do you mean?”

“You and the other sentient Reapers are tucked away down south while the younglings *you* created rampage up here. The Scrapers are tucked away up in their fortresses while we protect their food supply. You have more in common with them than you do me, I think.”

His gaze drifted back toward the mountains. “You’ve been up there?”

“Once.” Their patrol had saved the idiot son of an airship baron who’d gone on an adventure to the border and had almost gotten himself killed. She and Cam had gone up to represent the fort at the gala honoring his return. God, it seemed like an eternity ago.

“Did you like it?”

She thought about lying for the sake of simplicity, but her feelings about the Scraper cities were too complicated for a yes or no answer. “It’s different. Beautiful. Clean. At their parties, they serve so many different kinds of food, half the time you don’t even know what you’re eating. But… I don’t know. Somehow, it seemed wrong to enjoy it too much.”

“Fort Hill was luxurious compared to New Providence. I imagine the mountain cities are even more decadent.”

“They are,” she said. “They designed them to rival the old cities of Europe.”

“Our cities…there are only a few and they’re not like yours. For one thing, they’re old, older than the ones in Europe and large parts of them are empty. Even the sentient have trouble interacting peaceably with one another. We only gather when summoned.”

"Summoned? By who?"

His mouth twisted. "Tomas claims to be king but it means nothing other than that no one's managed to kill him yet to shut him up. He *is* old and very powerful."

Something about his tone of voice made her suspect there was more to the story than he was letting on—a worried note that alarmed her—but he seemed to shake it off. "I live south of the city. It's remote. I can hunt—" She flinched and he noticed. "I'm talking about animals, Abby. Few of the sentient still eat humans. For one thing, there aren't very many humans who have survived south of here except in small pockets living in the mountains. We own the southern lowlands completely."

"It sounds lonely."

His eyes glinted. "You think I'm pining for company? I have books. Occasionally I visit the city to stay informed about what's happening in the larger world."

He opened his mouth as if he meant to say more but then paused. Lifting his face, his nostrils flared like a hound scenting the wind. His black eyes narrowed to slits and he stopped moving quite like a man. His gait lengthened and smoothed. There was something about the way his muscles and joints worked together that marked him as a Reaper and, in his distraction, he'd stopped trying to hide it.

"What is it?"

"We're being followed," he said and then stopped abruptly. She reined in Harvey and swiveled in the saddle.

"You keep going," he told her. "In a few miles, you'll

reach a creek. There's a copse of trees where I planned for us to camp tonight. Don't light a fire until I return."

"Jake—"

He'd already taken off at a jog but paused to look back at her.

Slipping the rifle from its holster on the saddle, she held it out. "Take this."

He went very still, his dark eyes boring into hers, his expression completely blank. Slowly, he shook his head. "You keep that, Abby. You might need it."

She watched him go, torn because she'd never have let another Ranger go alone. But he wasn't another Ranger. He was a Reaper and well able to take care of himself. It didn't occur to her until she'd nearly reached the trees that the group following behind might not be Reapers at all. They might be Rangers following their trail. By now, there was a good chance that *someone* had reached a fort to raise the alarm. If they were Rangers, they might manage to kill Jake before she learned where he was holding the scientists. Or Jake…Jake might kill them first.

Fuck.

Harvey protested when she turned him and pushed him into a run. The poor horse could probably smell the water up ahead and was anticipating a rest, but there was no time for one. Jake had a twenty-minute head start and at a sprint he could run faster than she could travel on horseback. Abby bent over Harvey's neck and tried not to think too much about whether she was rushing in to save the lives of her fellow Rangers or the life of a fucking Reaper.

THEY WERE OUTLAWS, a ragged band of four men with horses that appeared healthier than their owners. That part was good, Jake thought. He needed a horse. He lay in the grass, palms flat to the earth, ready to propel his body toward the men when they passed. A hundred yards and closing. They were traveling at a fast clip, following the trampled trail of prairie grass he and Abby had left behind. The bits and pieces he heard of their conversation made his blood pound in his ears.

"I swear it was a woman, I don't care what she was wearing. The man was on foot and unarmed. She was wearing pistols and had a rifle strapped to the saddle."

"Was he her prisoner?"

"I don't think so."

The one in the lead spat. "And you lost sight of them."

"I had to take a piss. Where the hell are they going to go out here? They'll stop when they hit the creek and we'll catch them there while they're distracted."

Another voice, low and with a slow drawl said, "If nothing else, we get a pair of pistols, a rifle and a horse." A laugh that grated on Jake's ears. "Maybe a little fun if Johnny here is right and the skinny one really is a woman."

"She is."

"Well, I think—"

Close enough. Jake leaped from the grass, wrapped his arm around the nearest man's waist. He'd heard enough to know they were a threat and he wasn't letting these men get anywhere near Abby.

Plucking the man right out of the saddle, Jake didn't

even have to kill him. He just had to stand there, using the man as a shield as his friends opened fire. When they were forced to reload, he dropped the bullet riddled body to the dirt and grabbed the second man by the wrist. Eyes wild with fear, the thief tried to pull free, tried to turn his horse, but there was no room to maneuver.

The animals were startled, confused by Jake's sudden appearance, the gunfire and their masters' indecision. Jake ripped the man from his saddle and the riderless horse took off. Another thief followed and Jake let him go. He wasn't a peacekeeper. He wasn't hunting thieves and murderers for the sake of justice. He simply didn't want anyone on their trail. If they'd left him and Abby alone in the first place, it wouldn't have come to this.

A quick turn of his hand and the man's bone snapped. The gun thunked to the ground and Jake jerked the man forward. Turning on his heel, he hurled the body several feet into the grass. A dull moan from that direction told Jake the man was still alive, but he didn't have time to address that particular problem. The last thief to remain atop his horse decided to hold his ground.

Bad call.

Jake assessed the situation in a blink of the eye. A Winchester rifle was aimed at his skull. The man's hands were steady and his mount was at least momentarily still. The muscles around the thief's blue eyes tightened, and his finger moved infinitesimally on the trigger. Jake darted sharply right, faster than human reflexes could compensate for. His sudden lunge spooked the horse and the man swore viciously even as he settled his horse. Stubborn.

"Run," Jake growled, giving him a chance even as the smell of blood and fear clogged his nose. The rider was awake and gibbering, eager for the kill. But the stupid man just grinned at him and took aim again.

With a mental sigh, Jake stepped forward and batted the gun aside, hard enough to warp the barrel. The gun went flying and the man flailed, grasping for his pistol. His panic made him clumsy and it was the easiest thing in the world for Jake to reach up and fist his hand in the man's coat to pull him to the ground.

"You should have run," he said wearily.

"I will. I promise. Just let me go and you'll never see me again. Just—"

At the sound of hoofbeats, Jake lifted his head. He cursed when he saw Abby cresting the ridge. She didn't pause at the top even though her eyes flared wide. Her training was too ingrained to leave herself as an open target. She leaned over Harvey's neck and angled wide of the fight until she got her bearings.

"Damn." Jake looked down at the man squirming beneath his boot and then stepped back. "Leave your weapons and go. Go!"

The outlaw couldn't shed them fast enough. He scurried toward his horse as Jake watched Abby approach. Her gun was aimed at the fleeing outlaw, tracking him as he took off at a gallop, clumps of dirt kicking up in his wake.

When he passed out of range, her shoulders relaxed slightly and she turned to Jake.

“What the hell are you doing here?”

She inhaled sharply, lifted her rifle and swung the barrel to the left. Even as Jake turned to see what had caught her attention, she fired. The thunderclap of sound reverberated in his chest and he instinctively took a step back. Her aim was true, hitting the man standing behind Jake squarely in the chest. It was the thief with the broken wrist, the one Jake had disabled and then forgotten about. Somehow, the man had found another gun.

When Abby’s shot hit him, he stumbled back but still held on to the gun. He began to raise it, pointing toward Abby, and terror iced Jake’s veins. He hadn’t felt anything like it for such a long time. It momentarily immobilized him. Abby fired again and the outlaw’s shot went wide. Still stubborn, still clinging somehow to life, the man fell to his knees, making a sickening, gurgling noise as if trying to speak but the sound was coming out of the hole in his chest instead of his mouth. Jake took two steps—he was standing two fucking steps away—and wrested the pistol from the dying man’s good hand.

The outlaw’s face was corpse-white but his eyes were alive and pleading. For Jake to do what? He had no idea. There was nothing he could do…except bite him, and that would be no mercy. And he wasn’t feeling merciful. He felt stupid and sloppy and so goddamned tired it took an enormous effort to turn around to face Abby. Who’d just saved his life. By killing a human.

“I told you to wait by the river,” he snapped.

She stared at the dying man and he couldn’t read the expression on her face. When the thief finally crumpled to the ground, she blinked slowly, as if waking from a dream, and then looked around—at the slick puddle of blood and the gun in her hand—before finally focusing on Jake.

"He was going to shoot you," she said flatly.

He nodded.

She shoved her rifle into her holster and pulled on Harvey's reins. "I'll find you a horse."

THAT NIGHT THEY camped in a small stand of trees next to a quick-running stream. Silently, they worked beside one another and Abby wondered at how quickly they'd become a team. Jake took the horses and she fetched wood. He plucked their dinner right out of the water, tossing the squirming fish onto the bank for her to gut. He cooked while she swept the hickory nutshells from the bare earth and then shook out the bedroll they'd acquired from the thieves to check it for vermin. By the time it was all done and they sat across from one another, her thoughts kept turning to the expression on that man's face when he fell to the ground.

Jake poked at the fire with a stick but kept one eye on her. She always knew when he was watching her. She could feel it.

"You've never killed a human before."

"I have." There was that blonde woman near Jasper whose family had been ripped apart by Reapers. She was technically alive, bitten and bleeding but still clinging to life. Even if she hadn't been bitten, they couldn't have healed what had been done to her. She'd begged…

"That's why you hesitated in New Providence

even when you knew what Nelson and his friends had planned for you. You ran and hid like a rabbit just so you didn't have to pull the trigger."

"You don't know me. Don't start thinking that you do."

He didn't answer that. The fire popped and crackled as it ate up the dry wood. She tossed a stray stick into it and wrapped her hands around her knees.

"I should have made certain he wasn't a threat. I would have gotten to him eventually." He shifted, his boot scraping in the gritty soil. "Why did you follow me? You could have run. I *expected* you to run."

"I thought they might be Rangers."

A faint smile touched his lips. "You were coming to help them slaughter me."

"I don't want you dead." And because that was too profound a truth for her to contemplate, she added, "Besides, you're the only one who knows where those scientists are."

Shadows from the fire danced over Jake's skin, turning it golden. He'd set aside his hat and washed his face and hair in the creek. His hair was still damp, black as a raven's wing. Darker than the look he was giving her now.

"I'm sorry." He said it so soft and sincere somehow it only made her feel worse. Made her chest feel tight and her eyes itchy.

"You're a Reaper. Don't tell me you're mourning a dead man." If she hadn't been so bone-deep tired, she wouldn't have said it. But she was so stinking sick of it all. And this was Jake, after all. Why on earth she felt she needed to watch her words around him, she had no idea.

"I'm not." He leaned forward to toss another log onto the fire. "I haven't had much call to trust anyone. Not since I was changed, and there were few enough from before."

"But you trust me?" That teased a smile to her mouth and he returned it. "I already shot you once."

"I bit you. You might put a bullet in my head someday but I expect if you do, I'll have deserved it. That's all the trust I need."

He believed that and she didn't know… Yeah, she did. If she had to kill him, she could do it. All sorts of things she could do if she had to. An image of the outlaw clutching at his chest as he fell to the ground came to mind and she rubbed at a spot between her brows. "I need to get some sleep."

"Tomorrow night you'll have a bed."

When he turned her over to the scientists for their experiment. Important to remember that.

Pulling the blanket around her, she lay down on her side with her back to the fire. She fell asleep listening to the snap and crack of the dry wood and Jake's even breath as he kept watch over her.

Chapter Thirteen

A STEADY AND powerful wind swept down from the mountains and scoured over the flat stretch of rocky ground. There were few trees here, all of them stunted and leaning toward the east. It was as hopeless and barren a place as she'd ever seen, far enough south to be vulnerable to Reaper attack and with too little topsoil to farm. Everywhere she looked, rock poked from the earth like stripped bone.

There was more of the fine silty earth in the air than on the ground, and the wind whipped it mercilessly against every exposed patch of skin. Abby had a bandana tied around her face and her hat was shoved down as far as it would go, but the wind was still doing its damndest to tug it from her head. She wore gloves, but her wrists stung where the cuff of her shirt had pulled back. If the stinging wind bothered Jake at all, he gave no sign of it. His only concession had been to flip up the collar of his leather duster to protect his neck. His face was downcast, blocked by the brim of his hat.

Every time she tried to speak to him, the wind stole the words from her mouth and he pretended not to hear. *Bastard.* She knew he could hear a pin drop in a sandstorm. She also knew that he didn't want to talk about the scientists and the gruesome specifics of their plans for her. Fine. She was the coward who'd put off asking until now. She'd had the chance last night when they were sitting beside the fire, the day before when they were riding across the dusty plains. She'd put it off and put it off and now, when she couldn't ignore it any longer, Jake had withdrawn like a turtle hiding in a shell.

Her whole life she'd survived by only looking at the problem right in front of her. It was what kept her sane. One step at a time. One night. One fight. One kill. Then you put it behind you and walked away. She'd never had a say about where the next day would take her, she only had to survive it and she would survive this too. Damn it.

Glaring at Jake's profile, she shook her head. At least, she now had an answer for one of her remaining questions—why he'd been so certain no one would find his scientists. No one crossed the Barrens without good cause. Fifty miles without water or much in the way of food, unless you had a taste for snakes and lizards. It was a desert without even a solitary cactus to relieve the scenery. And these dustups were frequent, particularly at this time of year.

The wonder was that anyone had ever *tried* to settle here. Jake had mentioned a ranch and they'd passed through gates mounted with the bleached skull of an enormous steer not a quarter of a mile back. The rancher had probably staked his claim in the spring during the few weeks when the land came alive. She'd heard five or six years ago that some sort of cult had set up shop during a stretch of uncommonly wet years. Something about Moses drawing water from the earth. Squinting, she could just make out the dark shape of a building up ahead.

Riding directly into the open barn, she dismounted while Jake wrestled the doors closed behind them.

"Jake..." She didn't even know what she wanted from him. Maybe just a sign that he was still on her side.

"The horses first."

She swallowed a growl of frustration but turned her attention to Harvey. Even though they'd done their best to protect sensitive eyes and noses, the ride through the dust had been hard on the animals. That grit had worked its way in everywhere including under the saddles and bridle straps. They needed to get it off.

They worked in silence for a time. Until she glanced up to find Jake staring at her and his unguarded expression stole her breath. She'd swear that was concern there. Concern and regret and hunger...but not the creepy I-want-to-eat-you kind. It was the same kind of hunger she'd felt for him in New Providence. The one she'd tried to deny and ignore and destroy. When he looked at her like he was doing now, it rose up inside her just as strong as ever.

Jake took the heavy saddle from her hands and settled it over the rail as if it weighed nothing. And then, with the animals tended, he seemed at a loss.

"Is there a plan?" She tipped her head so she could see his expression beneath the shadow of his hat. "Or are you just going to toss me in there like you're feeding hogs?"

His mouth thinned. "You're frightened."

"I agreed to come," she said. "You're not the only one willing to sacrifice for a cure. Partners, remember?"

He took off his gloves and wiped a spot of sand from his jaw. The scrapes were already healed. The skin around her eyes burned like fire and she suspected it would remain that way for a few days before the sting went away.

"We're not partners," he said. "That was your word, not mine."

He didn't move and she couldn't leave the stall without touching him, which she was certain was a very bad idea. There was a tension in him now that she didn't like. It reminded her of that long night on the hill when his rider had simmered so close to the surface. She could almost see the creature in Jake's black eyes, watching her now.

Her pulse kicked up and she looked away, glancing at the door and then moving forward determinedly. He didn't like the word *partner?* Fine. Jake wasn't going to hurt her, not after all they'd been through. And he'd led her right to the scientists, that was the important thing.

At the last moment, he shifted his weight to block her path. Rather than barrel into him, she took a startled step back. There wasn't anywhere to go. Harvey was in the stall and huffed his annoyance, stomping his back foot restlessly. Jake used his bigger body to back her up against the wall. He didn't force her there, not with his hands. When her back hit the wood, the rickety old wall swayed.

"What do you think you're doing?"

"Before we go in there, there's something we need to have clear between us." He planted his hands to either side of her head and the wood creaked. He was just tall enough that she couldn't see his face with his head bowed the way it was. His arms flexed and he leaned in close enough for her to feel the heat coming off his body, smell the gun oil and leather scent of him. He was careful to keep his hips from touching her but when he inhaled, his chest expanded to brush against her breasts.

"My whole aim was to get you here. And I did." He raised his head enough to look her in the eye and the thing that shocked her most was that it was Jake, not the Reaper, staring down at her. "Those scientists are alive because they're useful to me, same as you. Don't make the mistake of thinking they're my friends or yours. You're not going to be able to believe everything they tell you."

"But I should believe you?"

"I didn't eat you. I didn't fuck you. I might not be your friend, but I do keep my promises."

She slapped a hand to his chest, hard, and he grabbed hold of her wrist to pin it to the wall. Caught her other hand and forced that up too. "Don't."

"This isn't you," she said evenly. "Let me go and get out of my way."

"You'll hear me out first, Abby. I don't want to see you get hurt."

"You brought me here so they could experiment on

me and now you're going to stand here telling me they can't be trusted? What is this, Jake? Are you having second thoughts?"

His warm breath touched her skin and made her shiver. "Those men in there are after a cure and will do anything to achieve it. Just because they're human doesn't make them good."

"I'm not an idiot."

"What you are is fragile and too damn brave for your own good."

"There's nothing fragile about me."

He studied her face, his dark eyes unreadable. When his gaze lingered on her lips, she thought for a moment that he might kiss her, but he just shook his head. "It's been a trial to keep you alive and here you are ready to climb up on the cross again. You want to know a secret? The reason your captain wants to lock you up in a fort? It has nothing to do with how many kids you can give him."

She tested his grip but there was no way she could break it. Jake didn't even have to strain to hold her. "You don't know what the hell you're talking about."

"It's because you're a liability."

"I pull my own weight."

"You might carry a gun, but you don't have the instincts of a killer. It's a wonder you survived this long."

"I killed Marston," she reminded him. "That man with his gun at your head."

"And you're shaking like a leaf just thinking about

it. The problem is you want to believe the best in people and sometimes it just isn't there."

That wasn't why she was shaking. She was trembling because with the wall at her back and Jake's body hard against hers, she was reminded of that alley in New Providence. And she was glad he still had hold of her wrists, because what she wanted to do was wrap her arms around his neck and hold on to him. She wanted him to tell her he cared and that it would be all right. That he'd be there with her and they'd see this through together. She wanted to feel his mouth on hers again. This time she wouldn't let him stop, even knowing he was a Reaper. And how fucked up was that? "You don't know what I'm thinking, don't pretend that you do."

Releasing her abruptly, he lifted his body from hers and stepped away. "You were planning a rescue. That's not going to happen. Those men don't want to go anywhere. Even if they did, I wouldn't let you take them."

She rubbed her bruised wrist. "Fuck you, Jake. I want the cure just as much as you or those scientists do, maybe more. Whatever it costs."

"Don't let down your guard." He hooked a bucket with two fingers and then walked toward the side door. "There's a working well. I'll fetch the water, then we can go meet the good doctors."

Waiting until she heard the door close, she bent her forehead to Harvey's neck. All the anxiety she'd been fighting since New Providence welled up inside her. "What the hell have I gotten myself into?"

It had seemed like a good idea at the time. She gave

a soft laugh. Those were the words Lyle had once told her he would carve on her tombstone. *It seemed like a good idea at the time.* Find out the truth and then escape, maybe take a shot at rescuing the scientists too. If Jake was telling the truth, then he wanted a cure as badly as she did. If he wasn't telling the truth… If there weren't any scientists and Jake had brought her to this remote ranch for his own nefarious purposes, then she'd never stood a chance anyway. She'd been a dead woman from the moment he set eyes on her in New Providence.

The plan made sense, but it didn't stop her from being scared down to her bones. She raised her head when the door opened and Jake's gaze shot immediately to her. Again, that strange mix of concern and hunger shadowed his eyes. Even though she suspected the hunger was only there because of the Reaper, she liked to think the concern was from Jake—the real person inside the monster. Turning back to brushing the dirt and sweat from Harvey's flank, she mentally kicked herself. In the back of her head, she could hear Doc's voice calling her a sentimental fool. And this time around she agreed with him.

"Where are the scientists?" She paused to stretch her back. He'd promised her a bed. Something, anyway, to look forward to. "I imagine they're anxious to get out of whatever hole you stuck them in."

Jake tossed his brush onto a crude table and gestured toward the door. "The cellar door's on the side of the house. Why don't you go inside and sit down? I'll herd them up when they're through cussing me out."

She considered following him, but this way she'd be

able to see the layout of the house without him looking over her shoulder. Tucking her hair back under her hat, she fumbled at the knot on her bandana. She didn't hear Jake come up behind her until his fingers brushed hers, swatting them aside.

"Let me," he said, voice low and gruff.

He barely brushed the skin on her neck, but a shock jolted through her body from her fingertips to her toes. What alarmed her most was that her reaction wasn't fear. And when had that happened? No matter how kind Jake was to her, no matter how noble she thought it was that he was trying to set this right, he was still a fucking Reaper. During the course of his long and wretched life, he'd done things she couldn't even begin to consider without feeling sick to her stomach.

Now that they were rejoining civilization, she had to stop thinking of him as her partner, as her friend. He'd said it himself he had no interest in being either. She pulled away from him before he was done retying the knot and the cloth sagged around her face. She pressed it to her nose with one hand. "It's not far, I'll be fine."

He nodded and pushed open the door. She ran all the way to the house.

A sorry excuse for a house. There was only one story and the shingles were long gone. Apparently the original inhabitants had intended to add a second floor. The floorboards for the second story offered some protection from the driving wind. Despite the shutters nailed to the windows and cloth stuffed in every nook and cranny, dust coated every surface. There was a lantern set on a small table inside the door beside a box of matches. She used her back to close the door and lit the lantern.

Lifting it, she walked through each room, noting the placement of all the doors and windows. There were two doors, front and back, and three separate rooms in addition to the main living area, all with double beds. The mattresses were moldy. She could smell that rich earthy smell as she passed through. Mice, mold and dust. She didn't imagine there'd be much in the way of fresh linens. "It's not like you're planning to stay," she reminded herself grimly.

No matter what Jake said, they'd be safer with the Rangers. Cap would know what to do about all of this and Abby wanted nothing more than to dump this into his lap, maybe with a self-righteous "I told you so" thrown in for sending her off alone in the first place. To keep her safe. *Ha.*

She heard a thud as the door banged open and she walked toward the sound. The sight that greeted her stopped her in her tracks. Light from the raised lantern bounced around the room, making her doubt her eyes at first. But it was no mistake.

Grubby, thin and accompanied by the rancid smell of stale sweat, three men pushed their way into the room. The leader's gaze fixed on her as he rose from a crouch. Jake lay on the floor, tossed there like a sack of flour. He was unconscious, possibly dead. Drawing her pistol with the ease of long practice, she aimed it at the head of the nearest scientist.

"I'd stop right there, mister, and explain to me what's going on."

His gaze flicked over her, taking in her uniform and gun. Slowly, he raised his hands. "You're a Ranger."

"I am. And who are you?"

He didn't answer immediately, just straightened to his full height to give her a short, formal bow. If she hadn't seen Scrapers do the same thing, she might have shot him for the sudden movement. "I cannot tell you how pleased we are to see you alive and unharmed. You've been traveling with this man?"

"I have."

"I regret to alarm you, my dear, but this man is not at all what he seems."

When he paused dramatically, she cocked an eyebrow. "I'm aware of what he is, *doctor*. What the hell did you do to him?"

The elderly man who'd been checking Jake's pulse stood. He took a long look at the gun Abby pointed at him and held up his hands. "You know he's a Reaper?"

"I know it."

He glanced down at Jake and shook his head. "He'll be fine. I managed to grab my bag on our way out of the fort and he never bothered to search it. I had one syringe filled with a substance we use to disable unruly Reapers. It lowers his blood temperature enough to disable the rider but will do him no permanent damage." He shouldered his way past the younger doctor and held out his hand. "I'm Dr. Karlson. This is Josiah Welks and the one over there is Robert Hamilton, my lab technician."

"You're the Fort Hill survivors he talked about."

Dr. Karlson's lined face hardened but he nodded, once.

Abby stared at his extended hand a good long time before setting the lantern down on a side table and holstering her gun. Shaking the doctor's hand, she said, "I'm very glad to find you alive, sir. He told me that there were survivors, but until this moment I wasn't sure whether to believe him."

Bushy gray eyebrows shot up. "And yet you came willingly?"

"I had to find out for certain, didn't I?" She glanced at Jake's prone body and quickly away. "Why did you wait until now to inject him? Why not do it *before* he locked you in the cellar?"

"As I'm sure you're aware, he's a very difficult man to surprise. We were trapped in that root cellar for two weeks and thought this might be our only chance to escape."

"He didn't plan to hurt you."

Dr. Karlson's smile thinned and Welks looked at her as if she was the stupidest creature to ever walk the earth. Perhaps she was. Because right now it took every ounce of her willpower to not rush to Jake's side and make certain he was all right for herself. The scientists, she reminded herself, were the men she was here to help, not Jake.

"He's a Reaper," the big man—the one Karlson called Hamilton—sneered at her. "I would think a *Ranger* would know better than to trust one of his kind."

"He hasn't hurt me. And it was my understanding that he's working with you willingly to find a cure."

Hamilton laughed. "Working *with* us? Is that what he told you?"

Dr. Karlson held up his hand to silence Hamilton and gifted Abby with a fatherly smile. "Jake does what he wants. He was always a difficult subject. Perhaps I should have listened to my peers and disposed of him sooner, but he was the oldest specimen we had available. I'm sure you understand."

No. But she was beginning to. "I understand that you'd be dead right now if not for him."

Karlson sighed. "Make no mistake, my dear. He saved us for his own purposes. They have their own political system, you know. Rivalries and alliances that go back for centuries. Perhaps he only wants us to work on a weapon to use against an enemy. Perhaps he wants revenge."

"Perhaps he does," she said. "Perhaps he wants revenge against you, for experimenting on him for *twelve years*. That's what you're really worried about. I'd be wary too if I were in your shoes. I don't blame you for that. But I'll warn you now, this is the first sentient Reaper I've come across and I won't stand aside while you slaughter him. I want to take him back to my patrol. I think it's important that my captain see this for himself."

Welks, who'd seemed content to let Dr. Karlson handle her, finally spoke. "You misapprehend the situation, my dear. Jake's sentience makes him more dangerous, not less. He preserved you for a purpose and it's a mistake to think that he has your—" He shook his head and gave a wry smile. "That he has *any* of our best interests at heart."

Possibly. *Probably.* But Abby couldn't shake her uneasiness with these men. Her gaze fell to rest again on Jake. His mouth gaped open and his skin was very pale, shiny with a sheen of sweat. He appeared so vulnerable lying there in the dirt. The sight of a vulnerable Jake disturbed her greatly.

Hamilton knelt down. He was a burly man with dirty blond hair and an old scar slicing down his left cheek. The way he shoved at Jake's shoulder—as if jostling a bag of grain—made her take an involuntary step forward. She checked herself as Hamilton pulled Jake's torso up and then, with a great heave, swung him over his shoulder.

"I'll secure him and fetch water." Hamilton looked to her. "Did you bring any food with you?"

She shook her head.

"There's a few jars left in the cellar," Karlson said. "Bring them up and we'll start the fire."

When Hamilton turned, the edge of the doorframe clipped Jake's temple. He groaned but didn't wake. Karlson touched her shoulder to draw her attention. "You have a seat, my dear. Tonight, you're our guest. Do you need medical attention? I can't imagine how terrible a time you've had of it these last several days."

She kicked her chair into the corner and set her hand on her thigh only inches away from the gun strapped to her hip. When Jake woke, she'd find a way to speak with him. He'd promised not to let these men hurt her and at the time, she'd taken it for a simple platitude. Now, she wondered. He'd told her the truth about Fort Hill, about the scientists he'd rescued, about the fact that they were well aware of the existence of sentient Reapers. It stood to reason that he was also right about the involvement of the Scrapers.

And these men…employed by Scrapers and then betrayed—what was it that they wanted?

JAKE SCREAMED AGAIN and Abby set her spoon aside. Once more… If he screamed one more time, she'd forget about trying to lure the truth out of Welks and she'd *force* it out of him. Jake should have warned her, damn him. She didn't understand the undercurrents of the relationships here. The way Welks and Karlson interacted spoke of deep dislike and bare tolerance. Hamilton, they dismissed as insignificant. But he worried her. There was a cruel glint in his eyes she'd seen once or twice before. Clearly, Jake had planned to manage them but since that hadn't worked out, she needed to figure out a way to talk them into returning with her to her patrol.

She caught the older man's eyes, Dr. Karlson, who looked only mildly uncomfortable with the sounds coming through the floorboards.

"What is Hamilton doing to him?"

Dr. Karlson turned to stir the coals in the iron stove. The room was heating nicely and the vegetable stew he'd assembled warmed in the pot. He'd given her the first serving but while her stomach growled, she couldn't eat. The noises coming from the cellar…they sounded as if they came from a wounded animal, not a man.

Karlson brought his own bowl to the table and sat across from her. "We're hobbling him the only way we know how." He must have seen the alarm in her eyes because he smiled and waved his hand. "Oh, no, child. No permanent harm will come to him. He's far too valuable for that. It's only that in these close quarters, we have to be certain that the parasite is disabled."

"He's controlled the parasite this far." She thought of New Providence, of how she'd wrapped herself around his body, of how he'd trembled beneath her hands. He hadn't lost control then. He wouldn't lose control now.

Karlson grimaced. "That is a wonder and a mercy. But, you understand, we can't take any chances."

He wanted to be in control and he didn't trust Jake. Fine. As long as they didn't kill him. She needed more information before she could decide how to handle this turn of events.

Clearing the dust from her throat, she said, "He told me that Scrapers were behind the attack."

The doctor's eyes narrowed slightly but he nodded. "That's why we followed him here rather than travel directly to another fort. If it's true, our lives are in grave danger should anyone discover that we're still alive."

"Do *you* think it's true?"

"I think it's a possibility," he said, carefully. "Welks

believes it's nonsense but caution is never wasted, as my dear mother always said."

"After you cure him..." Abby trailed off when he frowned. "What?"

"Hmm." He blew at the steam rising from his spoon and tested the heat with his tongue before filling his mouth. After he swallowed, he dabbed at his lips with a surprisingly white handkerchief he produced from somewhere about his person. "Jake's a poor candidate for this trial. His body has come to depend on the creature so completely that there's a good chance he won't survive the treatment. Of course, right now he's all we have to work with. Perhaps by the time we isolate the parasite from his spinal fluid we'll have another Reaper to test the serum on and Jake can continue as he is."

"He doesn't know that, does he?"

Dr. Karlson avoided her gaze as Welks entered the room, examining the fluid level in the biggest needle Abby ever set her eyes on.

"Perhaps you'd prefer his death?" Welks asked. "If you'd rather, we can promise to deliver him into your hands when we're finished. Consider it our payment for your services."

Keeping her gaze fixed on the needle, she held up her hand. "Wait there one minute, Doctor. I'm not interested in revenge and I haven't agreed to anything yet."

"Relax, child. This will put you to sleep and you won't feel a thing, I promise you that. You did come here to help us find a cure, did you not?"

"I'll talk to Jake first," she insisted.

But the assistant had made quick work of Jake and was back in the room. She'd been so distracted by Karlson's revelation and then by the sight of Dr. Welks and his enormous needle that she hadn't noticed the sneaky bugger slip in through the back door. Dr. Welks nodded to him now and Hamilton pinned her arms behind her back before she could bolt from her chair. She kicked out, but Josiah easily dodged the shot she aimed at his groin. Karlson cast her an apologetic smile and removed her bowl of stew from the edge of the table before it toppled. Welks slid next to the chair, gripped her hair and wrenched her head to one side to expose her neck. "You'll feel a small pinch."

The bastard was grinning. She'd kill him. She'd…

Chapter Fourteen

SHE WAS UNDERGROUND. Swallowing hard, she tried not to panic, tried to ignore the weight of the darkness pressing in on her. She hated this feeling—being surrounded by earth. Like being buried alive.

The ever-present sound of the wind was muffled down here and came from above her head. It smelled awful, not the rich scent of earth and root vegetables but the bitter musky scent of unwashed men, rotten food and human waste. She groaned and tried to hide her face from the smell.

The rock she was propped against shifted and she startled at the movement. A strong arm came around her shoulders to steady her and a whiskered chin scraped against her temple. Jake, it was Jake. She clutched at him as her memory slammed into place—the scientists, that needle, the screaming… And then nothing. *What did they do to me?*

"Shush, now." He brushed her hair from her face and she flinched.

Untangling her fist from his shirt, she touched his face, accidently bashing his lip when she didn't realize his head was bent. He grunted.

"Sorry," she whispered, trailing her fingertips over his eyelids, down through the hollow of his cheeks and across his lips. His skin was whole, maybe a bit scarred, but it wasn't the black and bloody mess it had been earlier. Even the scars would likely fade with time. "You've healed."

"Well enough," he murmured, breathing hot air across her fingertips. She flushed and withdrew her hand, reluctantly pulling away from his warmth. He caught her wrist and hauled her back down. "Stay here. It's cold and likely to get colder before dawn." A wry note touched his deep voice. "At least I left them with blankets."

A wave of dizziness swept over her and the next thing she knew, Jake's arm was wrapped around her back, holding her upright. She must have blacked out again. She shook her head to clear it, but it was like trying to beat back the fog. Her ears felt stuffed with cotton. Her tongue swollen and her limbs weighed down with rocks.

"Do you know what they gave to me? I can't…my arms and legs aren't working right. And my head feels like a balloon."

"I think it was a simple sedative," he said. "The scent is fading, but it will likely take a while longer for it to work its way completely out of your system. You shouldn't…don't try to move, okay?"

She let him settle her against him. He pressed her cheek to his chest and she let his warmth, the solid and steady beat of his heart, soothe her. It shouldn't comfort her; nothing had changed. He was still a Reaper. She was still a Ranger. Even injured and drugged, she should fight this.

During those quiet nights beneath the stars, she'd often wondered what this would feel like. A time or two when she'd woken trembling with the cold, she'd thought about lying beside him. For warmth, only for warmth. Each time, she'd managed to resist temptation. Now, she rubbed her cheek against his flannel shirt and closed her eyes.

"You know, I used to think that Reapers didn't have beating hearts."

He blew out a huff of laughter. "You have the strangest ideas."

"Doc and I argued about it once with me saying you were all walking dead. Never thought I'd learn the truth this way. I guess most people who get this close don't live long enough to tell the tale, huh?"

"You did. You've heard it before." She'd felt it, thudding against her breasts. In time with hers.

"Is this hard for you? Holding me like this? If there's a risk that you'll lose control, I'd rather be cold."

"They collared me." His breath stirred the fine hairs on top of her head. "It prevents the Reaper from taking over so there shouldn't be—*won't* be any problems."

"Karlson explained the collar." She remembered the sounds Jake had made, like a wild animal cornered and hurt. She started to lift her hand to his neck but let it fall to his chest. "Does it hurt?"

"I've been collared before," he said, which was not really an answer. "How are *you?* They drew blood from you, took a skin sample from your shoulder and a length of your hair." He paused. "I don't know what else they might have done."

A shiver chased over her skin and his arm tightened. "My head hurts, but otherwise I'm all right. I don't remember anything except the needle in Welks's hands. But…I don't think they hurt me. I would know, wouldn't I?"

He nodded and made a sound that might have been agreement.

"How did they manage to take you?"

"I left lye for them to use in order to control the smell of the latrine." His voice was low and bitter. She felt the deep rumble of it beneath her cheek. "Instead, they used it to make a solution to scald me with when I threw open the doors. It burned my skin and let them get close enough to knock me out. After all this time, I still underestimated them. It was a stupid mistake. I'm sorry."

"You're not the one who owes me an apology."

"I promised you'd be safe."

"You also told me to watch my back. You couldn't have known they'd try this."

"I should have known it. But I never thought that they'd hurt you, not like this."

A smile tugged at her mouth. "Because I'm human?"

"You're human. Female and a Ranger. They should be guarding you like treasure not tossing you into the cellar with a damned Reaper."

"You're collared," she reminded him. But they both knew that wouldn't stop him from hurting her if he really wanted to. "They must know you wouldn't hurt me."

"Or they're testing me…or you." He swore under his breath. "Both of us probably."

His hand on the back of her head kept her from looking at him. "What do you mean, Jake?"

He paused too long, thinking through whatever idea had occurred to him. In the end, he grunted and shook his head. "Nothing. It's nothing. They don't want us to escape and they don't trust you."

And well they shouldn't. Next time she saw Welks, she would shove that needle up his ass.

"We'll figure a way out of this," she told him. But it was hard to concentrate. Her head hurt so damn much. Gradually, she let herself relax against him. She knew there was a list of reasons a mile long why she shouldn't trust Jake, but none of them seemed to matter. Right now, she trusted him a hell of a lot more than she did the men upstairs.

JAKE CLOSED HIS eyes and tipped his head back to rest against the crude wall. With him collared, he was weaker than the average human man. And Abby was drained—literally drained—from the samples they'd stolen from her. He'd made her drink some water a little while ago and then, to his surprise, she'd snuggled her warm little body next to his again, slung an arm around his waist and a leg across his thighs and proceeded to drift off to sleep. She was snoring now, a soft and feminine sound he'd never once heard in his long life.

He let her rest, hoping she'd regain enough of her strength to get them out of this. He had little hope though. The scientists knew all his weaknesses, and they were far more ruthless than Abby could possibly imagine.

He should be racking his brain for a plan. Instead, all of his attention was focused on Abby—the warm weight of her limp body, the impossibility of the fact that she trusted him enough to be so vulnerable in his presence, the hope that it filled him with…and the sadness too. He'd never held a woman in his arms like this, one who trusted him to watch over her. It tore open something inside him that he'd kept locked away tighter than the rider. He traced the jut of her shoulder blade and the fragile curve of her spine, the sweet flare of her hips.

The smell of her surrounded him. Beneath the sweat and grime, he could smell *her.* Maybe it was pheromones that made him press his nose to her hair to breathe her in, but that wasn't all of it. He wanted her, no doubt about it, but he wanted *not* to hurt her even more. Pheromones didn't account for that. He didn't want to try to account for it. Not now.

He knew when she woke by the change in her breathing. She turned her face into his chest to wipe her drool on his shirt and he smiled. She didn't try to pull away, though he was prepared to release her.

"Jake?"

"Mmm?"

"Is it morning?" Fear made her voice tight and he hated the sound of it. "They said they'd come for me again in the morning."

"I'll get you out of here before then, Abby."

She was silent for a time. He could hear Welks strident tone berating Hamilton for something. Jake would get her out. He'd wring the cure out of Welks. And then he'd kill him. He'd very much enjoy killing Welks.

She stirred in his arms and he glanced down. She looked vulnerable, her eyes wide and her lips bruised. There was a streak of dirt on her chin. "You knew what they were like and you came back. You had to know you could die here."

"I thought it was worth the risk. I still do."

She wanted this to end as much as he did. He knew that by her reactions to everything he'd told her. He'd used that knowledge to manipulate her into following him. And even now, she didn't try to argue him out of dying if it meant there'd be an end to the scourge. He touched her hair, tentatively at first. When she didn't pull away or bat at his hand, he brushed the loose strands back from her face. She was frowning, struggling with something. After a moment, she said, "If we find a younger Reaper, maybe they can run their tests on him instead."

Ah… Karlson must have told her that he was too old to be cured. Jake wondered why she didn't ask him about it outright. She wasn't much for subtlety, his Abby. Surely she wasn't trying to spare his feelings.

"If I have to kill them to get us out of here, I'll do it," she said fiercely and it broke his heart to hear her voice shake. He wouldn't have thought that was even possible until he felt the ache in his chest.

"You don't know what you're saying."

"I want out of here is what I'm saying." Exasperation and determination were starting to win out over the fear.

He laughed. "On that we're agreed. But…Abby?

Leave Welks to me, if you can. He hasn't shared his secrets, not even with Karlson. I'll make him talk."

The wind had died down some while she slept, and light from the weak sun slipped through the cracks in the wooden doors. He'd reinforced those doors himself, but in his current state he wouldn't be able to break through them. Too much adrenaline, too much of an increase in his heart rate and the collar would release its poison into his nervous system through the needle embedded in his spine. And then he wouldn't be of any help to Abby or himself for hours afterward.

He squeezed her shoulders and released her. "Someone's coming."

"It's not morning."

She'd gone stiff as a board. He heard her heartbeat kick into a gallop and could smell the sharp bright scent of her fear. A snarl of pure rage rose up in his throat and he choked it back so as not to alarm her further. *His fault*, her terror was his fault. He helped her to stand up and then directed her toward the shadows beneath the door with a gentle nudge.

It was a sign of her exhaustion that she didn't fight him at all. Clenching his jaw, Jake willed his body not to react to the fear he felt for her. She was a Ranger, she could handle herself in a fight. She'd survived for years without his help. The doors banged open to reveal Hamilton's silhouette. He was a brute, one of Josiah's pets, a man who took pleasure in inflicting pain. Jake would have left him behind at Fort Hill, but there'd been no way to do that without endangering their escape. Hamilton had nearly broken Abby's neck dumping her unconscious body down here last night. The only thing that had kept Jake from doing his level best to kill Hamilton was the cold weight of the collar, the same thing that held him in place now.

"Where is she?"

"Come down and get her yourself, you little fuck," Jake snarled, hoping he'd do it. Collar or no, he could possibly move fast enough to snap Hamilton's neck before he was disabled.

Hamilton tsked and then in a fair representation of Josiah's more cultured tones said, "Language, Jacob. There's a lady present. Come out, little chickie, and I'll help you up. Dr. Welks would like to examine you again. Turns out there's an amona—anoma..."

"Anomaly," Jake said.

"'Sright. There's something weird about your blood. He said it was fascinating." Hamilton smiled at Jake, revealing an almost complete set of pitted yellow teeth. "And you know how the doctors get when they're fascinated by something, don't you, Jake?"

When Jake moved, Hamilton aimed the shotgun at his chest. "Come out now, little girl, or I start shooting. The shot *might* not kill him, but I'll make damn sure it hurts. Trust me darling, I know just where to aim."

The barrel of the gun dropped several inches and Jake paled. Still, he tried to give Abby a chance. Even armed, if Hamilton had to crawl down here to fetch her out, they could overpower him.

"Why would she care what the hell you do to me?"

Hamilton grinned. "The doctors think you raped her from here to Sunday, but I don't see it. She cares about what happens to you. I saw the look on her face last night when you were laying on the floor. She hid it well enough from the doctors but not from me. You either kept your dick out of her or she likes a good hard fuck. I reckon when the doctors are through with her, I'll find out for myself which it is."

Jake opened his mouth to deny it, but Abby stood up before he could speak, hands raised in surrender and squinting into the light. A growl erupted from his throat and he snapped his teeth together. He never thought to see her surrender to anyone and he hated to witness it now. *To be the cause of it.*

"Get back."

She spared him a brief glance. "I know what I'm doing."

Hamilton reached down to haul her up and Abby kicked his legs out from underneath him as soon as she was through the hatch. With a sharp cry of pain, Hamilton dropped her and she rolled beyond Jake's line of sight. He ran to the edge of the cellar but couldn't see a damn thing. He heard the heavy thunk of a fist meeting flesh. Hamilton's grunt of pain and then—*damn it*—Abby's strangled sob.

He leaped up to grasp the edge of the enclosure. He could feel the needle in his spine chill as the collar prepared a dose for injection. His heart thundered in his chest. Sweat dampened his brow. Rage flooded his mind. He flexed his arms to pull himself up even as the cold poison iced down his spine. Almost immediately, his fingers numbed and then he fell.

"Hamilton," he shouted. "You hurt her and Welks will kill you himself."

The words sounded slurred to his own ears. Hamilton laughed and slammed the door closed. His footsteps retreated. Just the one set of footsteps—he must be carrying Abby. Jake could still see, though he couldn't turn his head. His heart continued to beat, his lungs continued to draw air. His vision was preserved along with his hearing, but he couldn't so much as wiggle a finger.

He couldn't help Abby. Couldn't even cover his ears when she began to scream.

Chapter Fifteen

JAKE'S SKIN WAS ice-cold. Abby slipped her fingertips beneath the hem of his shirt and pressed her forehead to his shoulder. It was warmer there and she could feel the slow but steady beat of his heart beneath the palm of her hand. The muscles of his abdomen clenched.

She raised her head to see if he was awake. His face was slack, lips parted and eyes closed. While she'd managed to get her shoulder underneath him to flip him over, she couldn't move him to the mattress. His folded coat cushioned his head, but she was beginning to reconsider placing it there. She needed to warm him up.

Damn it.

What the hell had they done to him? What had they had the time to do when they'd all been working on her? When she'd regained consciousness to find him lying beside her, sprawled limp and lifeless on his belly in the dirt, she'd thought that Hamilton had shot him after all. But there were no bullet wounds that she could find and no blood, dried or otherwise. She considered trying to wrench the collar from his neck but, afraid it would kill him, she slapped his face instead.

"Jake," she said sharply. "I need you to wake up. Jake, come on. *I need you…*"

She choked on a sob and his eyelids twitched. She'd

never noticed his eyelashes before or the tiny fragile network of veins on his eyelids. Too delicate, too human to be a monster. Late afternoon sunlight filtered through the cracks making the stubble on Jake's jaw glint black and shiny. "Please."

He groaned and she pressed her palms to either side of his face. "Jake?"

He blinked. His eyes were cloudy, opened barely to slits and unfocused. His hands came up to circle her wrists, slid down to her elbows and then around her waist. He hauled her on top of him. "Warm," he murmured.

"You have to wake up." She tried to keep her voice stern, but she was anything but calm. There was precious little awareness in Jake's drugged gaze.

He pushed her hips down at the same time that he lifted his, grinding his erection into her belly. She gave a nervous laugh and braced her hands on the floor beside his head. "Just like a man, you can get your dick up but not your eyelids. Hey—"

One hand left her hip and fisted in her hair, yanking it all to one side and hauling her down. Jake's lips pressed against her exposed neck, his open mouth hot and wet. What truly alarmed her was how good it felt. Even though she knew he was half-asleep, her body didn't seem to care.

"Jake," she whispered. "It's Abby. You need to let go of me now."

If she could wedge her leg between his thighs, she could use her knee to— "Oomph."

He rolled, the full weight of his body crashing down

on top of her. She'd always been aware of his size, but not like she was now. He was taller than she was by nearly a hand, all hard muscle and solid bone. The hands that pinned her down were so incredibly strong that she wouldn't have been able to break his hold even if the doctors hadn't just torn her apart. *Oh, God.* He probably smelled her blood. How many times had Lyle warned her that sporting an open wound around a Reaper was like taunting a bull with a red cape?

"Your collar."

"Don't worry. It's spent." His words were slurred… or they might only have sounded muffled because he'd begun to work his mouth slowly up her throat to her jaw. One hand was still caught in her hair, the other reached for her waistband. When she squirmed to evade him, he groaned and flexed his hips, sliding his cock against her thigh in a slow, smooth arc.

The buttons gave one by one as he shoved the denim down over her hips. His mouth covered hers. Jake's tongue was in her mouth, his hand cupped between her thighs. He curled his fingers and the longest split right through her folds. She groaned and he repeated the movement except this time, he sank inside.

She squirmed at the insistent press of that one finger, opening her. Not gently but not roughly either. She could feel herself growing wetter with every stroke. Her muscles clenched around his finger and he grunted, pressed deeper. Her thighs opened to give him better access even as she asked herself what the hell she was doing. And then she came smack up against a very hard truth. She wanted this. Reaper or no, she wanted Jake.

Even injured and staring into the deep dark pit of an uncertain future, she didn't really want to shove him away. But she needed to. He turned his wrist, adding a second finger. She gasped and he didn't give her room to breathe. "You're so wet. I want to taste you."

"I don't…I don't think that's a good idea right now, Jake. I need to know that you're here with me. Do you know who I am?"

"Abby…I know you. Abby."

He froze, every muscle in his body locked tight. She lay there panting beneath a statue. Slowly, he withdrew his hand and lifted his weight from her body. A shudder ran down the entire length of his body and in a horrified tone of voice he repeated, "Abby."

She wanted to weep. She wanted to pull him back down on top of her but instead fisted her hands and pressed them against her stomach. She was such a fucking idiot to be hurt by his rejection. He hadn't known what he was doing or even who she was. She was a warm body and he was too drugged to realize what he was doing. Damn. *Damn.* She closed her eyes and listened to him move away from her. He'd come to his senses in time. At least one of them had.

Slowly, she sat up, withdrawing a few feet even though she knew the distance couldn't possibly matter. He'd said the collar was spent. She was trapped here in the gathering dark with a starving Reaper and she was wounded. She hauled up her pants and buttoned them while Jake sat across the room with his head in his hands.

"I'm sorry," he whispered brokenly.

She swallowed at the raw misery in his voice. He hated to lose control. He had to hate being powerless even more.

"I know it was the Reaper that made you hungry for me and I won't fault you for that when you've been fighting it all along," she said, working to keep her voice steady. "I blame those scientists for throwing us down here like this, not you."

He didn't comment, didn't move, and she resisted the urge to go to him and offer comfort. *Idiot.*

After an eternity, he rubbed his face and raised his head. "I meant that I'm sorry they took you. I couldn't move and—" His nostrils flared and his eyes narrowed. "They cut you."

She shifted uncomfortably. "Don't concern yourself about that."

"Abby," he growled in a warning tone.

There was nothing to talk about if nothing could be done. And it was too late to do anything about what had happened now. "You said the collar's spent. Will they need to reload it or can I get it off you?"

"You're telling me what happened."

"First things first." She closed her eyes when her voice cracked and gulped down a mouthful of air. "We need to leave. Can I get the fucking collar off you or not?"

Jaw clenched, he studied her a long time before slowly shaking his head. "I've never tried to remove a collar and I don't know what kind of damage it will do without the tool they use. There's no point anyway. They need to reload it before it'll work again. It will take me a few hours to shake off the effect of the dosage I got today."

"How many times did it shoot you?"

"Six. It holds six doses. By then they figure you're dead. No one's ever burned out a collar that I know of. The doctors might have been wrong about the dose or maybe they're using old cartridges, I don't know."

"Will you be able to get us out of here?"

"Yes. But not yet. I don't want to start banging at it until I'm sure I can break through."

"How long will that take?"

She hated the tremor in her voice, but she wanted to be miles gone by the time they came for her again. Apparently they'd never been allowed to work on a female Ranger before. Apparently even at Fort Hill there were ethical boundaries to consider.

She stared down at her hands. Jake had that determined look on his face again that meant he intended to press her about what had happened upstairs, and she didn't want to fight about it now. She was so damned tired of fighting all the time.

If she gave in and told him, she'd probably do something humiliating like start to cry. And she'd be damned if she let him see that either. She didn't want pity, not from Jake, not from a Reaper. Besides, a show of weakness like that might stir up his rider.

"Abby." His voice was so fucking gentle just the sound of it made a sob bubble up in her throat. But then he paused, seemed to reconsider whatever he'd been about to say, and only held out his hand. "Come here. I'm safe for now and you're cold."

Cold. Right. That's why she was shaking like a leaf. Allowing them both the lie, she crept across the space, tucking her arm to her side as discreetly as possible to stave off the pain. She curled against him and Jake held her as if he could protect her from the world. Even though she knew that was a lie, she placed her head against his chest and let the illusion lull her to sleep.

Chapter Sixteen

WHEN SHE WOKE, it was the dead of night. The house was dark and very still. Jake had pulled the mattresses onto the floor to create a nest for them. She hadn't woken when he'd done it. She hadn't stirred when presumably he'd moved her as she slept. He was lying next to her now, awake. She could tell by the cadence of his breathing and the tension in the muscles of his body pressed to hers.

His voice drifted to her, soft and low. "I know you're awake, but you should try to rest. They're all sleeping and the poison's starting to wear off. In another hour, I'll be recovered enough to take Hamilton when he brings food. Two hours and I'll be able to break through the boards on my own." He paused. "Are you okay?"

Stiff. Sore. A throbbing pain in her side. Scared to death. "I'm fine."

But when she rolled onto her back, a groan escaped her lips.

A huff of laughter came from the darkness. "Fine, are you?"

"Fine enough to try and escape," she whispered back. "We might not get another chance."

Jake's hand sought hers and she didn't try to pull

away. His hand was warm, steady, reassuring. "You have bones like a bird."

"On that hand," she said. "You're not sizing me up for a snack are you?"

"You're joking." He sounded half offended, half bemused. "I won't eat you."

She smiled into the darkness. "I know. Not tonight."

His thumb stroked over her knuckles. "I like your other hand too. They did a good job. Most people wouldn't notice."

"I notice."

A bed creaked almost directly overhead and she stiffened, wondering what time it was. She wondered when they'd come for her again. Jake squeezed her hand very gently. He was always careful with her. She should tell him that she wasn't as fragile as he seemed to believe, but she held her tongue. No one had ever treated her like she was delicate before and she kind of liked it.

"Neither of the doctors are early risers and it's not yet dawn."

Her muscles were slow to relax. The soft stroke of his thumb on her skin, bumping and dipping over her knuckles. Wide palm pressed to hers. Strong body. Jake was strong. He wouldn't let them take her again.

"When we get out, do we run or try to lock them up? I don't know that you'll be able to force them to work for you and after this, you can't trust them to work *on* us."

"I can get them another Reaper," Jake said. "Maybe I'll turn Hamilton."

She started to laugh but then stopped when he remained silent. "You're joking, right?"

"Hmm."

They lay there for a time, the Ranger and the Reaper, shoulder to shoulder, hands clasped, listening to the muted roar of the wind and the settling of the old house. Some awfully strange turns her life had taken in these past few weeks.

"We have to get them back to my patrol somehow. We'll be able to protect them and ourselves if we can make it to the fort."

He made a sound of disagreement but didn't argue the point. The plain truth was that he couldn't be on guard while he let those scientists shoot poison into his body. They could kill him and neither of them would be able to do anything to stop them.

"I know you don't like it, but what else are we going to do? You can't let them test the serum on you first. Karlson said…" She blew out a breath and then forced out the words, knowing they were going to hurt him but also knowing that he needed to hear the truth. "Karlson said the serum won't work on you, that the parasite is too much a part of your body for them to be able to kill it without killing you too."

He didn't speak right away. Squeezing his hand, she let him swallow that before continuing on in as gentle a tone as she could muster, "Think about it, Jake. You manage well enough on your own. You fooled all those people in New Providence. You fooled me. Maybe you just don't need their cure."

His thumb paused and then resumed its drift over her skin. "I can't fool myself."

"You could live forever as a Reaper. Even if the cure

does work on you, it's just a slow way to commit suicide."

"I've already lived for a very long time."

She fought the urge to shake him. Stubborn, his mind was set as stone. Maybe he did want to die after all. She gave it one last try. "Even if you survive their treatment, what are you going to do then? What's worth dying for?"

He was silent so long she thought she'd stumped him. He shifted and she could feel his gaze settle on her before he leaned back to tuck his free hand behind his head. "I always thought I might like to be a farmer."

She couldn't help the laugh that bubbled up at the image. And if it held an edge of hysteria, Jake kindly ignored it.

"What?" She could hear the amusement in his voice—he was trying to distract her. Accepting that she wasn't going to change his mind about trying the serum, she let herself be distracted.

"I can't imagine a less likely farmer."

"That's unkind, Abby, mocking my dreams."

She snorted. "The chickens would be too nervous to lay eggs and you'd scare the cows dry."

"You're probably right about that." He didn't sound particularly offended. "Why don't you let me worry about what I'll do once I'm free of the rider? You have yourself to think about. What will you do when there aren't any Reapers left to fight?"

That was a tricky question. What did she dream of except being done? She'd never wasted much time considering it. Crossing her legs, she rested her free hand on her stomach, avoiding the bandage that had come loose while she slept. She didn't have anything to fix it with, so she let it be. "I don't rightly know. Maybe I'll take up farming too."

"Not the city?"

"Having a cure will surely change the world, but not enough for me to fit in up there. And if the plains were free, I wouldn't bother to try. I'd make a new place, a better place. With all of the nice things and none of the bullshit."

Jake was silent and she tried to imagine what that kind of world would look like. She smiled wistfully into the darkness. "That's not ever going to happen, is it?"

A low sound rumbled in his chest, half growl. Tonight, it was a comfort rather than a terror.

"Not if you're going for perfection," he said. "But better? I have no doubt you could manage better than this."

"If I was in charge…" She trailed off when she heard a strange sound carried by the wind. She thought she'd heard something anyway and lay very quiet straining to catch it again.

"Jake?"

"You didn't imagine it."

She felt the tightness in his body as they both waited to find out what was coming. She shivered and Jake reached for her hand, twining his large steady fingers around hers.

"There are riders on the lane," he said, voice just above a whisper. "A half dozen and they're moving fast."

"Do they have friends this close?"

"None who'd lift a finger to help us. They might have sent Hamilton with a message while I was out last night. Josiah's benefactor owns men and land up and down the mountain."

"Who is Josiah's benefactor?"

"That's the question, isn't it? I know that he's wealthy, connected enough to be able to have Josiah placed at Hill on his say-so. I know he has men in the foothills." Jake met her curious look and shrugged. "Josiah likes to talk while he's working. Not even Marston could give me a name."

"They'd have to have been stationed close for them to get here so soon." And now she could hear the sound from the horses—the strike of hoof on bare rock, a man's voice lifted above the wind and then fell silent. The doctors would have heard that too.

"Is anyone from your patrol a good enough tracker to find you here?"

"Possibly." But it was unlikely. Once they saw Fort Hill, they'd have to address that before continuing to search for her.

Jake glanced her way, but his attention was clearly focused elsewhere. "If these men are from Josiah's benefactor, there's a good chance they're here to kill us all."

Her blood iced. "This is what you were talking about when you said I didn't get the big picture. You think Josiah's benefactor was the one who ordered the raid."

"I told Josiah he couldn't be trusted."

She stared at the floorboards. "They don't need to

know we're down here. They kill the doctors and their henchman and we break out later. I say good riddance."

Jake's laugh was low and devoid of humor. "Except that I still want the cure. I didn't do all of this to have nothing to show for it. Come on. We need to be ready for whatever this is."

He stood smoothly and then bent to help her up. By the time she caught her balance, she could hear the horses more clearly. They only had a few minutes. Jake guided her into the shadows beneath the door and then stood in the center of the room where whoever opened the door would see him first. Hands on his hips, he cocked his head slightly to one side, listening.

Jumping, he grabbed the door and when he lost his tenuous grip on the edge, fell lightly again to his feet. On his next try, he jammed his fingers into the big crack at the door's center and swung there for a moment until he found purchase with his other hand a little higher up. He'd just managed to brace his legs against the frame when the horses came to a jangling halt. The men outside dismounted as Jake began to pry the first board loose. With the noise from the splintering wood and squealing nails, she almost missed the leader barking out an order for his men to stand back.

"Jake," she cried. "Wait."

He turned his head, hanging from the doorframe like a gangly spider.

"I recognize that voice." Unless her mind was playing tricks on her, that was Lyle out there. She could barely contain the joy that welled up. She darted forward but then pressed her hand to her side when pain shot through her.

When she caught her breath again, she shouted, "Down here. Lyle! Cam! I'm here. It's Abby. Can you hear me?"

Jake dropped lightly to his feet. She caught his arm when he tried to retreat into the corner. A thud sounded from above as someone hit the door and then Lyle's voice echoed down. "Abby? Is that you? Thank you, Jesus." Then louder, "Cam, get the lock picks, we found her."

She cupped a shaking hand to her mouth. "There are three men inside the house. They'll have the key. You need to hold those men until I can explain what's happened. But don't hurt them… Don't kill them anyway."

"Tyler and Henry are inside talking to them. They say they're scientists from Hill. Do you know…well, hell, of course you know what happened there. Why are you locked in the root cellar?"

"I'll explain it all when you get me out. Just don't let those men out of your sight."

"Not going anywhere, sweetheart." He lifted his hand from the door. By the way the shadows passed between the narrow cracks, he was walking away. For the briefest of moments, panic locked her chest but she fought free of it. They wouldn't leave her behind.

And the next time she faced Welks, she'd be holding a gun.

A moment later someone rapped their knuckles against the wood and Cam spoke. "Lyle's taking care of it. The doctors clammed up as soon as they learned we were looking for you and I can't find the damned key. So let's see what I can do to get you out of here."

She turned to Jake and her smile faded when she saw the expression on his face. Or rather, the terrifying and complete lack of expression on his face.

"You can't hurt them," she whispered. "They're my friends and I'll make sure they don't touch you."

He didn't say anything, just nodded and turned his attention back to the door.

It seemed like forever—Jake staring at the door, her fidgeting and glancing nervously at him every few minutes. Cam fumbled at the lock and Abby tried to make up her mind on whether to warn him that there was a Reaper down here with her.

No. When the door opened and they saw that she was okay, then she'd attempt to explain the complicated truth. They'd see the proof of his goodwill when they saw her alive, well and whole. Maybe if she had Jake standing beside her…

Cam swore, long and colorfully. He banged on the door a few times with his fist, called down an apology and set back to work, muttering under his breath. A few minutes later, Lyle returned.

"You're still not done?"

"Fuck off, Lyle. I've got it. These tools are bent to hell."

"See, right there's your problem. Let me—"

"I know what I'm doing."

They could argue this until sunrise. Abby cupped her hands to her mouth and yelled, "Shoot it."

Lyle bent to the crack in the door. "There's enough room for you to take cover?"

She glanced at Jake who tipped his head toward the corner of the room and nodded.

"Do it."

"Stand aside then and cover your ears."

Jake snagged her shirt sleeve and pulled her in tight. Turning, he pressed her back to the wall and covered her with his body.

"Are you clear?"

She wrapped her arms around Jake's waist. "All clear."

The heavy kick of gunfire rendered her momentarily deaf. It was a familiar, almost reassuring, sensation. Jake's arm curved around her head as he pressed her face to his chest, protecting her from the shards of wood that rained down upon them. Cam fired twice before the lock fell with a thunk to the cellar floor, leaving behind a good-size hole in the door.

Jake's thigh brushed against hers as he started to withdraw but her hands lingered on his back. It was over. This whole nightmare. Cap would take it from here and he would know what to do. She looked up to find Jake staring down at her. His expression didn't give much away but there was a weight to his gaze that unnerved her. His fingers curved around her neck and the gentle touch stole all of her attention. "Whatever happens—"

Cam grunted when his feet hit the ground. "Who the hell is this?"

Jake spun, placing his back to her and facing Cam.

When the hard shove she gave to his shoulder didn't move him out of her way, she yelled to Cam. "It's fine. He's a friend. Jake. Out of my way."

Grudgingly, Jake let her out but caught her hand when she tried to step forward.

Not sparing her a glance, Cam settled his hand on his gun. Some people would be comforted by the fact that he hadn't drawn his weapon yet, but she knew exactly how fast he could fire. She slid neatly in front of Jake, ignoring the low growl rumbling in his chest. He'd said something about males triggering the aggressive side of the Reaper. Clearly, she'd underestimated the effect.

Cam's gaze flicked briefly to her. "Go on, Abby, you first. Tyler will pull you up." He raised his voice. "You ready, Tyler?"

"Yup." She could see the top of Tyler's red head and his long arm dangling down.

Abby shook her head. "I'm safe from him, but you're...not. You go first."

Cam hesitated, fingers caressing the butt of his pistol, weighing her determination.

"I've been down here with him for a long time and he hasn't hurt me."

Finally, Cam nodded and turned. Ignoring Tyler's extended hand, he jumped, grabbed the edge and hauled himself up. There would be more than one gun aimed at Jake's head when he climbed out of here.

Abby blew out her pent breath and turned to Jake. "Best behavior, all right?"

The muscles in her neck and shoulders tightened when he dropped his gaze. This wasn't her Jake. His eyes nearly glowed in the dim light and his expression was so rigid she barely recognized him.

"Go." The word passed his stiff lips in a whisper.

It took all her courage to turn her back on him. She could feel the weight of his gaze between her shoulder blades. The collar was spent and the Reaper was no longer asleep. But Jake was in there too, and he wasn't going to let her get hurt. She trusted Jake. He was a Reaper and she trusted him anyway.

Cam pulled her up and carried her several feet away from the opening before setting her on her feet. Immediately, he demanded, "What's wrong with him? Do we let him up or reinforce the door? He looks fresh bit."

She winced, stomach sinking. Jake wasn't going to be able to pass for human, not around Rangers. Not after the stress of being tortured. She felt sick because she couldn't put her family in danger. And she was pretty sure she knew how Cam would react to the truth. But she owed it to him anyway.

"He's infected, but—"

Cam shoved her behind him. She didn't even see him draw his gun but it was in his hand, aimed at Jake, who was already halfway out of the cellar. She grabbed Cam's elbow as he pulled the trigger, forcing the shot wide. Cam swore and knocked her aside. He called for Tyler, who raised his shotgun as she fell.

She hit the ground hard. Before she could rise to her hands and knees, a heavy weight fell on top of her, knocking the breath out of her and blocking her vision. She was flat on her stomach, spitting out dust. Grit dug into her palms when she tried to push herself upright but the weight on her back pinned her down. She recognized that weight, that warmth, the smell wrapped around her like a homecoming.

How had he moved so damned fast?

"Jake," she whispered frantically. "Get off me. They'll kill you."

His arms tightened and his body jerked as they *shot* him. Not the shotgun, they were probably afraid the shot would pass through Jake's body and hit her. Judging by the way Jake shifted, they'd hit his leg, probably the back of his knee. At this range, Cam would make sure it hurt.

"Cam," she hollered. "If you shoot him again, I will shoot you back, so help me God. You don't understand what's happening here and until you do, I'm in charge. Now back the fuck up."

She heard the shuffle of footsteps, Jake's breath in her ear and a door slamming closed. A moment later, Lyle snarled, "What happened?"

"She wants us to *not* kill the Reaper who's trying to maul her," Cam answered.

Lyle drew back the hammer on his gun. She'd heard the sound so often she recognized it instantly.

"But he's not mauling her." Lyle's voice dropped to a whisper. "Abby?"

"He can hear you and yes, I'm alive. Now put your weapons away and back up."

"Don't think that's such a good idea, sweetheart," Lyle said calmly. "You're not looking at his face."

"Then why hasn't he hurt me? I've been locked in a

cellar with him for days. He's been with me since New Providence."

A profound silence met that announcement.

"Go on," Lyle urged softly. "We're listening."

She dropped her forehead to the dirt. "Holster your weapons and go back into the house." When she didn't hear anybody moving, she yelled, "Now."

They didn't go quickly or willingly, but eventually they did go. The sound of their retreating footsteps came as welcome music to her ears, which was ironic considering how hard she'd been praying for rescue. Oh, and the fact that she was currently pinned beneath a Reaper. As little sense as her life had made before she left for Fort Hill, it seemed nostalgically straightforward compared to now.

She didn't try to move until Jake's breathing slowed down and some of the tension left the arms caging her. All the while she spoke to him, soothing nothings you'd say to a scared child. Because that's what he was—angry, yes, and on the brink of a violent rampage, but he was scared too. For her sake.

Was she really going to do this? Put her family in danger by bringing them a live Reaper? As much as she'd like to believe otherwise, Jake *was* a Reaper. And he wasn't tame.

"You have to let me up," she told him as calmly as she was able. "They're my friends and I have to go talk to them."

His arm flexed around her rib cage and nearly cut off her air supply. "Jake, you need to fight this. I know you can do it. This is Abby. You know who I am, right? Abby."

A rumble passed from his chest into her back and she felt his mouth on the side of her neck, his teeth scraping lightly over her skin. Back and forth, his tongue occasionally darting out like a snake's to taste her.

"Jake." She swallowed back tears. "Please."

It didn't happen right away. She lay as still as she was able while a six-foot-something Reaper gnawed delicately on her neck, his erection poking into her spine and his blood soaking through her pant leg. Two minutes or ten, she couldn't tell, but eventually he stopped. Eventually, his arms loosened and he lifted some of his weight from her.

"Abby?"

He sounded so bewildered it tore at her heart. Drawing in a jagged breath, she said, "Okay…it's okay. You're all right."

"I've been shot."

"You jumped on top of me. The only reason you don't have a bullet in your spine is because they couldn't get a good angle without hurting me too."

He lowered his head, touching his forehead to her shoulder. "It snapped too quickly for me to control it. These men…they may be your friends, but they're strangers to me. I saw a danger to you."

"I'm not hurt."

He inhaled, a quick shallow sniff like a dog scenting out a cat.

"You are."

"No." Then she remembered the wound in her side

and panic welled in a bitter black wave. She fought through it. Her losing control certainly wouldn't calm him down. It might very well enrage him beyond his ability to contain himself. "Wait."

He flipped her onto her back and she caught a glimpse of the black scowl on his face before he lowered his head. He pressed his nose between her breasts and inhaled more deeply. She shoved his head away…or tried to. He only moved lower, tugging her shirt loose and yanking it aside before she could grab it.

"Christ. They cut you."

His hands trembled as he brushed his fingertips in a feathery sweep across her abdomen. She dropped her head back to the ground, all of the fight draining out of her. Who was she protecting anyway?

"Welks wanted my reproductive organs, but Karlson convinced him that the risk of death was too high and they should wait until they were sure they were done with me…but not before he made the first cut. They only took a flesh sample and then stitched me up again."

"They wouldn't have stopped there."

Karlson had also convinced Welks that they couldn't afford to squander an opportunity to discover if a female Ranger was capable of carrying a Reaper-spawned child. She'd been so afraid that while she was unconscious… But Jake had been unconscious too. He didn't need to know about the doctor's plans now. It didn't matter. It hadn't happened.

She placed her palm against the side of Jake's face to draw his gaze up. "We're safe now. I'm safe and I'll do my damndest to make sure you're safe too."

"I couldn't protect you."

She didn't know if he meant that as a warning or apology. "I know. We made it anyway."

He sunk his teeth into the meaty pad of his thumb and cradled her head when she jerked. She'd heard Rangers talk about Reaper blood and the healing power in it. Whispers around the campfires. Dark stories for dark nights. She didn't know anyone who'd done it. She tried to turn her head when Jake pressed the bleeding wound to her mouth.

"It will heal you."

She couldn't open her mouth to argue but she glared murder at him. His gaze softened but his hold didn't. "A little bit, Abby. Do this and I let you up."

The whimper that escaped her throat only made him tighten his grip. "Please," he said softly. "If not for your sake then do it for mine. I'm not going to be able to let anyone near you knowing you're injured."

He was serious, she could see it in his eyes. She'd worn that same expression a time or two herself when she'd been stuck in medical working on a stubborn patient. She didn't want to take his blood. It went against everything she stood for. It would make her no better than a Reaper, a flesh eater like him. Jake's brown eyes pleaded with her, but it was the sound of the door opening that convinced her to open her mouth. Lyle had decided her time was up. If Jake couldn't convince him that he was stable, Lyle would kill him, she knew it. Jake pushed his hand against her teeth.

"One bite. It's faster and more potent than the blood alone."

Closing her eyes, she bit him and as soon as her teeth sank into his flesh, Jake pulled his hand back in a swift jerk that left a chunk of meat caught in her mouth. What terrified her most was that it wasn't as repulsive as it should be. Like sinking her teeth into raw steak. She gagged and he gave her a warning look even as Lyle called out.

"Abby?"

She chewed just until she thought she could choke it down. But when she tried to swallow, she actually did start to choke. Jake rubbed her throat and that seemed to help a bit. She managed another swallow anyway and wiped at her mouth.

"I'm fine, Lyle. We're coming. Give him another minute."

Lyle hesitated, but then the door closed again and she closed her eyes. Jake sat up and pulled her half across his lap. He untucked his shirttail and gently wiped her face. "I'm sorry."

"You are not," she growled. "Don't start lying to me now."

"I'm sorry I *had* to do it then."

She stared at him. As soon as she got up and talked to Lyle, everything was going to change. It already had. A tear leaked out of the corner of her eye and trailed into her hairline. She scratched at it and sat up. Already her side felt better. Her stomach very definitely did not.

"You have to let me go. I need to talk to them and try to explain all this," she told Jake. "Can I leave you out here alone?"

He stood, helping her up. When she was steady on her feet, he let her go.

"Go," he said. "Talk to your friends. I still recommend that we keep the scientists here."

"That's not going to happen."

His mouth twisted. "Warn them anyway."

She walked toward the house calling for Lyle, feeling the weight of Jake's gaze on her back with every step.

THEY WEREN'T LISTENING to anything Abby said, even though she was largely sticking to the truth. It took her an hour to convince them that Jake wasn't the cause of her injuries. The scientists had apparently told Lyle that they'd escaped from Fort Hill, rescuing her when she intended to stay and fight.

"I've seen it before," Dr. Welks said sadly. "It's because the Reapers appear to be human. Women particularly are prone to confusion, especially if they've survived rape. Humanizing the Reaper, convincing themselves it was something they desired…preserves the mind."

Abby bit back a curse and raised her eyes to the heavens until Welks finished speaking. When he was done, she fixed Lyle with a challenging glare. "Have you ever known me to be confused about how dangerous a Reaper is, Lyle?"

"No." He didn't look particularly happy with the admission and there was a question in his eyes that he apparently was too much of a coward to ask.

"Then trust me to know my own mind." She pointed at the bandage on her stomach. "Jake didn't do this to me, they did. Jake didn't rape me. He never hurt me at all. If these men were looking out for my welfare then ask yourself why the hell they caged me in the cellar with a live Reaper?"

Lyle turned back to Welks and lifted his eyebrows. "Doctor?"

Welks waved his hand dismissively. "He was collared and of no danger to her. She became violent and irrational when we tried to separate them."

"That's a load of horseshit," she snapped and then swallowed back her rage. It wasn't going to do anyone any good if this devolved into a screaming match. Not to mention the fact that her throttling the doctor was unlikely to convince anyone of her sanity.

"Jake's a Reaper," she said, holding on to her temper with both hands. "He was willing to let them experiment on him because he wants a cure too. *He wants it*, Lyle, and he can communicate that. You talk to him and you'll see I'm telling you the truth. These scientists knew all about the sentient Reapers and they didn't tell us shit."

Welks raised a hand. "That was not our decision. Our superiors felt it imprudent and unnecessary to reveal that to you. It doesn't make a difference. They're still infected, irrational, violent creatures that can be driven into a frenzy—as we all just witnessed when this one attacked Abby in the yard. Your superiors only thought to spare you the moral conflict."

Lyle snorted. "Go on, Abby."

She wasn't about to tell him Jake's theory about Scrapers being behind the attacks. Not yet. Not until

Lyle had a chance to talk to Jake himself. Lyle was smart. He'd see what she saw in Jake. Jake wasn't irrational or mindlessly violent.

Jake was barely a Reaper at all.

"Talk to him, Lyle. Jake can explain the rest far better than I can."

JAKE WENT TO the water pump to clean off the blood and grit. The icy cold water helped him to regain a modicum of control. He shouldn't have forced Abby to take his blood, wouldn't have if he'd been in his right mind, but the rider was still at the edge of his consciousness, enraged that there were men who'd come to take Abby away from him. He hadn't known his protectiveness toward the woman would trigger it like that. On raids… well, on raids it was unlikely that a human woman would survive the attention of one Reaper let alone several, but it happened and he'd never seen anyone upset about sharing. The meat, yes, the sex, no. And he wasn't even fucking her.

He bowed his head and dumped the bucket of water over it. Shaking the excess from his hair, he watched the dry ground greedily absorb every drop. He left his pants on. Damp as they were, the cold would do him good. Feeling eyes track his every move, he walked to the pack he'd fetched from the barn to remove a dry shirt. When he heard the door to the house open, he knew even before he turned around that it was Abby.

Strange how attuned he was to her—to her location, her safety, to her mood. She wasn't happy now. He pulled on the shirt and buttoned it as she crossed the yard. She would be considerably less happy if he was forced to kill her friends, but he'd do it if he had to. For a cure, he'd do anything. He couldn't afford to consider her happiness. Couldn't afford to consider his own.

She came to a stop directly before him and absently swiped the loose hair from her flushed cheeks. "Our patrol is camped just outside of Fort Hill," she said without preamble. "If we leave now, we'll meet up with them before nightfall."

"Nothing has changed, Abby. Those scientists are at risk as soon as anyone knows they've survived."

"They don't seem to share your concern on that front. They know we want the cure and they're willing to work with us on that but they think that you want revenge."

"I do." For what they'd done to Abby, he would kill Welks, Karlson and Hamilton without a twinge of remorse.

Abby's eyes narrowed and she set her slender hands on her hips. "We need them."

"For now, yes. What about your Rangers?"

She knew what he was asking. Was there a shotgun pointed at his head even now? She'd stopped six feet away from him. Not far enough away to stop him from killing her before a bullet took him out. He wondered if she knew that or if she was only keeping her distance to reassure the men watching through the windows. Even as the thought crossed his mind, she took a step closer. Behind her, one of the Rangers cursed softly and started walking in their direction.

She touched his chest and lowered her voice. "I won't let them hurt you."

It was the same promise he'd made to her only a few days ago. If she realized the irony in it, he saw no sign of it on her face. She likely was as earnest now as he'd been then—and equally as incapable of keeping her promise. He wondered if it was kinder to let her cling to the belief that her will could override two centuries of fear or if he should attempt to disabuse her of the notion.

"The way they see you…they're wrong." Her solemn gray eyes filled with concern and determination. There was a small crease between her brows he ached to smooth away. "*I* was wrong. You might be a Reaper but you're not a monster. Their minds will change too once they come to know you better."

He blew out a huff of laughter. "You're not going to be able to change their minds, sweetheart. They see me just fine."

"You could have killed me at any time on this trip."

"I planned to sacrifice you for a cure." And if he'd become increasingly uncomfortable with that plan somewhere along the way, well…he'd still brought her here, hadn't he? He didn't want her friendship or her trust. He sure as hell didn't deserve it and had absolutely no intention of trying to live up to her idealized view of his plans. He wanted a cure. That was the plain and simple truth. It was what he had to focus on now.

"You could have killed me down there, escaped and found another Ranger. You and I both know that. *Hamilton* knew it. That's why he used me against you."

"I am a monster," Jake said. "A Reaper. Don't you

forget it, Abby. If my control snaps, you need to be ready to pull that trigger."

He tipped her chin up. This was important for her to understand. Her eyes were wide and, despite all that they'd seen, very innocent. He didn't understand the how or why of it but he could sense her interest in him as a man, that sweet pure scent of arousal, the flush that came to her cheeks whenever he met her gaze directly. He'd wanted her to have confidence in his control so she'd take the risk of working with him, and he'd done too damn good a job of convincing her that he was safe. She saw him as a human man she wanted to fuck.

He sure as hell didn't have *that* kind of control.

Denial formed on her lips but instead of speaking, she shook her head and turned away to glare at the approaching Ranger.

She wasn't for him, as much as he might wish it could be otherwise. Jake shifted his attention away from Abby to face a man who looked like he'd just as soon kill him as say hello. This man had no doubts whatsoever about who and what he was dealing with.

Lyle put his hand on Abby's shoulder and yanked her back. "You said you weren't going to get too close."

Jake rode out the surge of possessive rage that filled him at the sight of the Ranger's hand resting on Abby's shoulder. It took every ounce of his already strained self-control to keep his instincts in check. The Ranger noted the look and his fingers flexed.

Abby jerked free. "Stop testing him, Lyle. None of us has the patience for it and it's not necessary."

Rather than argue the point, Lyle fixed Jake with a cold sharp stare. "Friend."

For Abby's sake, Jake kept his voice level. "Friend is a little presumptuous, don't you think?"

Lyle's eyes widened slightly and Jake realized that despite Abby's reassurances, until that moment, Lyle had doubted that Jake even had the capacity for speech. He recovered quickly. "Abby says you saved her life. If that's true, then it makes you a friend."

"I brought her here for the cure they promised me and I intend to have it."

Icy gray eyes narrowed and Lyle's hand drifted closer to his gun, but his heartbeat remained calm and steady. He wasn't going to draw. Jake took a step closer. "I'm coming with you. I didn't invest this much time and effort into chasing a cure to walk away now."

Lyle's jaw tightened and he jerked his head toward the house. "They say someone newly bitten will work better."

Jake laughed. "They would, wouldn't they? A youngling is far easier to control than I am. Easier to kill, too, if you still have a shred of conscience left like Karlson does. I'm seeing this through. You're not taking the doctors and leaving me behind. They'd be dead if not for me. Abby would be dead. The way I see it, you owe me."

"I don't owe you shit," Lyle said coldly, grunting when Abby elbowed him in the ribs.

Lyle's heartbeat picked up a bit and he shifted, opening up a sight line from the house. He was positioned so that he'd be able to shove Abby down if necessary and she must have seen the same thing because she stepped forward, directly in front of Jake. Smart girl… or idiot, depending on how you looked at it. She met Jake's scowl with one of her own. "Stop it."

"What?"

But she ignored the question and turned on Lyle. "You stop too. He's coming with us."

"We don't need him."

"We've never come across a sentient Reaper and I want the captain to see what it is we're dealing with. For our sake, we need to get to the bottom of what happened at Fort Hill. They killed at least fifty Rangers, and they had help. We can't afford to shoot him, not when he has information we need and he's willing to help."

His willingness to help them was not precisely the truth, but Jake didn't think that now was the time to interrupt. Abby had taken charge of the situation and Lyle seemed content—for now—to follow her lead.

The curtain shifted in the broken window and Abby shouted, "Henry, you shoot him and I shoot you, is that clear?"

There was no answer, but the ratty old curtain moved again and that seemed to satisfy her. She shot Lyle a look and some silent communication passed between the pair that made the Reaper inside Jake rattle at the bars of his cage.

Abby was his.

Except she wasn't. She regarded these men as her family. He was the monster who'd stolen her away and he had no claim to keep her. The sooner he came to accept that, the better.

Not for you.

Lyle wasn't happy, that much was clear. Suspicion and disgust were writ plain in the stark lines of his lean face. But he returned his attention to Jake. "Can you ride?"

"You'll need my horse to carry them." Jake lifted his chin to indicate the doctors. "I can keep up on foot."

Lyle rubbed at his jaw. "We can't have you running, do you understand me? I can't take the chance that you'll have a change of heart."

"You're not tying me up."

"They say they have extra cartridges for that thing around your neck," Lyle said, watching his reaction carefully.

"No," Abby said quietly but with a finality that made Lyle turn and stare.

"What the hell do you want me to do, Abby? Shoot him in the head to disable him long enough? What if he gets hungry while we're sleeping and decides he wants a snack?" His gaze flicked up to Jake's. "No offense."

"None taken."

"Offense taken," Abby grit out. "He's not going to eat anybody."

Lyle considered her a little too long. She wasn't doing herself any favors by siding with a Reaper. And in the end, her support wouldn't help. The other Rangers would simply stop listening to her opinion. Jake could sense Lyle's distrust, could scent it in his sweat, see it in his eyes and the tension in his stance. The only reason the Rangers hadn't attacked him yet was because their leader trusted Abby. Lyle seemed to realize that

Jake was trying to protect her, and he didn't trust the scientists any more than Jake did.

"Bring the cartridges," Jake said quietly, breaking their stalemate. "I'll load them before we go into your camp, but I'll need my strength for the trip."

Lyle nodded his acceptance. "When will you be ready to leave?"

"I'm ready now."

"And you, Abby?"

She was still fuming and Jake didn't meet her gaze when she looked his way. Best to break the unnatural bond that had formed between them now, before she got hurt and before he failed her again. Welks never would have gotten a jump on him in the first place if he hadn't been distracted by Abby's presence. Not that he blamed her exactly, but she was a weakness he couldn't afford. And, in the end, he had no future to offer her.

"Let's go." She stalked toward the barn. Lyle gave him one final hard look then turned to follow.

JAKE LEANED AGAINST a post waiting for them to ready the horses. The Rangers eyed him warily, hands never straying very far from their guns, and he ignored them. Well, he visibly ignored them. He couldn't help but hear their chatter, much of it about him.

Cam, the slender blond man who'd picked the cellar lock, wanted very badly to empty a round into Jake's skull and then tie him to a horse. It wouldn't kill him, which the Ranger seemed to realize, but brain matter didn't heal as completely as flesh. Despite the agreement he'd made with Lyle, Jake wasn't about to let that happen.

"I don't trust him either," Lyle said. "But, as far as I can tell, Abby was telling the truth about his control. I've never seen anything like it. He thinks and speaks just like a man. Can you—"

"Fuck that, Lyle. I don't care if he can sing opera and pilot an airship. He's a Reaper. It's not fucking safe."

"You talk to him then. You can see the Reaper in his eyes, but if you weren't looking for it you'd never know what he is."

"So he's wearing a mask. It don't change what he is."

A pause. "I'll watch him. Tyler and Henry have the scientists. Your job is Abby."

Tension crept into Jake's muscles no matter how hard he willed otherwise. Abby was his.

Maybe I should just let them shoot me in the head.

The jangle of harness echoed across the yard and the breeze carried her scent. She'd found soap and had washed away all the stale sweat and blood, had found a new shirt. He couldn't help but tilt his head to follow her scent. When he realized what he was doing, he forced his focus to return to the Rangers.

"...keep her away from him. I want to judge for myself how dangerous he is. And who's telling the truth here. We need to know what he's capable of."

"He's capable of hearing you now," Abby said, her voice sharp with exasperation.

Jake smiled but didn't bother to look up. He could, however, feel the combined weight of their stares settling on his shoulders. He should get used to the feeling. They'd be watching him closely from here on in.

After a moment, Cam swore under his breath and then Lyle shouted, "Come on out, Doctors. We're ready to go."

Chapter Seventeen

ABBY DIDN'T SEE much of Jake on the ride back to Fort Hill, which was fine. She needed the distance from him to regain her balance. It was strange having Cam riding beside her, darting worried looks her way when he thought she wasn't looking. Strange to have Lyle making all the hard decisions, like whether to send anyone after the Reapers whose fresh tracks they'd found heading south or to continue toward the fort. They kept going—they had neither the men nor the time to go hunting. Jake offered to kill the Reapers and catch up. Abby watched Lyle consider that for several minutes before slowly shaking his head no.

Jake shrugged as if it didn't matter to him either way. His gaze briefly met Abby's and then he walked away.

When she looked at Lyle, he said, "The closest town in that direction is Hardin. We sent a messenger to raise the alarm before we left Hill. Hopefully, they'll heed it."

"And if they don't?"

"Right now getting these men to safety and back to work is my priority." He frowned at Jake's back. "But, no, I don't like it either."

Lyle fell silent again and Cam went back to watching her. Neither of them asked exactly what the scientists had done to her, neither of them asked about Jake.

Fine. She'd save the whole story for Cap. It was fine that Jake was avoiding her too. He'd probably sensed before she did how uncomfortable the Rangers were whenever she tried to speak with him. They thought... Hell, she didn't know what they thought. She only knew that every time she supported Jake, they got angry and took that anger out on him. So she kept her mouth shut.

It took them two days to reach Fort Hill. The smell of charred wood still clung to the place but the captain—thank God—hadn't set up camp in the ruins. Instead, they were camped about two miles south, along the high bank of the Cedar River. When she woke that morning, Jake's eyes were glazed with pain and he was absently scratching at the collar. Apparently, Lyle had decided it was time to reload it with poison. She glared at him and he turned away without comment, ordering Henry to tie Jake's hands to the saddle horn.

Cam, already mounted, leaned down to tap her on the shoulder. "It's for show, Abby. You might trust him, but no one else will. It's for his protection as much as ours. I've never seen you doubt Lyle's judgment before."

She snorted and swung up onto Harvey's back. "Never?"

Cam ran a hand through his hair and reseated his hat. "Not like this." He paused, but she waited for him to spit out whatever had gotten stuck in his craw. "He's a *Reaper*. You shouldn't be picking him over us."

"This isn't about picking anybody. It's about doing what's right and making sure we get a cure."

He shook his head. "It's not about the cure for you. If it was, you would offer up that Reaper's heart as a sacrifice to those doctors, assholes or not. Right now, you'd rather rip out Welks's heart. And don't even try to tell me different. Why do you care what happens to him?"

"He saved my life."

Cam gave her a hard look and a blush crept up her face. "He's not all bad."

"You said he's been alive for almost two hundred years. How many people do you think he's killed all that time? How many has he fed on? Do you remember those babies we found last month?"

What was left of them he meant. Once he put that image in her brain, he leaned closer, adjusting his hold on the reins. "I don't want to see you get hurt."

"He won't hurt me."

Cam gave her a disgusted look and urged his horse forward. She watched him move up the line. No one took his place. It was as if she was tainted now. She rode alone the rest of the way into camp. Lyle ordered Cam to take Jake and then disappeared into Cap's tent. Doc emerged a moment later and stood waiting for her as she handed off Harvey to a waiting stable boy.

"I don't need medical care."

"That's good to hear," Doc said, voice rough but soothing. "I'm to make sure you're fit and then you'll have your chance to report. Are you okay?"

Cam stood outside the tent, legs splayed and arms crossed, watching her go. He cocked one eyebrow when he saw her looking over her shoulder and she swallowed a snarl of frustration.

"I will be, Doc. I will be."

Doc was quick but thorough in his examination. He

tsked over the neat and nearly healed scar on her belly. "That's too clean to have been a knife wound."

"Scalpel," she said curtly.

"One of the doctors did this?" He scowled. "Were you injured?"

"Not until they cut into me, no."

His lip curled a bit and his eyes narrowed, but he nodded. She dropped her head back onto the table and a moment later, he patted her shoulder.

"All done." He helped her sit up and handed her a clean shirt from his own trunk.

"There's a bath waiting for you behind the screen, and I set up the extra cot. You're officially under observation." When she opened her mouth to protest, he held up his hand. "Not my call. You need a good night's sleep. I'll let Cap know my professional opinion and you can track him down tomorrow. You know he's not one to make snap decisions. He'll interview everyone else before he gets around to you."

"I need to talk to him," she muttered, only slightly mollified by Doc's reasonable explanation. "I want this done and over with, Doc."

His expression softened. "I know. Are you hungry?"

She shook her head and he turned to leave, pausing as he reached for the flap. "Abby?"

"Yeah?"

"I'm glad you made it back."

SHE BATHED QUICKLY and dressed in freshly laundered clothes. Cursing the tangles in her hair, she braided it wet and went to track down Cap. She smiled when she saw Mason walking toward her. She glanced down at his arm and then quickly away. She couldn't ask about his injury. Among Rangers, it was considered very rude to comment on a restoration. Instead, she hugged him tightly—which he endured—and told him how happy she was to see him alive.

He patted her back once and she stepped away. "We thought you were dead."

There was an odd note to his voice that sharpened her attention on him, but the brim of his hat shielded his face from view. "Tough to kill me, Mason."

"That's what Lyle said. That a Reaper would take one bite of your rangy ass and spit you back out."

Her brows lifted. "Did he now?"

Mason seemed to belatedly realize that he'd insulted her and had the good grace to flush. "He meant it to be reassuring."

"I'm sure." She'd known Lyle a long time. Of course, he'd spare a moment for Mason. And by the way the boy said Lyle's name, it seemed he'd found a new hero. She couldn't regret that.

Mason shifted uncomfortably. "They haven't killed the Reaper yet. I was hoping that, if you don't want to pull the trigger, maybe you'd let me do it."

"I don't want to shoot him," she said and Mason looked at her sharply. "He didn't hurt me. Do you know where they're keeping him?"

Mason stared at her as if she'd sprouted horns. "Didn't hurt you?"

His incredulous tone made her uneasy and she shook her head. "He did not."

"He—" Mason swore under his breath. "Ben said you wouldn't let him put a bullet in his head. I thought that was only because you meant to do it yourself."

"He's sentient. He thinks like a man, can talk like one. He controls the Reaper inside him. We can't pass up an opportunity to study him. He wants a cure just as badly as we do. He saved those scientists."

"Yeah," Mason scoffed. "I've heard exactly about how he *saved* them. Locked them in a hole for two weeks is what he did."

"He got them away from that." She pointed at Fort Hill and even though you couldn't see it from where they were standing, Mason knew exactly where she was aiming. The doctors must have been very *chatty* for the whole camp to have their side of the story already. "Did you ever think that maybe those scientists don't have our best interests at heart?"

She knew it was a mistake as soon as the words left her mouth, but she was tired and frankly she hadn't expected an attack from this direction. Not from Mason. His lip curled just a bit as he answered her. "No, Abby, I've never thought the scientists working to find a cure weren't on our side. Do you hear yourself?"

Getting a grip on her temper, she managed not to answer that. She remembered Cam's advice and simply said, "Things aren't always the way they seem on the surface, you remember that, Mason. A lot of questions need to be answered before anybody puts a bullet in anyone's head. Where are they keeping him?"

"Near the supplies." She didn't miss his grimace. Well, fuck him. She'd made a promise to Jake that he'd be safe here and she would do everything in her power to see it through. It just...might be more of an uphill battle than she'd anticipated. The tents were struck all neatly in a row and she walked straight down the aisle. Half the patrol was out hunting the Reapers too stupid to have left the area, but the rest of the men didn't bother to hide their interest in where she was going. No one followed.

She saw Dr. Welks chatting with Doc outside a large tent erected beside the captain's. They sat in folding camp chairs with a small circular table between them. Dr. Welks lifted his tin cup in salute when she scowled.

When she reached the edge of camp, she cast around trying to figure out where they'd put Jake. She didn't see a tent. What—?

Her stomach dropped to her toes when she saw him. There was no tent, no shelter at all. They'd tied Jake to a fucking tree with one of the short iron chains they used to secure the wagons. She started walking again, her feet kicking up clouds of dust on the trampled earth. He looked like he was sleeping. Or hurt.

Lyle intercepted her as she approached. When she turned her shoulder to brush past him, he caught her arm. "Whoa, there."

Jake's back was braced to the tree. The collar around his neck glinted in the light from the setting sun. His knees were drawn up and his head hung nearly to his chest.

"What did you do to him?"

"Abby—"

She struggled, but Lyle tightened his grip and pulled

her away. She thought about digging in her heels, but there was no point. She couldn't take on the whole camp. Suddenly she understood the flat expression on Jake's face when she'd promised to protect him. He'd known all along. He'd known and he'd come anyway.

Lyle dragged her behind a half-emptied load of crates and released her when she struggled.

"Tell me."

"He's not hurt," Lyle said. "You had weeks to get used to the idea of him, give everyone else a few days. They'll see—"

"They'll see an animal if you keep him chained like one."

He reached out to touch her shoulder and she flinched away from him. "Is that how it is?" His expression hardened and his hand fell. "You know I wouldn't hurt you."

"I expected better from you, Lyle. I am sorely disappointed."

"I'm keeping you safe, whether you like it or not. Protecting all our interests. No matter who he is to you." His eyes darkened. "Those scientists say they can make a cure. If you put this…man ahead of that—shit, if you even put yourself ahead of that—I will be sorely disappointed in *you*."

"I want the cure," she said, dropping her gaze. On that point at least he was right.

"Then act like it."

"I want to talk to him."

"No."

Her head snapped up. "No?"

"Captain's orders. We keep him isolated until Cap decides what we're going to do with him."

Abby shook her head and her mouth firmed. "I'll talk to Cap first, then."

"He rode out, won't be back until well after nightfall. And that's only if he doesn't decide to camp elsewhere for the night."

She wanted to take out her frustration on the big man blocking her way, but that wouldn't be fair. Lyle was following orders and misguided as he was, he was only trying to do what was right. "Who's guarding him?"

The corner of Lyle's mouth tucked up in a half-hearted smile. "You planning on breaking him out?"

"I want to know that no one is going to do anything stupid." Like try to kill the Reaper chained like a dog at the edge of a camp within sight of the smoldering remains of Fort Hill.

"Me and Cam for now. Will and Carson are on for morning."

"Will—"

Lyle crossed his arms and frowned. "Is young but as levelheaded as they come. Carson will keep him in line."

Okay. Okay, then, it wasn't quite as bad as she thought, but still… *They'd chained him.* Every instinct urged her to go to Jake now, to touch him and hear him say in that rusted hinge voice of his that he was fine and that everything would turn out for the best. But that was a fantasy, because Jake had never…would never say such a thing. And maybe, just maybe, Lyle was right.

Maybe she needed to step back for a few hours to get her head on straight.

His hand settled on her shoulder again and this time she lifted her face to meet his sympathetic gaze. "Aw, come here." He tugged her into his arms, enveloping her in that smoky Lyle scent that she'd come to associate with home. He rested his chin on top of her head. "A few days and we'll have it straightened out. I'll keep your friend alive until then." His arms tightened. "He *is* a friend, right?"

"He saved my life more than once." She shrugged one shoulder. "And maybe that was because he needed a Ranger, but I still don't want to see him dead."

"He's a Reaper, Abby," Lyle said. "He'd probably be damn hard to kill anyway. At least not without raising a racket. Get something to eat. Talk to people and let them see you keeping your shit together. They trust those doctors who've been walking around shaking their heads in pity every time your name comes up. This isn't a fight you're going to be able to win with your guns drawn."

She laughed and pulled away. "That's the only kind of fight I know, Lyle."

"I know it." He patted her shoulder and nudged her back in the direction of camp. "Lord help us all."

SHE TOOK LYLE'S advice to heart and asked Doc to clear her so she didn't have to sleep in the medical tent that night.

"I'm not sick," she told him. "And I don't want anyone to think I am."

Doc scratched at his jaw. “I see. I talked to Dr. Welks this afternoon.”

“I saw that,” she said sourly.

“When you were supposed to be here resting under observation, yes.”

She lifted her chin. “You observed me, didn’t you?”

His mouth twitched. “Welks is a piece of work. Slick as a whore’s—” She gave him a sharp look and he snorted. “He’s a snake. But you’re right, some people will believe him based on his position alone. And he knows he’s untouchable, too, so long as he controls the cure. It makes my skin crawl knowing what he did to you. I’d hack him into little pieces and hand-feed him to your Reaper myself if I could get away with it.”

“Jake doesn’t eat people,” she said absently, hauling her tent out from the pile of her supplies one of the boys had dumped into the corner that afternoon. “And he’s not *my* Reaper.”

Doc raised his brows but didn’t comment, just bent and lifted the bundle when she pressed her hand to her side. “Be careful of him.”

“Jake?”

“Yes, be careful of your Reaper too, but I was talking about Welks.”

She grabbed an extra blanket from the pile and stood. “I’m always careful.”

“Clearly. You’re a paragon of circumspection. All those marks on your body are proof of it.”

Lifting the flap for him to pass, she grinned. “I’m still here, aren’t I?”

“That you are.”

Doc helped her set up her small tent alongside the others. While they ate, a few of the men sat down to ask whether the rumors about a cure were true. Her answers drew in others and before she knew it, half the camp was gathered around.

For the most part, they were innocuous questions. They all assumed that her injuries had been caused by Jake and when she opened her mouth to place the blame where it belonged, Doc abruptly changed the subject. He was of the opinion that they needed to speak to Cap first. He was afraid someone might try to take a gun to Welks if they knew the doctor had cut into her and didn't want to risk losing their chance at a cure. It wasn't right though. Jake had never hurt her.

She *needed* to speak with Cap.

When the men started to talk about their captured Reaper, she handed her half-full mug of coffee to Doc and climbed wearily to her feet. Doc stood with her and pulled her aside after she'd said good-night to the men. "You look pale. You holding up? Cap will have my ass if I let you push yourself too hard."

"I'm tired," she said, though the queasy feeling in her stomach had nothing to do with injury or illness. "If you see the captain tonight, tell him I want to talk to him."

"I'll do that." He touched his fingers to his hat. "Good night, Abby. Sleep well."

She patted him on the shoulder before walking back to her tent. Once there, she huddled inside, in the dark, listening as the men's conversation returned to its normal cadence. Deep voices and youthful ones blended into a lullaby she used to find reassuring. When she found herself straining to catch the words, she rolled and pulled the blanket over her head. It was a long time before she managed to fall asleep.

SHE KNEW CAP had returned by the expressions on the faces she saw when she stepped from the tent the next morning. She had a vague memory of a patrol riding in last night. The tired grunt and groan of men's voices and the jangle of harness. She'd been too tired to move and Cap wouldn't have been in any mood to talk to her anyway. Deciding to skip breakfast, she headed straight for the command tent.

There was no one waiting outside the tent, or in the first room, but Doc's voice drifted out to her from Cap's personal space. She stepped forward to rap on the one of the wooden supports, but Cap's rough question brought her up short.

"Is there a possibility of a child?"

Her hand froze an inch from the wood as she waited for Doc's answer. "She says not and I suggest you take her at her word."

Cap blew out a heavy breath. "A sentient Reaper. Never thought I'd see the day."

"Do you think he's telling the truth?"

"Not all of it," Cap said gruffly, "but what he's said so far…about the Council and Welks's anonymous benefactor rings true to me. I've already told you my own suspicions on that front."

"So we assume he's telling the truth," Doc said. "But still, I don't know—"

Abby knocked to announce her presence before stepping into the room. Cap's hand went instinctively to his gun before he saw who it was and relaxed. The smile he gave her was slight but real.

"You ought not surprise a couple of old campaigners like that, Abigail."

"I heard you outside," she said, tilting her head toward the flap. "There's no possibility of a child."

Cap's expression didn't change, but his eyes softened. "So I've been told. No one's ever been captured by a Reaper and survived. I wanted to be sure there won't be any...complications."

"A Reaper baby. Is that even possible?"

"I don't know, but I'm pleased to hear that we won't have to find out." He bowed his head and ran a hand through his hair. "Not that that's the only reason I'm pleased."

She waved his apology aside. "I understand. He didn't do anything to hurt me."

Cap studied her silently for several moments. "I've heard that you risked your life to shield him when you were found."

Lyle. She wished she'd been present to hear exactly how he'd chosen to paint that particular picture. "I wanted proof...wanted you to see a sentient Reaper for yourself, and Jake hasn't told me nearly everything he knows."

"About Fort Hill?"

She swept her arm out. "About all of this. About Fort Hill and sentient Reapers. About those scientists and what else they've been hiding from us, about the Council and the Scrapers who think they can move us around like pawns on a chessboard. We *need* Jake. And I trust him a hell of a lot more than I trust those scientists. And if you trust me, then you'll keep him out of their hands."

Doc remained silent, but she could hear his fingers tapping on the wooden arm of the chair. A nervous tic of his that had always particularly annoyed her. Cap fixed her with a measuring look. "Cam and Lyle are concerned that you've lost perspective."

She swore and Cap's brows drew together. He disapproved of women who swore. He never swore in her presence, although she'd heard him curse up a storm when he didn't know she was within earshot.

She held his gaze, letting him see how perfectly fucking calm she was. "I wouldn't lie to you."

"No one has accused you of lying."

"You've spoken to Jake," she said, as he returned to his desk.

"I have. He is…a revelation, but he's still a Reaper."

"Is that why you won't let me speak to him? You have him chained at the edge of camp like a rabid dog while the men who planned to experiment on me without my consent are walking around like they own the place. It's not right. If not for Jake, those scientists would have died along with the possibility of a cure. I would have died."

She stood there trembling, fingers braced to the edge of his desk, trying to get a grip on her anger. It didn't seem to matter to anyone that she had every right to her rage. Everyone saw it as a sort of hysteria. She supposed she had Dr. Welks to thank for that too.

"What I see is that you've experienced a trauma that has left you exhausted and unlike your usual self. I see a Reaper who has, for his own purposes, kidnapped several scientists and one of my Rangers." When she opened her mouth to protest, Cap held up his hand. "He kidnapped you. That you were willing to go quietly so you could locate the scientists is admirable. Reckless, but admirable. It doesn't change the fact that he planned to use you as a test subject. You understand that, correct?"

She nodded tightly.

"If he refrained from harming you, I have to assume it was for that purpose alone. That the scientists planned to use you as well is…equally distressing. But right now, the cure is more important than any of that. I'm afraid that justice, for you at least, will have to wait." He folded his hands on the desk and regarded her levelly. "And for that I am deeply sorry."

She wasn't after justice. Well, after the cure was in their hands, she had a bone to pick with Drs. Welks and Karlson—but she intended to see to that herself. She was after something else altogether. "You stationed guards around Jake."

Cap nodded. "For his protection as well as our own."

"They barred me from speaking with him."

Something changed in his expression and she couldn't immediately identify it. His neck flushed a bit and he stared down at the table for a long moment before lifting his gaze. "That order was issued at his request."

At first, she just stared at him, uncomprehending. "What do you mean?"

"Jake said that your presence makes it difficult for him to control the Reaper. *He* asked that we keep you away. I'm not curtailing your freedom in any way, only his."

She swallowed. Cap was watching her curiously and it took everything she had not to let him see how much that hurt. She nodded tightly. "I see."

"Frankly, I didn't think you'd want to see him or I would have told you earlier."

"I wanted…" She'd wanted to see Jake, to speak with him, to touch him, to know that he was unhurt. She'd made him a promise she meant to keep. She wasn't scared when she was with him, even if he was Reaper. She knew that he'd never hurt her.

He had though, just not in any way she'd seen coming.

"I wanted to make sure that he hadn't been hurt," she said. "I don't trust the scientists."

"Nor do I," Cap said wearily. "Is that all?"

"Yes, that's all." What else was there to say? Jake was done with her and she was an idiot to be disappointed over that.

Leaving the captain's tent, she avoided the small group gathered around the campfire and walked toward the river, hoping the fresh air would clear her head. She walked upstream for about a mile until a mass of straggly bushes blocked her path. Sitting down on an overhang, she watched the water slip past beneath her feet. The river was sluggish here and brown, low because of the drought. She sat there for a long time, staring at the glossy rocks and swirling eddies, her eyes burning and chest tight. But she didn't cry. She'd promised herself after her first kill that she'd never shed another tear over a Reaper.

And that was another promise she meant to keep.

Chapter Eighteen

IT TOOK THEM nearly two weeks to travel to Fort Dougan. Not the closest fort, but it was home. They hid the scientists inside a sealed wagon normally used to transport Reapers. Abby thought that was marvelously ironic. When Lyle slammed the iron door shut on the good doctors, the justice in the sound kept her smiling for miles.

Jake rode like a man, his collar hidden beneath the turned up collar of his duster and an artfully placed bandana. That would not have been his doing. Someone—probably Cap—had decided it was better not to remind the men what Jake was. She took that as a good sign, even if Jake's hands were still bound and secured tightly to the saddle.

Two weeks had passed with the patrol and not once had Jake looked at her, let alone tried to speak to her. Now that they were home, she was restless and on edge. She wasn't sleeping well. Bags had taken up permanent residence under her eyes and she'd lost weight. As Doc had so crudely pointed out yesterday, there was no jiggle left anywhere on her.

She watched Frank in the ring putting a new horse through its paces. The mare was a beauty, with a coat so dark it appeared black until the sunlight hit just right and picked up the red. One white foot. Abby was thinking about claiming her to replace Marley. She rested her chin on her folded arms and sighed when she heard approaching footsteps. A moment later Lyle leaned his forearms on the fence next to her.

"I'd like for you to reconsider, Abby. Stay here for this round and rejoin the patrol once you're fully recovered."

"I'm recovered. Ask Doc, he cleared it. My injuries are completely healed. Did Cap put you up to this?"

"No. This is me worried about you. When we saw Fort Hill…" He turned his face away from her and after a moment, cleared his throat. "There was the fire, but we found signs of a fight in the ash with fresh blood. Part of a uniform. I knew it was yours by the stitching on the sleeve, you know the one?"

"I know the one." She'd sent him to the mercantile store with a list of supplies after a scuffle outside Tribulation and he'd brought her pink thread as a joke. She'd used it to mend the bullet hole in her shirt. "I'm sorry, Lyle, but that's about your fear not mine."

"Maybe," he allowed and fell silent as the mare passed near enough to touch. "Is it the Reaper? If you don't want to see him, I can make sure that you don't."

She didn't like the ominous sound of that. "Sitting here isn't going to make me better. I want to move on, forget about all this." She wanted to forget about Jake. Which was impossible to do when she was wretchedly aware of how close he was. She'd caught a glimpse of him two days ago when Cam had let him into the courtyard for sun and exercise. He'd looked pale and too thin.

She'd wanted to go to him. Feed him. Yell at Cam for letting him fall into such a state. No one would appreciate that. Least of all Jake.

Lyle nodded. "All right then. We leave at the beginning of next week. I'm taking a small group. Cap's staying here to guard the scientists. We'll be gone a full month. You're in?"

"I'm in."

THE COLLAR TRIGGERED AGAIN—the cold knifing down his spine and into his brain, a surge of rage as the Reaper responded to the pain, collapsing into the foggy numbness they told him would be his existence if they were ever able to successfully administer the cure. Welks seemed to take particular delight in explaining that. The doctor was a bastard through and through. He'd make a fine Reaper if he survived the incubation period.

"I sometimes wonder if you've become addicted to the coolant. You look as dazed as an opium addict. It would explain why you were so eager to hand yourself over to us again." Welks locked a steel cuff around his wrist, his pinched face coming into Jake's line of sight for only a moment. "There are easier ways to commit suicide, you know."

Not for his kind. Jake smiled, or at least, he thought he did. He couldn't feel the muscles in his face move. He didn't want to die, but his long life had given him a somewhat fatalistic view of things. He'd seen too many others die, had killed too many himself, to be much excited by death either way. This was only something he wanted to finish. Not guilt, as Abby had suggested.

Only a tipped scale he needed to see balanced. He didn't believe in many things, but order was one of them, justice, balance. And his kind was a blight on the land, one he'd unwittingly helped to release.

Welks returned with an enormous needle. Jake felt a cold sting as it pierced his flesh. Even through the fog in his brain, he felt an aching pressure. "We need more bone marrow as well as a sample from your spleen." A flash of white teeth. "Short day. We should be ready for the first trial by week's end when the patrol returns."

Abby had ridden out with that patrol. Jake had watched her go, splinters of wood biting into the palms of his hands from the fence rail, legs locked with the effort it took not to run after her. She hadn't tried to see him after that first day back and he'd been grateful for that. Since then, he'd only caught stolen glances of her. He'd hear her laughter drift to him on the breeze. When he'd last spoken with the captain, it had been the day before she left and she'd been in the office less than an hour before his meeting. He'd barely been able to give his report. Her scent had been everywhere, and it was very hard to talk when you were doing your best not to breathe.

She was better off. He'd returned her to her home and her family. Balance restored. The captain insisted that the scientists only work with volunteer Rangers and even then he closely supervised the doctors, approving every procedure.

Five more extractions and then Welks picked up his scalpel. "Is that what it is? This is somehow pleasant for you?"

It felt like Welks only traced a finger along the edge of his rib cage, but fire bloomed along the trail. Jake grunted.

Was this pleasant? "No."

Welks cut again, deeper this time. He smiled. "Good."

Chapter Nineteen

THE REAPERS THAT had attacked Fort Hill scattered after the massacre, wreaking havoc in a wide arc from the fort to the border. Most of them were long gone already, leaving a trail of burned ranches and dead livestock in their wake. Before she'd left on this patrol, Abby had received word from her sister that they'd made it safely back to the ranch. She hoped there'd be another letter waiting for her by the time she returned to the fort. Even then, she wouldn't truly be able to lay her worries to rest until she saw Amy and the kids again.

Reapers didn't leave behind any dead to bury. You were either taken as food or you were infected. Their patrol had mostly run cleanup this time around, gathering the newly bitten still in the first throes of infection. Reapers were slower during their first few weeks, disoriented and weak. The Rangers' job, per Captain's orders, was to round up as many as they could take alive and put down the rest. The hope was that they might be able to cure this batch.

She'd been guarding the wagon of chained Reapers with Cam when the scouts reported a band of fifteen to the west, heading south fast. If Alden hadn't been directly in their path, Lyle probably would have let them pass. Not that they didn't generally kill whatever Reapers they found while on patrol, but they'd already lost one man, they had this delivery of newly infected Reapers to make and they were short a dozen men. Abby swiped the sweat from her eyes and reloaded the rifle. She laid it beside Cam's prone body along with what was left of their ammunition.

"We're almost out," she told him. "I'm going back for more."

Dropping behind the rocks, she passed quickly to where the horses were tethered. She grabbed one of the smaller cases from the wagon bed because, already, things were beginning to wind down. The sound of gunfire echoed down the canyon, reverberating inside her chest. A familiar sound, comforting in its own way. It meant her brothers were still standing and that there was one less Reaper running around loose.

Keeping her head low, she returned to the spot on the rim of the canyon where she and Cam had set up shop. He was splayed out flat on his stomach, sighting down the barrel of his gun. After a moment, he popped off another shot and then swore softly under his breath.

He was a good shot, much better than she was. She watched their backs, keeping his gun loaded and one eye on the wagon of younglings who were growing increasingly frantic as the fighting continued. Even from this distance and with her dull human nose, she could smell the blood. The Reapers were frenzied.

"Let me know when you want to trade off," she offered.

"I'm good. Unless you want to take out a few. There's only a couple left and they're cornered."

She raised her brows. "And you missed?"

"I'm trying to get the one wedged behind that rock. He twitched."

"Ah."

Cam lifted his head and studied the scene below. She didn't look. She'd seen it before. After a moment, he pulled back onto his haunches and then dropped down to sit next to her.

She passed him her water skin and took a bandana from her pocket to wipe the sweat from her forehead. When Cam returned the skin, she dumped some water on the bandana and wiped again. Cam lifted his chin. "Do you think they'll settle down on their own?"

"I hope so. The chains should hold…"

She trailed off as the wagon began to sway ominously. The noise coming from inside, hissing and snarling, increased in volume.

Cam shook his head. "I'm more worried about the wagon. The wood will break before the iron does."

The Reapers were as secure as the Rangers had been able to make them. If any broke free there was nothing Cam or Abby could do but start shooting the escapees. So they sat tight, grabbing what rest they could while the cleanup crew worked below. From here, she could almost pretend they were just chopping wood. The swing and thunk of the axe hitting home. The wet sound… She swallowed. Well, it wasn't really wood, but she clung to the illusion.

This patrol had been particularly difficult. Every Reaper she looked at, she couldn't help but wonder in some small corner of her mind about the man he'd once been. Lyle had probably been right in urging her to stay at the fort a while longer. Not that she'd ever tell him that. It was also entirely possible she'd never be able to kill Reapers with as clear a conscience as she'd done before the captain had sent her to Fort Hill.

"Still thinking about that kid?"

She winced. "I hadn't been, no."

"Shit," he muttered. "I'm sorry. You looked so grim, I thought…"

It was no wonder really. Thinking about Jake again. No matter how she tried to avoid it, he was always in the back of her mind. The scientists were trying to isolate the parasitc from his body to use to recreate their cure and she knew firsthand exactly how brutal their experimentation could be. Jake could be dead by now.

Lyle had tried to talk to her about Jake the first day or two out on patrol, but he'd been smart enough to accept her terse answers at face value and let it drop. Cam for all of his good looks could be skittish around women, particularly distraught ones. He'd grown up inside the Fort where there were very few women around. His mother had been a Ranger. Normal women probably seemed as alien to him as Reapers. Not that she was normal.

Slanting her head to block the sun, she smiled at him. "Don't worry, Cam. If I was looking for a shoulder to cry on, yours would be the last one I'd aim for."

He jerked back like she'd slapped him. "What's that supposed to mean?"

"I didn't mean it that way." She knocked into him with her shoulder. "I know you care, I meant it to be reassuring. It's a fact that you'd rather take on a horde of Reapers than handle a weepy woman."

He dropped his gaze to his hands hanging between his knees and when he looked back up, the expression on his face made her heart hurt. He *was* worried about her. "I wouldn't mind if you cried on my shoulder…if you needed to."

Ducking her head before he could see the tears that pricked her eyes, she fiddled with replacing the cap on her water skin. Tucking her legs up to her chest, she wrapped her arms loosely around her shins and rocked a bit. "Thanks, Cam. That…" She cleared her throat. "That means a lot to me. But you don't need to worry. I'm okay…I *will* be okay."

"Shit," he said. "I can't get the sight of that little boy running after us out of my head now."

It took her a minute to figure out what he was talking about. At one of the ranches they'd passed two days back, they'd found a youngling wandering around, howling in the ruins. He'd killed the family's milk cow but had only half eaten it. The carcass stunk to high heaven and was crawling with maggots. She'd been so sickened by the sight that, at first, she hadn't seen the Reaper running full tilt toward her. She'd been the one standing closest to his food, triggering some territorial reflex that lured him out into the open.

When she did see him, she'd shot his knees out from under him and John and Ellis had brought in the chains to shackle him. Unfortunately, that was right about the time the rest of his family returned. They'd been visiting the wife's sister's house only five miles distant when the Reapers attacked. The wife and her two teenage daughters had survived along with a son, about eight years old. He saw his father being chained, saw the blood and gore all over his hands and face and knew instantly what it meant. The women had recoiled but not the boy.

Despite all that blood, the little boy had only seen his papa. And when it was time to ride on, he'd run after them for a good two miles before falling to his knees in the dirt. Abby hadn't looked back. It wasn't an image she'd wanted to take with her. Apparently, Cam *had* turned around. What bothered her was that in her mind, it made sense. The creature in their wagon was not that boy's father any longer. The Reaper would kill his son and feed on the body. She knew it. Reapers weren't human. But in her heart, she could relate. When she looked at Jake, even now, she didn't see a Reaper either.

She dropped her chin to rest on her knees. "Maybe they'll be able to cure him."

Cam looked at her, brows raised. "You believe that?"

"Yeah, I believe it. They'll figure it out eventually and there will be cure."

"God, Abby. I hope you're right." He rubbed at his face. "The thing that I wonder about is where we're going to put all of them until that happens."

"What do you mean?"

"Now that there's a chance at curing them. I mean, the ones who are a danger, of course, we have no choice but to kill them, but...like that man. If his family knew there was a chance at a cure, they'd likely have tried to pen him and turn him over to us. How many people are going to get infected because they went for the capture instead of the kill? And what are we going to do with all the extra Reapers?"

She hadn't considered long-term. "If Welks can't recreate his serum or if it doesn't work, we'll have to go back to business as usual."

Cam grunted, but it didn't exactly sound like agreement. Yeah, she didn't know how they were supposed to do that either. Hope was a tricky thing.

Something cold touched the back of her hand and she stared at the droplet caught between her knuckles before squinting up at the dark clouds. Of course, today would be the day when the skies opened up to end the month-long drought—when they were on the road with loaded wagons. Lyle shouted at them to ready the horses and Cam stood, holding out his hand and pulling her to her feet. Lyle and the rest of the patrol met them at the head of the trail leading back toward the Fort.

"Messenger from the captain," he said tersely. "We can't stop to rest. They need us back at the Fort yesterday."

She drew her horse in closer as Cam asked, "What happened?"

Lyle mounted and then whistled sharply, signaling everyone to do the same. Once he was satisfied that everyone was moving fast enough, he turned back to Cam. "Scouts reported a large band of Reapers on the move, coming up from the south but avoiding the towns in their path. We wouldn't have known they were coming if Cap hadn't stationed someone to watch the ford at Jasper."

Reapers didn't swim well and the ford was one of the few spots on the wide river that was shallow enough to cross on foot. Cam's jaw clenched as he came to the same conclusion she had.

"Fort Hill," she whispered.

"We don't know that yet," Lyle said.

She shook her head. "How do they know we have the scientists? Jake said that the Scrapers were the ones who told the Reapers a cure had been discovered. We've been watching the scientists too closely for them to have gotten a message out and even Welks agreed to the precautions Cap demanded."

Cam's lip curled but he didn't look directly at her. Lyle's expression was oddly gentle. "Jake was at Fort Hill too, Abby."

She pulled back. "He wouldn't call the Reapers down on us."

He didn't bother to argue with her, only swept his gaze over his worn-out troops to make sure everyone was keeping up.

"Lyle," she said, and he reluctantly returned his attention to her. "How would he even have contacted them?"

"He's one of them, Abby. Until last month, we didn't even know there were sentient Reapers. Maybe they have ways of communicating that we don't know about. Don't fret over it. We don't know what happened. Maybe they'll have it figured out by the time we reach the fort."

If the fort was still standing when they reached it.

She saw the same thought haunting Lyle's eyes before he turned his horse to prod the stragglers.

JAKE STOOD BESIDE the captain on the ramparts overlooking the plains. The fort had been built upon a slight promontory. The surrounding area was very flat and they'd cleared the land for several miles in every direction so as not to impede the view. There was a small town to the north, inhabited mostly by women who were either attached to one or another of the Rangers or who hoped to bear a star-marked child. They'd been evacuated yesterday, sent north to Clayton. Messengers had been dispatched to all the nearby forts, but it was unlikely that any help would arrive in time. At least Abby was gone.

A river curved gently around the southern side of the fort. Rain-swollen from yesterday's downpour, it would serve as a barrier of sorts to the Reapers the scouts said were on their way. The rain would help, provided that it continued to pour, and the sudden drop in temperature would help too. There'd been a chill in the air that morning that promised winter. Even though his rider was currently suppressed by the chemicals the doctors were pumping into him, Jake could still feel the compulsion to run south. Faint now, but it would only grow stronger as the temperature fell. If the fort survived the next few days, the changing season would grant them a temporary respite from Reaper attack. Until spring anyway.

The captain turned his head and rain sluiced off the brim of his hat. "How did they know?"

Jake had his suspicions but he couldn't prove anything. He'd heard Welks tell Hamilton that he had no intention of remaining imprisoned in a run-down border fort for the rest of his life. Welks had complained about everything—the dirt floors and the bland food, the lack of available women. The motivation was certainly there, but Jake couldn't figure out how Welks might have contacted his benefactor. He still didn't know who Welks's benefactor was.

Jake met the captain's accusatory gaze with a cool one. "I don't know."

The Cap grunted. "I'd like to believe you. Both that you don't know and that you didn't have anything to do with this. Doc thinks I should lock you up anyway."

"Why?"

"Morale is low enough as it is and half the men suspect you signaled for the attack."

"How would I have done that even if I'd wanted to?"

Cap grimaced. "It doesn't matter. They won't fight beside you."

"Convince them otherwise. You're down twenty men and your defenses won't hold, not against the size of the group coming in."

"The patrol is on its way in."

Jake's hands clenched on the rough wooden rail but he forced his voice to remain casual. "I thought they were still a week out."

"They made better time than I thought they would. They should be back by nightfall."

"Abby?"

Something flickered in the old Ranger's expression

that Jake couldn't read, but he nodded. "She's with them."

Jake turned away to look out over the river. Abby… A part of him rejoiced at the chance to see her again, even if it was only the stolen glimpses he caught as she crossed the yard or through the cracks in the door of his cell. But he sure as hell didn't want her trapped in the fort with death at the door.

"If you won't let me fight, then let me get Abby away from here. We'll make copies of the research and—"

"You trust Welks to commit his serum to paper? He's not about to let anyone else claim the glory for his work. Karlson gave me what he could and I already sent that with the messengers yesterday. If we fall, hopefully it will be enough for someone else to pick up where they left off."

If we fall… Abby would ride into the fort just hours before the Reapers arrived. Nearly two centuries he'd been alive. He'd thought himself numb to fear.

"There's a cellar beneath the fort. It has access to an escape tunnel that lets out a few miles north. I'll place her there as your guard."

"Please," he said, and the captain's eyes widened. Jake didn't give a fuck, he'd drop to his knees if he thought it would make a difference. "You can still send her away. There's time."

The corner of the captain's mouth lifted. "Trouble follows Abby even when I try to drive her away from it. Look what happened with you. No, I learned that lesson."

"These walls are going to fall."

The captain gave him a hard look and Jake met it dead-on. What did he have to lose? If not for Abby, he would simply leave the fort. He'd developed a tolerance to Welks's injections, had managed to lift the key off Hamilton this morning when the report came in about the attack and would be able to disable the collar before it disabled him. Perhaps he would still leave, find out who was behind this attack, see what he could discover from the other side. He should probably attempt to rescue Welks a second time, though the prospect of that turned his stomach.

The captain turned away as Karlson walked up. The deceptively fragile-looking old man smiled warmly. "I beg your pardon, Captain. But we require Jake's presence in the lab."

"Doctor. You've saved me the trip. I'm afraid you'll have to do without Jake's services for a time. You can take him to the lab but I'll need you to remove his collar."

Karlson paled but to his credit didn't immediately object. "Captain?"

"Reapers will be here by midnight. We need every man who's willing to fight. How's work on that weapon coming along?"

Karlson's eyes darted from Jake to the captain. "We'll need more dry ice and I've had trouble calibrating the spray mechanism properly. We simply don't have all the necessary parts and your blacksmith—"

"Has other duties to attend to. Try to make do with what you have. You might want to stop by the armory and pick up a gun."

Karlson looked appalled by the idea but nodded anyway. He turned for the stairs, gesturing for Jake to accompany him. There was something immensely satisfying about the sweat that beaded on Karlson's forehead as Jake followed him toward the lab.

Chapter Twenty

IT WAS LATE afternoon when they returned to the fort. Puddles filled the low dips in the road, reflecting orange and pink light from the setting sun. The rain had stopped less than an hour ago but already the dry earth had absorbed much of the rainfall. The clouds had lifted leaving behind a sticky, humid heat. As uncomfortable as that was, what alarmed Abby was the stillness of the land as they approached Fort Dougan. It reminded her of the area around Hill after the massacre. She was greatly relieved when the intact gates of her home fort finally came into view.

Dust clung to her face and neck, the backs of her hands. Her scalp itched and her clothing felt heavy and abrasive against her skin. When they came into the yard, Lyle dismounted and left them with a clipped order to get some rest. Abby watched him walk with a brisk stride toward the captain's quarters. She wasn't walking briskly anywhere. Groaning as she dismounted, she passed Pepper off to a stable hand and stumbled toward the women's barracks, slow and stiff as an old woman. It felt like the rain had rusted out all her joints. They'd ridden through the rain for hours, only stopping when it became necessary to pry the wagon free of the sucking mud. Impending Reaper attack or not, the only thing that filled her mind at the moment was a soft bed. A bath first if she could manage it.

"Abby," Cam called. She turned. "We're to report back by midnight. That's when they expect the Reapers."

"So soon?"

He held up his hands. "I'm just the messenger. Try and get some sleep."

She nodded and walked across the yard to the house that served as the women's barracks. Barracks was really too harsh a term for the quaint home. It was a two-story structure with private rooms and a shared parlor. She was the only star-marked woman at the fort; the other five were employed by the fort in one capacity or another.

Haddy and Amelia were sisters who'd lived there for as long as anyone could remember. They ran the place and seemed to regard the other women—and most of the young men—as their personal charges. There was Jane, a mysterious beauty Cam brought back with him after leaving to attend to some family business last June. Abby didn't know why the captain agreed to let her stay on and didn't know Jane well enough to ask. Louisa was softheaded but sweet, and Jennifer was Haddy's granddaughter, soon to be married to the town blacksmith.

Haddy was seated in her rocker on the front porch. When she saw Abby, she set her knitting aside and rose to meet her at the top of the stairs. Folding her into a hug that smooshed Abby against an ample bosom, Haddy bundled her inside. She clucked her tongue at the state of Abby's sodden clothes and helped to peel her leather coat from her shoulders.

"We heard the patrol come in. Amelia's already drawn your bath. You can go right upstairs if you want or if you're hungry there's stew in the pot."

Abby had her foot on the bottom tread of the stairs when the smell of freshly baked bread reached her and she reconsidered. Changing course, she started down the narrow hallway toward the kitchen.

"I think I'd like food first, if it's no trouble."

"No trouble at all."

Haddy followed her down the hall. "Go out back and wash your hands at the pump then."

Abby followed orders and by the time she made it back to the kitchen, a bowl waited for her on the table. Haddy set a cutting board down beside it, plucked a towel off the loaf of bread and lifted her knife.

With a frown, she pointed with the tip of her knife toward the folded napkin and Abby spread it across her lap. It was always strange to return home. Haddy and Amelia both expected good manners of her. She sometimes wondered if that wasn't the captain's influence—part of his campaign to make a lady of her. She didn't usually let the sisters fuss over her so, but they seemed to enjoy having someone to take care of. Tonight, she had neither the energy nor the inclination to fight them.

Taking a bite of the stew, she sighed in appreciation as the meat nearly melted in her mouth. It was simple food—meat, potatoes, carrots, some of Amelia's jarred tomatoes—but it eased the ache in her belly. Haddy poured them both tea and sat down across from her at the table.

"Did everyone make it back?"

Abby shook her head. "We lost Daniel."

"The new boy from Dixon?" There was a note of relief in Haddy's voice that Abby could not fault. It was always bad when they lost someone but easier if the Ranger was new, as that meant there'd been less time to grow attached to him. She nodded and Haddy sipped at her tea while Abby ate. When she was finished, Abby got up to wash her bowl.

Haddy took it from her before she reached the sink. "Head upstairs, dear. You look plain tuckered out."

Thanking Haddy, she paused with one hand resting on the back of the chair. Haddy's brows lifted and Abby hesitated. She shouldn't ask. It shouldn't make a difference and it would only cause Haddy to worry. But she *needed* to know. "Jake…the Reaper, is he still alive?"

Haddy's expression didn't give anything away, but she reached out and caught Abby's hand to give it a good squeeze. "I saw him yesterday speaking with the captain up on the wall. He's alive. Now go on. Leave the clothes in the bathroom and I'll take care of them. You've fresh in the dresser."

Abby went through her bath half-asleep, but she managed to scrub off the worst of the dirt before pulling on a shirt and climbing into her bed. A horde of Reapers would attack in a few hours—it barely touched her. She'd see Jake again soon. The thought warmed her from the inside, a bright and shiny thing that she held on to as sleep claimed her.

If Jake had tried to picture Abby's room, he never would have imagined anything so sweet. It was a comfortable room, undoubtedly inhabited by a female. It smelled like her—Abby's scent—along with a touch of the lavender she must use in her soap. The freshly swept wooden floor was covered by a large braided rug. Abby's hair was undone and spread across her pillow. This was the first time he'd ever seen it clean and loose. The sight made him want to run his fingers through it to see if it was as soft as it looked. He'd like to bury his face there and breathe her in.

She lay abed with a softly colored quilt tucked beneath her chin. Her gun belt was looped over the post of the gleaming brass frame. Now that he'd seen this place, he would always think of her here. Taking two steps farther into the room, he sat down beside her hip. Her body shifted ever so slightly, his weight on the mattress drawing her toward him.

"Abby." He shook her shoulder. "Sweetheart, you have to wake up."

"Jake?" Her voice sounded fuzzy and confused.

Blinking open her eyes, she rolled onto her back. Hair mussed, gray eyes wide and sleepy. Warm, feminine, soft. Abby. His heart skipped before settling into a thick, heavy beat.

"Are the Reapers here?" she asked, not recoiling from him in horror, not even questioning what the hell he was doing in her bedroom.

"No. They're not here, not yet."

He touched her knee, covered by the light cotton quilt. He could feel her warmth through the fabric, feel her slide beneath his fingertips when she stretched like a cat and yawned. She woke up slow as the sunrise. He'd missed that—watching her wake up. He'd missed every single damned thing about her.

"They won't come until after the moon sets. They'll attack then, when we'll be at a disadvantage, tired and blind. The darkness won't slow them down."

"But not yet?" She rubbed at her eyes. "I was having the worst nightmare…"

When she sat up, the blanket pooled around her waist and the thin shirt she'd worn to bed gapped open in the front. Heat slowly rose up his neck. When they'd ridden together, she'd always kept her breasts bound. They were loose now. He could see her nipples peak beneath the fabric when the cool air hit them.

His fingers wrapped around her thigh just above the knee. Not something he planned. It seemed as natural as breathing to reach for her and when she didn't object, he moved his hand higher on her leg. His thumb settled into the seam where her leg met her hip. Just a few inches to the right… He could feel the heat of her.

"It was only a dream." He squeezed her leg reassuringly, trying to ignore the give in her flesh. "I came from the ramparts and it's quiet out there."

She looked past him to the window, framed by frilly curtains. It was dark already, but they still had a few hours left.

"What are you doing here?" The strange catch to her voice tugged at his heart—what was left of it—almost as much as the look she turned on him. "I thought you didn't want to see me."

"Did you?"

"Jake."

"Sweetheart, you know exactly why I made that request of your captain. Don't pretend otherwise."

"I'm not pretending. I'm giving you the benefit of the doubt. At first I thought you locked me out. That you'd gotten what you wanted and had no use for me anymore."

"That wasn't it." He'd hoped to come in, bundle her up and send her off to safety. He should have known better than to think she wouldn't want to talk about this. Subtle as a gunshot to the chest, his Abby. She didn't shy away now.

"Then what was it? Were you just too chickenshit to say what you had to say to my face?"

He might have gotten angry at the jab if he couldn't feel her trembling beneath his hand. That was anger, yes, but hurt too. If it made her feel better to slice at him, he could stand it. He kept his voice steady. "I'm a Reaper and you're a Ranger. That's the plain truth. Call me a coward if you want to, but I was never so chickenshit that I couldn't face the truth."

"The truth…" A frown formed between her thin straight brows as she adjusted the angle of her body so that she faced him fully. When he removed his hand from her thigh, she caught it to hold him in place. "The truth is that I thought I was falling in love with you." He made a rough sound of denial, but she continued. "When you locked me out, it broke me. That's the plain truth you couldn't face. I know what you are and I know exactly what I am, so don't try to tell me this was all about protecting my tender feelings."

Like a bullet. She never had hesitated to pull the trigger when aiming at him. *I thought I was falling in love with you…* He shook his head. "It wasn't about protecting your feelings. It was about saving your life."

"Then why come now?"

"To ask you to leave." He forced himself to meet the accusation in her eyes, the anger. She had a right to it and he hadn't come here to make excuses. "You still have a few hours, you could be well away by the time the Reapers get here."

"You're asking me to abandon my post."

He'd known it coming to see her that she'd be difficult to convince to run, but he'd still had to try. Had to see her at least one last time. "I want you to live."

"I'm not the one who keeps handing himself over to Welks trying to punish himself."

He breathed out a soft huff of laughter. "I'm not punishing myself. I want the cure, Abby, that's all. You're the one with no sense of self-preservation."

"Maybe that's true." Her smile was sad and sweet. It didn't so much soften the anger in her eyes as give it another layer of complexity. "Maybe I'm the biggest fool on God's green earth for thinking there was something more between us than just a common goal."

He flinched. "You're not a fool."

She stared at him for a time and when she seemed to realize he had nothing more to add to that, the fight drained out of her. She blinked twice and then looked at the window again before shaking her head and returning her gaze to him. "It's fine. I understand you don't feel the same way. You should go now."

He hesitated. "Abby…"

"I'm not leaving the fort, and I need to get some sleep."

She tugged at the blankets, but his weight meant she could only pull them so far. He didn't like the look on her face. Tired. More than that…beaten.

"Shit."

Her head snapped up and her eyes narrowed.

"You want to know why I locked you out? I knew you felt it too. That…attraction same as I did, even after you knew what I was. I knew you didn't want to feel that way, not for a Reaper, but you still always treated me like a man. It's been so long since anyone's looked at me like that…you can't know what it meant to me. The only way to honor that, to honor *you* was to break the connection. Even after all this…if we survive the attack, if Welks is telling the truth, I can't be cured. I'm no damned good for you."

She was silent for a full minute, eyes narrowed, considering. His throat tightened and his stomach churned. He shouldn't have said any—

"Did it work?"

He frowned in confusion at the whispered question.

"Were you able to break it? Do you not feel any kind of connection to me now?"

Fuck. Her gray eyes were wide and vulnerable. Her lips trembled slightly though her chin was up. This woman did not back away from *anything.* It hurt him to see her so close to unraveling.

"It doesn't matter."

Her brows drew together in a frown. "It matters to me."

A lock of honey brown hair fell into her face and she pushed it impatiently aside. The curl settled on her shirt just above her breast. He couldn't resist the impulse to reach up and trace the curve of it with his fingertip. He couldn't do it. Maybe that made him a coward. Maybe weak. But he couldn't make himself hurt her. Not again. Not like this.

His breath slipped out in a rough sigh. "I'm here, aren't I?"

"Are you here because I'm a responsibility or here because you care?"

He watched the subtle movement of her throat as she swallowed and his mouth went dry. He should lie to her. If there was any chance she was staying here because of him, he should lie his ass off to save her life. But the look on her face—full of every good thing he'd ever wanted out of life—kept him to the truth.

His voice fell to a gravelly whisper. "I'm here because I couldn't fucking stay away."

A small sound escaped her and he could see the tears brightening her eyes. He didn't want her to cry, not over him.

She lifted her hand to touch his cheek and he felt it as a blessing. "Then stay."

He held himself still as her fingertips feathered across his skin, sliding back to brush his ear and then catch in his hair. He allowed himself to be drawn closer. There was a question in her eyes. On her parted lips.

One kiss. He could have just one kiss.

He dipped his head to brush his mouth over hers, soft as a breeze. Then, when she didn't jerk away in disgust, he kissed her again, more firmly. He tangled his hand in her hair and angled her head so that he could delve deeper, slip his tongue past her parted lips and drink her in.

Her tongue touched his tentatively and he hummed in approval. One of her hands fisted in his shirt to pull him in closer. Her other pressed against his thigh to lean up and into him.

He kissed her breathless and then pulled back just enough to set his forehead to hers. "I did it to keep you safe. Not because I didn't want you. Because I wanted you too damn much."

"Safe?" She repeated incredulously. "There isn't any such thing as safe, Jake. Not down here. I could have died on that patrol."

"I know."

"I could die tonight."

He knew where she was going with this and didn't answer her right away. He only wanted to touch her for another few seconds. Then he'd force himself to leave.

"Like a virgin being sent off to war?" He smiled gently. "I'm not a naive schoolgirl you can talk out of her bloomers, sweetheart. It's more complicated than that and you know it."

"I'm not a virgin, but I do want you. Very much. I'm a grown woman and I'm willing. I know the risks and you don't need me anymore for your experiments. Why hold yourself back now?"

Her breasts tempted him and she must have seen that because she snagged his hand and pulled it to her chest, turning toward him so that he had free and open access to molest her as he would. He dragged in air past dry lips. She arched, her perfect breast fitting neatly into his open palm.

"I could hurt you."

"You won't."

His jaw clenched. "But I could."

She felt wonderful, soft and giving…willing. Eager even, restless as she kicked off the covers and hooked her fingers through the belt loop of his pants as if afraid he'd bolt. He *ought* to run.

"When I first came here, your captain asked me if we'd…been intimate. He was worried that you'd conceive a Reaper baby. I didn't even know that might be possible. I won't take that risk."

She shook her head. "It's the wrong time for me to conceive, and I have an herbal tea I can drink to make certain of it. Doc's lover in New Hope gave it to me. Lucy. She's a whore and swears by the remedy."

Sick as it was, he felt a slight twinge of disappointment. There was something very satisfying about the thought of filling Abby with his child.

She caught his gaze. "There's risk everywhere, Jake. Let me decide which ones I'm willing to take."

Her legs were bare, pale compared to the brown skin on her hands. He sat there frozen while she rose to her knees and straddled his lap.

"I want you."

She began to undo her shirt. Button by button, revealing inch after tantalizing inch of smooth white skin. He remembered that day in the hills when she'd done the same. Not willing to leave anything to fate, she'd grabbed on to the reins with both hands then and had forced him to make a choice. Accept her as his partner or give in to the Reaper. Much the same choice that she was forcing him to make now.

He couldn't resent her for it, either. She wouldn't be Abby if she didn't fight for what she wanted.

But could he give her what she wanted? God knew why she wanted him, but she did. And if he actually did hurt her…he'd be lost. More broken than the Reaper had ever made him.

The tails of her shirt lay across her thighs. She'd exposed a pale line of skin from neck to navel but was waiting for him to make a choice. With trembling hands, he reached for the collar, slipped his hands beneath the loose cloth and eased it down her shoulders, closing his eyes briefly at the shock of warm flesh beneath his fingertips.

He touched her. Traced the lines of her face before skimming his hands down her throat to her breasts, her stomach and finally the curls between her legs. He paused with his hand covering her mound and closed his eyes…measuring, waiting. The rider remained silent, just as it had for days.

"I've never made love to a woman." He almost choked on the admission, but she deserved it. "I was only fourteen when I was infected. And then…I don't remember much of anything that happened when the rider had its grip on me."

"The Reaper?"

"It's dormant. I don't know when it will wake but if anything would rouse it, this would be it." He swallowed hard. "I can't do this."

"You can."

He wanted to. God, how he wanted to.

He couldn't stop himself from staring at her. Lithe and smooth, sleek as a cat. Firm muscles beneath soft skin. Perfect breasts. Her nipples pebbled beneath his gaze.

"Jake?"

There was a raw vulnerability in her eyes, a fragile hope and something else that made his heart swell in his chest. And he knew that he had to try. He wanted her to know that she'd owned him from that first moment in New Providence. He wanted to show her how different things might have been if he'd been free to pursue her.

Pressing his palm to her back, he urged her up and forward, dipped his head to catch her nipple on his tongue. Drawing her into his mouth, he sucked at her gently until she moaned and clutched at his shoulders for balance. When her hand moved to the back of his head, when her fingers twined into his hair, he turned his head to lavish the same attention on her other breast.

She rocked her body against his erection and he had to stop for a moment. Slow. If he was going to do this—and apparently he was—then he would damn well do it right. Even if it killed him. Pressing his face to her neck, he kissed the spot above where her pulse thrummed and breathed deep.

The pure rich scent of desire flooded his nose and his mouth. It made his already hard cock throb almost painfully. She tugged at his hair and he lifted his face.

She kissed him. Softly at first, skimming her tongue along his lower lip and then sucking it into her mouth. He groaned when, tentatively, her tongue dipped inside his mouth. His hands grabbed on to her hips and he held her tightly to him. She grew bolder and he trembled beneath her, feeling the heat of her body through his trousers as her mouth moved on his.

Reluctantly, he peeled her away. "You're certain?"

Her wet lips curved into a wry smile. "Are you?"

"No," he answered honestly. "But I'm not turning back."

She lay down on the bed. His body twisted to follow her. His knee on the bed, thigh pressed between her legs, lowering himself atop her with a hissed exhalation. Bearing most of his weight on his arms, he bent his head. He was still clothed, thinking that would help. Maybe it did, but he was still nearly overwhelmed by the flood of sensation. The vibration of her heartbeat pattering away, the rush of blood through her veins, through his veins as his cock stirred. The heat and smell of her. Her hands rested on his shoulders, kneading at muscles that had suddenly locked tight.

"Jake?"

A groan rattled in his chest, but he managed to lift his head. She was smiling at him, a shy uncertain thing that tore at his heart. "Why do you want this, Abby? I don't deserve you."

"Let me be the judge of that."

Her thighs slid wider and she shimmied her hips, working him tighter against her. Her hands slid between their bodies and he pulled away, because the sensation was suddenly overwhelming, because he wanted to see her. All of her. Rocking back onto his knees, he smoothed his hands up her thighs to her hips. "You're beautiful."

The smile faltered. "You don't need to say that to me."

"I've never lied to you, Abby. Have I?"

"No." He could hear the frown in her voice though he wasn't looking at her face any longer. "You haven't, but…"

He slid his palms over her abdomen and then lower. His thumbs stoked downward, through soft curls until he found the top of her slit. She arched into his hand.

"And it's not the Reaper talking, if that's what you're thinking. You suggested that once before and I shouldn't have let it pass. I can tell the difference between what the Reaper wants and what I want. The Reaper wants to throw you down and devour you. Swallow every scrap until there's nothing left."

Her voice dropped to a whisper. "And what do you want, Jake?"

"You." How could she not know it? "To love you. To worship you. To protect you." He ran a fingertip along the sweet curve of her waist. "Just to be near you. You make the rest of the world fall away."

She tried to drag him on top of her, but he caught

both of her hands to raise them above her head. His cock strained against his trousers. Rubbing against her did nothing to relieve the ache. It only made the rider fight him more desperately for control. He wouldn't… couldn't let that happen. When Abby lifted her hips to grind against him, he pulled away from her and released her hands, setting his elbows to either side of her rib cage and tasting her throat.

She clutched at his shoulders but, seeming to finally accept that he wasn't going to budge, stopped trying to pull him closer and simply clung to him. In his long, long life, he couldn't remember anything ever feeling as perfectly *right* as this moment.

Closing his eyes, he nudged her chin up so that he could taste her jaw, kiss his way down her throat. There. He'd waited forever to lick her there. He lingered for just a moment. Smiling when she shivered, he moved on, closing his teeth gently over her collarbone and nipping lightly. She moaned softly and he had to pause for a moment to beat back the Reaper.

When it was safe, he slid his cheek along the smooth side of her breast and then, turning his head, took her nipple into his mouth. Her back arched and he slid one hand beneath her, lifting her to his mouth.

"Can you take your clothes off?" Her voice was husky, sexy as hell. "At least your shirt…"

He shook his head, dipped his tongue into her navel and shifted his body lower, sliding his arms beneath her thighs. "I can't, Abby. I want to. I can't."

Parting her with his hands, he swallowed the growl

that rose in his throat. A moment. He kissed her thigh, nuzzled closer as he got a handle on his reaction, locked the Reaper away as tightly as he could manage and then tasted her, softly at first. Gently traced the edges of her folds with his tongue, dancing across the hood of her clit and then delving deeper into slick heat.

She lifted her hips, demanding a firmer touch but he wouldn't be rushed. He stretched his left arm out across her abdomen to hold her in place as he teased her. The sounds she made…soft moans and heavy sighs, the way her breath caught when he touched her just so… it was the most damnably erotic thing he'd ever heard. His balls felt like lead weights. His cock ached with the need to take her. It was funny, as old as he was, all of his knowledge of female anatomy, everything he knew about how to pleasure a woman was theoretical. All of it came from the books he read or from disjointed memories he'd rather forget.

This wasn't anything he'd ever expected to feel—fear that he might lose control, worry that he wouldn't please her, an overwhelming need to be closer. He wanted to be free of his clothes. He wanted to feel her skin slide along the length of his body, but that wasn't going to happen. He could do this for her though. Tenderly suck at her clit while she rocked against him, stroke his thumb down her folds until he found the entrance of her body. He shifted his weight so he could turn his hand. Slowly, he slid one finger inside her. She went momentarily still and then pressed against him. He withdrew and timed his thrusts to the flick of his tongue, varying the pressure until he found what seemed to please her best.

"I want you, Jake. I want you to feel your skin, your body. I want…" She gasped as he slid another finger inside of her. "More."

Abby… He smiled even as he swallowed a groan. Of course she would guess his mind. "Take this, sweetheart. You know that I want you now, don't you? Or are you going to deny it again?"

"Jake."

"I can't, Abby. Not while this thing is still inside me."

The sound she made, equal parts hunger and frustration, nearly did him in. He pressed his cheek against her thigh. Her fingers tangled in his hair and he pushed her higher, curling his fingers to drag his fingertips along her inner wall. Smiling at her gasp, he did it again. Keeping to that steady pace even when she began to tug at his hair and grind herself against his mouth.

"Let me do this." This he could manage. This he could give to her, to them both. "I want to feel you come."

She was close. He could hear the hammer of her heart, feel the quiver of her thighs against his cheek, scent the flood of moisture from her body. And he almost did lose it then. When her body called to his, when she begged for him to fill her.

But he held back and a second later, her body stilled as her orgasm swept over her. Her muscles clenched on his fingers, her hips bucked and she cried out his name. Pleasure swept through him too, despite the pressure in his groin. *His* name was on her lips. It echoed in his ears.

When she settled, he kissed her one last time and pulled back so that he could see her face.

"Jake…what about you?"

"Did I please you?"

She gave him a lazy and sated smiled. "You know that you did." She touched his cheek. "I don't need slow, if that's what you're worried about. We can do slow later once you know this will work. Then we'll test your limits."

"Test my limits…"

"Carefully." She reached for him. "Maybe I can—"

He never found out what she was going to suggest. The alarm sounded then, one faint clang followed by a louder and heavier one as the bell picked up momentum. Abby cursed under her breath and released him. He pulled back, listening to her scramble off the bed while he pressed the heels of his hands to his eyes.

When he looked up, she was fully dressed.

"We'll try this again later."

She smiled. A bright hopeful smile that made him want to haul her back onto the bed and finish what they'd started.

"Later," she repeated and her smile faded. "Promise me, Jake."

He rose from the bed and kissed her instead. Already, he could feel that cold touch in his mind, the dark whisper of the Reaper telling him to ignore the clamor, telling him to pin her to the mattress and take what he wanted from her body, to gorge himself in sex and violence.

He ignored the Reaper and he didn't make Abby any promises.

Chapter Twenty-One

THEY WERE UNDER ATTACK. The alarm had sounded well before midnight when a flare from the first watchtower went up. That had given them an hour leeway and they'd fought through the night, successfully battling off the first wave. A brief thunderstorm had passed through a few hours before dawn, dousing the Reapers in a cold, driving rain. They'd retreated for a time only to return now just as the sun was rising.

The land surrounding the fort was fertile, but twenty miles south it turned to desert. The Reapers looked like they'd come straight through the desert, like they'd been traveling for days to do it. Gaunt with red-rimmed eyes, they swarmed toward the fort. The river was wide and deep below the fort but rather than file across the bridge, they ran right into the water like herded cattle. Many of them never resurfaced.

Abby stood on the ramparts beside Jake. Shoulder to shoulder, his warmth seeped through the thin fabric of her shirt. Haddy had taken her coat to beat the dust out and Abby hadn't wasted any time looking for it. Later—if there was a later—she'd find a few minutes to track it down.

Jake made a noise that sounded suspiciously like a growl. He was angry, she knew that. At Welks, who still denied trying to contact his benefactor, at her for refusing to leave while she had the chance. At himself because…well, because he took everything on his own shoulders. But he was still hanging on to his control.

She fired, watched long enough to see the impact. A good shot. Left eye. The Reaper dropped almost immediately and was shoved under by the others behind him. Jake took her empty gun and pressed a freshly loaded one into her hands. As she bent her head to take aim, he leaned over the wall and went so suddenly still that she lifted her head to see what was wrong.

His eyes tracked some movement below but when she tried to follow his gaze, she saw nothing out of the ordinary. She could feel the tension in him, so strong he nearly vibrated with it.

Touching his arm to draw his attention, she asked, "What is it?"

He didn't answer immediately. His broad tipped fingers gripped the wood railing, making it creak as he leaned farther out. After a moment, he straightened, swearing viciously as he turned to her.

"Marston is down there."

"That can't be possible." She stared down at the roiling crowd of bodies below. She couldn't make out individual faces but had no doubt that Jake could. "*How* could that be possible?"

"A solid shot directly to his spine, there shouldn't have been enough left to heal."

"There wasn't. I saw him die. You did too. And they're still so far away. Maybe—"

"It's him," Jake interrupted flatly. "I know it is. He wanted to make sure that I saw him."

She tried to ignore the memories that flashed through her mind. Marston's hand on her breast, his mouth, his teeth… Her heart faltered. She forced herself to draw a deep and steadying breath, blew it out slowly. He was down there. Within range. She was up here on the wall with a gun in her hands. Jake at her side and eighty Rangers at her back.

"I don't see him. Can you take the shot?"

He shook his head. "He's out of range. As soon as I saw him, he moved toward the western wall. He fucking waved at me."

Which meant he'd been looking for Jake. That he knew about the scientists. "So, Welks may not be the one to blame for this after all."

Son of a bitch.

"Marston would have known to follow me. He knows I want the cure. If he's been watching…it's likely that he knows everything by now." Dark eyes fixed on her. "He's old, bored and he holds a grudge. *Fuck.* I should have made you leave."

"I made my choice and there's nothing I can do to change it now." She stared down at the Reapers, searching for Marston even though she wasn't sure she wanted to see him. Shoving aside the panic rising inside her, she turned from the wall. "Come on, we need to tell the captain what we're dealing with."

They found the captain conferring with Jace, the fort carpenter, about reinforcing the gates. As soon as they broke the news to him about Marston, Lyle called for them to join him on the wall.

Cap cupped a hand to his mouth. "Can it wait?"

Lyle shook his head, his expression so grim he nearly looked like a stranger. "It's not good."

"Fuck," Cap muttered under his breath and grimaced when his gaze fell on Abby. "Walk with me."

Jake and Abby fell into step beside him as he headed toward the stairs leading to the ramparts.

"You told me he was dead."

Abby flinched at his tone. "We thought he was. There wasn't time to burn the body."

By the time they reached the top of the stairs, he'd sorted through the implications of it. He scratched at his beard. "He followed us then. You think he knows about the scientists?"

"That's what we think, yes."

The captain scowled at Jake. "If he's sentient, can you reason with him? Convince him that Welks and Karlson are dead or that the rumors of a cure were false?"

Jake shook his head. "He's sentient. Not sane. He won't turn back, not now."

"If we kill him, will it make a difference?"

"Only if he's alone. If there's no one driving them to attack the fort, they'll go after easier prey. But—" he swept an arm out to indicate the hundreds of Reapers outside the gate, "—there could be another sentient out there, I don't know. I've been away from the city for too long to be able to recognize them all on sight. Marston always liked to work alone. He wouldn't ask for help if it meant letting people know he'd failed at Fort Hill."

Cap's mouth thinned and he nodded shortly. "You two are the only ones who know what he looks like. Patrol the walls and see if you can put a bullet in him. If you do, let me know and I'll risk sending out a team for the decap."

He left unspoken the accusation that if they'd done that the first time, they might not be in this situation. There'd been no time and his head had been attached to his body by a flap of skin. That's the way it had seemed anyway. Even knowing there was nothing she could have done differently, guilt made her stomach turn. Something brushed against her fingertips and then a large warm hand enfolded hers. Everything in her settled and she squeezed Jake's hand back.

"Cap," Lyle called out again. "You need to see this."

Cap clapped her on the shoulder and moved toward the wall. When she tried to follow, Jake held her back. "There's nothing you could have done. We barely escaped Hill with our own lives."

"I know that."

"And it's no use putting your life at risk to make up for something you never did wrong."

She gave him a pointed look. "You're going to lecture me about trying to paying off debts I don't owe?"

He grimaced. "That's different."

She knew that. Not guilt. Not because he wanted to die. Jake was doing this because the man he was couldn't look at this world and not try to do something to set things right. She lifted onto her toes and kissed him, full on the lips, in front of everyone. His hand caught her hip and steadied her. He made a rough, surprised noise. When she pulled away, his brows lifted slightly. His dark eyes met hers. Warmth, there. Hunger. Faint amusement.

She took a step back and, ignoring the stunned looks on the faces of the few Rangers near enough to have witnessed the kiss, she tugged on his hand. "Come on. I want to see what this is."

This turned out to be a strange knot of Reapers about a quarter mile distant. She'd noticed the grouping earlier but had taken it for a frenzy. Reapers often attacked their own wounded when there was no other prey immediately available. Bodies coiled in a thick knot but as she watched, they moved steadily forward. Jake passed the glass to her and she squinted down the barrel.

"What are they hiding?"

Occasionally they'd part just enough for her to see the sheen of dull metal. It appeared to be a thick iron material like the kind used to construct bank vaults and steam engines. It had to be on wheels for them to be able to move it. Even then, after yesterday's rain, she was surprised they were able to move it at all without getting mired. It was difficult to see past the Reapers, which she now realized was what they intended.

"It's what they'll use to blow the gates," Jake said loud enough to draw Cap's attention.

"Explosives?"

"The outer shell is meant to protect the mechanism

from gunfire. It's a clockwork fuse that will drop the shields a few seconds before the device detonates. It's a drone, aimed for the gates, though it could blast directly through the wall itself. The younglings are only clearing a path for it. They used something like it at Hill."

"If we shoot enough Reapers in its path, maybe we can slow it down enough to detonate farther out," Lyle suggested.

"You can try," Jake said, then shook his head. "They'll do whatever they need to do to get it here. You can see how they're already avoiding the area directly in front of the drone. I'd aim for the wheels instead of the younglings."

"You can't even *see* the wheels."

"They're down there," Jake said. "It's either that or wait for the shields to drop and hope you hit something that disables the bomb instead of setting it off."

Cap swore, glanced at Abby and then flushed slightly. To Lyle, he said, "Go ahead and spread the word to aim for the wheels. Make sure all of the civilians are behind the second wall. Tell them to stay at the rear of the compound and that they need to be ready to take to the tunnels." He turned back to Jake. "I didn't know your kind had any use for explosives."

"That's Scraper technology," Jake said. "Not a Reaper design."

DANIEL, WHO'D JUST turned sixteen, was the one who blasted a rear wheel and halted the progression of the load of explosives inching toward their gates. The fort breathed a collective sigh of relief that lasted through midday. The Reapers dragged their broken machine out of the range of fire but by early afternoon, the armored cart was slowly wheeling toward them again.

And wasn't that disconcerting? That the Reapers were able to repair the kind of complicated machinery used only up in the Scraper cities. Already, they were closer. This time, the younglings made sure no one got a good bead on the wheels until the drone was nearly to the gate. When it was less than twenty feet away, Reapers began to retreat beyond the blast zone. A sort of fatalistic numbness settled over Abby as she watched the bomb begin the climb up the slight incline that surrounded the base of the fort. Bullets pinged off the heavy metal shields but did no real damage. Troy had fallen because of a horse. They got an iron armadillo. She saved her own ammunition for the Reapers.

Jake was in the yard arguing with the captain. Cap stared at the ground, one meaty hand rubbing at the back of his neck. As if he felt her eyes on him, he looked up and grimaced before turning away. That broke through the fog surrounding her. Something was going on. Lyle came up, said something and the three of them moved off together, walking toward the captain's quarters.

They were definitely up to something. Something they didn't want her involved in, which meant someone she loved was about to do something stupid. An awful feeling settled in the pit of her stomach. She had a feeling she knew exactly who that stupid someone was.

And he was shutting her out again.

THE CAPTAIN'S QUARTERS here were Spartan compared to the ones at Fort Hill. Of course, Captain Schmitt from Hill had been something of a prick. A small man who didn't want anyone to forget his station. He'd surrounded himself with old maps and glittering brass scopes. He'd considered himself a collector. Had weapons from every continent hanging on the wall, none of which had done him a damn bit of good when the Reapers attacked.

Captain Jones by comparison had a small bookshelf in the corner, a desk large enough to use for strategy and an old map of his patrol area that took up most of one wall. Not a collector's item. It was beginning to yellow at the edges and had been torn in the lower right corner. That wasn't what told its age though. The dark lines marking where the border lay was what gave it away. Six different colored lines, each farther north than the last.

As Lyle and Cap argued in low furious voices, Jake sat, stretching out his legs and folding his hands across his abdomen. He hoped they wrapped it up soon. He didn't like leaving Abby on the wall while he was down here, relatively safe. Her eyes were bloodshot from searching for Marston, who Jake knew wouldn't be so careless to show his face again now that he'd made his point.

The captain had called him into this small meeting after seeming to finally accept that the walls were going to fall before help arrived. *Now*, the Rangers were willing to consider other options…when it was nearly too late.

Jake didn't gloat. He felt absolutely no pleasure in having been proved right.

"Karlson says his contraption is nearly ready."

"To test." Cap glowered at his lieutenant. "I'm not betting lives on it. Not when we can send Jake out through the tunnels with the scientists."

He didn't recall having volunteered for that. Lyle glanced his way and then back at the captain. "That's betting lives too. Except now you're talking about putting all our money on a Reaper."

Jake took no offense. Lyle had never tried to hide his distrust, which Jake suspected had more to do with Abby's feelings toward him than anything Jake had done. That kiss she'd so openly given him on the ramparts hadn't helped much, he suspected.

The captain opened his mouth to argue, snapped it closed and then moved around the desk to sit down. He rubbed his face. "Maybe that is what I'm talking about. But Jake has proven himself."

"How?"

"By saving the scientists in the first place. By saving Abby."

"He *saved* her for them to experiment on," Lyle grit out.

Cap's brows rose. "I don't see how that contradicts my point. He wants the cure and he's best equipped to see that they survive this."

Lyle glared at him. With a sigh, Jake turned to Cap. "I can't take Welks out through the tunnels. Assuming Marston followed me all the way from Hill, he's been here for some time. I'm sure he's found the tunnels by now."

"I sent a man down there less than an hour ago," Lyle said. "They're clear."

"Which only means he's watching them. Hoping that I take the scientists and run. It would be the easiest way for him to see that he gets the job done this time around before he destroys the fort. It's what I would do."

Cap paused to consider that, his dark eyes narrowed. The flame from the lantern sitting on the desk guttered a bit when a draft caught it.

"Hell." Lyle ran a hand through his hair. "Maybe we give him what he wants. Just tie a ribbon around Welks's neck and toss him from the wall."

Jake smiled at that mental image. Surprisingly, the captain smiled too—a slow, genuine smile that caused both Lyle and Jake to stare at him for several uneasy seconds. Just what they needed at a time like this. For the captain to lose his ever-loving mind.

Jake shook his head. "I could try fighting past him, but I doubt I can take Marston and whatever Reapers he has guarding that tunnel. Not alone and not while protecting the scientists too."

"What if you weren't alone?" Cap reached behind him and pulled a map out of wooden tube. Rolling it out, he said, "There's more than one tunnel. Look here." He tapped the map. "This is the main escape branch, but these were used for drainage."

When Fort Dougan had first been constructed it was at the confluence of two small rivers, little more than creeks really. Ranger engineers had diverted the smaller northern course to create a single larger river that flowed to the south side of the fort. Large enough to act as at least some small protection from the Reapers. Abby was right—water didn't stop them, but they avoided it when they could, primarily because it lowered their body temperatures. The tunnel system Cap traced with his finger was a vestige from the early days of the fort when they'd been necessary for drainage during the spring when the twin creeks would rise and occasionally flood the plain.

"You're talking about an ambush."

Cap nodded absently, still examining the map. Jake bent his head to do the same but after a moment pulled back in disgust. "None of these get me out of here. I'd come out in the middle of the fight. And they'll know about those too. You're guarding them right?"

"We collapsed most of the tunnels," Lyle said. "Except for these two. They're both barred and locked. Will has them rigged with explosives, trip wires halfway down. If anyone gets in, they're not getting back out. But—" he looked up at Cap, "—I can send Will in to disable the explosives and we can get out that way if we need to."

"Into the middle of the fight," Jake repeated.

"You wouldn't be going that way. If you leave down this main tunnel…the one Marston is watching, we can send a team out through each of these. They open near enough to each other that we can fight our way to you. At the very least, we'd cause enough of a distraction to give you and your team a shot at Marston."

He wasn't talking about placing the scientists at risk

then. He was talking about launching an attack, one that actually might stand a chance of succeeding. Just a few problems. "So your plan is to send armed Rangers with me pretending to be the scientists?"

Cap nodded.

"Marston knows what they look like now."

Lyle touched his gun. "But he'll have to get close enough to take a look, won't he? I can act as one of the doctors, pretend to be unconscious. Could you carry me that last distance?"

Jake blew out a huff of laughter. "I think I could manage it."

Cap rapped his knuckles on the desk. "You pick the men, Lyle, and have Will ready to disable the triggers. I'll order Abby to the cellars to guard Welks and Karlson. That's the safest place in the fort right now. We do this." He stood. "What do we have to lose?"

"Half your fighting men," Jake said quietly. "The fort if they use those tunnels to get in after we disable the explosives."

The captain held his gaze steadily. "Are you in or out, Jake? I can't order you to help us."

Jake rose to his feet, meeting the captain's glower with one of his own. "In. But I do have one condition."

JAKE CLAMPED A hand around Abby's wrist before she stepped into the courtyard. She kicked up a fight until she realized who held her, and then let him pull her along for a few feet before digging in her heels and demanding an explanation.

"Where the hell have you been?"

He looped an arm around her waist to get her moving again. It wouldn't take the Reapers long to breach the outer walls now. Everything was in motion. Only this one last thing for him to take care of.

"What were you talking to the captain about?"

He glanced down at her.

"We're going after Marston."

She blinked in surprise but while she processed that, she continued to follow him without protest. "How do you expect to find him?"

"We think he might be waiting for someone to make a run with the scientists."

"You. He's waiting for you to make a run with the scientists. Through the tunnel system?"

He smiled. Clever Abby. She knew him as well as Marston did. Better. She grabbed his arm but he kept walking, away from the walls and the sound of gunfire. "You're planning to run into him alone? That's the plan they talked you into?"

"Not alone. I'll have a team with me. And two others to keep the rest of the younglings in that area busy for a few minutes."

"A few minutes." She cursed so viciously, he glanced down at her and smiled. Her brows rose, waiting for his challenge. When it didn't come, she said. "It's too dangerous."

They'd reached the edge of the main keep and Jake swung her around, pressing her back against the rough wood wall.

"It is dangerous."

She grabbed his hips, fingers digging into his skin

even through the denim. "I don't want you to go. Marston scares the shit out of me. He's crazy."

"I know."

She searched his face for a moment. A shadow passed behind her eyes and some of the fight seemed to drain out of her. "You already said yes, didn't you? And this is goodbye. Let me guess, I'm guarding the scientists, right? Haddy and Amelia? The last one holding a gun."

He threaded his fingers into her hair and tipped her face back, shivered as her fingertips drifted down the side of his face. Gently, he took her lips, sank into a slow, deep kiss. When he pulled away, there were tears in her eyes. "Jake…"

"It's your call, Abby. I told the captain I'd do it. I'd rather have you with me, even going after Marston. Your captain wants you to stay with the scientists. It's up to you. Partners."

Her eyes widened and then narrowed. "Is this some kind of trick?"

"Trick? No. But there aren't any good options. There's risk everywhere, remember? Nowhere's safe. And I wanted it to be your call."

Her hand came up to the back of his neck and she pulled his head down for another kiss. This one fierce and wild. Her breasts arched to press against his chest and her tongue claimed every last piece of him. He grabbed her ass and pulled her up, rubbing her against his aching cock. When she finally pulled away, they were both breathing hard. Lowering his head, he touched his forehead to hers.

"What's it going to be?"

He growled when she nipped at his lower lip. "I'm coming with you."

Chapter Twenty-Two

JAKE HEFTED LYLE'S limp body higher into his arms and lengthened his stride. Abby trailed a step behind him. The others were still waiting within the fort. They'd give them a fifteen-minute lead before following. Jake had insisted on that. Any sooner, he'd said, and Marston would be able to smell and hear them coming. Lyle was meant to play Welks. He feigned unconsciousness because they were grasping at anything that might give them an edge. She was herself. Marston knew she'd been traveling with Jake. He wouldn't be surprised by her presence, might be distracted by it. They hoped anyway.

She shivered again. It was cool in the tunnels beneath the fort. The floors were covered in a slimy muck and the walls were damp. She could smell rat feces but couldn't hear the telltale scratch and twitter that signaled live animals. The rats were probably long gone by now. They'd likely run at the first whiff of Reaper. Smart creatures, rats.

"It's low here," Jake murmured. "Watch your head."

She ducked but after several feet, the ceiling to the tunnel opened up and she could again walk normally. By her calculations they were directly below the western wall. Up ahead the tunnel curved gently to the north. A mile and a dozen feet of bedrock separated them from the fight, but she could feel the vibration of it through the earth. She hoped the walls held. Just another hour. If this mission failed… If this mission failed, it wouldn't matter if the Reapers broke through. This was truly their last hand to play.

Another two miles and the tunnel narrowed before opening to a crack in the ground beside a tumble of stone. The light stung her eyes and she blinked rapidly, willing them to adjust. Searching the area around them, she held her gun at the ready, expecting a Reaper to jump out at any minute, but the area was clear. They stood just above the dry creek bed from the diverted river.

She looked to Jake for direction but he shook his head, lifting his face to scent the wind. They couldn't wander far from the tunnel entrance. They were the bait. In another twenty minutes, a band of Rangers would push through. Marston would have to come to them.

"I want to see the fort," she said, climbing to the crest of the small hill to get her bearings.

The fort was a little more than five miles distant and the area surrounding it was alive with Reapers. Strange to see it from this angle. She crouched down, pressing her fingertips to the dry earth, letting her gaze drift over the ugly view.

The sky was flat and low, but there'd been no rain. No sign of a storm that might drive away the Reapers for a time. The fort looked tiny from up here, a small wooden box surrounded by hundreds of men who showed no signs of fatigue.

Removing a glass from the sleeve strapped to her arm, she adjusted the eyepiece for a closer look. She could see more of that steel armadillo from this angle. It was shaped somewhat like a bullet, flat on the back end, pointed at the other. If Reapers ever found a gun big enough to shoot something like that, the forts wouldn't stand a chance. It was set on a low wagon bed, four wheels, the tops protected by armored shields. No wonder the wheels had been so difficult to hit. She swung the glass wider and her attention fixed on the gate. Something happening there.

She froze, thinking they'd found a way in, but the gates were still intact. There was also a very definite gap that widened as she watched. Even from this distance she could hear the Reapers lift their voices in triumph as they surged forward.

"Fuck."

Jake came up beside her. He set Lyle down—none to gently, she noticed. But Lyle was a good actor. His eyelids didn't so much as twitch as his arm flopped across his chest.

"What is it?"

"I don't—" *Damn.* They might have to make a run for it after all. As the gates opened wider, she could see smoke drift through the gap in the great wooden doors. "Someone set fire to the fort. They're trying to get out."

Lyle did flinch then but stilled almost immediately.

"That doesn't make sense," Jake murmured. "The

Reapers wouldn't have done that, not yet. A fire with all the men inside the fort robs them of their food."

"Maybe it was an accident," she suggested. Or maybe one of the men had done it on purpose, she admitted to herself. Having seen Fort Hill after the massacre, she could sympathize with the desire to escape that fate by whatever means necessary. But she hated the idea that one of her brothers might have made that choice for everyone else.

She didn't protest when Jake took the glass from her shaking hand. She watched his back while he scoped the fort but after reassuring herself they were still alone, her gaze was drawn back around.

Jake was right. There was something…off about the fire. She couldn't see any flames and the smoke hung low to the ground instead of rising into the dreary sky. And…

"Why aren't they stopping the ones fleeing the fort?"

"Those aren't Rangers running. They're Reapers. And the smoke is tinged pink. It's not a natural fire."

As they watched, a wagon came into view from the direction of the main gates. Rangers surrounded the wooden cart in a protective phalanx. It was difficult to get a good view of the wagon from this distance. There was a bulky metallic object in the bed, the source of the smoke…one of the sources anyway. Smoke billowed out from the contraption and seemed to be driving the Reapers away.

"That's not… Is that Karlson's weapon?"

"He pulled it off after all," Jake said under his breath. "I'll be damned."

"An argument could be made that you already are."

That voice...

Abby rose to her feet slowly, the blood draining from her face as she turned. Marston strolled into the clearing, naked as the day he was born. Covered in dust and sweat, he looked exactly like a youngling except for the broad smile on his face and the calculation in his cold blue eyes. There were a dozen Reapers behind him, slinking low to the ground, moving like a pack of jackals. And though they fixed their wild eyes on the pair of humans just a few feet away, none of them attempted to dart past Marston.

She'd asked Jake about that once—about the control Marston was able to exercise over the younglings. He'd explained that it wasn't truly control. Marston surrounded himself with the nearly sentient and those with enough intelligence to be afraid of an older Reaper. Eyeing them now, Abby wasn't certain how much she trusted that fear to keep them at bay. The others—the younglings—merely needed to be pointed at a food source.

"I see you brought your...pet," Marston said, his hungry gaze fixing on her.

She couldn't stop the quake in her shoulders. Even though she'd expected to see him again, there'd been no way to brace herself. Her body remembered his hands, his mouth. Her skin crawled, but she repressed a shudder. Her fear would only distract Jake. She knew that.

Marston knew it too. He winked at her before returning his attention to Jake. "I didn't expect to find her alive. What are you doing, feeding her your blood?"

Jake kept his silence. They were positioned well enough. If Marston kept moving forward, it would place him directly between them and the tunnel. The other Rangers would be able to come up behind the pack. Of course, that would leave Jake, Abby and Lyle cut off but… Well, no one had ever argued that it was a *perfect* plan.

Marston laughed and took another step. "Tell me this, then, and perhaps I'll let your little pet live—that new weapon, what is it?" At Jake's neutral expression, he rolled his eyes. "Yes, I saw it too." He lifted his chin to indicate the glass still in Jake's hand. "I'd wager my equipment is a good deal better than yours. This is their second pass through the gates. They retreated once, but it appears that was only to refill the tank. The smoke disables us but doesn't seem to affect the Rangers at all, even the ones not wearing masks. Why is it?"

"I have no idea."

Which was the God's honest truth, Abby thought. No one had put enough faith in Karlson's weapon to ask him more than a few cursory questions. *Karlson* hadn't believed he'd finish it in time. Apparently, imminent death could serve as a powerful creative motivator.

"Well, I suppose it doesn't matter now…" Marston tipped his head to one side, trying to get a better look at Lyle. "I knew you'd bring me Welks. I've been waiting here all night for you to scurry out of the tunnels with him. And you brought the girl too. That was kind. It took me days to heal from the wound she gave me. If you hadn't killed so many of the younglings, they'd have finished me off before I could defend myself."

Marston's gaze shifted to meet hers and he smiled. His message was a loud and clear—*I owe you.*

Jake growled low in his throat. Marston laughed. "I didn't plan to draw out her death but I could use her to break you, couldn't I? You fancy yourself in love, Jake? With a human. That's—"

"He doesn't love me," Abby said, drawing Marston's attention.

Jake frowned at her, but she ignored him. The more time they spent chatting, the more time the Rangers had to get here. It was their job to distract him.

"No?" Marston tipped his head to one side. "I admit I don't see the appeal myself, but he does seem to have formed an attachment."

"You think he hunted me down because he's in love?" Abby's lip curled. "He's not a fool, you must know that."

"He *is* a fool, human. A self-loathing fool who's chasing a cure that will only kill him in the end."

"He's not after a cure," she said, palms sweating on the barrel of her rifle. "He was never after the cure."

"Ah," Marston said softly, a world of menace in his tone. "I see. You think that I'm the fool here. That's a mistake, little girl. Don't waste my time. You're not the only loose thread I intend to clip today."

She laughed and was gratified by the way his eyes changed. Even from here she could see the way they dilated, the black of his pupils expanding until the blue was a thin faint rim. Marston's Reaper was so much closer to the surface than Jake's. She couldn't afford to forget that. Not again.

A youngling tried to slip past Marston's invisible territorial line. Marston grabbed the Reaper by the shoulder and, with a flick of his wrist, sent him hurling back into the pack where the others kicked and snarled at him. Such casual violence. She blinked and tamped down the fear that threatened to choke her. She'd forgotten how strong he was…

As if sensing her reaction, Marston smiled. "If not a cure, then what is he after?"

"Me. That part's truth. He was after me all along, but it's not about love."

Marston scoffed. "I think you overestimate your charm."

"He wants a child. Like him. Of his own blood."

Jake's body went rigid. He'd be angry with her. But, hell, she already had a target painted on her as far as Marston was concerned. This wouldn't place her in any *more* danger, it would only keep Marston talking.

Marston's gaze flicked to Jake. "Truth?"

Jake let the silence draw out for a few moments before he sighed and shook his head. "You've always known I want more than this life. I want to keep her, but I'm not willing to die over her."

"You think she can carry a Reaper without it killing her?"

Jake shrugged. "Only one way to find out."

Marston stared at them for a moment and then lifted his hand. "You're carrying her. We leave from here. The rest can have the fort."

Jake stiffened. The plan had been for Lyle to shoot Marston when he came close enough to check his identity. Marston was already beginning to turn away. "What about the doctor?"

At the question, Marston looked back. "What about the doctor? Let the younglings have him."

The pack understood that. At Marston's words, they surged forward even as the first Ranger stepped from the tunnel, gun raised, and began to fire. Jake pushed Abby aside and she scrambled on elbows and knees toward the boulder just a few feet away, wedged up against the trunk of an old oak.

Lyle was right behind her. Guns drawn, he blew the head off the Reaper flying toward them.

"They're after you, Lyle." She grinned, hitting the next. "Damn it. You led them right to me."

He grinned back. "Honey, I'm sure they'd rather have a taste of you than me."

And for the next few seconds, it was all they could do to hold their ground. When she could afford to tear her gaze away, Abby looked for Jake.

"Did you see where he went?" she demanded of Lyle.

"After Marston." He squeezed the trigger and she felt his body flinch with the recoil. His eyes narrowed. He shifted the barrel a bare inch to the left and fired again before glancing her way. "By the old creek. There's no way to reach him right now. He'll be fine."

He wouldn't be fine. Marston fought dirty and Jake was too weak. He'd been locked up for weeks and before that, twelve long years of captivity and torture. To Lyle's mind a Reaper was a Reaper, but that's not how it worked.

She caught a glimpse of raven dark hair, the breadth of his shoulders, the line of his back. It was just a flash of movement, but she'd know Jake anywhere. He went down. The Reaper who'd attacked him had pushed him right off the ledge above the dry creek bed. And though she hadn't gotten a good look at the Reaper who followed him down, she knew who it had to be.

When she tried to stand, Lyle caught her arm and hauled her back down. "Where the hell do you think you're going?"

"He needs help." Half the younglings were down. Between them and the fort, she could hear the sound of gunfire, which meant the other two parties had also emerged from the tunnels successfully. With any luck, they'd be here soon. But not soon enough to save Jake from Marston.

Lyle cursed savagely but let her go. "Go on." He set himself behind the boulder. "I'll cover you."

She ran, trusting him to do it. Five steps and there was the first shot. Something heavy landed behind her, but she didn't look back. She ran straight for the edge, going over without looking and landing hard in the creek bed that turned out to be much, much shallower than she'd expected. With a grunt, she rose from a crouch, ignoring the sting in her ankles as she turned around.

There. Jake and Marston were about two dozen feet away. She lifted her gun but couldn't get a clean shot from this distance. Jake rolled, managing to use his legs as leverage to hold Marston to the ground for a moment. He reared back and dropped his elbow sharp and fast into Marston's nose. She heard the crack as the bone broke. She hurried toward them, the loose stone sliding under her boots. Just as she took aim again, Marston twisted his body and Jake went down.

Jake wouldn't win this fight. Abby could see that even as she looked for her shot. Marston was strong, Reaper strong, extraordinarily fast. And he hadn't spent the past several weeks—the past several *years*—being experimented upon by sadistic doctors. He would kill Jake if she didn't find a way to stop him. They were moving too fast, skidding down the hill a few more feet as she followed, tracking them with her gun.

"I'm going to end you," Marston snarled, and jerked to one side before she could pull the trigger. Something snapped with a hollow pop and Jake gasped in pain. Abby swore and repositioned herself.

Marston pulled back so he could reach Jake's neck and Abby took the shot.

She hit him in the forehead. It punched through his skull and Marston jerked. For an instant, his gaze locked on hers, eyes wide with shock. A snarl curled his lip and panic swirled up inside of her, screaming that he wasn't dead.

She dropped the rifle and pulled her pistol, hitting him again when he lurched forward. His clawed hand caught his weight as he fell. His eyes didn't leave her. She shot twice more in quick succession before Jake shoved him aside. She took an involuntary step back as his body toppled forward.

Hands lifted, Jake came to his knees. "Abby?"

"Move," she whispered. "He's not dead. He's not—"

Gently, Jake closed his hand around hers and guided her arm down. "He's dead. I can hear it, remember? His heart's not beating. He's not drawing breath. He's dead and this time we'll make sure he stays that way. It's all right now." He rose to his feet with a grunt of pain. "It's all right."

The arm he wrapped around her shoulders was shaking and when he drew her to his chest, she could feel the tension in him. A fine tremor running the length of his long lean body. With all of the violence around them, he was likely fighting off the Reaper. But when she tried to give him space, his arm tightened and he pressed a kiss to the top of her head. "Jake?"

"Just one minute," he murmured. "I need to know you're not hurt. Let it sink in."

She took her hand and pressed it between her breasts. "Feel this then. Can you hear it?"

"I hear it. The gunfire's stopped."

By the sound of men's voices above, they'd won this round. If Jake was right, the rest of the younglings would begin to clear now that Marston was dead. And if not…well, they still had Karlson's invention.

"Come on," she said. "Let's get back to the fort."

Jake swayed a bit and she noticed that he was holding his arm awkwardly against his side. Slipping her head under his shoulder, she wrapped an arm around his waist. They turned to find Lyle standing on the crest of the hill, gun in one hand, ax in the other.

"Clear up here. You need help?"

"We need to borrow your ax."

Chapter Twenty-Three

JAKE LEFT ABBY sleeping in her frilly bed, hand tucked beneath her cheek, short lashes like tiny spikes against her pale cheeks. She was exhausted and she needed the sleep. He was a pragmatist not a coward for leaving her now. So he reminded himself.

As he walked silently across the floorboards to ease open the door, he couldn't help but reflect that Abby never would run like this. She met things head-on. When he'd kidnapped her, he hadn't wanted to tell her his plans, thinking she'd only fight him harder. But once she knew the truth, even understanding the risk to herself, she'd still helped him every step of the way. She didn't run when the fort was under attack. She didn't run from him.

And apparently he didn't have the willpower he'd thought he had, because he couldn't keep avoiding her. Which left only one solution: Welks had his serum brewed up again and Jake meant to take it. He'd told Abby the truth about that—it would kill him or cure him, but either way she would be safe.

He paused on the porch steps to pull on his boots before starting toward the lab. He'd toss Welks out of his bed and do this now, before Abby woke up and tried to talk him out of it again. He glanced back at the house and stopped. That dark window, open to the night, white curtains fluttering with the breeze. Abby warm and naked in that soft, girly bed. Maybe…

"Not thinking about breaking in, are you?"

He turned. Lyle. Jake hadn't even heard him come up behind him. Living among humans was making him soft. "No."

Lyle stretched and his back cracked in three spots. It was late, but he smelled of horse and sawdust, not woman. A lot of the men were in the small town situated outside the fort walls, helping to welcome back the returning townspeople, paying special attention to the brothel. Lyle was in charge of directing repairs. With Marston dead, there'd been no one to direct the attack and the Reapers had quickly scattered. Reinforcements had arrived yesterday to help with cleanup. The fort was beginning to return to normal.

"I'm taking the serum."

Lyle huffed a soft laugh. "It's midnight."

"Good a time as any." Jake glanced at Lyle, who was looking up at Abby's window.

"I see," he said, clapping Jake on the shoulder. They started walking again toward the lab. "She's going to kill you if the serum doesn't do the job, you know. And that is not exaggeration. Have you seen her with a gun?"

"She won't shoot me."

Lyle shook his head. "Wouldn't be too sure about that, my friend. Welks figure out how to keep your brain from turning into strawberry jam?"

"He has the serum. The five younglings he's tested it on so far are all stable."

Lyle was silent for a few paces. Thousands of stars looked down on them. Someone up on the ramparts coughed as they passed beneath him. "So do I tell her this was suicide?"

"Fuck you, Lyle. Don't tell her shit. Better she thinks I'm a selfish prick if it goes badly."

"Are you? She thinks she's in love. I've never seen her like this. Something happens to you, I don't want her broken."

Jake reached for the doorknob, but Lyle slammed his hand down on the wood to hold it closed. He could rip off that arm and shove it down Lyle's throat to shut him up without even breaking a sweat. Lyle knew it too, but he kept his hand there just the same.

"I don't want her hurt either. But all it would take is one slip, a distraction, the tiniest lapse of concentration." Jake shook his head. "I couldn't live with myself if I hurt her. So yeah, I'm the selfish prick who wants to be with her, so I'm doing this. Now get the fuck out of my way."

Jake grit his teeth while Lyle studied him. It would be ironic if, after everything, Lyle was the one who finally pushed him over the edge. And Abby… Abby would be very upset if he killed her friend.

It didn't come to that. After a moment of tense silence, Lyle reached down and turned the knob for him, pushing open the door. "Good luck."

A SLIGHT BREEZE stirred the curtains of the sick room and Abby lifted her head to breathe in the clean crisp air. The smell of horses outside mixed with the smell of the stew Haddy sent over for her dinner and made Abby acutely aware of how rank she smelled by comparison. She should bathe, but she couldn't leave. Jake was going to open his eyes any minute now and she wanted to be there when it happened.

She rested her head on the bed beside his hand, cool to the touch. "You're a stupid man, Jake. I should just leave you alone with Welks. He's been standing around polishing up his drills and scalpels, you know, just waiting to get a crack at you. I've barred the door so far, but if you don't wake up soon I'm going to hunt down a Reaper and force him to bite you. Just see if I don't."

Three days, he'd been out. She'd been frantic in the morning when she'd woken up in her bed alone, Jake's scent still on her pillow, on her body. She'd rolled over to kiss him and he'd been gone. Stupid. Stupid. Stupid.

"And cowardly too."

"I knew you'd say that." A touch to her hair, fast and light as a hummingbird, shaky as one too. She looked up. His eyes were still closed.

"Jake?" God, she hadn't imagined that touch, his voice. Please let her not have imagined it.

His throat worked as if he was trying to swallow. There were dark circles under his eyes, and his face was pinched with pain. His head fell to the side and his eyes opened to slits. "I feel like shit."

She gave him a shaky smile and he got all blurry. "You're not immortal anymore, you fool man."

His lips twitched. "I love you too, sweetheart. Lyle warned me you'd put a bullet in my head."

"Did he?" She *knew* Lyle had been in on it. "I'll chamber one for him too."

Slipping an arm beneath his head, she lifted him so he could take a sip from the cup of water she pressed to his mouth. "Are you…how do you feel? Normal? Is it—?"

"Gone, Abby." He smiled. "It's gone. Only me in here."

His eyes were already drifting closed, but he didn't let go of her hand. He tugged her closer…or tried to. God, he was so weak. And she was too, because she climbed right onto the bed with him, tucked her head on his shoulder. His lips brushed the top of her head. "I'm safe now."

LYLE WAS SITTING on the porch swing outside the women's barracks when she finally left Jake to bathe. Reaper senses or not, he'd be able to smell her now. Jake was sleeping peacefully and Doc said he was going to be all right. Welks and Karlson had injected the other Reapers with their serum and were already demanding more test subjects. They still wanted to run tests and make certain that there were no side effects. And even though everyone was still holding their breath, half-afraid that the serum would prove to be another fake, it was becoming increasingly apparent this was a genuine cure.

Lyle stood when she climbed the steps, but she waved him down and sat beside him. He stretched an arm behind her and tugged at her braid.

"I heard Jake's going to make it."

She elbowed him in the ribs. Hard. "I heard you knew what he had planned and didn't tell me."

"That was between him and you, Abby. And I thought he was doing the right thing. It all turned out in the end."

"If it hadn't turned out, would you have told me you knew about it?"

"God, no."

They fell silent for a few minutes, listening to the sounds of the camp waking up around them. The morning air had a nip to it. Winter was coming on fast—they'd have to repair the fort before the first snowfall. The Reapers would be back in the spring and they had to be ready for them by then.

"Do you think we'll be able to stop them? Really end this?"

"Karlson said once they perfect the serum, he can produce enough of the stuff to keep a supply in every town, every homestead eventually. Of course, Welks wants to sell it. They haven't decided on a price."

She snorted. "That will keep them from making new Reapers, but what about the old ones?"

He kicked the swing into motion. "You worried about losing your job?"

"Hell, no. I want…" She smiled. "I want to start planning a life."

He grinned back at her. "Good for you."

A small group of men rode past, led by Garrett, who touched his fingers to his hat when he saw them watching. She coughed at the dust that kicked up behind them and Lyle waited for the noise to die down before he said,

"We'll hold the border. Inject the Reapers we can and kill the ones we can't."

She pictured all those ragged half-crazed men wandering the countryside. "How do they go back to a normal life after that?"

"I'm hoping maybe Jake can help us figure that one out. It'll be an adjustment for him too." He glanced at her and shook his head. "You truly never did see him as a Reaper, did you?"

No. She never really had. "He's different."

"That he is. Cap requested a meeting with the Council. Welks and Karlson will be done with their tests soon and they'll need to come up with a plan for distribution. He's hoping to take Jake."

She frowned, not liking the idea of Jake leaving so soon. Lyle touched her shoulder and she looked up.

He smiled, gray eyes crinkling at the corners. "You can go too if you want. Knowing how you feel about Scrapers, I think Cap assumed you wouldn't want to. But I'm sure you'll be welcome to ride along."

"I'll think about it." She yawned. Maybe she'd steal a quick nap before a bath. There was one other thing she'd been meaning to ask Lyle. "What's going to happen with Welks? Cure or no, he had a hand in what happened at Fort Hill."

"Maybe. There's still no proof of that."

At Abby's rude noise, he held up a hand. "We need him for now and by the time we have the serum, he'll probably have found a way to land on his feet."

"He's a rat."

"Cunning animals," Lyle agreed, placidly. "He did

give up the name of his benefactor. Although that's not much of a concession now. With the cure, it'll be damn hard to go after either one of them."

Something in his tone made her nervous. "Who is it?"

"John Williams."

She startled. Even she recognized that name. "The former secretary of defense?"

Lyle's mouth twisted. "Ironic, ain't it?"

"Why would he…" She tried to wrap her mind around that bit of information. John Williams was a born Scraper and an aristocrat. Although he'd retired from his post to pursue business interests, he still had friends on the Council and family at every level of the government.

"We can't touch him," Lyle said. "Not yet and not without proof."

She stared at his grim face. "You can't mean to let him get away with it."

"First things first. We get that cure out there."

"And then?"

Lyle's gray eyes turned hard and very cold. "We find proof."

Chapter Twenty-Four

THEY BURIED THEIR DEAD, chased off the rest of the Reapers and sent messages up and down the line informing the other Rangers of Jake's conversion and the new weapon Karlson had invented. The first leaves were falling from the trees and the doctors planned to use the winter months for research, manufacturing, outfitting the other forts and demonstrating their devices.

Jake's Reaper was truly dead. Every once in a while there was a distant look to his eyes as though he held a finger to the wind. But he smiled more. He didn't hold himself back. And he was happy, genuinely, purely happy.

A happy Jake was a sight to see. When he grinned at her across the common hall, it sent a thrill of anticipation chasing all the way down to her toes. When he was working with the men to rebuild the fort, shirtless and covered in grime and sweat, every muscle in his body straining, he seemed content and at peace. When he was driving deep inside of her, trying to hold himself back until she shattered, she knew herself to be the happiest woman on God's green earth. All of it only winched the ropes that bound them together tighter.

It was Jake who insisted on the wedding. No matter how Abby argued that it was against the rules for a

Ranger to marry, Jake insisted. Cap made an exception for her, saying that he was going to need all the help he could get keeping her in line. And what better guardian for her than a Reaper? *Former* Reaper.

Guardian her ass.

She thought that Cap making the exception for her was going to open up a whole bag of trouble for him. But when she'd expressed that opinion, he'd given her a patronizing smile and told her it wasn't her problem.

She was going to enjoy rubbing his face in that some day.

During the ceremony, Cam stood beside Jake and Lyle held Abby's hand until Jake claimed her at the altar. Doc watched from the back, standing with his arms crossed over his chest while Haddy cried in the front pew.

Bill and Amy were there too. Amy watched the ceremony with a soft smile on her face while Bill tried to keep the boys from fidgeting on the wooden bench. Though Amy still had some reservations about welcoming a former Reaper into the family, Jake was slowly beginning to win her over and the boys were ecstatic. They followed Jake around everywhere. Secretly, Abby suspected they were waiting for Jake to eat someone, but they were having fun doing it. And Jake tolerated his small shadows with a patience that warmed her heart.

There was a celebration afterward with people crowding up to them both to offer congratulations, most of whom Jake didn't know. Hell, she didn't know half of them. Lyle said they needed something to celebrate, some sign that there was still living to do and a future to look forward to. Funny that the wedding of a Ranger and a Reaper should be the thing that would give them hope.

They slipped away as soon as they were able, back to her room in the women's barracks for now. Jake, she knew, was already making plans to build their own house. He lay nude and delicious propped up on all her lacy pillows and she straddled him, tracing her fingertips over a new scrape on his chest.

"You'll get old."

He smiled. "With you."

"And weak."

"I married a Ranger. She's a crack shot. I expect that she'll be able to protect me." He caught her hand, turned it and pressed a kiss to the inside of her wrist, eyes glinting with dark promise. "And I'm not old yet."

"Or weak." He tugged, pulling her so that her breasts flattened against his chest.

She smiled and flicked her tongue over the nipple that happened to be near her mouth. She smiled when he grunted. "Oh yeah?"

He rolled, pinning her beneath him and making the springs on the small bed creak plaintively.

"We should oil that."

"Later," he whispered against her skin before tracing the lower curve of her lip with his tongue. "If you really want me to fix it. It hides that sound that you make."

"What sound?"

He grinned. "Half pant, half moan, half—"

"I do no such thing."

He ran his nose up her neck and bumped her chin out of his way, trailed kisses down the same path and then moved lower. He turned her so that she lay on her stomach and slipped his arms beneath her. His chest slid against the back of her shoulder and his legs twined with hers. He nipped at her earlobe. "Listen."

She turned her face to tease him back, but he stole the words from her mouth as he eased himself inside of her. He was still being gentle with her. So very sweet it made her heart ache even now that it was in his hands. And a few moments later, she heard the sound he was talking about slipping from her lips in a breathy rush of air. His laughter rippled through her, telling her he'd heard it too.

The sound of Jake laughing was the most wonderful thing in the world. It still always caught her by surprise, shot right to her heart and then ricocheted around in there. She'd fallen in love with the man inside the monster and now that the monster was gone, the man was fully revealed. Strong, honorable and good-hearted. Someone who could accept all of her, the hard edges and the insecurities, the hidden hopes and fragile fears. Someone she could build a life with in this new world where Reapers could be cured. Though it still amazed and befuddled her, she knew that Jake loved her. He saw the real *her* and loved her anyway.

She'd always sworn that she'd never make the mistake of falling in love, but she didn't really mind being proved wrong.

"Jake?"

"Mmm."

"Do that again, please."

He drove deeper, hand sliding beneath her body to move between her thighs. His long, clever fingers found her clit and circled there as his cock pulsed inside of her, driving her closer to the edge. "My pleasure, sweetheart. Anything for you."

* * * * *